AN OXFORD ENEMY

An utterly gripping page-turner

FAITH MARTIN

writing as

MAXINE BARRY

Originally published as *Dear Enemy*

JOFFE BOOKS

Joffe Books, London 2020
www.joffebooks.com

First published in Great Britain 1997
as *Dear Enemy*

This book is a work of fiction. Names, characters, businesses, organisations, places and events are either the product of the author's imagination or are used fictitiously. Any resemblance to actual persons, living or dead, events or locales is entirely coincidental. The spelling used is British English except where fidelity to the author's rendering of accent or dialect supersedes this. The right of Maxine Barry to be identified as author of this work has been asserted in accordance with the Copyright, Designs and Patents Act 1988.

Please join our mailing list for free Kindle books and new releases.

www.joffebooks.com

We love to hear from our readers! Please email any feedback you have to: feedback@joffebooks.com

ISBN: 978-1-78931-483-0

I'd like to thank Mr Steven Neasham for his invaluable help with the legal matters that arise in this novel.

CHAPTER 1

Keira Westcombe's hand trembled slightly as she carefully picked up the single creamy-white gardenia that the florist had delivered barely ten minutes ago. She lifted it slowly to her lips and breathed in its beautiful, heady fragrance. As she did so, her heart skipped a beat. Somehow, the single white flower made everything seem all too real. Suddenly the moment was upon her, and she was . . . well, quite frankly, scared. There was no other word to describe it, she thought to herself, with a rather ironical twist of her red-painted lips.

But perhaps it was only to be expected. They said everyone got cold feet at times like these. If Jane, her best friend, had been here, Keira knew she could have expected a lecture. As it was her friend and stalwart ally from school days had married a South African man and gone to live far away in her husband's country. It was a shame that she was too heavily pregnant to fly over for the occasion. Even though she knew Jane wouldn't approve of what she was about to do, her friend's solid, comforting presence might have helped calm her jitters. But now there was no one to distract her, and she began to really *think* about what she was doing.

With a pang of panic, she closed her eyes and felt the cool petals brush her cheek. She could almost hear Jane's voice, half exasperated, half worried. '*I told you your ridiculous sense of duty would get you in trouble one of these days. And now look what you've let yourself in for.*'

Only now, when it was far too late to do anything about it, did Keira feel close to the edge of real panic. In the back of her mind she knew that she could still chicken out, and who would really blame her? After all, the potential for disaster seemed enormous.

Then she shook her head and opened her eyes once more, their grey-green depths firm with renewed resolution. Now was definitely *not* the time to lose her backbone. There was far too much at stake. And not just her own future, either. But the future of the reserve. The future of all the creatures depending on her. The villagers who relied on her. She was just being selfish, letting fears and self-doubts cloud her usual clear, logical reasoning. Whatever Jane might say, Keira did have responsibilities. And, yes, damn it, she knew her *duty*. It might sound old-fashioned to Jane, and perhaps to others, but they hadn't been raised to be Lady Penda, and all that entailed.

Unknowingly, her slender back straightened and stiffened. No. She was doing the right thing. She'd thought so two weeks ago, and she thought so now.

Didn't she? Her shoulders slumped for a moment. Then, with a soft exclamation of self-disgust at her shilly-shallying, she straightened once more to her full height, and walked, still clasping the flower, to the full-length mirror, where she looked at herself critically.

Her wedding dress was beautiful.

The shoulders of the gown were of the finest Cotswold lace, a pure and dazzling white, contrasting with the tanned skin of her elegantly straight shoulders beneath. It had been a long hot summer, and on this day in September the sun was still shining brightly. Working outdoors had always given her a healthy complexion, and beneath the white lace her skin glowed like deep, sweet honey. The satin of the bodice gave way to a tight, V-shaped waist emphasizing her slender lines before falling to a voluminous skirt that swished and swirled in a thrilling, slightly alien way whenever she moved.

Used to practical jeans, she felt strangely lost in the beautiful dress. As if someone had hijacked her personality and wrapped it up in white silk.

She forced herself to laugh at her rather morbid fantasies, and moved closer to the mirror. The satin underskirts persisted in feeling cold against her silk-stockinged legs. Unable to prevent herself, she shivered, and almost dropped the precious flower.

This was not how she'd expected to feel on her wedding day. But then, she supposed wryly, she was lucky to be getting married at all. Most of the men she'd known — and there hadn't been that many — had taken one long look at all they'd be taking on in marrying Keira Westcombe and decided it was way too heavy a burden.

She twirled the gardenia thoughtfully, and perhaps a little sadly. Her father, who'd had a passion for all sweet-scented flowers, had loved gardenias above all others.

He'd even converted one whole greenhouse for them. Now, of course, the Heronry's greenhouses grew only practical fruits and vegetables. She'd wept bitterly in the privacy of her room the day she'd had to ask the gardeners to remove the gardenias, but, as always, practicality came first in Keira's life. It had to. She couldn't afford to waste a precious penny.

But on this, of all days, Keira had ordered a gardenia for her hair . . . She twirled the single stem in her hand, her eyes turning to emerald as unshed tears sprang once more into their depths. She wished for the millionth time that her father was here to see this day. His death, three years earlier, had left her feeling utterly bereft, and even now, so many long lonely days later, she could still feel his absence, like a gaping wound in the fabric of her life.

It was, people had kindly assured her, only natural. Her mother had died when she was less than a year old, leaving her daughter with no memories of her. Her father had never remarried, and, as an only child, Keira had not only inherited the property and titles due to the Westcombes, and all the hard work they entailed, but also the full extent of her father's love, wisdom and protection.

Now she missed him more than ever. What daughter didn't want her father to walk by her side down the aisle and give her away to the man— And there her thoughts came crashing to a sickening halt. For she knew how that scenario was supposed to end. Her father was supposed to give her away to the man she loved. Except, of course, that she *didn't* love Lucas.

'Oh, stop it, Keira,' she murmured angrily, and lifted the gardenia to her hair. The hairdresser had done a wonderful job with it, she thought determinedly. Her hair was naturally raven-black, and so long she usually just-gathered it up in a ponytail and pinned it on the top of her head. She'd never bothered to get it cut — had never, in fact, visited a hair salon in her life. Once, just after leaving college, Jane had called her a typical nineties woman — an 1890s woman! Keira could remember her saying it, and her own laughter. Now it didn't seem quite so funny any more.

The hairdresser she'd hired this morning especially for the occasion had taken one look at her newly washed waist-length raven tresses and thrown up his hands in delight. Out had come the curling tongs, and other, more mysterious instruments of his trade, together with a babbling commentary on how fabulous she was going to look. Now, gazing at the mass of gentle curls and waves that glimmered like ebony against the whiteness of her dress, she felt another frisson of shock.

The beautiful, mysterious-looking bride in the mirror was so far removed from the down-to-earth, capable woman inside, it was almost . . . obscene. It was as if she were offering Lucas a sham, a mere replica of herself.

And, worse than that, she knew Lucas would not mind. For Lucas did not love her, either.

Keira took a deep, shaky breath. 'Get on with it, girl,' she murmured to her reflection, checking the back-to-front image of the clock in the mirror and realizing she had only a few minutes left before the chauffeur-driven car was due to collect her. Silly, she supposed, to travel the few hundred yards to the village church in her own rather ancient Rolls-Royce, but everyone would expect it. The lady of the manor had certain obligations to live up to, even on her wedding day.

Especially on her wedding day . . .

With a snap of her pretty white teeth, she moved the gauzy veil to one side and pushed the gardenia into one tight curl, just by her left ear. Replacing the veil, she could see the flower glowing, like rich dairy cream, in the darkness of her hair. She looked stunning. One very detached part of her mind was able to tell her that, without vanity or real pleasure.

Oh, Lucas, she thought, and almost, *almost* surrendered to the impulse to call the whole thing off. But Lucas knew she was marrying him for money, as surely as he knew his own reasons for marrying her. And they had nothing to do with love . . .

In that bleak moment of total honesty with herself, Keira wanted nothing more than to run. To run far away from the Heronry, from the village, from the reserve . . .

The reserve.

Keira's eyes darkened to stormy grey. No, she would *not* run away. Besides, Lucas was counting on her, and he'd been so wonderful. He had gone against the dictates of his own family to propose to her, and here she was, acting like a prima donna in a rather bad tragic opera.

She shook her head grimly at her own wide-eyed reflection, and then walked steadily to the door. If her legs felt leaden in their unaccustomed high-heeled shoes, what did it really matter?

She opened the door onto the long sweeping gallery, and walked past Gainsboroughs, Turners and Stubbses to the wide, sweeping staircase. The Heronry had been her home for the whole of her life. She'd actually been born in her mother's bedroom, as had all the Westcombe babies for the last three centuries. The house itself was Elizabethan in structure, but had been completely modernized inside, just before she was born. Her father had been a practical man, as well as a devoted historian. Sensible central heating, as well as structural strengthening, would keep the house habitable for the Westcombe descendants for generations to come. But it still gobbled money at an alarming rate . . .

She walked down the stairs, carefully clutching the banisters for support. Her hands felt cold against the ancient walnut. The carpet beneath her feet was old, red and thick, and as she stepped onto the flagstone hall, she glanced up automatically at the chandelier. As a child, she'd loved the tinkling crystal light. It had been a focus of magic for her, especially on the rare occasions when her father had entertained, and a ball had been held. Now, though, the chandelier was just a brass and crystal fixture. No breeze came from the open door to make it dance and sing.

No magic today, it said. And it looked disapproving.

Keira hastily looked away from it, and crossed the hall to the open doorway. A broad, sweeping gravel path led to two huge double gates of wrought-iron, fixed between sturdy gateposts. On top of each stone pillar was a huge round ball of granite, and on Hallowe'en, so local legend had it, those two balls swapped places. As a child, she had often sneaked out on the night, firmly taking her courage in hand, and positioned herself in the rhododendron bushes to watch the huge stone balls float across the gate to change places.

She'd never caught them out, though. Her father had said that it was because they were too wise; they knew that she was watching, and craftily waited until, defeated and sleepy, she returned to her bed.

She'd told that story to Rex, when she'd thought they had something special. Before he'd learned just how little money she really had, and just how much the house, gardens, estates and, of course, the reserve, would cost to run.

Exit Rex.

'Ready, My Lady?' a deep Oxonian-burred voice asked respectfully, breaking into her reverie and making her jump visibly.

'What? Oh yes, Sid, thank you,' she said quickly, giving him a wide smile. Sid Johns had been handyman-chauffeur at the Heronry ever since she could remember, and now his thick-set body was slightly stooped, his white hair growing sparse.

The ancient Westcombe Silver Ghost Rolls-Royce had been lovingly polished and shone like a real spectre, and when he opened the door the smell of freshly waxed leather rose to meet her. She smiled as he helped her in, and for a moment their eyes met. Then he stooped to help arrange the white frothy train around her feet.

Sid shut the door with a gentle snap and an implacable face, and walked around to the front. She noticed, suddenly and unbearably touched, that he'd got out his old chauffeur's uniform. His wife must have moved the buttons back for him, for although the grey velvet looked strained it managed to meet over his rounded girth. He even put on his carefully starched cap before setting off. As he started the engine the car gave a purring growl, then moved slowly up the gravel drive. Impulsively, Keira turned and glanced back at the house.

In the mellow September sunshine its ancient walls glowed a pretty rose-pink. Many-faceted lead-paned windows gleamed in the light. Already the creepers climbing the walls were beginning to lose their greenness and held a hint of copper and bronze. But the formal rose-beds were still awash with blooms — pink, red, orange, yellow and white.

The reception was being held at Green Acres, Lucas's huge, modern house in the neighbouring village of Tunner Leigh. Since Lucas had agreed to move into the Heronry, and since they were getting married in her village church, she'd agreed that it was only fair to hold the festivities at his house. Even though most of his things had already been moved into his room in the west wing of her Elizabethan manor.

Her own room was in the east wing, of course . . .

She noticed Sid's eyes slide across to meet hers in the mirror, and she couldn't help but wonder what he must be thinking.

When she'd been growing up, Sid had been the man who taught her to ride her father's horses. The man who showed her where all the best apple trees were, just ripe for scrumping. His wife, Bessie, was officially their housekeeper, but was more like a beloved aunt. She'd taught Keira how to cook rhubarb crumble and make holly wreaths at Christmas.

'Mr Harwood will make me very happy, Sid,' she said softly.

'Ah, I dare say he will, My Lady,' he agreed. But his voice was deadpan, and she knew him well enough to know that this meant scepticism.

The car swept out of the gates and there was old Mrs Sedgewick, standing on the grass verge, waving her white hankie. Her father had told her that she'd done exactly the same thing — it must be thirty years ago now, she mused — when he had married Keira's mother.

Deeply touched, Keira instinctively leaned forward and waved back. Ahead lay the village of Upper Rousham.

Upper Rousham had belonged to the Westcombes ever since the very first Westcombe had built the Heronry and the farm workers' cottages that comprised the village. Herons had been making their lofty, twiggy nests in a small copse behind the house for centuries. Besides the main lane, lined with thatched, tiled and beamed cottages, there was the village church, which had been built due to the largesse of her great-great-great-grandfather; a pub called, not inappropriately, The Stone and Heron; a village school, again funded by Westcombe money; a thriving greengrocer's; a working mill; a butcher's shop and a part-time bakery.

And all of them relied on her for the upkeep of their buildings, the maintenance of the lanes, the low rent for the elderly. And it all took so much money, time and effort.

Mr Greenslade and his six Yorkies stood a few yards further down, just coming out of his pretty honeysuckle-covered cottage, and the dogs began to yap excitedly at the sight of the huge, silent car. Again, Keira smiled and waved back as the old man raised his walking stick in the air in celebration.

She leaned back against the leather seat, her hands cold in her lap. Her eyes gazed out across the countryside, focusing sharply on the field opposite the road. A team of draught horses patiently ploughed the land. The man who walked behind them looked as muscular, as quiet and patient, as the team he led. His hands were steady on the reins, but as the car went past in his peripheral vision, he lifted his head.

He didn't wave, but Keira smiled nevertheless. Aidan Shaw had been her 'horse man' for nearly three years. She'd thought long and hard about converting her home farm to horsepower, and when a local news programme had run a story on thirty draught horses that had been left homeless, she'd taken them on and advertised, without any real hope, for an experienced draught-horse handler and farm manager in one of the magazines devoted to the breed.

No one had been more surprised than Keira when a Yorkshireman with excellent credentials had applied for the job. Now the horses' love and trust for him, coupled with the truly excellent job he'd done on making the farm show such a good profit, meant that the job was his for as long as he wanted it. Sometimes Keira was not quite sure just how long that would be. Aidan was a quiet man who kept himself to himself, but she couldn't help feeling that he had a hidden agenda. Sometimes she was afraid he would leave. And no one, she knew, understood horses and the old-fashioned farming methods better than the gruff Yorkshireman.

But today, she knew that he, at least, would not be judging her . . .

All too quickly, the car swept past his patiently traipsing figure. And there, up ahead, she could see the Penda Stones.

The Penda Stones were as ancient as Stonehenge, according to local historians, and indeed were made of the same South Wales bluestone as the monument's smaller fixtures. It was the only megalithic monument in Oxfordshire, and only slighter smaller than the stone circle at Avebury, in the neighbouring county of Wiltshire.

Even though she'd grown up with the mysterious stone circle, every time she went past its silent, granite grandeur, she felt a shiver of . . . kinship. It was hardly surprising. Her 'title', if it could be called such, came from the Penda Stones.

Legend had it that King Penda, who'd been King of Mercia in the seventh century, had fought a great battle on the site of the stones, and, out of gratitude to a Westcombe ally, had granted him title of the land, ownership of the stones and the title of 'Lord of the Stones' for perpetuity. It was a fine legend, but, like most wonderful stories, she knew it had little basis in fact, and her father, on realizing that his only daughter would be his heir, had been scrupulous in teaching her both the legends and the facts behind the Westcombe legacy.

To begin with, he'd told her seriously on her tenth birthday, the stones were authenticated as having been erected any time between 2600 and 1600 BC. Long before the time of King Penda. And Penda himself had probably never travelled as far south as Oxfordshire, he'd lectured her scrupulously. After all, she had a duty to pass on the title some day, and ensure her own heir understood the history.

The title the Westcombes had enjoyed ever since the house had been built, of 'Lord — or Lady — of the Stones', was just as nebulous. It was not, for instance, listed in *Burke's Peerage*, since it had not been granted by an official monarch. But it hardly mattered. To the locals, Keira was Lady Penda, and nobody seemed to much mind whether it was official or not. Certainly not Keira herself. Her snobbery quotient was zero.

But, whether her title was official or not, her obligations to the village and villagers of Upper Rousham were. Her father had stressed this to her time and again, and made her promise on his deathbed to always look after the Westcombe inheritance. She'd had no trouble promising that she would; after all, she'd been raised with this aim in mind. But she'd always known it would not be easy.

A lot of her tenants were old farm workers, who had pensions to fall back on and little else, and lived virtually rent-free. Even though the farmland for miles and miles around belonged to her, and she rented out no less than six farms, her expenses were terrifying. The church alone, which was no longer in the diocese, applied to her whenever the lead needed replacing, the clock needed fixing or the windows needed renovating.

It was hardly surprising, then, that the whole village had turned out to witness her marriage. A stranger might have found this feudal, not to mention demeaning. But the stranger would have been wrong. It was not subservience that brought them. Nor tact, nor even canniness. Keira was genuinely admired and respected for what she had done for the village.

Not only were low rents for the elderly the order of the day, but her policy of renting to locals and children of locals had won her many friends.

Upper Rousham, situated on the outskirts of the Cotswolds, had the rolling-hill views to match. Clusters of oak and deciduous woodland gave way to well-managed farmland and unspoiled rivers. She could have made a personal fortune selling off her land, but nobody who knew her well — though few really did — would ever believe she'd be so greedy.

Instead, she'd done her best not to let people down, while making sure every enterprise she owned paid its own way and then some. It was the only way she could ever hope to keep herself from bankruptcy.

The pub had been rented to a man who was dedicated to real ale, and was packed nightly with seekers of traditional beer.

The mill, which might have been renovated into a millionaire's home, she'd kept intact, and rented it instead to an enthusiast who had got the mill working again. The building now purchased Westcombe farm grain to produce organically grown, traditionally ground flour which sold to health-food stores at very healthy prices.

The old bakehouse had been let to a baker, who baked delicious fresh bread every morning. It hadn't taken long for the word to spread, and now the modest little bakery had customers flocking in from as far afield as Banbury and Woodstock. Once again, she'd managed to make an unlikely enterprise pay.

And from such humble beginnings things had begun to pick up a momentum of their own. A butcher, who was a master sausage maker of some fame, had heard about the village and applied for a cottage to be converted into a shop. And recently Keira had let a cottage to an artist, who hoped to set up a small gallery.

All too quickly, it seemed to Keira, the Rolls-Royce pulled up outside the tiny wooden porch that led to the equally tiny church, and the last few stragglers moved quickly inside at the sight of the car.

Keira emerged into the crisp September air. The church's arched wooden door, studded with brass, stood invitingly open. Inside, she could hear the faint sound of organ music. She knew that Bessie would have done a good job with the flowers, and that the church would be festooned with them.

By her side, Sid waited. It was his very patience which, in the end, stirred her. She glanced at him, took a deep breath, and held onto his offered arm. Rather tightly.

* * *

Fane Harwood checked the needle on the speedometer of his E-type Jaguar, saw it already touched seventy, and glanced at his watch. He cursed silently to himself as he read the dial. Nearly three o'clock already. He was never going to make it in time. If only he hadn't been so far out of touch, in the depths of Colombia, his father's letter might have reached him sooner!

It had been so unexpected, that letter. And even if the news it contained had been somewhat startling, if not downright unsettling, Fane had been glad enough to receive it.

Eight years was a long time to be estranged from your own father. And any olive branch, no matter how diffidently offered, deserved to be accepted.

He overtook a trundling petrol tanker, just swerving back in time as a somewhat battered Montego came around the approaching bend and tooted angrily. Fane impatiently cursed the narrow country roads. He passed a signpost and jammed on the brakes. Bicester. Wasn't he supposed to turn off there somewhere? He grabbed the map. Where *was* Upper Rousham anyway? His chocolate-brown eyes narrowed in frustration.

The wedding must have started by now. His father must have thought he'd torn the invitation up. Hell, he half-wondered if he should have done just that. This wedding seemed so . . . *bizarre.* So unlike the man he remembered.

He sighed deeply, then glanced up and noticed the other arm on the weather-worn wooden country signpost: Upper Rousham two miles.

Two miles, and the E-type Jag could eat them up like a tiger. His spirits rose, and a wolf-like smile split his austere, handsome face. He rammed his foot down on the accelerator, jerking the wheel around to take the impossibly tight right-hand turn, and the car leapt like a panther, as if sensing its master's urgency as he headed towards the sleepy little village.

* * *

Inside the church Keira shivered as she stood in front of the aisle, and promptly told herself it was just the cold. All English churches felt icy inside, even in high summer. Her eyes narrowed as they adjusted to the poorer light. She heard the 'Wedding March' begin, as if in a dream. It seemed to be such a long way off. She blinked hard and held on tighter to Sid's arm and, slowly, her head cleared.

Mrs Darling was a fine player, and the music flowed sweetly and solemnly from the old organ. Ahead of her, almost as one, the packed pews of people turned to catch their first glimpse of her. There were several audible gasps.

She knew all these people, of course — had known most of them all her life. So the few strange faces amongst them fairly leapt out at her. Lucas's friends and relations, of course. People she'd never met in her life. What must they be thinking now? Angrily, she shook the thought away. What did she care what they thought?

She forced herself to smile yet again, but her face felt stiff and uncooperative. Inside, she still felt guilty. She couldn't shake the sensation that she was nothing but a fraud. But she was not really cheating anyone. Certainly not Lucas, who had approached this whole affair like a business transaction. *But aren't you cheating yourself?* a sad little voice asked, deep in the back of her mind, refusing to be silenced.

By her side, Sid had the keys to the Rolls in his pocket. She could still . . .

Keira stiffened, took a deep breath, and began the slow, halting glide up the aisle so peculiar to brides.

Ahead of her, two men waited. One was old and stoop-shouldered, his silver hair shining uncannily bright in the dark church. Beside him stood an attractive middle-aged man, with pale blond hair and laughing blue eyes. The laughter left his eyes as Keira approached, and his gaze ran appreciatively over her.

He was not the only one, of course. As she walked up the aisle every man there looked at her with admiration. The women looked at her with varying expressions of envy, fondness or puzzlement.

All except one.

Seated at the back, she was dressed in powder-blue. Her white-gloved hands twisted around a matching white handbag, and her hazel eyes bored into the bride's back, an expression of pure venom etched on her features. But then, slowly, a smile twisted her painted lips as she thought about her father's lawyer, who was going to be so very helpful in the near future. Keira Westcombe might think she was getting things all her own way now, but soon . . . soon she'd wish she'd never set foot in this church!

By her side, the woman's husband shifted restlessly, wishing he was somewhere else. Anywhere else.

Keira, thankfully oblivious of the hateful, frustrated gaze, kept her own eyes fixed firmly on the vicar.

The Reverend Martin Jones had christened her, and now he watched the little girl he remembered, all grown up, walking towards him in her wedding dress.

He should have felt happy. Instead, he glanced at the groom and tried not to look as worried as he felt.

Keira came to a halt in a state of rather numb resignation. She'd made her decision, and she was sure it was the right one. If Lucas could still go ahead and marry her, in spite of everything, then she owed him nothing less than the same defiant courage.

She turned as the best man stepped forward to stand beside the groom. The vicar began the opening words of the ceremony.

* * *

Fane swung the car into the narrow turning, almost clipping the hedgerow of red-berried hawthorn. The powerful car practically flew down the road. He briefly saw a man leading a team of horses, and was mildly surprised that anyone should choose such a back-breaking form of farming in this day and age.

Up ahead he saw a ring of stones, and the sight momentarily had him standing on the brakes. There was something very pagan about that ring. It looked ancient and regal, and somehow magical, even in the mellow September afternoon. On a cold winter's day, with bare trees around it and crows cawing, it would be like something straight from ancient legend. But then he saw the church. Above the purr of the engine he could hear no sound of bells; as he'd feared, the ceremony had already begun.

Inside, the best man was handing over the ring. His blond hair fell across his handsome face as he passed the plain gold band to the silver-haired man by his side.

Keira looked up into the seventy-two-year-old face of the man who would soon be her husband, and felt him slip the ring onto her finger. As she listened to him making his vows, she suddenly realized how wavery his voice was. It crackled with the dryness of autumn leaves and she felt her heart lurch in tenderness. Her hand squeezed his, and he looked at her with surprise.

She smiled at him tremulously. In that instant she realized that she really did love him. She loved him as she loved Sid. As she had loved her own father, almost.

With a shaky sigh, she took her own ring and slipped it onto his finger, the knuckle slightly enlarged by arthritis, and repeated her own vows in a clear, firm voice.

'With this ring I thee wed . . .'

It was so quiet in the church suddenly. Over by the pulpit, she could hear a wasp buzzing in the roses.

'I now pronounce you . . .'

Behind her, Keira heard the door open and close. In the silent church, footsteps echoed on the cold stone flags. She wondered who'd come so late, but only idly. It hardly mattered now.

'. . . man and wife. You may kiss the bride.'

In the rear of the church, Fane Harwood leaned wearily against the last pew. Well, at least he'd made it in time to see his father kiss his new bride. From the back of the church it was hard to see her clearly, although Lucas had said in his letter that he was marrying a woman some years younger than himself.

Reading of his father's upcoming marriage, Fane had felt a coolness pass over him, even in the Colombian heat. He'd known he was being totally unfair in thinking the worst, but he'd managed to catch his sister on the phone in between airports, and Jennifer had been scathing about this Keira Westcombe. Of course, Jennifer had always taken it for granted that Lucas would leave her a considerable fortune, and so couldn't be expected to be overjoyed at the fact of their father's second marriage. But Jennifer had bitterly told him that the Westcombe woman was notoriously 'cash poor'. At that point the connection from South America had become so bad that the static had finally caused him to hang up.

But, after eight years of silence between them, Fane knew he was in no position to second-guess his father's feelings or motives, much less those of his new bride, whom he'd never even met.

And just because he himself had once been engaged to a woman who had wanted nothing more than a bank balance and carte blanche to live like a duchess, it didn't mean that his father was being equally as blind now. He tried to tell himself that he was being unduly sceptical and narrow-minded. Nevertheless, he felt his uneasiness returning.

Keira and Lucas signed the register, Lucas's hand shaking as he held the pen in a clumsy grip. He glanced up at her and his eyes were gentle as she added her name. Then, together, as Mr and Mrs Lucas Harwood, they turned to face the church.

The organist began the triumphant music. Now on Lucas's arm, Keira began the walk back down the aisle.

Halfway down, her steps faltered.

There, at the back of the church, was a man she'd never seen before, and her eyes fell on him like a moth's wing against a candle flame.

Suddenly the sea of avid faces disappeared. The flowers receded to vague coloured clouds on the periphery of her vision. Her husband of a few minutes ceased to exist.

Keira, in a split second, took in every inch of him. He was tall — so very tall. Lean and dark, with thick, unruly hair that looked as if he'd just thrust his hands through it. His face was thin, saturnine, hawk-like. The lips were cruel, but she knew, with some kind of female magic, that they'd be soft against her own.

Her heart had stopped beating for a fraction of second. Her pulse had become suspended. Her eyes met his in an explosion of green and brown.

Fane Harwood felt himself sway, and he quickly reached out and grabbed the back of the pew.

He had not expected this.

Over the telephone yesterday, with the thousands of miles separating them, he'd heard plainly the spite in his sister's voice as she'd described Keira Westcombe as beautiful.

But this woman was . . . beyond belief. The sight of her seemed to almost assault his eyes; the aura surrounding her engulfed him. He felt as if he were drowning, and, although he took a deep, shaken breath, he couldn't summon up the desire to try and save himself.

In that small village church, Fane stared at the woman who was his soulmate. In that single, devastating instant, his instinct told him the truth of it in a way that he could never mistake.

He was looking at the love of his life.

And at his stepmother.

CHAPTER 2

Lucas Harwood had purchased Green Acres, a large, modern house on the outskirts of a neighbouring village, when he'd retired and first moved to the area six years ago.

Lucas had been something of a legend in the city, having inherited his father's modest construction company back in the fifties. The various booms since then had enabled him to build up Danelink into a very successful company. He had, of course, always intended to leave the company to his own sons. But things had not worked out that way.

Now, as the big Rolls-Royce led the wedding procession through the village and onto the gravel-swept drive, he wondered how it could all have gone so wrong. Most of it, he was honest enough to admit to himself, was his own fault. When Fane had walked out all those years ago, Lucas had convinced himself that his son would eventually have to forgive him for the mistake he'd made. Even so great a mistake . . .

But one year had gone by, then two, and Lucas had been forced to face the fact that the split was not going to be as temporary as he'd hoped. And so he'd followed Fane's progress at a distance, becoming as proud of his son, and his accomplishments, as any father could be. But Fane had never known that. Lucas had tried several times during the last eight years to write to him, but had never been able to bring himself to post any of the letters. His sense of guilt had been insurmountable. But now he was running out of time, and Fane's unexpected appearance at the church, which could surely only be a good sign, had lifted his heart like nothing else could have.

If only he'd been able to have a word with him then and there. But the photographer had been busy arranging them into various groups, and when he'd looked around, he hadn't been able to see his son anywhere. But now that Fane was here at last, surely they'd be able to sort things out?

As for his eldest son . . . Lucas sighed deeply. He very much feared that *he* was lost for ever. Alice, his first wife, had been so *adamant* that Lucas would never again be part of their lives, but under the circumstances . . . Oh yes, he'd try again. He had nothing left to lose now. What a rotten husband he had turned out to be, to both of his wives.

He felt a hand touch his briefly, and he turned to look at his bride of only an hour. This, his third wife, would have nothing to complain of. This time he'd make sure of it.

Keira smiled at him, no doubt wondering why he was looking so gloomy, and he felt himself smiling back. Keira had always been able to do that to him. She was so uncomplicated. So clear-sighted. So . . . well, Keira.

She turned now to look out of the window, her eyes very accurately 'reading' the land that lay around them.

Lucas had bought a lot of land over the years. After selling Danelink for millions in the boom years of the early eighties, he could afford to. Like many a businessman before him, he knew all too well the benefits of landownership. And, to be honest, he liked the safety and prestige it bestowed upon him. Businesses might rise and fall, stocks and shares might swell and crash, but land was for ever. It wasn't hard to understand Keira's devotion to her own estates. And what she'd done with it was truly remarkable. The Westcombe Nature Reserve was a credit to her.

At the start of his retirement Lucas had been content merely to employ farm managers and sit back, relax and act the retired gentleman farmer. Until he'd met Keira Westcombe. She'd been just twenty-one then. Her father, Michael, had invited him to one of the famous Westcombe Balls, and his first sight of the 'Lady of the Stones' had taken his breath away. With a somewhat roguish twinkle in his eye, Michael had happily introduced him to his daughter.

If Lucas had expected to indulge in the usual meaningless social chitchat, he'd soon been set straight. Keira knew more about land management than any of his own estate managers. He'd been instantly intrigued, of course, and over the years had come to see for himself the sense and profitability of her 'green' ideas. When someone made sense, Lucas habitually listened, and it had been totally his own idea to dedicate some of his land to expanding the nature reserve. He only wished he could have helped her without putting her through this ridiculous marriage fiasco. But, as things stood . . .

'Are you all right, Lucas?' Keira's soft voice brought him back from his memories, and he reached across to take her hand in his. At the coldness of its touch he frowned a little, and glanced at her quickly.

'I'm fine,' he lied, appalled by the weakness of his own voice. He knew why it had become so quavery, of course, but he refused to think of that now. 'The question is, are *you* all right?' he asked softly, and watched her chin come up in that delightfully pugnacious way of hers.

'Of course I am,' she said firmly. 'Why shouldn't I be?'

Lucas shrugged. 'I just thought that days like this were supposed to be somewhat trying on a girl, that's all.'

Keira smiled wryly. 'I'm a woman, Lucas,' she chided gently. 'And as for wedding-day nerves . . . well, they hardly apply to us, do they?' The last few words sounded tense, perhaps even slightly defiant, and he quickly hid a gentle smile.

'No, Keira, they don't,' he agreed softly. Twisting in the seat to face her, glad that her handyman had raised the glass partition behind the driver's seat, thus giving them privacy, he met her somewhat wary eyes with a firm glance.

'I do hope you haven't got it into your head, my dear, that now we're married I'm going to suddenly go back on our deal and turn into some kind of raving, slavering beast,' he murmured, putting as much rogueish good humour into his voice as he could manage. He was relieved to watch her face relax slightly.

'A slavering beast?' she echoed, with a wry twist of her lips, one eyebrow rising delicately into her hairline.

Lucas chuckled. It was a wheezy sound, so unlike his usual hearty laugh, but Keira didn't seem to notice, and for this he was glad. She was obviously badly in need of some reassurance, and he was determined to give it to her in these few moments of peace, before the reception began and the fun-loving chaos commenced. 'We've been friends, you and I, for a long time, haven't we?' he mused quietly, and Keira nodded.

That was true. Ever since Lucas had first moved to the area, he'd been a regular visitor at the Heronry — at first to see Michael, then, after his sudden death of a heart attack, to comfort Keira.

'And you've put me right on many a thing, haven't you?' he added, his voice rich with genuine amusement now.

Keira, too, remembered their first meeting at the Ball, when she'd told him in no uncertain terms what she thought of his plans to uproot hedges. She laughed, beginning to feel a lot happier about things. Trust Lucas to understand, and to be so kind. 'And aren't you glad now that you didn't go ahead with it?' she asked, and thumped him playfully on the arm.

Lucas smiled. That was better. Much more like the woman he'd come to know and admire above all others.

'So, you know you can trust me,' he finished, and the simple statement made her feel ashamed. He was saying that he was going to honour their agreement that this was to be a marriage in name only. That he would never renege on his agreement about the land . . .

Keira glanced at him quickly. 'I know,' she said, her voice quiet and dignified. 'I'm sorry. I suppose it is nerves after all. I didn't mean to insult you. To insult . . . us, and what we're doing.'

Lucas nodded. 'I know that. And so long as neither of us starts trying to change the rules we agreed upon, then . . .' He shrugged.

It was hardly the most romantic thing to say to your bride on your wedding day, but it was the sweetest thing Keira had ever heard. She chuckled delightedly. 'Aye aye, sir,' she said, and saluted smartly.

'Clever dick,' Lucas said indulgently. If only Jennifer had been more like her. Instantly his face clouded at the thought of his only daughter. 'I wish Jenny hadn't come,' he said aloud, then realized how hard that must have sounded, and winced. 'I don't mean to be heartless,' he corrected himself quickly, although Keira didn't look at all shocked, just a little sad. 'I know she's my daughter, but she's so . . . angry at the moment. Somehow I've managed to turn all of my children against me, one way or another.' For a moment his sense of failure was so acute it felt like a physical weight in his heart.

'It's not your fault,' Keira said staunchly. 'Besides, she'll come around, once she gets used to the idea.' But though she tried to keep her voice cheerful and optimistic, she didn't really believe her own words. It was because of Jennifer and her greedy machinations that Keira and Lucas had been forced to marry in the first place. Somehow Keira didn't think she'd appreciate the irony of it if they told her so.

When Lucas had called around to see her, almost a month ago now, it had been painful for him to admit what Jennifer had done, but he'd thought he owed Keira the whole truth, especially as he was about to propose marriage! And so, haltingly, Lucas told her how Jennifer had tried to have him declared incompetent to handle his own affairs. She'd lined up doctors and applied for a court order to force Lucas to take tests. Of course, she was only doing it because he'd told her that he was going to endow the reserve with some land, and she couldn't bear to see her inheritance diminish.

She was only after his money, Lucas had told her glumly, defeat rife in his voice, as Keira had listened, appalled.

Of course, she knew Jennifer liked to live life to the full, and Patrick, her husband, only had his salary as an Oxford don with which to indulge her. Although that would be considered good by most people's standards, it was hardly enough to satisfy Jennifer. She wanted diamonds and furs, and luxury cruises. As the daughter of a millionaire, she'd always felt entitled to them, and resented her father's refusal to give her an allowance after her marriage.

'I'd always spoiled her,' Lucas had said sadly. 'I thought, with her marriage, she might change, but . . .'

Although Lucas had taken and easily passed the doctors' tests — for of course there was nothing *mentally* wrong with him — his daughter's duplicity had shaken him.

And worried him.

He'd wanted to give both land and a sum of money to the Westcombe Nature Reserve while still alive, but feared Jennifer would only use it as an excuse to re-instigate her legal battle against him, and he just couldn't face going through all that humiliation again. The only alternative was to donate the land to Keira in his will.

But even then, he knew that Jennifer would probably be able to successfully contest any such will in court. Nowadays, judges never seemed to take the testator's wishes into consideration, and Lucas was determined that Jennifer would get no more than her fair share. Which had led to his proposing marriage to Keira Westcombe.

At first, Keira had thought her old friend had been more affected by his daughter's treachery than she'd realized. Only when he'd pointed out the advantages and terms of the arrangement had she gradually become convinced.

Lucas was old and lonely. He wanted to live out his remaining time at the Heronry, a house filled with company, laughter and real kinship. He did not, he'd hastily assured her, want a physical relationship. He knew that it had taken courage, dedication and commitment for her to turn all the

Westcombe lands into an official wildlife sanctuary, and he sincerely wanted to help her expand it. Donating some of his land that lay on her southern borders would be an ideal way of doing it, especially as the River Cherwell ran right through it. He wanted to make sure that Keira got it, and what surer way was there than to marry? He would make a will, leaving her the tract of land and a generous sum of money to be donated towards the upkeep of the reserve. The rest of his fortune was to be divided equally between his children. No court would then contest her right to inherit the land and money, especially in a will that was so patently fair to both widow and family.

It had been too good an opportunity to turn down.

Now Keira sighed as she heard the first of the cars pull up behind them.

Sid opened the door and helped her out, Lucas following, trying to hide his wince at the pain that shot across his stomach and seemed to lodge, nastily, between his ribs.

On the gravel drive, the wedding guests quickly began to congregate like brightly coloured birds, twittering and laughing, but none of them, human-like, wanted to make the first move inside.

Bessie moved shyly up to Keira's side, and Keira gave her an exuberant hug and an affectionate kiss. The two women looked at each other, their eyes watering. Bessie was the closest thing to a mother Keira had ever had, and she was glad of her presence.

'Right then, let's get on inside,' Lucas said, just loudly enough to get action but not sternly enough to sound bossy, and slowly, happily, the wedding party trooped indoors.

Green Acres, as might be expected from a construction millionaire, had been built on a grand scale, and had a large hall as well as several salons and, more importantly, a vast, old-fashioned dining room. This was set out with tables forming an open-ended square, and at the top table stood the cake. Keira looked at the five-tier ivory and green creation, and shook her head in bemusement.

The dining room had two sets of French windows, which were now standing open, leading onto a paved patio. On that patio an eight-piece orchestra had set up, and now began playing a soft, melodious Strauss waltz. Waiters circulated with trays. In the salons, groups sorted themselves into family and friends, and soon everyone was chatting, happily sipping fine champagne and munching on delicious canapes, hors d'oeuvres, nuts and candied fruits.

Keira found herself feeling strangely left out. Lucas was talking to his old cronies from the city, who were no doubt congratulating him on acquiring such a beautiful and young wife. Her lips twisted as she wondered what they must be thinking, and then, once again, she shrugged fatalistically.

What did it matter? She and Lucas knew what they were doing, after all. Besides, she had other things on her mind. With Lucas's land she could divert the river and make an off-shoot miles long that could be filtered at both ends, making it habitable for otters. It had always been one of her more ambitious dreams to see otters returned to the Oxfordshire countryside. Of course, the filtering equipment needed would cost a small fortune, and she'd have to find a reputable company to—

Her thoughts came to a sudden and abrupt end.

He was there. Right in front of her, just to the left of a group of women who were discussing some television programme or other. He had his back to her, but she'd know him anywhere. Her heart began to race, making a slow, feverish heat seep into her blood. She swallowed hard.

When she'd first seen him in the church, she'd thought she'd been about to faint. He'd seemed to be so much more . . . *real* than anyone else. It had only been nerves, of course; she'd realized that as soon as she'd stepped out into the fresh air and posed for the photographs. It had been silly to be so spooked. Her feeling of . . . kismet . . . had just been an aberration. She'd been full of doubts about marrying Lucas, and feeling a little guilty about having had a church wedding when it had been, in reality, little more than a business deal, and it was only natural that her mind should decide to play tricks on her.

Having sorted all that out to her satisfaction, she had, nevertheless, found herself looking out for the stranger as the photographer had arranged and cajoled them all into position. But she'd never once spotted him, and now she'd almost begun to doubt that he had ever been there. There had been something almost . . . magical about his appearance in the church. She wondered vaguely if there were any legends in the family history about Westcombe brides being courted by ghostly lovers.

But now here he was again, very much in the flesh. She could see the dark blue material of his jacket wrinkle over his shoulder blades as he reached across one of the many laden tables for a glass of champagne. She saw the hard plane of his cheek appear as he half turned, the glass rising to his lips. So strong was the connection between them, she felt that she could almost taste the cold tang of the wine on her own lips, and she licked them nervously.

Something very weird was going on. And she didn't like it.

She had the childish impulse to find Lucas and have him reassure her, once again, that she had not made a hideous mistake. She wouldn't even mind if Jennifer should decide to sidle up to her and start pouring venom into her ears. At least it would be something normal. Something she was familiar with. Could cope with . . .

Fane Harwood gently lowered the drink back onto the table, his whole spine tingling. He felt as if someone had just poured a mixture of hot wax and ice cubes down his back. Slowly, he began to turn.

The room was unfamiliar to him, since he hadn't so much as set foot in his father's most recent home. The walls were covered with flowered wallpaper and lined with country scenes. The carpet was a solid green. It was full now of food-covered tables, flowers, people and noise. But the woman in white was immediately the focus of his attention. Yet it was not the wedding dress, that most evocative of gowns, that made her so prominent. Nor her nearness. Nor even, he supposed, her beauty. But something else. Something that only *his* eyes could see made her stand out like a poppy in a field of cornflowers.

Their eyes met.

Again.

Keira's heart stopped beating for a fraction of a second.

Again.

Fane Harwood silently but graphically cursed.

Again.

Keira, somewhat dazed, shook her head. She hadn't realized she'd done so, but he noticed it at once, and it echoed his very own thoughts. This couldn't be happening. This couldn't mean what they thought it did. It was . . . just a trick of the light. A twitch of unsettled nerves. It meant nothing.

Like hell! Fane's lips twisted into a somewhat grim smile. He'd followed the line of cars back to this place in a state of tense caution. And the more he'd thought about the scene in the church, the more angry with himself he'd become. He was a grown, sophisticated man, for Pete's sake! He wasn't, he simply *wasn't* going to let himself be taken in by a fortune- hunter again, no matter how beautiful she looked in a wedding dress. And he couldn't believe that she could be anything else. A woman of her age and beauty marrying an old man. His *father*!

And yet . . . he wanted to believe there was another explanation. He felt a hot shaft of terrible confusion wash over him, but he pushed determinedly away from the table and began to move towards her. He moved like a jaguar might move, Keira thought nervously, his limbs a mere extension of his mind's wish. And his only wish, for better or for worse, was to get closer to her.

Keira instinctively took a step back. She was vaguely aware of the unconcerned chatter about her, of the sweet music from the orchestra out on the patio, and the sound of her own heartbeat, thudding rather sickeningly now in her breast. An instinct as old as time screamed in the back of her mind: *run.* But it was already too late.

Way too late.

Fane had no idea what he intended to do, until he felt his arm go around her waist. Keira found herself turning, her rooted feet leaving their spot at the pressure of his leg against hers.

'Dance?' Fane asked, his deep-timbred voice hitting her body like a hammer-blow, making her blink.

'What?' she said, her own voice as thin as gossamer.

The waltz was one she was unfamiliar with, but as his fingers changed their pressure, just slightly, on the left side of her waist, she found her body swinging around into his; it was as if the language of the music had bypassed her brain altogether and gone straight to her flesh.

Fane felt the cool silken stiffness of her dress press against him. Beneath it, he could just sense the heat of her body. His heart leapt. His nostrils dilated as the scent of fresh gardenias tantalized his senses. Instinctively he tightened his grip on her and reached for her free hand, which was hanging, limp and useless, by her side. The moment his fingers found it her wrist twitched, as if receiving a bolt of electricity. He saw her eyes — her incredible sea-green eyes — widen, and felt a sense of almost profound joy and relief flood him.

So, he was not the only one who felt this way. Whatever madness had assailed him in the church, whatever residue of it that was still, even now, working in him, at least he was not the only one afflicted by it. And he was savagely glad. If he had to suffer, he did not want to suffer alone.

'I suppose I could claim a guest's privilege to kiss the bride?' he murmured cheekily, and felt her stumble as he took the first gliding step.

'I don't think that would . . . well, I don't know you,' Keira heard herself stuttering, and cursed her tongue-tied stupidity.

With the first pressure of her breasts against his chest, Fane felt a jolt shoot through him. He'd been in Japan, building a bridge over a gorge, when he'd felt his first earthquake. Although the epicentre had been miles away, he'd literally felt the earth moving beneath his feet. It had been the most uncanny, eerie and downright frightening experience of his life, and had left him feeling disorientated for days. Now he felt the exact same sense of astonishment. Except it was not the ground that moved, but something deep within him. Something he hadn't even been aware of before. Had the woman in his arms been any other woman but this one, he might have been thrilled. Excited by this new sensation. Now, he only felt . . .

Keira saw his lips tighten ominously, and she wondered what it would feel like to have those lips on hers. They were thinner than her own, and looked harder. Stronger. More . . .

'That's no hardship. My name's Fane,' he said quietly, watching her like a hawk for her reaction.

Keira's eyes widened. Fane. Wasn't that the name of Lucas's son? He'd told her that he'd written, asking him to come to the wedding, but he'd also told her they hadn't spoken for years.

'Fane?' she echoed. 'Lucas's son?'

'None other. So you see, if I don't have the right to kiss the bride, who does?'

Keira felt panic nibble at her consciousness, but at the same time became aware of a strange silence around her. Only dimly at first, because her mind, her heart, her soul, were too much taken up with the man who held her in his arms. But the silence grew more intense, demanding that she pay it attention.

And suddenly, in one awful realization, she knew what she was doing. She was dancing. The first dance. Which she should be starting with her husband. Tradition demanded it. She stumbled and tried to draw away. But Fane, too, was aware of the disapproving silence around them, and ignored it completely. Let them stare.

'Please,' Keira said, her voice ragged. 'I shouldn't be dancing with you.'

He glanced down at her, surprised by the panic in her voice. And she was looking up at him with eyes that seemed to be wide with . . . shame? Fane felt it hit him like a body-blow. It had felt so perfect, holding her in his arms. He didn't want her to make him feel guilty, damn it.

'I'm sure Dad won't mind,' he said drolly, and watched her wince. 'After all, you are my . . . stepmother.'

Keira stumbled again, and closed her eyes. She began to feel quite sick.

'Are you all right?'

The voice was outwardly amused, and when she forced her eyes open to look at him, he was wearing a cruel smile. Keira recognized the steel and strange anger that lay underneath it, and understood it only too well.

'Let me go,' she said, quite firmly, but quietly enough to reach only his ears.

'Why?' he said, equally softly, his eyes openly mocking her now. 'You don't really want me to.'

And Keira knew that she didn't. No sooner had he said it than she realized it was nothing more than the truth. She had to put a stop to this. Now. But her body trembled with a weakness she'd never known before. Desperately she cast around for a defence, any defence, against this devastating stranger.

'I want to dance with my husband,' she lied, as calmly as she dared.

'You have a funny way of showing it,' Fane said softly, his eyes narrowing.

Keira flushed in unhappy guilt.

'I expect Dad is as wealthy as ever?' he began to probe, none too tactfully, turning her into a tight series of steps that he executed with perfect timing and grace, seemingly unaware that she was like a wooden doll in his arms. 'As he probably told you, we haven't kept in touch, but I can't believe he has let retirement slow down his money-making activities. Dad always was lucky with the stock market.'

Keira stiffened. 'If you're assuming that I married your father for his money . . .' she began grimly. Then went as white as a sheet. He was quite right. Hadn't she done just that? For one sick instant, Keira wanted to burst into tears.

He noticed her sudden pallor at once, of course, and allowed himself a slow, burning, sexy smile of triumph. But he felt anything but victorious. Damn her, couldn't she at least pretend to be a loving bride, a woman totally misunderstood by a cruel and cynical world? Instead, she was looking at him like a stricken deer. He wanted to shake her. To kiss her . . .

'It's none of your business why I married Lucas,' Keira said at last. With no excuses to offer him, she only had defiance left.

For once, his own smooth dancing steps faltered. None of his business! The cheek of the wretched woman!

Keira gasped as his hands tightened on her waist, and then he all but lifted her off her feet as he swung her in time to a particularly sweeping piece of music.

'Well, I have to give you ten out of ten for nerve,' Fane finally managed to rasp. 'And let's see. Ten out of ten for intelligence, too — unless Dad's gone senile. He never was easy to fool, so you must be good. And ten out of ten for self-control. It can't be easy for a woman to let an old man touch her and pretend to be pleased about it. Ten out of ten for looks, of course. I can't wait to see how you score for perseverance. Or do you intend to just wait a year and then go all out for a very profitable divorce?'

Keira felt her heart fall to her feet. This was . . . appalling. She wanted to slap his damned arrogant face for being so cold-blooded, and at the same time cry on his shoulder, because she knew, deep in her heart of hearts, that she couldn't really blame him for what he was saying.

'If you don't let me go,' she warned, her voice impossibly choked, 'I'll . . .' And there she trailed off helplessly.

'You'll what?' he goaded. 'Scream?' His hands tightened on hers as he swung her around in a graceful arc. 'Don't let me stop you,' he offered, as the music swelled to a sweet crescendo.

Keira knew when she was beaten. But, oddly, at the same time, she felt a strange kind of power begin to awaken within her. An age-old, feminine power that she'd never even suspected had been a part of her before. For she knew, without quite knowing *how* she knew, that she could hurt this man just as much and as easily as he could hurt her. But she had Lucas's happiness to think about. She simply couldn't let his son think the worst. But how could she tell him about Jennifer? That, surely, was Lucas's decision. 'For your information, I happen to care about Lucas very much,' she said, trying desperately to salvage something from the situation.

'But you don't love him, do you?' Fane shot back, needing her to admit her own duplicity, so desperately needing her not to say yes.

Keira's eyes darkened. 'As a matter of fact,' she said softly, 'I do love him.' But not . . . oh, not as she now knew she *could* love someone. Like she could love *this* man. If she was ever given a chance . . .

Fane drew in a hissing breath. Even though he didn't believe her, *couldn't* believe her, it still hurt. Grimly, he forced himself to laugh. 'Don't tell me,' he drawled, 'pigs can fly, and fairies really do live down at the bottom of the garden.' His eyes narrowed into dark slits. 'And, of course, you're perfectly entitled to wear white.'

Keira felt so utterly weary, suddenly. No, she wasn't entitled to wear white. She had loved Rex, and had happily and confidently looked forward to their marriage.

There was just no getting through to this man who was her husband's son. She felt her eyes fill with tears, and instinctively tried to free her hand to wipe them away, but Fane's fingers tightened just as instinctively on her wrist. When he looked down into her tear-bright eyes, he felt like such a bastard that he wanted to shake her. If she could play on his father's heartstrings even half so easily as she played on his, no wonder Lucas had married her.

'Why are you being so . . . vicious?' she asked at last. 'I haven't done anything to you.'

Fane couldn't help it. He threw back his head and laughed out loud. Not done anything to him?

The music saved them both by coming to an abrupt end. Keira stepped back and he let her go, his reluctance obvious. She turned, and saw her guests look quickly away. There was a sudden babble of embarrassed talk.

Keira reached for a glass of champagne with a shaky hand and took a generous sip. By her side, Fane watched her with defiant but puzzled eyes. Her tears had nonplussed him. He'd hadn't expected her to be so . . . vulnerable. She really was a remarkable actress. Except when he'd accused her of marrying for money, she hadn't been in the least prepared for it. Of that he was sure. He just couldn't figure her out — and that worried him.

Lucas, who'd been out in the garden showing an old friend his fuchsias, had come in during the last few bars, a little surprised to see his bride dancing so soon and wondering why she hadn't come to fetch him. Then he saw who it was she was dancing with and smiled with pleasure. He'd half feared Fane wouldn't show up at the reception, and he wanted to talk to him so badly.

Slowly, with more difficulty than he'd like to admit, he made his way to his now isolated bride. Keira saw him, and almost wilted with relief. Although she had turned her back on Fane very decisively, she was all too aware that he had not moved away. Not that she'd expected him to do the decent thing, of course. Her newly awakened instinct had already told her that this was not a man who cared about the conventional. He might look civilized in his expensively tailored Savile Row suit, but she knew a savage when she saw one. Now she could feel his presence like a hot ember beside her.

'Lucas,' she said, reaching for him like a drowning man reached for a lifeboat. She took his arm in a strong grip.

Lucas glanced at her, surprised.

'Hello, Father.' That deep-timbred voice once more cannoned into her body, burrowing its way through, heating her blood and settling in her bones like a tender ache.

She'd never heard such a deep, rich, expressive voice before in her life.

'Fane,' Lucas said, a little stiffly now that the moment was on him. 'I didn't know you were here.'

Keira knew how desperately Lucas wanted to be reconciled with him, and wished miserably that she could have made it easier for him. It broke her heart to see Lucas smile so warily at his son, when she knew he wanted nothing more than to hug him but didn't dare.

Then Lucas glanced down at Keira's pale, tense face. 'I see you've already met my son,' he said gently. Her eyes were stricken, and he glanced quickly at his son, wondering what had happened. Something obviously had.

Lucas had always been proud of Fane, in spite of their differences. He was strong and intelligent, and a handsome devil. A son any man would be proud to call his own, in fact. And he was looking at Keira like a hawk looks at a tasty dove.

Lucas felt the pain in his chest tighten. Fane and Keira . . . But after the first second of shock, he felt, absurdly, like laughing out loud. After all, it was so . . . perfect. Two of the people he loved most in life. Why shouldn't they get together? But he was jumping way ahead of himself. There was so much he and Fane needed to sort out first . . .

He glanced from his wife to his son, and back to his wife again. Then he reached for her hand. 'Come on, my dear,' he said comfortingly. 'Let's go and cut our wedding cake.' To Fane he said quietly, 'I'd like to talk to you, son. Later?' There was such a wealth of appeal in his eyes that Fane found himself nodding. Besides, his father looked so much . . . older than he'd expected. With a start he realized that Lucas was in fact looking rather ill.

Keira was so relieved to be getting out of Fane's disturbing orbit that she smiled a sweet, grateful smile at Lucas; it fairly radiated from her face like a precious stone.

By her side, Fane drew his breath in a deep, painful hiss. He could only watch helplessly as his father led her away.

‘I see Fane has had his usual effect on a pretty young woman,’ Lucas probed casually as they made their way to the top table.

‘He certainly has a way of making his presence felt,’ Keira agreed ruefully. She smiled as the photographer took their picture cutting the cake, and for the next few hours tried, unsuccessfully, to put Fane Harwood out of her mind.

She was aware that Fane and Lucas had disappeared into Lucas’s study, and so could just about force herself to eat and drink, dance with other guests, chat to friends and generally look as if she was enjoying herself.

Around eleven o’clock, things began to wind down. She and Lucas had decided a honeymoon was hardly appropriate, and Lucas, in particular, was glad. He wasn’t in any condition to travel and was glad to move into the Heronry as soon as possible. As they prepared to take their leave, Sid brought the Silver Ghost around to the front.

Drawing away from Lucas and the crowd of well-wishers, Keira walked a few paces into the garden, glad of the darkness and fresh air. She leant against an ivy-covered wall and took a long, shaken breath. At last this nightmarish day was over and could be put behind her.

‘You look exhausted.’ A voice spoke from behind a huge rose bush beside her and she gave a quiet cry, spinning around, recognizing the voice instantly. Her shoulders came back, bracing herself for the worst. Fane noticed the gesture and smiled grimly. He held his hands out in a gesture of peace. ‘It’s all right. I won’t bite. Dad’s asked me to come to the house tomorrow. I just wanted to warn you.’

‘I’m surprised. I’d have thought a surprise attack was more your style.’

In the darkness, she saw his teeth flash white. ‘I deserve that. But Dad and I have talked a little tonight and he’s told me all about the Heronry. And . . . the land you own.’ The admission seemed wrung out of him, and Keira couldn’t help but smile grimly.

'Ah. So you don't mind your father marrying an upper-class gold-digger, then?'

Fane's smile vanished. 'That wasn't what I meant,' he snarled.

'No?' she challenged. 'Forgive me, but that's what it sounded like.'

'You don't pull any punches, do you?' he said, and there was grudging admiration in his voice now.

'I didn't notice you wearing kid gloves this evening,' she said coolly, and in the darkness Fane laughed. It was a cool, unamused laugh.

'No, I suppose not.' He sounded bleak all of a sudden. And, somehow, in the space of a heartbeat, the night had become dangerous.

She moved restlessly. 'I'd better be going.'

'Of course. I wouldn't want you to be late for your wedding night. You must be looking forward to it so much.'

'You bastard!' Keira snapped, then flushed. What was the matter with her? She couldn't let him keep getting to her like this.

Fane knew he was acting like the bastard she'd called him, and he knew why, of course. He moved closer, the light from the porch casting his face into dramatic shadows.

'Tell me again that you love him,' he said softly. 'Really love him, as a wife should.'

But Keira couldn't.

And they both knew it.

CHAPTER 3

Blaise Clayton reached into the fridge for a tin of cat food and smiled down sympathetically at the ravenous feline winding her silky grey tail around her calves.

'All right, Keats, hold your horses, puss,' she murmured, and crossed the kitchen to extract a can-opener from one of the drawers. The moggy followed faithfully, miaowing pitifully. Can a hungry cat miaow any other way? she wondered, with a rueful twist of her unpainted lips.

Blaise nodded in satisfaction as she put the full dish of food down and watched her pet of only three days get tucked in. She'd gone to the animal rescue shelter less than a week after moving into the cottage. She'd felt in urgent need of company, and a warm, soft, purring body to cuddle had seemed just ideal. And, somehow, the thought of rescuing a full-grown cat from an institutionalized life had appealed far more to her than buying her very own kitten.

Now, she thought with some smug satisfaction, her altruism had paid off. The moment she'd seen the five-year-old grey-striped she-cat in the cattery, she'd known the moggy was for her. Its previous owner had thought the kitten was a he, not a she, hence the rather odd name, the sanctuary had explained. Unfortunately that owner had died, and no one had wanted to look after the cat.

Now Blaise reached down and stroked her pet's back, and as she did so, utterly cat-like, Keats's rear end rose happily as her mistress's fingers touched the base of her spine and curled around her tail.

'Now who, I wonder, called you Keats?' Blaise asked softly, as the green eyes swung her way. 'And why? Fancy yourself as a poet, do you, hmm?'

The cat purred and continued eating, and Blaise laughed. That was what she liked about cats. They had such good common sense.

She sighed and reached for the kettle, thinking only now about her own breakfast.

For years she'd made porridge, or pureed fruit. Her mother had only been able to eat basic, carefully prepared menus, and now, suddenly free from such restrictions, Blaise felt once again an arrow of loss shoot through her. It was only to be expected, she knew, but still it took her by surprise.

Her hand shook as she poured water into the kettle, and she stared at her offending limb balefully.

Enough of that. Her mother had been gone for months now. The funeral was over. The house had been sold. She'd come to a new part of the country to start afresh. At least, that was the theory.

But, at thirty-six, it was easier said than done.

Blaise walked back to the fridge and deliberately reached for a carton of eggs and a plastic-wrapped piece of bacon. She'd never cooked herself a traditional English breakfast before. And, she reminded herself determinedly, as she reached for a couple of tomatoes and a few mushrooms, the longest and hardest of journeys started with the shortest and simplest of steps.

As she cooked, the cat leapt onto one of the padded kitchen chairs and washed her pretty face, watching her new mistress with indulgent eyes.

Had other eyes been watching her, they, too, might have been just as indulgent. At five feet five Blaise was not tall, but she moved as a taller woman might, with a lithe economy and grace. Her hair was a short, unruly mop of naturally light blonde curls, and she had the blue eyes that went with it. Many men had found her heart-shaped face, generous mouth and warm heart appealing.

None had found the prospect of a sick and totally dependent mother-in-law the least appealing. Consequently, Blaise's knowledge of men was not vast.

'Ouch!' Blaise yelped as a spiteful bit of bacon fat spat at her from the frying pan, hitting her square on the wrist. She rubbed it ruefully and stepped back.

Porridge began to look good again.

She made a mental note to buy one of those round wire-mesh things that fitted over frying pans and protected cooks from killer bacon, then neatly cut the tomatoes in half and added them to the fat.

She sniffed, admitting to herself that it really did smell rather good.

Behind her, Keats sniffed too. Some of that bacon had her name written on it, or she was no judge of humankind.

Half an hour later, feeling pleasantly full and just a little guilty at her gluttony, Blaise collected her mass of bulky belongings and shut the door carefully behind her, checking it was locked. The cat, who was still finishing off the last of the bacon, leapt loyally onto the windowsill to see her off.

When Blaise turned at the wooden gate to drop the latch back in place, she glanced up, her heart lifting at the sight of the cat in the window. She somehow made the cottage look like home. Even though it was only rented.

Blaise had previously lived in one house for all of her life — a neat semi on the outskirts of Birmingham that her father had bought back in the sixties. When he'd died, the house and his insurance had enabled his wife and only child to just about get by.

Which was just as well, since Mary Clayton had, within a year of his death, contracted a long, lingering illness that had prevented Blaise from working.

It had been partly because she'd needed to stay at home, and partly because she'd needed to answer the call of a natural talent, that Blaise had turned to full-time painting as a career.

In the beginning, of course, it had hardly paid. Blaise, tied to the house, had been rather strapped for subjects. And, like most things, building up a passable finesse in the competitive world of art had taken practice. Years and years of it.

But eventually her bowls of fruit; vases of flowers; seas and landscapes painted from memory, photographs and imagination, had begun to sell. At first only to friends of the family, who had probably felt sorry for her, but who had also known, nevertheless, a finely painted picture when they saw one. Then, a few years ago, she'd managed to persuade a local gallery to take a few. Then a shop or two.

Soon, Blaise had been earning enough to save some money for the first time in her life.

Not that she'd been able to do anything with her newfound money and independence, of course. For a start, she'd never been able to learn to drive — lessons cost money, which they'd been ill able to spend. Moreover, lessons would have taken her out of the house for hours at a time, and they hadn't been able to pay for carers to patient-sit. And Mary simply couldn't be left alone. Her ailment had affected her breathing, and if an alarm should go off, indicating something was wrong, somebody had to be there to push the right ventilator buttons or administer the right drug.

Nor had Blaise been able to spend her newly acquired money on a holiday. Her previous experience of holidays had all been as a little girl, before her father had died and the advent of her mother's illness. Weeks spent at Margate, or Weston-Super-Mare. Idyllic days building sandcastles and eating sandy ice-cream cones. The funfair and candyfloss.

As an adult, Blaise had never been away on holiday, and going abroad had been a dream akin to winning the lottery.

People had pitied her, although she hadn't been aware of it. To Blaise, her life had been perfectly normal. She'd loved her mother dearly, and her mother had needed her. She'd suffered so much that Blaise didn't begrudge her a single day of the life she'd devoted to her.

Blaise had had her painting. She'd had a roof over her head. If she hadn't had a man in her life, or all the usual trappings one might expect a woman in the 1990s to have, she hadn't missed them. Now, she supposed, she could have it all, but she was in no rush.

She'd been distraught when her mother had finally died, although she'd had plenty of warning. The kindly doctors had seen to that.

Now, as was only natural, Blaise felt a little lost.

She'd spent the week after her mother's death in a state of limbo, but the funeral had allowed her to say a final goodbye, and with that goodbye certain facts had gradually become clear to her. That she didn't want to stay in the house was the first of them. She'd come back from the cemetery to a place full of lingering, painful memories. It had been a wrench to take the first step of contacting an estate agent, and the day she'd seen the 'For Sale' sign go up in her garden she'd felt a moment of panic.

But the neighbours had been kind and supportive. It would do her good, they'd said, to make a fresh start. She was still young, they'd kindly assured her, and she still had time to make a go of her life.

If their tact had been questionable, their affection had not. Old Mrs Simms, who'd lived next door on the left, had lived in her neat semi ever since Blaise was a little girl. Consequently, she looked on Blaise like the daughter she'd never had. She'd been sad to see her go, but, like everyone else, also secretly relieved.

It was not good for a woman to live so long without a man. To live without the prospects of a home life of her own, a *family* of her own.

Blaise had immediately started looking around for somewhere else to live. At first, spending long, lonely nights poring over a map of Great Britain, the task of picking somewhere had seemed huge. Not to mention extremely daunting.

But, little by little, she'd reasoned it all out. For all her scatty appearance, Blaise had a good head on her shoulders. She didn't like city life, and Birmingham had been encroaching on their own particular suburb for some time. Trees had perished, and more housing estates had taken their place. She wanted somewhere full of light and space and greenery. Obviously, then, a small town or even a village.

And she wanted to paint something other than bowls of fruit and vases of flowers. She wanted rolling landscapes and panoramic views that she didn't have to paint from photographs. The Lake District? Too cold, she'd thought, with a shiver. Too far away from what she was used to.

Something a bit more . . . cosy. A bit more . . . safe. She'd smiled at that thought, but she knew herself well. She was hardly the adventurous sort.

Her clothes were considered bohemian by her friends, but that was only because she'd always bought her wardrobe in charity shops — it was all they could afford, and consequently she took what she could get. Brightly coloured dresses that were too big for her that nobody else wanted. Trousers that didn't match tops, scarves that kept her warm but looked . . . different. Anybody looking at her, she knew, immediately classed her as the typical artist — rebellious, bohemian, slightly wild. In fact, she was as sensible as semolina.

And what she'd been planning to do with her life now leaving her home and everything familiar — was already enough of an adventure, thank you very much!

So . . . the Cotswolds, then? Why not? She'd pictured in her mind's eye canvasses filled with scenes of haymaking, bubbling brooks and bluebell woods. As a painter, she loved painting beautiful things. Abstracts were not for her. Besides, she knew without false modesty that she was *good* at painting beautiful things. And, if critics thought her work a bit chocolate-boxy, well . . . sod 'em!

So, the Cotswolds it had been. And, since she wasn't sure that she'd settle, she'd decided to rent rather than buy. After all, with the money from the house, Blaise, for the first time in her life, was financially quite secure.

It had been sheer chance that she'd heard of the unusual village of Upper Rousham.

The lady who ran the local health-food shop had been chatting to a fellow bean-curder when Blaise had walked in, and she hadn't been able to help overhearing their conversation. The proprietress had just got in this 'fabulous' ground flour that would make 'simply divine' bread. It came from the mill at Upper Rousham. Did her 'favourite customer' know about it? Apparently not.

Blaise had listened to the two women talking in growing fascination and excitement as she'd learned about this village in Oxfordshire that was keeping up traditional values. There'd been no new houses built there in 'centuries, my dear', and the corn was grown without pesticides, and milled by 'real stones, can you imagine?' in a 'real, working mill'.

The more she'd heard, the more Blaise had been seduced. She'd rushed home and grabbed the map, and — with a little difficulty — finally located the tiny village. In the north-west of Oxfordshire, it just brushed shoulders with the Cotswolds. It was halfway between Oxford itself and the ancient market town of Banbury.

A few days' research in the libraries had yielded the information that the village was owned by one person — a certain Keira Westcombe. Quickly, and with growing excitement, she'd learned more. Keira Westcombe had turned her land into an official nature reserve and wildlife sanctuary. And — the clincher as far as Blaise was concerned — the village had its own stone circle.

Blaise had never seen Stonehenge, or the other ancient stone circles in Wiltshire, and just the mention of a megalithic monument had set her heart pounding. She could see her canvasses now — such a sight demanded more than one painting. A winter scene, with bare trees and a flock of rooks, circling over the ancient stones. And perhaps — why not? — a sunset, with the stones like great black obelisks against a fiery sky. Her artist's soul had surrendered to the images then and there.

She'd written that very same day to Keira Westcombe, stating that she was an artist of some renown — which was, perhaps, a little cheeky, but in one sense strictly accurate — and was hoping to relocate to a rural setting. She was looking for rented accommodation in a scenically challenging area, and did she have any cottages available?

Blaise had not really expected to be so lucky. Common sense had told her that a village as unique as Upper Rousham was bound to be popular, and her chances of getting in were probably zero. Especially as she'd read that Keira Westcombe's cottages were nearly all rented out to local families and farm workers.

But, for once in her life, Blaise Clayton had been lucky. A cottage had become vacant, there were no locals interested in it, and Keira had quite fancied the idea of the village having its own resident artist. Blaise had received a letter, almost by return of post, asking her to come down and see Lady Keira Westcombe for an interview.

Blaise had been at once jubilant and terrified. She hadn't realized that the owner of Upper Rousham had a title, and she had no idea what to wear, what to say, or how to play it. She'd never had an interview before in her life.

In the event she'd worn her best smart outfit — not a hard choice, since she had only one — taken the train to the neighbouring village and walked the mile and a half to the Heronry. Luckily it had been a fine day.

She'd been so fascinated by the huge, fluttering shapes of the birds and their unlikely twiggy nests high in the trees that she'd been late for her appointment. She'd been shown into a cosy study by a round, pleasant woman — obviously the housekeeper — and had immediately started babbling apologies to the most beautiful woman she had ever seen.

She'd expected Lady Keira Westcombe to be . . . well . . . more like something out of P.G. Wodehouse, she supposed. Tall and fat, grey-haired and imperious.

Not a woman who could have been a fashion model.

Keira had taken one look at the blonde-haired woman, listened to her rather breathless description of the herons, and how marvellous they'd look on a spring canvas, with daffodils and bluebells in the foreground and the lofty, stick-like nests of the herons above, and decided then and there to give her the cottage.

The 'interview' couldn't have been less interview-like if Blaise had planned it. The housekeeper had returned with tea and caraway seed cake, and *stayed.* Keira Westcombe had introduced her as Bessie, apparently seeing nothing odd in a servant staying to chat with the guests. The afternoon had fled as Keira described the work that went into the nature reserve, and Blaise unexpectedly found herself describing her life with her mother, and how she came to be looking to start a new life.

Bessie had even brushed away a tear or two, and heaped more cake upon her. Blaise had eaten it with pleasure.

Then and there, the two women — the lady of the manor and the artist — had looked around the vacant cottage. It was in the middle of the village, not far from the church. It overlooked rolling hills on one side, a copse to the left, the church on the right and the village road on the front. Since the village road was a no-through road, and was lined with flowering baskets, dry-stone walling and cottage gardens frothing with every kind of cottage garden flower known, Blaise had fallen in love with it on sight. How different it was from the Birmingham suburb, with roaring traffic, litter and crime.

She'd moved in less than a month later. Soon all her admittedly meagre belongings had been unpacked, and that was when she'd gone to the animal sanctuary to collect a pet.

The Claytons had traditionally always kept dogs, but pet hairs had been no good for her mother's condition, and the family dog had been taken off their hands by relatives.

Blaise had gone to the shelter with a dog in mind, but one look from Keats's green eyes had changed all that. The cat had leapt down from her heated pad of a bed, sashayed up to the wire netting and stuck one soft grey padded paw to the wire. Blaise had knelt down and touched it, and the deal had been cemented.

Now, on this crisp morning, Blaise walked away from her pretty cottage, a blank canvas under one arm, an old school satchel full of paints hanging off one shoulder, a fold-away seat and a bag of mints in one hand, and set off down the village road.

She knew just where she was going.

To the stones.

She'd deliberately kept her mind on the move, and had conscientiously spring-cleaned the empty cottage before setting up home. She'd resisted the impulse to explore until all the furniture was in, the bed made, the clothes put away in the wardrobe and the kitchen stocked with edibles from the village shops.

It had been marvellous to be able to walk just a few yards down the street and get all she needed from a small, delightfully old-fashioned butcher's shop, greengrocer's and bakery.

At first, she hadn't known the bakery existed, for, unlike the butcher's and greengrocer's, there had been no charming hand-painted sign hanging up outside it.

Instead, the beautiful red ironstone building had simply exuded the most wonderful smells, and she had simply followed a small line of people in through what she had thought of as the front door of a private home.

Well, it had been a front door, and the baker did live in the house as well, but the bottom of the three-storeyed home had long since been turned into a huge old-fashioned kitchen. It also had a newly built counter, where the baker's wife held court like a queen.

There were 'Mr Cowley's special doughnuts', fresh from the oven, and 'that bloomer for Mr Spikewell,' who was 'goin' fishin'' and needed some good bread for his sandwiches. Not to mention some good bait. Roach, so Blaise had learned that first day in the village, loved good bloomer bait.

She'd bought two crusty rolls for her lunch, and had been about to buy a bigger loaf to see her through the week when the baker's wife had kindly told her that they were open every day, and why not just buy bread as and when she needed it, when it was fresh and still warm from the oven?

Blaise, used to supermarket sliced loaf, had been over the moon.

Now, though, she girded her loins, so to speak, and deliberately turned her nose in the opposite direction as she walked past the ironstone bakery. Nevertheless, the smell of freshly baked bread had her stomach rumbling, in spite of the fact that it was pleasantly full of bacon and eggs.

She paused at the church and looked at it with longing eyes. It was old, she knew that much, the oldest parts of it dating back to the 1200s. With its wooden porch, leaning walls and slightly twisted spire, she longed to paint it, but she knew she had to ration herself.

She also wanted to paint a village scene, the Heronry itself, the old water bridge and mill . . . The list was endless.

Today, she'd promised herself her first close-up look at the Penda Stones.

As she turned, she felt something soft touch her cheek, and she just managed to catch a piece of pink paper as it flew past her on the autumn breeze.

She looked at the piece of paper, cut into the shape of a horseshoe, and smiled. Confetti.

Of course, the wedding had been last Saturday.

Blaise glanced at the church again. She'd had no idea that Keira Westcombe had been due to get married the same week that she moved in to her new cottage. She'd heard the church bells, of course, and thought how wonderful they'd sounded, but it hadn't been until she'd gone to the shops to stock her empty kitchen that she'd heard the latest news. It was never 'gossip' in the village. Villagers loathed gossip.

During the morning, she'd learned that Lady Penda had married a man in his seventies, who owned a lot of land locally. She'd learned his daughter didn't like it, that Lucas Harwood was moving into the Heronry, but into a different wing from that occupied by Keira, and that some mysterious stranger had shown up and seemed intent on causing trouble.

Blaise had staggered home, awash with news, bemused and a little concerned. She'd liked Keira Westcombe almost on sight. Nervous of beautiful women, knowing that she herself could only be described as 'pretty', Blaise hadn't expected the lady of the manor to be so approachable.

The thought of her marrying someone so much older was . . . none of her business, Blaise thought guiltily, and, with a sigh, hefted her canvas a little higher under her arm and turned firmly away.

She'd have to remember to drop Keira a little line, congratulating her on her marriage.

She headed to the end of the road, where a stile gave way to a country footpath. It was no more than a track across the field, probably made by sheep, and the baker's wife had told her that it led straight to the Penda Stones.

Of course, she'd seen the stones from the road the first time she'd come to Upper Rousham. They dominated the village, looking across at it from the bottom of a hill. The first sight of them had made her heart leap, and she'd longed to get closer. To see for herself the individual shapes. How many stones there were. What pits and indentations they had. Were they covered with lichens? Now, her curious artist's soul could finally find out.

She'd just followed the path around a copse of beech trees when she glanced up from her wet, grass-encrusted boots and stopped dead.

There, in the field, were two Shire horses, pulling a plough.

For a moment Blaise thought she was seeing things. For a second she was half-convinced that she'd overdosed on pastoral beauty and was hallucinating.

Then she heard the jingle of the harness, and one of the huge beasts snorted gently, and she knew she was not suffering a time-warp or seeing ghosts.

A flock of crows and — absurdly — seagulls, noisily and greedily followed the progress of the plough, and the man guiding it.

Blaise, without thinking about it, unfolded her easel, set up the canvas and reached for her marking pencils. Within the space of a minute or two she was outlining rough shapes.

There was something about the scene that was so . . . touching . . . she felt her breath catch. The man was large and solid, like the land itself, and the horses so obviously trusted him. For long minutes at a time she simply sat and stared at them, their stout hearts and stouter bodies working in harmony to plough the land.

Aidan Shaw kept one eye on the Ransomes YL, a single-furrow plough, another eye on the wheel in the rut, and — somehow — a third eye on the lie of the land. It took years of practice to plough a straight furrow, and his were as straight as dies.

And then he saw her.

She was sitting on the edge of the field on one of those precarious-looking folding stools, wearing a deep purple dress and a grey raincoat. She had an easel and canvas set up in front of her. Through the beech trees behind her the sun caught the top of her head, turning her mass of blonde curls to the colour of buttercups.

Aidan hastily averted his eyes and kept them on the earth in front. It was good, Oxfordshire earth, reddish and fertile. He was used to the slightly harder soil of Yorkshire, but he didn't mind. He'd been glad of the job — a job he'd never expected to be offered — when he'd come south in search of answers.

He'd been lucky to find his father living so close to a farm that was on the lookout for a man who knew how to work a team of horses. He'd hardly been able to believe his luck when he'd first met Keira Westcombe and she'd offered him the job of horse man on her farm, the Westcombe home farm, which was the biggest of them all. Now, after almost three years, he'd still done nothing about those 'answers'. Perhaps he didn't want them after all.

He got to the end of the field at a slow, steady, plodding pace, using the plough trace and whippletree as equalizers, careful to ensure that each horse pulled no more than his fair share of the load.

When he came back, she was still there, her head bent over the canvas, and there was such an air of concentration about her that he felt safe giving her a longer, more lingering look.

She was not thin, he noticed, and was glad. He found it oddly distressing to look on women who'd starved themselves to look like whippets in the name of some perverse fashion. Nor, he saw with pleased surprise, was she wearing make-up. The cool wind, which bore unmistakable traces of autumn, had whipped her cheeks into a ruddy, healthy glow. Her hands were moving rapidly across the canvas, and as her head started to rise, Aidan quickly looked away.

At the bottom of the field he turned once more, his eyes instantly seeking her out.

She was still there.

An hour had passed.

As he approached her for the third pass he stopped and reached into his overall pocket for a spanner; he bent down to make an adjustment on the plough. The spanner he carried fitted every nut and bolt on the machine, which was just as well. He straightened and glanced at his watch. Time to water the horses.

Blaise looked up, surprised to see the plough stationary and the ploughman walking away from his animals, who stood with patiently drooping heads.

Blaise watched him walk to the end of the field and pour water from what looked like plastic gallon containers into two huge galvanized buckets.

When he came back, Blaise, on a sketchpad now, quickly captured the image.

Aidan put the buckets in front of the horses and watched them drink. They were a good pair, these, one a Clydesdale, the other a Suffolk Punch. Aidan loved his horses. He loved his job here, and knew he was lucky to get it. There weren't many jobs around for a man who could work with horses.

When he and his mother had moved to Yorkshire, when he was only six, they'd lodged on a farm, and the farmer there, who'd refused to work with tractors, had slowly, but almost inevitably, taught the growing boy how to carry on the old traditions. And Aidan had been only too glad to learn, for he'd hated the special school he'd had to attend, and he still hated socializing to this day. A life on a farm, with animals who didn't judge or sympathize, was his idea of paradise.

Yes, in spite of his good references, he knew how lucky he'd been to get another job working on a farm with horses. He owed Keira Westcombe a lot.

He glanced up to find that the woman was watching him openly now. But, instead of feeling instantly self-conscious and wary, he was uncharacteristically curious.

Cursing himself for being a fool, he nevertheless found himself walking towards her.

As he got closer, Blaise began fidgeting on her stool. Suddenly, and rather belatedly, she realized just how alone they were. The village was a good half-mile away. He was a big man, too, she saw nervously, at least six feet tall. His hair was very dark but . . . yes, there were chestnut highlights in those dark locks.

He began to smile as he got closer — a rather shy, slightly anxious smile — and in that instant Blaise felt all her nervousness disappear. This man was not going to hurt her.

His eyes, when he finally drew level with her, were an unusual hazel colour, neither brown nor green.

'Hello,' he said, somewhat diffidently, 'you must be the artist who moved into Glebe Cottage?'

Blaise blinked.

There was a slight . . . not lisp, exactly, but a slight . . . flatness in his voice that took her by surprise.

She nodded. 'Yes. Blaise Clayton.' She held her hand out brightly and he took it a shade awkwardly. Her hands were exquisitely shaped, he noticed, and the handshake itself was firm and strong. He found his fingers curling around hers in a gesture so natural it had him drawing his hand back more sharply than he'd intended to.

Blaise frowned, a little surprised by the rejection, but shrugged and smiled again. 'I expect the village grapevine's been at work?' she asked ruefully. She was beginning to learn how the community worked.

Aidan watched her lips carefully, relieved to be able to read them so easily. She had a very pretty mouth.

He nodded and smiled. His deeply tanned face creased in unexpected places as he did so, and Blaise felt a pleasant warmth steal across her back, sidle up her ribs and lodge in the area of her heart.

'I'm afraid so. But people around here mean well,' he assured her. And he meant what he'd said. Coming from a small Yorkshire village, Aidan had known what to expect from village life, and when he'd first moved here, and changed the land from tractor-worked to horse-worked, he'd expected to be the intense focus of attention. But he'd also expected it to eventually wear off, as it had. Now he was totally accepted here. And if any of them knew of his . . . difficulties, they kept it to themselves. At least, as far as he knew.

Blaise laughed. 'I think you're right,' she said. 'Everyone seems very helpful. My next-door neighbour offered to manure my rhubarb for me yesterday. It came as a bit of a shock, since I didn't know I had any!' The garden back in Birmingham had consisted of two pocket-handkerchief lawns, front and back.

Now, she realized with a slightly panicked start, she'd have to learn how to manage a cottage garden.

Aidan chuckled. It was a rasping, rather uneven sound, but Blaise liked it. She liked it enormously.

'Don't tell me you're a city girl?' Aidan asked, surprised at himself. He was finding it quite easy to talk to her, a phenomenon unknown to him. He didn't feel at all awkward or anxious to be away. And he rather liked that.

When he'd first come over, he'd told himself it was just to get it out of the way. No doubt she'd be expecting him to come and introduce himself and mention her painting. It was only polite. And Aidan didn't want to do anything to draw attention to himself.

Not yet, anyway. Not until he'd figured out what he intended to do. Of course, Keira's marriage had thrown him. He wasn't sure, now, how he intended to proceed. Instinct had told him to continue patiently watching and waiting. And keep his head down.

Now, though, he found himself genuinely interested in this stranger. She was not as young as he'd first thought, and he liked the straightforward way she met his eyes.

'I'm afraid so,' Blaise said. 'Or at least a suburb gal,' she added with a laugh.

Aidan didn't quite get the last words, so he covered it by nodding at the back of the canvas. 'May I look?'

Some artists, he'd read, didn't like their unfinished work being looked at. In fact they could get quite antsy about it.

But Blaise merely smiled and nodded. 'Go ahead. It's only a rough outline at the moment, though, so don't be too disappointed.'

Aidan stepped forward and looked down. It was a medium-sized canvas, about two and a half feet by three feet, and although it contained, as she'd warned him, a mere outline of himself, the horses and the landscape behind, he could see at once that it was good.

Obviously, she wasn't merely an amateur who liked to 'dabble'.

Although what he knew about art could be written on a horse rein, he could see for himself that the proportions were good, the figures anatomically correct and, more importantly, somehow alive. He, who knew horses well, could almost see their sinews shiver, could almost watch their manes blow in the wind and their ears twitch.

'Are you going to be in this field long?' Blaise asked, and, when he made no move to look up from the canvas or answer her, added a little nervously, 'Only, I'd like to go the whole hog and get a full-fledged painting out of it. It's so . . . earthly.' She fumbled for the right word, wondering if she'd found it.

She'd never expected to be presented with a scene right out of history, but, after watching the man and horses at work for an hour, she'd gradually realized that it was a scene that was far more than just 'quaint' or 'old-fashioned'. She could smell the earth that was being turned. The raucous calls of the birds were tangible. And she wanted to get the sheer . . . *aliveness* of the scene transferred to canvas. She simply couldn't get that input from an old black-and-white photograph of days long gone.

This was here and now.

Keira Westcombe was a businesswoman who made a good living out of organically grown produce. It was a modern story, and an ancient one, and Blaise wanted to capture it all.

Aidan looked up from the canvas and glanced at her. 'It's good,' he said. 'The horses really are like that.'

She'd been unnerved by his silence, but at his words she instantly forgave him.

Having had no formal training — she'd never attended an art school in her life — she was prone, she knew, to a lack of self-confidence. Those few simple words from a man who knew his subject made her day for her. And the man himself, a little voice piped up mischievously in the back of her mind, would make any girl's day!

'Thank you,' she said simply, and beamed a happy smile at him. 'I'd like to carry on with it. Will you be here tomorrow?'

Aidan blinked in the brilliance of her sunny smile, and had to drag his mind back to the work at hand. He glanced at the field. 'It'll take a good day or so to finish this field,' he said, and saw her face fall. He smiled tenderly. 'Then another day to do the next field.' He nodded past the hedge to the neighbouring field. 'Then another day . . .'

Blaise began to laugh. 'I'm glad. You don't mind being immortalized on canvas, then?'

Aidan turned from the field and looked at her. 'Well, I'd best be getting back. The horses will be wondering what's keeping me.'

She nodded, a little puzzled. He wasn't one for answering questions, obviously.

As he turned and began to walk away, she realized she didn't even know his name. And suddenly she desperately wanted to. And if he'd always lived here. And if he was married . . .

'I'll be here for a while,' she called gaily. 'Perhaps you'd like to come back to my place for lunch?'

Aidan kept on walking. He didn't so much as look back over his shoulder.

Blaise frowned, wondering what she'd said wrong. Perhaps he was married after all, and was just being tactful in pretending not to hear her.

It was a depressing thought.

CHAPTER 4

Colin Rattigan stepped from his car and glanced up at the house. It was, he had to admit, an impressive sight. In the trees high overhead a single heron landed, a surprisingly delicate and graceful operation for such a big bird.

For all its beauty, Colin wished he were somewhere else. Anywhere else. He had a good idea why one of his oldest clients had asked him to come and see him, and he could feel a fine sheen of sweat begin to form on his upper lip and forehead. But there was no way he could get out of it now. Rattigan, Hearst and Clarence, Solicitors, had been representing the multi-millionaire Lucas Harwood for nearly ten years. And when Lucas Harwood called, you jumped.

But at least he could console himself that *she* wouldn't be there. Jennifer Goulder, the she-cat from hell, was still at loggerheads with her father, so at least he wouldn't have to face that harridan.

At least, not yet. He felt his stomach lurch unpleasantly, and cursed the day he'd gone into law.

He found the old-fashioned bell-pull and rang it, the sound of the chimes echoing within. He shivered and turned up his coat. There was a nip of frost in the air this morning — the first of the season.

He waited patiently while he was no doubt being scrutinized via a very discreetly placed camera in the ivy, and wondered idly what kind of security system they had in place. He heard the solid click of a lock and the door was opened by a round, red-cheeked woman, who wouldn't have looked out of place in an advert for country cider. He gave his name, which obviously meant little to the housekeeper, and told her, somewhat nervously, that he had an appointment to see Lucas.

He was shown at once to a very charming room, half book-lined, with a large grate and a roaring fire. As he settled into an old but extremely comfortable leather sofa, he began to understand why Lucas had moved into his bride's establishment. The house had charm, atmosphere and warmth, something that Green Acres, for all its modern conveniences, lacked. And, if what Colin suspected was true, Lucas had probably wanted the company and comfort a place like this had to offer.

'Colin, good to see you. I hope you can forgive me for not inviting you to the wedding, but we wanted to keep it as small and informal as possible, didn't we, darling?'

Colin, on hearing the dry voice of his client, rose abruptly, almost knocking into the low coffee table and upsetting a vase of late chrysanthemums. He swivelled and found himself gaping at the woman standing quietly beside her husband.

He'd been told, of course, that Keira Westcombe was a famous local beauty. But it hadn't prepared him for this woman, who was svelte, with hair as dark as plain chocolate, and so beautiful she took his breath away.

She smiled at him now, a polite but gracious smile.

When Bessie had found them in the dining room, just finishing off breakfast, and announced a Mr Rattigan, Lucas had told her at once who he was, and, naturally, what he had in mind. As a new bride, Keira knew, she would be meeting a lot of Lucas's friends and acquaintances over the next few months, and Lucas had wanted her there as he gave the solicitor his instructions, even though she'd demurred.

Now she inclined her head back towards the sofa. 'Please, take your seat again, Mr Rattigan,' she said quietly, coming to the chair opposite the sofa and sitting down, careful to cross her legs and keep her long mustard-coloured suede skirt pulled down across her knees.

There was something about Colin Rattigan that puzzled her. He seemed almost . . . well, scared.

'Thank you,' Colin said, slightly flustered, and sat down, reluctantly dragging his eyes away from her to those of his highly amused client. Colin flushed.

'Thanks for coming, Colin,' Lucas said easily, and eased himself into the armchair next to his wife. 'As you know, Keira and I recently married, and of course, I now want to have a new will drawn up.'

Colin, even though he'd been expecting it, felt his heart sink, but forced a bright smile onto his face and reached into his suitcase. This meant he'd have to call Jennifer tonight. He didn't dare do otherwise. If she found out about the new will, and that he hadn't called her . . . he dreaded to think what she might do.

'Of course, and may I offer my congratulations?' he heard his own voice responding pleasantly, and he licked lips gone suddenly dry. He unfolded a large legal pad, and was glad to see that his hand wasn't trembling all that much. He looked up expectantly.

Keira began to feel acutely uncomfortable. She knew Lucas would always keep his word, and she was uneasily aware of what the lawyer must be thinking. The gold-digger making sure of her ill-gotten gains.

She looked down at her hands and tried to tell herself she had no reason to feel guilty. But Fane Harwood's face kept floating across the back of her mind. It was as if he was here, and she could see the cold, sneering smile growing on his face.

Lucas kept it as concise and as simple as possible, leaving the land he and Keira had agreed on to her, together with a sizeable donation to the Westcombe Nature Reserve, and dividing the rest of his property and fortune equally between his children. Lucas found his voice becoming very dry towards the end, and began to cough slightly.

Colin looked at him speculatively, and with some alarm. He quickly finished scribbling the last of the terms, and when his pen stopped Lucas leaned forward slightly. 'I may . . . sometime in the near future, make a codicil to the will. Another beneficiary. But I'm not sure yet.' He coughed again and leaned back, breathing deeply.

Keira was curious about who the mysterious beneficiary might be, but she'd die before she'd ask. Lucas was a man of dignity and of his word. If he had secrets, she was more than willing to let him keep them in peace.

'Oh, that's fine,' Colin said, trying to keep his voice light and cheerful, then spoiled the effect rather by swallowing hard. 'Er . . . when would you like me to bring this new will over for signing? As you know, we'll need independent witnesses . . .'

Lucas smiled dryly. 'As soon as it's ready.'

Colin nodded with apprehension. He didn't know *exactly* what that bitch Jennifer was up to, but he knew that it would be bad news for Colin Rattigan. If only she hadn't found out about the gambling debts. And, far worse, if only she hadn't bought his markers from that treacherous crook who ran a casino . . .

'And Bessie and Sid can act as witnesses,' Lucas said, getting rather slowly to his feet. Colin was more than happy to take the hint, and he rose quickly, shaking Lucas's hand with far more vigour than necessary and smiling rather sickly in Keira's direction before more or less bolting for the door. Keira barely had time to reach him before seeing him out.

Lucas watched him go with some amusement, then winced as a pain shot through his chest. Slowly, and with infinite gratitude, he sank back down on the chair, feeling much more settled in his mind now. He had a doctor's appointment tomorrow, and who knew what that would bring? So he'd better move fast about the matter of his firstborn.

Keira reappeared, her face rather bemused. 'He's a bit highly strung, isn't he?'

Lucas grunted. 'But he knows his stuff; that's all that matters.'

Which was true. Colin Rattigan was a very competent lawyer. It was rather unfortunate, though the newlyweds didn't know it, that he had Jennifer Goulder's best interests at heart, and not those of his client.

* * *

Fane Harwood turned his car down the gravel drive, just avoiding a Mercedes that was coming too fast in the opposite direction. He pulled onto the lawn with an angry shake of his head. He didn't recognize the other man behind the wheel, who gave him a vaguely surprised look in passing.

Fane wondered if he was Keira's lover, then shook the thought away. He could drive himself crazy, letting stray thoughts like that have easy access into his head.

Besides, his father lived here now too. Surely not even she would entertain her men-friends so openly?

Fane parked the E-type Jag outside the big wooden doors, the gravel spurting out from beneath the wired wheels as he slammed on the brakes. In one lithe movement he was outside the car and striding towards the door.

In the salon, Lucas and Keira were still together after Colin Rattigan's visit, when Bessie showed Fane through the door.

'Another visitor, Keira,' Bessie said, her eyes twinkling. She hadn't missed the dancing scene at the wedding reception any more than anyone else had, and, although she was too old-fashioned to approve, she did rather like the look of Lucas's son.

Fane was oblivious to the housekeeper's roguish approval, for the sound of Keira's laughter had transfixed him for a moment. His eyes rapidly took in the scene. She was sitting in a huge leather chair, looking a picture in a mustard-coloured suede skirt with a cream blouse and a cameo at her throat. Her dark hair was upswept in a loose, practical chignon. She wore no make-up, but then, she didn't need it. Her skin was flawless, her eyes the only jewels she needed. She was leaning across towards Lucas, who was on a sofa opposite her. Her face was relaxed and happy, and she was looking at his father with affection in her eyes.

It was not what he had come to see. It was not what he *wanted* to see, but he knew it should make him feel relieved. It shouldn't make him want to feel like striding across to her and shaking her until that hair of hers fell around her shoulders in a raven cloud . . .

'Fane!' Lucas said, his voice rich with welcome. 'Come in, son, come in!' He went to get up, then thought better of it, and watched his son with eager eyes as he approached, somewhat warily, he thought, and took a seat on the sofa.

'I'm not too early, I hope?' he said, with almost savage politeness. He leaned back, trying not to look at her but unable to do anything else. What was it about her that could drive all common sense right out of his head?

Keira, who'd sagged into her chair the moment her senses had recognized his voice, felt her body tingling as if it had just been slapped.

Lucas laughed. 'Of course not. You can come any time, you know that. Can't he, darling?' Lucas glanced at Keira with a confident smile, knowing that she would agree with him.

And with that smile, that said so much, Fane felt a pang of pain hit him like a body-blow. Because his father had every right to feel so sure of himself. Keira was his. His wife.

For her part, Keira smiled weakly but valiantly. 'Of course your children are always welcome here,' she murmured, and stared at the wedding ring on her hand. She had to keep a clear head about this. He was Lucas's son. To deny him access to her home was unthinkable. But, at the same time, she longed to do just that. Something told her that this man was dangerous. So very dangerous to her sense of balance. He was a threat to every defence she could erect.

In medieval days the Westcombes had been able to keep out marauders by using men-at-arms, moats, bows and arrows and boiling oil. Now, glancing across at Fane and meeting the threat and sexual challenge in his eyes, how she longed to be able to do the same!

But here she was, calmly giving him leave to treat her home as his own.

Her eyes flashed as he smiled wolfishly. She had the uncanny feeling that in that one electric moment he'd been able to read her mind, and it left her feeling thoroughly rattled. She rose lithely to her feet, then wished she hadn't as she realized she hadn't the faintest idea what she was going to do. In silent panic, she grappled for something, anything, to say.

'Would you like some . . . tea . . . er . . . ?' She could hardly call him Mr Harwood, although she longed to keep the formalities between them. There was safety in civilization, after all. Or at least there was in theory. But, at the same time, she found his name — such a simple, easy syllable — stuck in her throat.

Fane's lips twisted. His dark eyes seemed to glimmer, deep in their pupils, like pieces of jet. He was enjoying her discomfort, she realized, the way a connoisseur enjoyed a pedigree port.

'The name's Fane,' he said, leaning forward just an inch closer and dropping his voice to a conspiratorial whisper. 'I'm sure you can manage to use it — if you really try.'

Lucas felt the electricity between them, and wasn't sure if he should be dismayed or glad.

Keira drew in a sharp breath, knew that he'd heard it, and fought back the urge to scream. 'Fane,' she finally managed to grind out.

'And I'd love a cup of tea,' he said casually, leaning back against the settee and looking around him slowly. 'And what a charming room you have here.'

Keira shot him a furious look. Now he was being facetious.

'Yes, isn't it?' she agreed sweetly, and did something she never had. She walked to the fireplace and pulled on the bell-cord. Fane smiled grimly. So, she wanted to play Madam Bountiful, did she? The gracious, long-suffering lady of the manor, tolerating the loutish oaf?

He'd give Her Ladyship something to suffer over, all right.

'So, son, tell me all about Harwood Construction.'

Fane glanced at him, surprised his father knew about his company, and was struck again by how grey and old he was looking.

'There's not much to tell. I started off small, just a local building outfit, really. Times were tough, but a bank loan, together with some brickies and chippies who really knew what they were doing, meant we put up good houses. Word got around, and I was able to expand. I hired a good architect, and we slowly managed to get bigger and better commissions. Highrise blocks. Some bridge work. I managed to wangle a few big jobs abroad and . . .' Fane shrugged. 'We did well.'

Lucas chuckled. 'Now that's an understatement, if ever I heard one.' It had taken guts, determination, know-how and years of hard work to build up a company as huge and well-respected as Harwood Construction. That Lucas knew only too well. 'I hear that job you did on the new dam in South Africa went down very well.'

Fane smiled, a little tightly. 'It hasn't cracked yet. And I had no idea you were keeping tabs on me.'

Lucas sighed. 'Why wouldn't I? You are my son, even though at times it might have seemed as if I forgot as much.' Lucas met his eyes levelly, and then tried not to wince as a pinch of pain nipped at him.

Fane looked at him just as levelly. 'Are you feeling all right, Dad?' he asked softly, and Keira, too, glanced quickly at Lucas, seeing what his son saw. A pale, tired, ill-looking man.

She bit her lip anxiously. The wedding and all the fuss must have been affecting him more than she'd thought. She should have made allowances for it, she thought guiltily.

Lucas smiled tiredly. 'I'm fine. Stop worrying. It's probably just . . . all the excitement,' he added, grappling for an excuse. The last thing he wanted was for Fane to find out how very ill he was. Or Keira, for that matter.

Fane opened his mouth, then suddenly closed it with a snap. He turned to look at Keira, and on his face was such a look of thunder that Keira, who'd been about to retake her seat, suddenly took a quick step backwards instead.

He was looking at her as if he wanted to kill her. His lips curled back, reminding Keira of the snarl of a wolf. For a second, she couldn't understand what had caused it.

Then he turned back to his father. 'You should take it easy,' Fane gritted. 'I know you're still . . . *honeymooners*,' he spat out the word as if it were the deadliest of poisons, 'but even so, at your age, you shouldn't . . . overtax yourself.'

And in that instant Keira felt a nameless wave of horrible emotion wash over her as she suddenly realized what he was thinking. That his father was so tired and ill-looking because . . . well, because she'd been tiring him out in bed, a wry voice in the back of her head finished the thought for her. She went red, then white, but refused to back away from anything, no matter how unpleasant or humiliating.

Quickly she rallied. Her chin lifted. Well, if that was what he thought . . .

'Lucas, darling, perhaps you should take it easy today,' she said quietly, making both Harwood men suddenly turn surprised eyes on her.

Lucas's eyes were full of amusement, and perhaps a little gentle admonition. He could see the way things were going between these two, and his instinct was to try and smooth things down a bit. But he remembered what it was to be young and so attracted. His eyes melted at the thought.

Fane's eyes were like bullets.

'After all,' Keira added softly, 'we don't want anything to upset our honeymoon, do we?' And she reached out to squeeze his hand.

As she did so, she glanced down at Fane's own hands, which had been lying placidly across his lap, and saw them suddenly clench into fists so tight his knuckles were turning white.

Keira met his eyes bravely. 'Your father's a very . . . remarkable man,' she said, with deadly sincerity.

Fane felt himself leaning forward. He wanted only to get his hands on her. The light was coming through the diamond-paned window, turning her hair to raven-wing blue. Her face was pale, but so composed he longed to smash that coolness of hers to smithereens with a kiss that would leave her gasping. He wanted to hear her cultured, quiet voice break out into one of abandon, one of animal pleasure, as his hands caressed her. He wanted to take the power she had over him far away from her and—

'You rang, Keira?'

It was Bessie at the door. No doubt she'd been surprised to hear the bell ring in her kitchen, for neither Keira nor herself could remember the last time a Westcombe had actually rung for service. Michael Westcombe had always wandered into the kitchen to make his own hot drinks whenever he wanted, a practice Keira had continued.

'Yes please, Bessie,' Keira said, feeling guilty and oddly embarrassed now. 'If you have time, do you think you could bring in a tea tray? Mr Harwood's son has just dropped in to . . .' Kill me, she thought, or something worse. 'To . . . er . . . say hello. I was hoping you might have made some of your delicious shortbread?'

Bessie, who knew Keira like a daughter, caught on at once. Her backbone stiffened and her ample bosom swelled. 'Certainly, My Lady,' Bessie said magnificently. 'Would the young master like some fruit cake as well?'

At this, Fane ground his teeth so hard it was audible. Keira wanted to burst out laughing and hug Bessie at the same time, but she did neither. Instead she turned a perfectly composed face to Fane and raised a gentle, questioning eyebrow.

'Would you care for some fruit cake . . . Fane?' She added the last syllable with obvious effort.

'No,' Fane gritted, 'the *young master* would not care for some fruit cake.'

'Just tea, please, Bessie,' Keira said, her dark eyes glowing her thanks.

Bessie nodded her head impressively and silently withdrew. Lucas, who'd come to know the kind-hearted, fiercely loyal housekeeper well, felt like applauding. It was, without doubt, the finest performance he'd ever seen. He hoped his son appreciated it. But through his amusement he also felt a shiver of unease. Things could so easily get out of hand between these two young people. They were both so alike — fiercely determined they were both right. Lucas only hoped that, whatever their problems, they'd sort them out quickly.

Fane watched her like a hawk as she finally sat back down in her chair. She was much closer to him than she would have liked, but with Lucas right beside her she felt safe enough. For the moment, anyway.

'So, son, what are your plans now?' Lucas asked diplomatically, determined to change the subject onto less fiery pathways.

Fane dragged in a rather ragged breath and tried to regain his usually iron-willed self-control. It was not as easy as he'd hoped. He forced himself to lean back against the sofa and ran his hand through his hair in an unconsciously harassed gesture.

'Well, at the moment I'm putting up at the Randolph.' He mentioned the prestigious hotel in Oxford as if he were staying at a bed and breakfast. 'But I'm going to see a flat in Woodstock this afternoon. It's on a three-month lease, and I was thinking of taking a break.'

At this news Lucas's face broke into a relieved smile, and Keira's face fell like a bad soufflé. Three months? He was going to be around for three months?

'I haven't had a holiday since starting up the company,' Fane said, his voice slightly weary now. 'Oh, I've seen the world, all right, and recently I've been in South America, but you can't call building a mansion in the middle of a Colombian jungle a holiday.' He grimaced. 'Besides, I've got one of the most competent teams going. They don't need me back. All the specs are done, the foundations are laid. I have a foreman I can trust to oversee the actual construction. Now seems as good a time as any to take a little time out and relax.'

As if he'd be doing much of that with Keira Westcombe around. No, Keira *Harwood* around. She was part of the family now.

He smiled grimly.

Lucas wondered about that smile, but he was too happy to worry about it. He still kept contacts in the building and construction world, and knew the Colombian mansion was being built for one of the rich governors, an anti-drugs campaigner who needed an isolated, fortress-like place deep in the jungle. He was sure Fane's company would build him a remarkable home. And, even though the construction workers were being well guarded by the military, he was glad Fane was out of it.

'I think that's a splendid idea,' Lucas said heartily, determined to look on the bright side. 'You can easily fall into the habit of letting work take over your life.' His smile faltered. 'You can get to the point where building the next building, making the next million, going onto the next thing can become more important than anything. More important than the things that really do matter. It's a vicious trap. Believe me, I know.'

Fane looked up at him, and a strange look passed between the two men. 'Yeah, I guess you do. And Mum, she knew all about that too, didn't she?'

Lucas nodded. Keira saw his blue eyes fill with tears and she made an instinctive move forward, not sure what to do. But Fane saw her, and held up a warning hand.

'Yes, your mother . . . I can't tell you how sorry I am for what I did to her,' Lucas said. 'I tried to tell you at the time, but . . .'

'I left,' Fane said flatly. 'I know. I couldn't do anything else. At the time I was so angry I just . . . had to leave.'

Keira bit her lip. She had the uncomfortable feeling that she shouldn't be here. That she shouldn't be listening to what was obviously painful, personal family business. 'I think I'll just go and see what's keeping Bessie,' she began, half getting out of her seat.

But Lucas blinked, and then turned to her, waving her back down. 'No, my dear, it's all right. Fane has every reason to be angry with me. I never told you this, but Emily, Fane's mother, she . . . well, she committed suicide.'

Keira felt herself go pale, and she took a quick, steadying breath. 'I'm . . . so sorry.'

She didn't know what else to say. Lucas had told her very little about his marriages. Or about the reason for his estrangement from his son. Jennifer, she knew all about, but this latest revelation . . .

It explained so much.

Lucas turned back to Fane, who was looking at Keira with a curiously guarded expression.

'I know I was responsible for it,' he admitted. 'I knew she wasn't well. I knew I was spending too much time at the office, over that inner-city renewal project Danelink was working on. I should have been there.'

Fane slowly nodded. 'Yes, I think you should have been,' he said quietly. 'But then, I wasn't there either. I was doing that architect's course, remember? And Jennifer was out somewhere, at a party. None of us were there for her.'

Lucas sighed deeply. 'Fane, I never told you this, but your mother . . . well, Emmy had been ill before. When you and Jenny were only babies. You probably don't remember. She . . . spent some time in a hospital.'

Lucas bit his lip, wondering if he was doing the right thing in telling him now.

Fane stared at Lucas, a mixture of surprise, pain and finally pity crossing his face. 'No. No, I don't . . . remember her being away.'

Lucas sighed again. 'I know it's no excuse. I should have been able to read the signs. But that night she . . . took the pills . . . I really didn't notice anything odd in her behaviour.'

Fane shook his head. 'I think it's time we let the past be just that, Dad,' he said softly. 'The past. It's time we moved on. Mum wouldn't have wanted us to be apart so long, I've always felt that. It's just that . . . well, we said some pretty harsh things to each other, and as the years passed it just seemed harder and harder to make that first move to get in touch and . . .'

Lucas leaned forward, his voice gruff now. 'I know. Believe me, son, I know. I'm only glad that you're back now. And . . .' he reached across and took Keira's hand, not at all surprised to find it so cold, '. . . things have a way of working out.'

Fane dragged his eyes away from the sight of their held hands. It had felt good to cauterize the old wounds once and for all. The last thing he wanted to do was stir up new troubles now. Except . . . dammit, he couldn't just let his father make another huge mistake. But what the hell could he do about it?

He glanced at Keira, willing his heartbeat to stay steady, and cursed silently as she turned those eyes on him. Those sea-green eyes that could drown him so quickly.

'I'm glad things have worked out for you,' he lied. 'I hope you and Keira will be happy.' The words were so patently insincere that Lucas had the absurd urge to laugh out loud. He knew what Fane had to be thinking, of course. That he'd been taken in by a beautiful fortune-hunter.

'I'm glad you came just now, actually,' Lucas said, as casually as he could manage. 'I've just had my lawyer in.'

Fane tensed. 'I expect that was him I passed in the drive.'

Lucas nodded. 'I dare say.' He glanced at his fingernails, tried to think of a way of putting it tactfully, then decided there *was* no tactful way of putting it, and said bluntly, 'I've had him make out a new will.'

Fane's eyes shot daggers at Keira, who was staring down intently at her hand, clutched in those of her husband.

'Of course you have,' Fane said, his voice so toneless it was the most insulting thing Keira had ever heard.

'I've left some land and money to my wife, of course,' Lucas said grimly. 'The rest, which is the bulk of the estate, is to be divided equally between my . . . children.' He hesitated over the last word, wondering if now, after confessing so much, he should confess the last of his secrets.

But Fane didn't give him the chance. 'I don't know why you're telling me all this. It's hardly any of my business.' His voice was cold now, as cold as ice, as cold as the look in his eyes.

'Of course it's your business,' Lucas said calmly. 'I'm leaving you a lot of property.'

As those words suddenly sank in, Keira tried to keep the look of dismay from her face, but she knew she hadn't succeeded. She'd had no idea Fane was in the construction business, and now, as she fully comprehended just what that might mean, she had a horrific vision of him building housing estate after housing estate right next to the reserve. She knew it was stupid of her, not to mention selfish, but she couldn't help but feel a sick horror slowly overcome her. So many people living right next door to her fragile, eco-sensitive reserve was a nightmarish thought. The cats people kept as pets could decimate a songbird population alone, not to mention field mice and voles. Her new barn owl releases would be in danger of starving. And that was only one way in which all her years of hard and painstaking work could be put in jeopardy.

Fane saw the misery in her face as clear as day, and he found himself furious and sick with disappointment. What had she expected? To inherit all of his father's wealth and land? Someone that greedy, someone that cold-hearted and manipulative, deserved all that she got.

So why wasn't he feeling triumphant that he had read her so right? Why wasn't he jumping for joy that his father hadn't been taken in completely by her, but had still managed to keep his grip on what was fair?

Aware that the silence had grown, Fane dragged his eyes from hers. 'Thanks, Dad, I appreciate it,' he said, but his voice sounded more hollow than victorious. He hardly needed the inheritance, of course. Though still a young business, Harwood Construction was worth millions, and it was privately owned. It was almost as big as Danelink had been, and was growing by the year. A few thousand acres of land in the green belt meant nothing to him. Except that it meant he could keep Keira West— Harwood from getting her greedy hands on it.

Lucas glanced at Keira, surprised by her sudden pallor. Something had obviously upset her, but he couldn't think what.

'You're welcome, I'm sure,' Lucas said, struggling to comprehend what had just happened.

Keira could hear the grandfather clock ticking ponderously on the wall. She could hear the sound of Fane Harwood's heavy, angry breathing. She could hear the thud-thud of her own heart.

For a long time she said nothing. Should she ask him outright what he planned to do with the farmland? She knew she had a valid point to make about her nature reserve. If people didn't protect the land and conserve it for native wildlife, then soon there would be no wildlife. And then there would be no life, period. And that she simply could not allow to happen. Not when she was in a position to do something about it. As Lady Penda, she had a duty not only to the village, but to the land. To the creatures that needed that land to live. And no one would stop her. Not even when the man trying to take her dream away from her was Fane Harwood.

The door opened and Bessie walked in, a laden tray in her hands. She glanced at Keira and almost stumbled at the tenseness of her face. She quickly put the tray down and took a step towards her.

'Thank you, Bessie,' Keira said, and gave her a long, level look. Bessie interpreted it at once, nodded and withdrew, but cast a vicious stare at the oblivious Fane as she did so. Perhaps he wasn't such a catch after all . . .

Fane continued to stare at her, willing her to challenge him. He was leaning forward on the sofa, and the light fell across one side of his face. It emphasized the hawkishness of his nose, and the flat plane of his cheek. In the shadows, his eyes glittered.

Keira reached for the tea tray. 'Milk and sugar?'

Fane rose slowly. 'No milk. No sugar,' he said flatly.

Keira poured the brew, her hands, he noted with chagrin, rock-steady. From her sitting position, she lifted the teacup over her head and handed it to him. He took it, and the delicate porcelain looked flimsy in his hands.

He moved across to the window and looked out. Herons circled over the river. In the beeches he could see a squirrel, busy collecting beechmast. On the bird table greenfinches swung on a nut-holder. In the distance the Penda Stones glowered down at him. He felt, suddenly, an intruder in this paradise. For one brief second, he wanted to leave her to her paradise and never come back.

But the moment quickly passed. She was the interloper, not him. She'd married a man old enough to be her grandfather in order to get money, power and land.

And it was time that Keira realized that in *Fane* Harwood, at least, she had met her match. She might be able to twist Lucas around her pretty little finger, but . . .

He turned back from the window and found her looking steadily at his father with a thoughtful, rather pensive look on her face.

In fact, Keira was wondering if she could ask Lucas to sound his son out about his future plans. But the peace between them was still so fragile, so hard-won, that she wasn't sure it would be fair to put him in the middle. Besides, she was used to fighting her own battles. She knew that starting and maintaining a nature reserve might make her a crackpot in many people's eyes, but it had come to mean the world to her. And she would defend it to the last drop of power she had left.

As he watched, a look of total calm and confidence settled over her lovely face, and he had the strangest feeling that if only he could read her thoughts, he'd find out something extraordinary.

He put the cup and saucer down with a loud crack. 'It's time I was going,' he said flatly.

But he'd be back.

The unspoken words hung on the air like a threat. Or a promise. Keira, who now that he was going suddenly felt an insatiable urge to feast her eyes on the sight of him, wasn't sure which it was.

'I'll see you out,' she offered politely, rising lithely to her feet. If her knees felt more like blancmange than cartilage and sinew, she gamely ignored it. Out in the hall, she preceded him to the huge front door, very aware of his eyes boring into her back.

'You may think you have the upper hand now.' His voice feathered across the huge hall in an eerie echo. 'But we've a long way to go yet.'

At the door, with one hand resting on the big iron handle, she turned slowly around. If he expected her to cower and simper, he was in for one hell of a shock. Keira was a woman of the country. A Lady of the Stones. She'd watched stoats chase and kill rabbits. She'd seen butterflies caught in spiders' webs. She knew how the harsh laws of nature worked. They were terrible, and they were ancient, and they were miraculous. And she knew that in a battle of any kind it didn't pay to be the prey.

She forced herself to watch implacably as he came closer, keeping her feet planted firmly in one spot. She allowed not a tremble to pass through her body, nor a flicker of unease to cross her eyes. 'Yes,' she finally said, when he drew level with her. 'We do have a long way to go.'

Fane found himself torn between admiration and frustration. She was unlike any woman he'd ever known. After his disastrous engagement he'd gone wild and had affairs with some of the most courted and beautiful women in the world — Italian fashion models, American film actresses, television presenters. None of them had affected him like this woman. And he knew why.

She had so much power of her own — the ancient power of being lady of the manor, as so ably demonstrated by Bessie. Also, the power of being a beautiful woman. This last power she could exercise just by turning those sea-green eyes on him. She could make him want her with an ease that terrified him.

But . . . did she want him? Fane wasn't sure. He had believed it instantaneously in the church during that incredible moment when their eyes had first met. Now, he was not so sure.

Did he just want her so much that he had fooled himself into believing that it was requited? Suddenly it was vastly urgent that he know. Before Keira could even guess what was happening, he reached for her, his arms curling around her waist and dragging her across the few inches that separated them with contemptuous male ease.

She just had time to draw a quick, stunned breath, and then his head was swooping over hers, blocking out the light. She saw the flame of jet in his pupils and the next instant her own eyes were feathering closed as his lips found hers.

She could feel the hard, scorchingly hot length of his body, pressing from the shoulder touching his, to her breasts, crushed against his chest, to their hips, grinding against each other, and on down to where their knees and then their ankles touched. Every nerve in her body leapt into clamorous life. At the same time a languorous, almost drugged feeling seeped into her head, turning her brain from a bright, reasoning machine into a blissfully uncaring traitor. She felt her back bend as her spine melted, and her lips trembled beneath his. His tongue, a moist, hot invader, darted past her lips and met her own.

She jerked in his arms in helpless reaction. Against her mouth, she heard him groan. The tiny vibration of it passed into her and raced down her throat, lodging in a deeply feminine, melting place somewhere between her thighs.

Her legs immediately gave way, and he instinctively took her weight in his arms. Her hands were suddenly full of his hair, and she dimly realized she was holding his head in her hands, her palms running flat against his skull, his dark, unruly hair cool and silky against her skin.

He bent her right back as the kiss deepened. Her mouth opened wider, and she felt her nipples hardening into diamonds against him.

Fane groaned again, a deep, animal sound, like someone in pain. It was the sound of it that shocked him back from the precipice, and he suddenly thrust her away. Keira fell back against an ancient, bulging wall that felt as cold as ice to her back.

She dragged in a huge breath, her eyes wide and grey-green and totally stunned.

For a long, long moment Fane stared at her, feeling no victory. For he knew that his own eyes must hold the same look of stunned, shamed desire.

But at least now he knew.

'Yes,' he said, as if in answer to some unasked question, and walked forward. He yanked open the huge wooden door, the ease with which he did so giving silent testimony to the frustrated strength still coursing through his body. 'We have a long way to go, you and I.'

He turned and looked at her, his eyes clouding in reluctant tenderness. She looked like a bruised flower.

But she was made of iron. He had to remember that.

'And I, for one,' he said with a growing, now-familiar wolfish smile, 'am going to enjoy the journey.'

CHAPTER 5

Lucas smiled amiably at the receptionist as she rose to usher him into Leslie Coldheath's office. The room was typical of many a Harley Street doctor's office — wooden panelling, shelves full of learned medical tomes, colourful pot plants, a cosy-looking sofa and chairs, and a big desk.

Rising from behind the large wooden expanse of desk was an equally large man. He was not young, but looked it, and was in obvious hearty health. Lucas and Leslie had got along famously ever since Lucas had first consulted him thirty years ago, and Leslie was now as much friend as doctor. Therefore, when Lucas had first felt seriously ill, several months ago, it was hardly surprising he had gone straight to see his trusted friend. And, although a local doctor might have been more convenient, Lucas had never regretted it.

Back then it had concerned a simple complaint, easily cleared up. Now, they both knew, they were dealing with something vastly different.

'So, Lucas, how are you, then?' Leslie asked, reaching across to shake hands. It was not as facetious as it might have sounded, and Lucas answered him as he was meant to.

'The tiredness has become more noticeable. And the chest and stomach pains are increasing.'

Leslie nodded. Lucas's hand looked old, liver-spotted and arthritic in his own meaty paw. His patient was also thinner and paler.

It was all to be expected.

'I hear congratulations are in order,' Leslie said, as diplomatically as he could.

Lucas subsided gratefully into a big, comfortable leather armchair opposite the desk, and laughed.

'I know what you're thinking, and you're wrong,' he admonished, waiting to continue as the receptionist tapped, entered at the doctor's permission, placed a tray of tea on the table and quietly withdrew. The first-class service was one of the perks, and Lucas quite liked the blend his doctor served.

He helped himself liberally to milk and sugar. At this stage of the game there was no point in stinting himself.

Leslie watched him, a wry smile on his face. 'And how, pray tell, do you know what I'm thinking?' he challenged.

Lucas sipped and snorted. 'Easy. You've heard my bride is youthful, beautiful and charming. You're thinking I've tied the knot in some last-gasp effort to stave off the inevitable, or recapture my youth, or some other such rubbish, and that I've been spending wild nights shortening my time on earth like an out-of-control lecher. True or false?'

He shot a white, wiry eyebrow up into his hairline, and gave the doctor a gimlet-eyed look.

Leslie put his hands up in surrender. 'All right, I admit it. But the grapevine has it wrong, I take it?' His voice was carefully casual, and Lucas chuckled at his caution.

'It does. I married Keira for purely practical reasons. There's been no lechery, nor will there be. For one thing, she knows nothing of my illness, and I don't intend to tell her. And if we should start . . . er . . . cavorting about, she'd be bound to notice that something was wrong. Besides, the marriage was a business arrangement, nothing more and nothing less.'

Leslie looked at him thoughtfully. 'This has something to do with Jennifer's attempt to get power of attorney, doesn't it?' he asked quietly. When Jennifer had tried to have Lucas declared incompetent several months ago, it had been to Leslie, as his long-term doctor, that Lucas had turned to refute the claims of mental incompetence.

And Leslie had come through for him.

Now, Lucas smiled wryly. 'Partly. But it's much more than revenge, or even pride. I forgave her long ago, you know. I spoiled her rotten, as my only daughter, so I'm as much to blame as she is for how she turned out. No, I was determined to save the land, not get back at my family. Have you heard of the Westcombe Nature Reserve?' he suddenly asked, seemingly out of the blue.

Leslie shook his head.

Lucas sighed. 'You city-slickers! Keira Westcombe, or I should say Keira Harwood,' his eyes twinkled, 'owns an Elizabethan mansion and the village of Upper Rousham, barely a mile from Green Acres. She also owns several farms and many square miles of land. A few years ago she legally turned all her land into a nature reserve. Don't get me wrong, she's no green fanatic. As a matter of fact, she's got a sound business head on her shoulders. But she's also the kind of woman who, if she's going to do something, does it to the very best of her ability. She'd feel she was cheating herself, and others, if she didn't.

'So, for several years now, she's banned all pesticides and chemical use on her properties. She hired a Yorkshireman to train and oversee the farmhands in using draught horses on the home farm. She banned fox-hunting and hare-coursing on her land as soon as her father died and she inherited. You should have seen the fireworks that took place between Keira and the Master of the Hunt! As she said to me, there are now more foxes in towns and cities than in the countryside, and before she went ahead with it, she got proof positive that the Hunt was breeding foxes just to release and then kill them.

'I tell you, she's quite some woman, Les. If you could just see what she's accomplished — I've never known anyone work so hard. When I first retired to Green Acres there was barely any wildlife around, and, as an ex-city slicker myself, I was pretty surprised. I had visions of Bambi coming down to the garden for breakfast, not a virtual wasteland. But over the years . . .'

He stopped and coughed, a dry, rasping sound that had the doctor frowning. Lucas caught the look, shrugged, and carried on determinedly.

'She's increased the barn owl population by twenty percent already, just by leaving old and disused barns as they are. Because there's no chemical usage, there's plenty of mice, voles and other prey for them to catch. The RSPB have made her an honorary member. There's been an increase in badger setts, and bat numbers are now safe.'

Leslie smiled. 'Bats? I'd hardly have thought . . .'

But Lucas hastily headed him off. 'If you want to hear the gen on bats, you should come to dinner at our place one night,' he chuckled. 'Keira can give you all the information about pipistrelles that you could possibly need. You'd be surprised how fascinating bats can be. Believe me, when Keira is the one doing the telling, drying paint can be made to sound intriguing.'

Leslie laughed. 'I can see the lady's made quite an impression on you.' He'd been a little alarmed to hear his terminally ill patient had married a much younger woman, but now he could see from the flush of happy colour in Lucas's cheeks when talking about her that the new bride was proving to be a much better tonic than he could ever prescribe.

'So, I take it you agree with her?' Leslie probed gently. Funny, he wouldn't have thought a construction millionaire would be so easily swayed. Even by a beautiful woman.

Lucas snorted. 'I know what you're thinking, but she's no castle-in-the-air idealist. She runs her farms at a profit, and her village projects are practical as well as environmentally friendly. Upper Rousham's thriving! But that goes hand in hand with what's really closest to her heart. The land. She's set up a hedge-planting scheme, refilled ponds and turned drained marsh back into marshland again. Already we're getting botanists coming from all over the world to study the orchids and other rare flora to be found there now. So, when this business with Jennifer came up . . . well, you can see why I wanted to donate a good portion of my land to the reserve. Keira deserves it. She's *earned* it, dammit!'

Leslie smiled. 'Well, I'm glad to see it's all working out. Er . . . will you be telling her about . . .'

But Lucas shook his head emphatically. 'No. I don't want her to know.'

Leslie knew better than to push it. 'Well, I think we'll have that jacket and shirt off, if you don't mind.' He reached for a stethoscope. 'I'll have a quick listen.'

Lucas rose rather painfully to his feet and began unbuttoning, muttering good-naturedly, 'Anyone would think I'd married Lucrezia Borgia. You're as bad as my son.'

Leslie paused, glancing up from the instrument in his hand. 'Fane's back?'

Lucas grunted. 'He is. We've . . . talked. Things are mostly working out between us, I'm glad to say, but yesterday, when he came around, he and Keira staged their own fireworks show.'

But the angry words were belied by a rather fond glint in his eye. Leslie wasn't surprised. He was glad that sad business about Emily hadn't kept them apart until it was too late.

Leslie had a feeling that Lucas was feeling more ill than he was letting on. He wondered if he'd told Fane the true situation. Somehow he doubted it.

Twenty minutes later, after a thorough examination of his patient, his slight frown had turned into a furrow of frowns, and as Lucas put his shirt back on, he looked at him grimly.

'It's worse, isn't it?' he said at last, his voice flat.

Leslie carefully washed his hands, his back turned towards him. 'We always knew it was going to get progressively worse,' he prevaricated. 'We talked all this over months ago. I'd like to do some more tests.'

Lucas nodded. 'But it's gone on a lot faster than you thought?' he persisted. 'Hasn't it?' he added, when the doctor's silence continued to stretch.

Leslie slowly turned around, drying his hands on the towel and meeting the fierce-eyed look with an assessing gaze. Doctors trod a fine line when it came to dealing with the terminally ill. What worked for one didn't always work for another. As a general rule, it paid not to let the patients know too much.

But . . .

Slowly he nodded. 'Yes, Lucas, I'm afraid it has. And there are two things you can do about it,' he continued quickly. 'Admit yourself to hospital now, today, and undergo some radical drug and perhaps radiation therapy. It'll probably give you another couple of months or so on top of what you already have left, but you'll need to stay in hospital, and the therapy . . . well, it's not pleasant.'

Lucas licked his dry lips and returned slowly to the chair. His legs felt rather weak all of a sudden. 'And the second choice?'

Leslie shrugged. 'You go home, I prescribe stronger drugs, and you . . .' he trailed off.

Lucas nodded. 'And if I go with that? How much longer . . . ?'

Leslie sighed. 'A few months. I shouldn't think much more.'

Lucas looked at him sadly. 'Not a very long marriage.' It was the first thing that came into his mind, and he frowned slightly. Strange, but he'd not thought of that until now.

Just how *would* Keira feel, being widowed so soon?

* * *

Blaise made her way to the last field in what Aidan called the 'lower thirty', well prepared for a picnic. Back in her old home picnics were only to be countenanced in the summer, and then it was a very special day out. A treat to be savoured and long looked forward to.

Now, a picnic was no longer such a fanfare-type occasion. She had in her basket a thick piece of plastic and a blanket, for now the grass was autumn-wet, and she needed a good ground covering. Her hamper was full of bakery-fresh bread rolls, a hunk of Mr Farthing's special cheese, made at the home farm, a jar of real pickled onions from the grocer's shop, apples from her neighbour's tree, and a pat of fresh butter.

She'd been painting Aidan for four days now, and today she was determined to get him to sit down to eat a meal with her. If he didn't feel comfortable coming to her home, well . . . you could learn a lot from the old saying about the mountain and Mohammed.

She hummed to herself as she carried her burdensome picnic bag, easel, paints and satchel. Many of the villagers now stopped to chat, having got used to her laden figure setting off each morning to capture Aidan and his horses.

Mrs Keene, the same lady who'd kindly and tactlessly informed her that Aidan was not married and nor did he have 'any young lady in tow' nodded and gave a knowing, rather pleased smile as they passed on the street.

Instead of finding it intrusive, Blaise found herself remembering instead how every village had once had a matchmaker in olden times, who'd been a very valued — and highly paid — member of society. No doubt modern times had robbed Mrs Keene of her true vocation. But who was Blaise to go against the wishes of a matchmaker?

She climbed over the stile, laboriously trailing her things behind her, and glanced across at the now-familiar sight of the man and two horses. She'd learned, through watching, that the horses were rotated every four hours or so, and that the home farm must have at least two dozen or so heavy horses.

A keen observer, she'd also noticed how the horses always walked within the ruts they'd made and wondered how long it had taken Aidan to train them to do something so clever.

She set up her canvas, which was now half covered with paint, and glanced anxiously at the sky with growing confidence. She'd already become better at predicting the weather — it was strange how quickly she was adapting to country living. It was as if she'd been born for this kind of life. A few scudding clouds were forming low on the horizon, but she gauged she had a good hour or so of sunshine before they became a problem.

Aidan, who'd been keeping an eye out for her while telling himself that he was doing no such thing, raised an arm in greeting and carried on ploughing, his heart a little lighter now. He knew he was beginning to look forward to her presence, and knew, too, that soon the painting would be finished. And then . . .

But he didn't finish the thought. He'd lived a lonely life, and didn't regret it. Or at least he never had until now.

At eleven, the clouds had progressed from horizon to overhead, and Blaise, with a sigh, put her paintbrushes down. The vagaries of nature were a pain, and not something she was used to, having always painted indoors before, but she would put up with that and a lot more to get the results she could see taking shape before her very eyes.

On her canvas, she'd captured the changing colours of autumn far better than she could ever have hoped, and her first attempt at horses had been something of a revelation. She loved the way they moved, the patience and loyalty they showed, and she didn't flatter herself when she believed she'd captured that in paint. But, for all that, it was the figure of the ploughman, she knew, that made the painting.

She'd given Aidan a solidity that went further than mere blood and bone. Oh, she'd captured his handsome face and the strength of his broad shoulders, but she'd also given him a dignity that went hand in hand with the man who was at peace working with the land. When it was finished, she just knew, instinctively, that it was going to be the best piece of her career so far. Perhaps she'd take it to one of the galleries in Woodstock. During the tourist season in high summer she might get a very good price for it. If she could bear to part with it, of course!

'Hello, you look happy.'

The last word came out rather lopsided, and the voice was instantly recognizable as Aidan's. She glanced up, saw that the horses were busy drinking, and nodded at the canvas.

'You can see for yourself why,' she offered.

Aidan looked away from her lips and walked around to look at the half-finished painting thoughtfully.

It was good.

'No wonder you're looking so smug,' he said at last, his eyes narrowing on his own figure. He was taller than he'd thought of himself, and more good-looking. He glanced at her, smiling as she blushed, then watched curiously as she opened up a big bag.

She spread out a plastic groundsheet, then a blanket, and lifted out a Thermos of tea. Bread rolls, butter, cheese and apples followed. When she looked up, she was just finishing a sentence. '. . . and so I thought you might like to join me for an early lunch?'

Aidan felt a familiar shaft of unease lance through him as he translated her seemingly innocuous question. If he agreed, he'd have no quick get-out if things started getting . . . out of hand. But, on the other hand, the rolls looked lovely, and as she unscrewed the Thermos, he could see steam rising from it temptingly.

Who was he kidding? He simply wanted to stay in sight of her laughing blue eyes a little longer.

Why not?

He folded himself to the ground, careful to keep his heavy muddy boots off her blanket, and watched her break open a bread roll, spread some white butter all over it, spear a pickle with a wooden toothpick and break off a hunk of cheese.

It was his kind of picnic, and it was a little disconcerting that she'd instinctively picked all of his favourites.

He took his plate and thanked her, and for a while they ate hungrily and in companionable silence. He kept a careful watch out of the corner of his eye, and the moment her head lifted he turned to look at her.

'You know, I've always thought painting in the country to be a summer kind of thing,' she said. 'But half the cottages in the villages are brimming with colour now, more so than back in August, when I first came to see Lady Westcombe about renting the cottage.'

Aidan licked a piece of butter off his finger, unaware that Blaise found the gesture was doing strange things to her insides. She hastily averted her gaze and told herself that she was just imagining the sudden urge she'd felt to help him lick his fingers.

'It's the mums and dahlias that do it,' Aidan said helpfully. 'I've got plenty in my own garden. They love the Indian summer we've had.'

'Mums?' Blaise said innocently, unaware of how she'd made Aidan stiffen.

But there was nothing else for it. The difficult word had to be attempted. 'Chrysanthemums,' he clarified, but the word came out sounding more like 'chissums' to Blaise's ears.

Nevertheless, she instantly understood it, and wondered if it was his slight speech defect that made Aidan so shy. She rather hoped not, but she knew how cruel children could be, and she would have bet her last set of watercolours that he'd been teased something rotten as a child. No wonder he'd gone on to work with horses. She'd bet they never let him down.

'Oh, right,' she said, determined not to even notice the slight slur in his voice. 'I dare say I'll have to try and do something with my own patch, but I'm no gardener. I'm dead scared of hoeing out a plant instead of a weed!'

Aidan smiled, loving the way she laughed. It looked so carefree and easy, and made her eyes sparkle like blue forget-me-nots. 'This time of year it's easy to see what's a weed and what's not. A plant is either fully grown or going over by now. Weeds will still be growing. I'll come and give you a hand, if you like,' he offered, as naturally as breathing, and then he hesitated, surprised to find he had spoken without thinking it all out first. It was another first for him.

She smiled across at him and he bit into a pickle, deliberately glancing across at the horses. They'd finished their water, but were still waiting patiently, heads hanging drowsily in the quickening breeze.

Blaise shivered and reached for her cardigan. 'I suppose I'd better pack the canvas away, in case it starts to rain.'

Aidan continued to look at the horses.

She shrugged and moved towards the easel, and felt him start beside her. His head turned quickly to hers, and she realized her movements had caught him by surprise.

She felt her lips twist ironically. She knew she was hardly a sparkling conversationalist, and years spent talking to nobody but her ailing mother had probably made her more boring than normal, but even so, it would be nice if he actually paid her some attention!

She carefully covered the canvas, and when she turned back, he was already on his feet, brushing breadcrumbs from his dirty blue overalls.

'Well, thanks for the lunch,' he said, feeling awkward once more. He knew it had been a mistake to stay.

'Oh,' Blaise said, aware of a deep disappointment. She longed to have him stay just a little longer. With the breeze blowing his dark hair across his face, he looked suddenly very beautiful, standing looking down at her. His skin was leathery, and she longed to explore it. To trace the wrinkles at the sides of his eyes that deepened so devastatingly when he smiled, which, alas, was not often enough. She grappled about for an excuse and reached for the Thermos. 'Wouldn't you like some more tea?'

Aidan blinked. He knew he'd read her lips correctly, but for once it was not her words that demanded his attention. Instead, something else nudged at him, a voice that insisted that she actually *wanted* him to stay. He could hardly believe it, but he knew he wasn't mistaken. He was sure she'd been casting about for some excuse to keep him near. It made his eyes water with choking gratitude, and he quickly blinked.

Nobody had ever actively sought his company before, except perhaps his mother, dead for many years now.

Suddenly he felt strangely afraid. No, not afraid exactly, but . . . disconcerted. His life seemed to be changing, and he wasn't sure he wanted it to.

'I . . . can't stop,' he said, and wished that he could hear his own voice, just to reassure himself that it was coming out all right. 'I have to see to the horses.' He indicated them, and at once felt guilty for his cowardice.

Blaise's pretty face fell. 'Oh. Oh, of course you must see to them,' she agreed, and began to pack away the things. 'Perhaps,' she said, bending down to repack the cheese, 'we could meet in the pub for a drink one night?' She raised her head and smiled. 'But only if you don't have any other plans.'

Aidan took a step back. 'No, I don't have any plans.'

Plans? What had he missed?

Blaise immediately brightened. 'OK. Shall we say tonight?'

Aidan fought back the panic, the words of his old teacher coming back from all those years ago. 'If in doubt, ask, lad. *Ask*.'

But it was an easy thing for a teacher to say.

'All right,' he agreed, wondering what he was agreeing to. 'Where?'

Blaise blinked, puzzled, and then shrugged. 'I don't know. By the bar, if you like. I don't suppose the Stone and Heron is so big that we'll miss each other!'

The pub! Aidan thought. Of course, he should have guessed. He nodded. 'OK. Tonight, then, about . . . eight?'

Blaise nodded happily.

It was only when he'd turned away that Aidan realized he'd never been to the Stone and Heron since moving into the village. As he walked back to the waiting horses, he wondered what would happen if they met up with others and everyone started talking at once.

Then he shrugged. It wouldn't be the end of the world. Not with Blaise there . . .

* * *

Fane parked the car in the middle of the village and glanced up at the big house. But he had no intention of calling in today — not after that fiasco yesterday. He could still feel the touch of her lips on his, even twenty-four hours later.

No, today he was on a reconnoitring mission. If he was to take on Keira Westcombe — he refused to give her his own surname — then he had to do some research. As a piece of practical advice, 'Know thine enemy' had a lot going for it.

He reached inside for a light jacket and locked the car door firmly after him. It was one thing to be told that there was no crime in the village, but it was another thing altogether to leave his beloved E-type unlocked.

Briskly, he set off for the nearest gate. It was a traditional five-bar country gate with a sturdy iron lock-and-catch mechanism. On it was a white square sign:

Westcombe Nature Reserve
Please remain on footpaths

He'd heard from one of the locals that Keira had turned all her land into an official nature reserve, and he wondered what tax boffin had put her onto it. No doubt by signing a few official papers she'd managed to secure some kind of financial coup for herself. He doubted it actually meant anything in reality. He'd have to look into it. In due time, when he inherited the land adjoining it, it might pay him to do the same thing. Perhaps there was some kind of subsidy involved. Didn't the government pay farmers to let land lie fallow nowadays? Perhaps it was sheer laziness on her part. If she didn't have to employ farm workers, she'd save huge amounts of money.

He smiled grimly at the worthless sign, agilely sprinted over the gate, and set off up a sheep path towards the nearest grove of trees.

As he approached, he could see that one of the trees was a walnut, and that already several large nuts lay on the ground. He shrugged and put some into his pocket, ducking his head as he went under a low branch and set off deeper into the shadows.

A flash of red shooting up a tree trunk stopped him dead in his tracks. He was so used to seeing only silver-grey squirrels that for a moment he stared at the tufted-eared creature in amazement. The red squirrel stopped and watched him warily. Fane reached into his pocket for the walnuts, looked back at the squirrel, which began angrily chattering away, and couldn't help but laugh. He tossed the nuts back onto the ground. 'OK, OK,' he said, 'I didn't realize it was your patch. No need to tie your tail in a knot.'

He continued walking, in sudden good humour. Although the sun had gone in and grey clouds began to roll in the sky, he felt unaccountably cheered. Harwood Construction was based in London, and he'd left that office this morning, for once glad to leave the hustle and bustle of the city behind him. Now, the walk through the peaceful woods gradually began to ease the tension out of his shoulders. He ducked under the last of the low-lying tree limbs and emerged onto a grassy knoll.

To the right were the Penda Stones, and he stopped to look at them.

According to Jennifer, it was the Penda Stones that gave Keira her title and status and were the real reason why the locals all revered the Westcombe family. And as he looked at the grey stone circle, he felt a pleasant but cool touch feather down his back. It was almost as if the stones were trying to tell him something . . . He had been about to investigate the megalithic monument a little closer, but now, for some unaccountable reason that only his subconscious knew, he turned away and instead headed towards a large disused barn.

As he approached it, his builder's mind took in every detail. It was still fairly sound, with an intact roof and the usual slits for ventilation. But its entrance was half tumbledown, with the remains of a stable door at the bottom. Something, he saw, had chewed a way through the bottom plank, and as he leaned on the top, which came to his waist, he heard it creak alarmingly under his weight.

If the building were his, it would soon be converted into a country home. He looked into the gloom, imagining a mezzanine level, perhaps a large open-plan area with a huge stone fireplace at one end. It would then easily sell for . . .

But his profit margin was quickly forgotten as, out of nowhere, or so it seemed, a large white ghostly figure suddenly moved across the darkness within. For a second he felt the hairs on the back of his neck rise, and then he felt a breeze as a heart-shaped face flew out of the darkness at him. He ducked instinctively, then swivelled as the barn owl shot past him. No doubt the squeak of the door had awoken it, and the figure of a man in the light had frightened it.

Fane watched the bird go, his heart pounding in primordial delight. It looked like a wedge of white and gold in the air as it dipped below the hedge and was gone. It was only then that he realized that he hadn't heard it. Used to the pigeons of Trafalgar Square, he'd expected to hear a flutter of wings. And yet, even more ghost-like than ever, the bird had passed him in total silence.

'I never even heard the wind in its feathers,' he said aloud, astonished.

'You wouldn't,' a cool, slightly wary voice suddenly spoke up beside him, making him jump anew. He turned, already knowing who it was. No one else had a voice that could warm his blood at the first syllable.

'Don't sneak up on me like that,' he snapped.

Keira glanced at his tight, angry face and smiled gently. 'I'm sorry. I didn't mean to.' Seeing the look of open scepticism on his face, she sighed deeply. 'I mean it. I've spent years perfecting a quiet walk. You don't get to see much wildlife if you go tramping about like a herd of elephants.' As he continued to look at her sceptically, she sighed deeply. 'Honestly, I didn't realize I was doing it.'

Fane's eyes narrowed. 'I see.' He thought about the red squirrel. Weren't they rare in England? Could it really be that she was serious about this nature reserve thing? With his mind still filled with the beautiful owl, he asked reluctantly, 'Why couldn't I hear it?'

Keira accepted the olive branch willingly. She, too, could vividly recall their earth-shattering kiss of yesterday, and she was just as anxious to eradicate it from her mind as he was. Well, sort of.

'Barn owls hunt at night. Their prey are mostly mice and voles. If they could hear the bird coming, they'd be able to avoid it and the owl would starve. So nature equipped most owls with softer flight feathers that don't make a sound.'

Fane's eyes narrowed suspiciously. 'You sound very knowledgeable,' he said slowly. What role was she playing now?

Keira shrugged. 'I've been managing the reserve for several years now. I should be.'

Fane smiled ruefully. 'Yeah, right. You and an army of managers.'

Keira's smile faded. 'There are no managers. I hire three wildlife rangers to help me keep a check on everything, though. And from time to time forestry people are invited in to check on the health of the trees. If I need experts on a particular subject — like badgers, for instance — I can always find somebody to call in. I have a good network of contacts within the RSPCA and other wildlife organizations. But *I* run the reserve. Westcombe money pays the wages of the rangers, and Westcombe money funds the animal hospital.'

Fane continued to look at her, searching her face for lies, and Keira suddenly realized why he looked so disgruntled.

She laughed grimly. 'What's the matter, Fane?' she taunted. 'Did you think the reserve was just a paper empire? Were you hoping to find out that I only put my name and title to it and nothing more, as if I were patronizing a charity?'

Fane said nothing. There was nothing he could say, for that was exactly what he had thought. He simply hadn't been able to believe that such a beautiful and elegant woman would stoop so low as to actually get her hands dirty. Now, looking at her muddy wellingtons, he wanted to throttle her. Or kiss her. Or both.

Keira felt her shoulders droop dispiritedly. There seemed to be no getting through to him. He was determined to think the worst of her. 'As a matter of fact, I do lend my title and name to several charities,' she said wearily. 'And I do attend meetings and hold fundraisers at the Heronry. The Autumn Fayre is this Saturday — a kind of village fete. The Westcombes have given it for centuries, and the Heronry gardens always play host to it. But this wildlife reserve is all mine. My idea, my responsibility. Perhaps you'd like to see over it some time?' she asked, but without any real hope he'd take her up on it. The last thing Fane Harwood wanted was to see how wrong he'd been about her. Nevertheless, she had to make the effort. 'I'd be more than willing to take you on a guided tour.'

'Thanks. I'll take you up on that some time. I imagine running a place like this takes a lot of money,' he added, watching her closely.

Keira gave him a long, level look, a hint of sadness lingering in her eyes. 'You're determined to see some ulterior motive in everything I do or say, aren't you?' she said wearily. 'But I'm not the Wicked Witch of the West, Fane. I'm a woman, just like any other. I make mistakes, and sometimes I do things I regret.'

'Like marrying my father?' he slipped in silkily.

Keira's lips twisted. 'I was thinking more of . . . loving the wrong kind of men.' Rex, for instance. Although she'd been young and could be forgiven for that. She was hardly the first young girl to be taken in by a practised charmer. But now there was Fane, and she had no such excuse. She *knew* he was dynamite. Her husband's son . . .

Fane felt the colour drain from his face. 'Men?' he echoed, his voice a snarl. 'Just how many *men* have there been, Keira?' he asked, taking an angry step closer to her. The thought of her with anyone else . . .

Keira laughed; a harsh, bitter laugh that stopped him dead. 'So now I'm the local tramp, am I?' she snapped, raising her chin in defiance but nevertheless taking a quick step backwards. He was so damned tall . . .

'Sorry to disappoint you,' she drawled with desperate bravado, 'but before you . . . your father,' she hastily amended, 'there was only one man. He promised to marry me, and look after me, and all the rest of those lies you men like to tell women. But when he saw how expensive it was to keep the Heronry going, and how much like hard work it actually was to run a farm, he soon changed his mind. So, I've had a young and handsome man, Fane, and much good it did me. And you'll just have to forgive me,' she dropped her voice in warning, 'if I say that I'm more than happy, *genuinely* happy, with your father.'

She was appalled to find angry tears in her eyes, and she quickly dashed them away. What had possessed her to talk about Rex to *Fane,* of all people? Now she'd just given him another reason to despise her. She turned away, wishing she could take back every word.

Fane stared at her pale and miserable profile, suddenly lost. What could he say? He'd never expected someone as beautiful, as hard and sophisticated as this woman, to have had an unhappy past. It left him feeling strangely wrong-footed.

'I'm sorry. I didn't mean to pry. It's none of my business,' he said inadequately.

'No, it isn't, is it?' She seized the lifeline at once, and stiffened her spine, turning to face him once more. 'So let's leave it, shall we? And, by the way, I meant what I said about showing you around.' If she could just get him to see how vulnerable the reserve was, how very much help it needed to survive, she'd have accomplished something other than making a damned fool of herself. Besides, she needed to keep her mind on business. And keeping the nature reserve as some kind of buffer between them would give her at least a fighting chance of survival as far as dealing with this handsome, treacherous, *appealing* man was concerned.

Fane felt stung by her coldness. Damn her, he'd make her private life his business if it was the last thing he ever did.

'Right. But don't think you're going to turn me all green and soft in the head,' Fane snapped. 'I'm not in the market to be lectured.'

Keira gave a frustrated sigh. 'Believe me,' she said, goaded beyond measure now, 'I wouldn't dream of trying to teach *you* anything.'

Fane's eyes blazed into black fire. 'Why, you arrogant, little upper-class bitch! Just who the hell do you think you are?' He reached for her, intending to do . . . he knew not what, but this time she was quicker than him, and prepared. Like a fleet deer, she nimbly stepped to one side and backed away.

'I think not,' she said coldly. 'Not again.'

Fane, his hands full of air, let them fall back to his side. He looked at her — so beautiful in ancient jeans and an old black sweater with holes at the elbows — and shook his head.

'No,' he agreed. 'I think that point has already been proved.'

Keira smiled grimly. Did he think she would let him take the upper hand so easily? It was about time she taught him that he was not the only animal in the jungle with claws. 'I'd have said that it had been proved to our *mutual* satisfaction, yes,' she agreed, and watched his hands curl into fists. So she hadn't missed the tell-tale hardness in the lower part of his body. He didn't think she would have.

'You're a cocksure little madam, aren't you?' Fane whispered, above the excited thundering of his heart. He had to admit it to himself — he was *glad* that she was serious about something, at least. Even if it was only a plot of land. She had fire in her, and depth. And, although he should be angry to discover that she was not simply a shallow little money-grabber, he wasn't. He was curiously relieved.

Keira felt like laughing out loud. Sure of herself? If only he knew. Fane Harwood terrified her. Thrilled her. Excited her. But he hardly inspired self-confidence . . .

'Let's just say,' she said sweetly, 'that I know how to defend what's mine. And if you think I'm going to let you build a concrete jungle right next to my land, then you'd better damn well think again!'

Fane dragged in a swift, ragged breath as his whole body became suffused with seductive heat. He hardly heard her last few sentences, for his mind was filled with an image of her as a tigress, protecting her territory. 'I'll just bet you know how to keep what's yours,' he gritted.

And wished, suddenly and with a fierceness that was so incredibly sweet, that she regarded *him* as belonging to her . . .

CHAPTER 6

Blaise sighed over her wardrobe's meagre selections and promised herself a shopping spree soon — perhaps in Bicester, the old market town which she had yet to explore.

As it was, she reached for her prettiest skirt, a long, pleated creation in cream and lilac, and donned a deeper purple top. Not the most fashionable of outfits, but it made her fair curly hair look fairer and curlier, and her eyes more violet than blue.

Next she donned a dab of powder, a touch of lilac eyeshadow and a slash of lipstick. It took her all of five minutes to get ready. So much for the chauvinist male presumption that it took women hours to prepare for a night out!

She returned to the kitchen to ladle out the little hard fishy biscuits that Keats loved so much and stood watching the cat happily crunch away. Then she glanced at her watch for about the hundredth time.

She knew she was being ridiculous — after all, she was just popping out to the local pub for a drink with a man she was painting. But, in spite of stern lectures, Blaise knew it was more than that.

Hence the giddy-schoolgirl nerves!

It was still only seven-thirty, and it would take her all of two minutes to walk the short distance to the Heron and Stone.

Or was it the Stone and Heron?

Blaise had never been to the pub before. Since it was *the* social high spot of the village — in fact, the *only* social high spot of the village — she supposed she'd better get acquainted with it sooner rather than later.

Her days of lonely isolation were over.

She left the cottage, with the faithful cat once more on the windowsill to see her off, and made her way up the village street. It was dark now, at this time of year, but she could still smell roses on the night air.

For October, the season was fantastically mild. She wondered, with a shudder, if this was the first manifest sign of global warming, and determinedly pushed the awful thought away. Nevertheless, she made a mental note to support one of Keira's green causes when the first opportunity arose.

The pub was pleasantly full, even at so early an hour, and she stood in the doorway looking around. She'd heard it was a gathering place for real ale aficionados, and she wondered how many brews were made from the farm's barley. Perhaps Aidan had sowed the barley seeds that made the beer one old man was happily slurping over in one corner.

It was a lovely little thought.

The first thing she noticed on stepping up to the wooden bar was the odd but welcome absence of raucous noise, and she looked around, slightly puzzled. The room was old, with bulging walls and low-beamed ceilings, and then she realized that there were no noisy slot machines or jukeboxes, or those hideous, flashing-light monstrosities that children seemed addicted to.

Instead there were clusters of lamps on the walls, throwing out pools of gold light, pretty coloured fairy lights over the bar, giving it a permanently festive look, and, in one corner, a piano that someone was tinkling on very effectively.

What was the tune? Something . . . rather lovely. 'Stranger on the Shore', she recalled, and smiled nostalgically. One of her mother's favourite golden oldies.

Horse brasses hung on the walls, along with ancient farming implements. The floor was covered with centuries-old tiles, giving a pleasantly uneven feel to the place. It was great for lovers of authenticity, but she wondered with a smile how people leaving the worse for drink felt about it.

She was still smiling when she leaned on the bar. The landlord's wife, a round-bodied, round-cheeked woman, seemed to know her immediately, as Blaise had expected, and asked her what she'd like.

The list of real ales was mind-boggling, and, not surprisingly, Blaise opted for wine. She was then promptly offered a list of delicious-sounding home-made varieties as well as the more ubiquitous labels available in supermarkets.

It turned out Michelle, the landlord's wife, was a dab hand with wine, and Blaise, intrigued, ordered the elderflower champagne.

'Not that we can strictly call it champagne, luv,' Michelle said, winking as she handed over a generous glass of delicately coloured wine. 'The la-de-dah champagne-makers over in France would object. But it'll always be elderflower champagne to us, luv. Right?'

'Too right,' Blaise said quickly, catching the woman's quirky spirit. She took a tentative sip under Michelle's confidently watchful eye, and gasped. It was wonderful. Nectar. It had such a . . . floral taste. She knew elderflowers were those creamy flowerets that lined the English countryside verges every May and June, but she'd never guessed they could be turned into such ambrosia before.

'It's marvellous,' she said, her accent unknowingly increasing its Birmingham twang.

Michelle nodded, her eyes turning speculative. 'I'll keep 'em coming, shall I? Will a gentleman friend be paying?'

Blaise smiled openly. Talk about nosy! But she didn't mind. Instead she nodded. 'I'm meeting Aidan.' She looked around, but once again could see that he hadn't yet arrived.

Michelle looked surprised. 'The horse man?' she asked, her voice matching her look.

Blaise glanced at her, openly puzzled. Surely, since Aidan had lived in the village for a few years, he was better known in the pub than that?

She nodded. 'He's not a regular, I take it?' she asked, and Michelle laughed.

'Never set foot in the place since he arrived,' she agreed, but she didn't sound particularly bolshy about it. Her next words confirmed why. 'Mind you, I hear he hasn't set foot in any other pub around here, neither. Perhaps he's teetotal. I hear some of them Yorkshire types are. Live right up in the hills on the moors with no pub for miles — they grow up without good liquor. I expect that's what it is.' Then her round, rather bovine brown eyes softened as they took in Blaise's pretty purple outfit, and she nudged her playfully. 'I'm glad to see you're teaching him better manners, Blaise.' And she laughed and winked, and left to serve a group of farmhands who'd just wandered in.

Blaise took her drink thoughtfully over to a quiet corner table that was bathed in soft golden light and set her fluted glass carefully down, careful not to spill a drop. Her face was pensive. Why didn't Aidan mix more with the locals? She herself had been here barely a month, and already the landlady was calling her Blaise.

He must be very standoffish to keep his privacy in such a friendly place. Why was that? She sensed a mystery, and Blaise loved solving mysteries.

Aidan, unaware of Blaise's thoughts, was walking slowly up the street, his steps slowing the closer he got to the pub. He could see it up ahead, well-lit in the darkness, the red-leaved creepers that marched across its stone facade highlighted by the carriage lamps circling the pub gardens. The sign, showing a well-painted heron and one of the Penda Stones, swung in the breeze, creaking slightly.

He stood looking at it for a long time. To most men a visit to the local pub was hardly an event. But Aidan was not most men.

He never had been.

He sighed, then smiled at himself ruefully. Taking a deep breath, he walked up the path to push open the side door. He emerged into a side bar and nodded at one or two men. There seemed to be a dominoes match on, and many of the farmhands who worked with him watched him in open surprise as he made his way towards the main bar.

Aidan was well-liked by the men on the farm. At first, when they'd heard that Lady Penda was changing from machinery to horses, there'd been a lot of consternation and fear for jobs. The arrival of a Yorkshireman to oversee them had caused even more anxiety.

But they'd been quickly won over. Horses meant more work, which meant more employment. The demand for organic food, instead of diminishing, as some people had scornfully predicted, had instead grown, meaning higher wages. And Aidan had proved to be a very patient teacher where the care and handling of horses was concerned. And it was not only the horses that responded well to him. He had a gentleness that had soothed the younger lads, and a competence that had reassured the older men and allowed them to follow where he led without any resentment.

And, although life on the farm was now much harder work, the horses had quickly worked their magic on all who now used them. As Aidan had told them that first morning he'd joined the Westcombe home farm, there was something immensely satisfying about getting up at dawn on a fine spring morning to groom and harness horses, then lead them out onto the land to start a whole new cycle of life.

And, as the years had gone by, and Lady Penda's reforms had matured, lads who'd grown up in the village had got to see things they'd never seen from a tractor seat before. Stoats and weasels, skylarks' nests that were scattered in the fields, fields that were never turned until the chicks had fledged. Owls and hawks, foxes and pheasants. Of course, there was no game-shooting on Westcombe lands.

Aidan, however, was unaware of the friendly but curious eyes that followed his progress, and when he emerged into the main bar, he stopped dead in his tracks. It was much more crowded in here. He saw Michelle, whom he knew to speak to, and carefully turned to look at her as she moved across to him.

'Well, hello, stranger,' she said, her eyes running over him in an appreciative gaze. She'd been twenty years happily married, but that didn't mean she couldn't ogle a hunk every now and then. Bert, her hubby, ogled the ladies on the sly!

'What can I get you?' Michelle asked, and Aidan smiled.

'What can you recommend?'

Michelle was about to list a whole wad of oddly named real ales and beers, then quickly changed her mind. Why make life difficult for the poor chap just when he seemed to be coming out of his shell? Instead, she reached for a beer glass and pulled him a pint of ale that had been brewed in Chipping Norton. She handed it over and turned to open the till, careful to turn her head back towards him as she quoted the price, so that he could read her lips.

It had been her friend Mavis, if she recalled rightly, who'd first told her that Aidan Shaw was deaf. She supposed that by now the whole village probably knew, but nobody talked about it much. If a man didn't want to talk about his private business, well . . . folks around here were more than happy to let a man live his own life the way he liked it best. But her generous heart was glad to see him socializing a bit at long last, and she had no doubts as to who she could thank for that!

Aidan saw the till open and took out a five-pound note. Michelle gave him the change, then nodded knowingly to the corner table, her eyes twinkling irrepressibly. 'She's waiting.'

Aidan swung his head around, his eyes instantly finding her. The lamps made her hair glow like molten gold, and turned her outfit from purple to orange. He picked up his pint and walked towards her.

Blaise watched him approach, her heart hammering pleasantly. He was dressed in simple clean jeans with a bottle-green jumper. It made his hair darker and his hazel eyes greener. He moved like a big elk, she mused, packed full of muscle, solid but graceful.

He pulled the seat out directly opposite her and sat down. It creaked slightly. He looked, Blaise saw at once, incredibly nervous. And, once again, she couldn't understand why. Where did this shyness come from? He was, she supposed, in his late thirties, and was incredibly good-looking. Well, she thought so, anyway. He had a romantic job that kept him really physically fit and seemed to have everything he wanted in life. So why this awkwardness around people? A minor speech defect just couldn't account for it. Perhaps the slurred voice was due to some medical condition? Hadn't she read that a stroke could cause a lisp? Then she firmly bit back the angst. She was being stupid — no stroke victim worked with cart horses! She was letting her past experience with disease and illness warp her sense of judgement.

Nevertheless, she knew Aidan was hiding *something* from her. From the village. Why had he left Yorkshire?

She was determined to get to the bottom of the mystery. And it was not just idle curiosity that urged her on. She was beginning to understand that Aidan Shaw was becoming more and more important in her life.

Oh, she knew what the sceptics would say. She was so afraid of becoming an old maid that she was clinging to the first real man she'd met since being freed from a life of near-seclusion. And a part of her that was deeply honest couldn't deny it was a reasonable argument. She *was* actively looking for a relationship. She *did* want love and, in time, a family, and everything else that most women wanted.

But she knew, for all that, that even though Aidan *was* the first man she'd met since her mother's death, he was not just . . . an experiment. He was an incredibly complex, difficult-to-understand, hard-to-get-close-to man. If all she wanted was a boyfriend, she'd be far better off casting her fishing net further afield. She knew she was reasonably attractive, and could land quite a few acceptable fish if she put her mind to it.

But they wouldn't be Aidan.

She smiled at him, glad that he wasn't a mind-reader. She'd probably be scaring him witless!

'I like this place,' she said, looking around. 'Michelle brews some of the finest wines.' She glanced at her pale cream-coloured sparkling glass. There! For an opening conversational gambit, that was about as non-threatening as you could get.

Aidan nodded and took a sip of his beer. It was surprisingly good. 'She doesn't serve bad ale, either,' he agreed, and then promptly stared down into his glass.

Blaise grinned. She couldn't help it. This was going to be like pulling teeth. He glanced up at that moment, scared in case she was talking and he wasn't watching her lips, and caught the wide grin.

It was infectious, and he found himself laughing openly. 'What's so funny?'

Blaise shook her head. 'Nothing. Us.'

Aidan's smile faltered. 'What's wrong with us?'

Blaise's blue eyes darkened. 'Nothing that I know of.' Aidan stared at her so hard she wondered if she'd got lipstick on her teeth or something. Then, slowly, he leaned back on his chair.

'Blaise—' he said, and then stopped abruptly. No, he couldn't do it. He couldn't tell her.

Blaise felt herself tense. She leaned forward quickly, her hand coming out naturally to cover his. She sensed he'd been about to say something important, and instinct screamed at her that she must hear it. It was imperative. She couldn't have said why she thought so, she only knew she suddenly felt as tense as a bow string.

But again Aidan shook his head. 'It's nothing. I . . . Tell me what brought you to the village. Was it just the scenery?'

The last word came out like 'sheery', but she was aware only of a tense feeling of bitter disappointment. But she wouldn't give up. Blaise had lived a lifetime of not giving up, even when all the odds were against her.

So she forced herself to lean back and smile away the chagrin. She began by telling him about her life in Birmingham. Her father's death, her mother's illness. The house, the kind neighbours, the men who'd met her and liked her, but who had quickly left when they discovered what came with the package of being with her. She told him about her self-taught career — the paintings she'd started, laboured through, finished and then rejected as being no good.

She told him about the first painting she'd ever sold to a friend of the family, so it didn't really count. Then she told him about the first painting she'd sent to a gallery. The first painting the gallery had sold for her. She told him about her mother's death, the funeral, the selling of the house. She told him about overhearing all about the lovely, unusual village in Oxfordshire, about her meeting with Keira and the housekeeper.

She held nothing back as she took him from her first childhood memories to the day she'd set up her easel in the field to paint the man ploughing the land with his horses.

By the time she'd finished, Blaise was on her third glass of elderflower champagne. Aidan was feeling as humbled as a fallen oak, and fighting a near-irresistible urge to return her courage and honesty and relate his own life story.

But how could he, when things stood as they did? Especially now, when he'd heard that Fane Harwood had returned to the village. So far, try as he might, Aidan had been unable to 'accidentally' run across Fane and check him out for himself. He wasn't looking forward to it, remembering only too vividly his first run-in with Jennifer Goulder. He'd been so looking forward to seeing her . . . and she'd turned out to be cold and superior.

Now he was wary about meeting up with Fane. He was already concerned by some rumours being told about him. It was a minor scandal, about the way Fane had opened the dancing at Keira and . . . her husband's wedding. Rumour now had it that Fane was thinking of building new houses on Harwood land. He wasn't sure how true that was, but . . .

He glanced up and found Blaise's soft blue eyes watching him carefully.

'You looked so . . . serious all of a sudden,' she said softly, then smiled. 'Sorry. I didn't mean to stare. I think this elderflower fizz of Michelle's is more potent than you might think.'

Aidan grasped the lifeline like a sinking man. He glanced at his watch, truly surprised to see that it was nearly half past ten. Time had flown by as he'd listened, alternately appalled, amused and respectful, to Blaise's life story.

Now he rose slowly to his feet. 'Time to leave,' he said softly, and held out his hand.

Blaise took the huge hand immediately, loving the way the strong fingers curled around hers. She stumbled, just slightly, and banged her leg on the table getting up.

'Careful,' Aidan smiled, wondering if she was just a little tipsy.

Blaise walked beside him across the uneven floor, smiling goodbye to Michelle as Aidan left their glasses at the bar. The landlady waved at them cheerfully, her eyes bright as she watched them go.

'Well, there's a first,' Bert, her equally round and cheerful husband, grunted by her side. 'Never thought I'd see him in here.'

Michelle smiled. 'They'll be back,' she said, watching the couple disappear into the dark night. She sighed deeply. What it was to be young and in love.

Or middle-aged and in love. She gave Bert's bottom a frisky pat.

Outside, Blaise shivered a little. The night was still balmy, but it had been warmer inside the friendly inn than she'd realized. Aidan saw her movement, and frowned.

'You should have brought a coat.'

Before she knew what he was about, he pulled off his sweater and draped it over her shoulders, tying the sleeves into a loose knot over her breastbone. The sweater still held his warmth, and she could smell soap and just a touch of aftershave — cool and tangy — rising up from the material. The sweater was so big on her it covered her back and arms and immediately warmed her.

'But you've only got a shirt now,' she said, and quickly picked up the pace. 'Please, come back to my place and I'll make us something hot to drink.'

Aidan, walking behind her, said nothing.

It was but a few hundred yards to her cottage, and she turned in at the gate and walked to the door without slacking her pace. When she had opened the door and turned back, Aidan was loitering uncertainly at the gate. The full moon turned his head into a mixture of dark shadow and silver light.

'Come on in,' Blaise said softly.

Aidan saw her lips move and walked forward, his heart beating strong and sure in his chest, his mind insisting that he was being a fool. A fool playing with fire.

When he got closer, she went inside and held the door open, giving him no other choice but to follow.

He found himself in a cottage similar to his own. Low-ceilinged, well-built, cosy. She led him to the kitchen, which was definitely chilly. He glanced at the unlit boiler — a black, decorative, but still functional affair — and frowned.

'You have no fire.'

Blaise put on the kettle and glanced at the iron furnace. 'I don't know how to use it,' she admitted ruefully. 'I don't have any trouble with the living room; it's centrally heated and I just turn a knob. But Harry next door says I'll save on fuel bills if I use the fireplace, like he does. He offered to cut me some wood, but I wouldn't know how to go about lighting a real fire. Although it would be nice to have one around Christmas time. To roast some chestnuts and sit around it listening to carols and things . . .'

She was babbling, and knew it, and she flushed. Aidan had his eyes fastened to her lips like glue, and no doubt he thought she was mad. She turned back to the cabinets and ladled out the drinking chocolate.

'I could teach you how to lay a fire and keep it going,' Aidan said. 'All it needs is newspaper, some kindling, logs and coal. Once it's got going, all you need to do is keep feeding it logs. Keira has a sustainable forest system going on the edge of her land, and one of her men comes around the village every week in winter, selling logs at a good price.'

Blaise turned slowly around, and her smile was tender. She was glad that she was not the only one babbling.

Their eyes met. With his dark green jumper still across her shoulders, clashing hideously with her purple outfit, Aidan thought he had never seen a more lovely woman.

Her eyes were the colour of summer sky. She moved slowly across the cold kitchen towards him, and Aidan shifted nervously, like one of his horses might at the approach of an unknown piece of harness.

But there was trust in his eyes as she reached up to him, and when she circled her arms around his neck, drawing his head closer to her, he bent willingly.

Blaise tilted her face back and up that extra inch and kissed him.

She wasn't all that good at kissing, not having had a great deal of experience in it, but the moment she touched his lips with her own it ceased to matter. She stopped worrying about whether their noses would hit and bounce off one another, or whether he was thinking how bossy she was to be the one to instigate the kiss, or any of the other hundred and one irrelevancies that had journeyed with her across the space of the kitchen floor.

Instead, all that mattered was being in his arms at last. She felt him shudder, once, as their lips met, and then his hands were on her back, his palms warm against her skin through the layers of clothing. He pulled her closer to him with an easy strength that was thrillingly new to her. It felt good to be held by strong arms. Surprisingly, fundamentally good.

She pressed closer, opening her mouth wider, inviting more.

Aidan responded, his eyes closing, leaving him in a world of dark silence where only the feel of her mattered.

A strand of hair was against his cheek, cool and deliciously tickling. Her lips felt warm and tender under his own. He could detect the sweet floral taste of elderflowers on her breath, and it intoxicated him.

He moaned, but never heard the sound. But Blaise did, and she shuddered in her turn.

Her head swam in a warm, pleasant eddy.

Slowly, reluctantly, she drew back, wanting to look at him. Aidan's eyes slowly opened. Their hazel depths looked a little dazed and just a touch unfocused.

Her own eyes looked like Ceylon sapphires.

Aidan drew in a deeply ragged breath. He'd never kissed a woman like that before. It was . . . soul-changing.

But, as their eyes held, he understood with a flash of insight that it was only soul-changing because it was Blaise that he had kissed. Open, honest, pretty, generous, kind-hearted Blaise.

Who deserved the best.

Who deserved so much better than . . . *him.*

Blaise felt the coldness the moment he stepped back, out of her range. She wanted to cry out, to reach out for him and physically drag him back, for it suddenly felt as if he was moving out of her world, not just out of her kitchen.

'Aidan!' she said, but he was already turning away.

Quickly she slipped off the jumper. 'Here, you forgot your sweater.'

But he didn't turn back for it.

Determinedly she followed him to the door. He stopped abruptly and glanced down, and Blaise saw with relief the way Keats had wound herself around his legs. The little grey cat was standing on his shoes, her tail curled around one leg, her cheek pressed against his other knee, rubbing sensuously. She was purring loudly.

Aidan reached down to pick her up, and gently stroked her white chin. The cat's purr turned as loud as a lawnmower.

Blaise could have kissed the animal! Her pet had just earned herself a salmon supper for life.

She moved forward. 'Looks as if you've made a friend,' she said, keeping her voice deliberately light.

Her shadow, falling across the wall, alerted Aidan to her presence and he swung around.

Blaise nodded at the cat. 'She likes you. I always thought cats were supposed to be standoffish.'

Aidan forced himself to smile. He wanted to put the cat down and take her mistress back in his arms. He wanted to feel close to Blaise again. But he kept the distance firmly between them.

'I have a way with animals,' he said, and gave the cat a scratch on top of her head that had her going into wriggling fits of feline bliss.

Blaise held out the jumper and Aidan put down the cat to take it. Keats meowed loudly in protest. Aidan took the jumper but made no move to put it on.

'Well, I'll see you tomorrow then,' Blaise said awkwardly, and saw Aidan's eyes leap. 'I mean . . . in the fields. To finish the painting . . .'

Aidan took a deep breath. 'Oh, yes. Right. I hope it's nearly finished.' When she looked puzzled, he forced himself to shrug nonchalantly. 'Ploughing's nearly over.'

'What, so soon?' Blaise cried, dismayed.

Aidan shrugged. It sounded cruel, but sometimes you had to be cruel to be kind. 'There've been three other teams besides mine ploughing the other fields. But it'll take a day or two to finish up,' he admitted finally, unable to withstand the disappointment in her eyes.

Blaise immediately brightened. She was a born optimist. A lot could happen in a few days, after all. Especially when a gal was determined that it should!

'Great. Well . . . tomorrow, then.'

Aidan looked at her, wishing that things were different. But they were never going to be different. It was a fact that he'd long ago come to terms with. Something his father had never done.

He nodded at last, aware that she was waiting for some kind of response. 'Yes. Tomorrow.'

He turned and left, the cat determinedly following. Blaise watched the man and cat go, and wondered if Keats would be spending the night curled up on Aidan's bed.

Lucky cat!

* * *

Colin Rattigan sighed as he carefully checked through Lucas's new will. He had typed it personally, his instinct for self-survival dictating that no secretary should be aware of the document's existence. Although, at this stage, he could genuinely claim ignorance of any wrongdoing, he knew it couldn't last.

He sighed deeply and pushed the legal papers into his briefcase, locking it carefully.

The solicitor lived in a large modern house in Woodstock, but it had been heavily mortgaged to pay for his gambling fever. Now Jennifer Goulder, as holder of his markers, could take the house away from him at any time she wanted, as well as everything else he had. Including his reputation. She must have spent her last penny on those damned markers. And it was for certain that she wouldn't have paupered herself for no reason. No, she had something in mind, all right. And whatever it was, it wouldn't look good for Colin Rattigan.

But there was nothing else for it. He poured himself a huge whisky and soda and picked up the telephone, his hand shaking wildly. On the other end of the line, a cool female voice answered after the fifth ring. 'Hello?'

Colin gulped a mouthful of whisky. 'Hello, Mrs Goulder, it's Colin Rattigan here.' He cleared his throat nervously. 'I know you . . . wanted to be informed the moment your father changed his will, and—'

'He called you in to rewrite it?' she interrupted briskly, not in the mood for pleasantries.

'Yes.'

'You have a copy of it?'

Colin glanced guiltily at his briefcase. 'Yes.'

On the other end of the line Jennifer Goulder's eyes narrowed thoughtfully. 'I see. You haven't done anything . . . official yet, have you?' she added, her voice glacial now.

In his mortgaged home, Colin Rattigan drained the last of his whisky and looked longingly at the still half-full decanter. 'No, Mrs Goulder,' he said hoarsely. 'I haven't.'

'Good. You can stall for a few days, can't you?'

'Stall?' Colin echoed, but without much hope. He winced as he heard her soft, tinkling laugh.

'What part of the word "stall" don't you understand, Colin?' Jennifer purred. Then, abruptly, her playfulness ended. 'I want you to keep that document safe. Make no copies of it, and, if Father gets impatient and calls to ask for it, tell him it'll take a little while longer. Is that clear?'

'Yes,' Colin said miserably.

'Good. I'll be calling in to see you in a few days' time. I'll tell you what I want you to do then.'

She hung up abruptly, and for a moment or two Colin stared at the buzzing receiver in his hand before crashing it down on the cradle angrily. Then he made himself another drink, neat this time, and ran a shaky hand through his hair. He took the will from the briefcase and walked to his safe, hidden behind a mirror, and locked the only copy of Lucas Harwood's last will and testament carefully away.

CHAPTER 7

The annual Autumn Fayre was a tradition going back longer than Keira could remember. It was a well-organized affair, unlike the June Fayre, which was held on the first of the month on the village playing field, and which was an impromptu flower-show-cum-six-a-side-football extravaganza.

The Autumn Fayre had always been held in the grounds of the Heronry. The famous gardens were open free of charge to village residents and at half price to out-of-towners. A huge marquee was always erected on the formal lawn since, in mid-October, the British weather was apt to be wet, windy, or both. There were, however, exceptions to this rule, and when Keira threw back her curtains that morning, the sun was shining benevolently in one of those rare, incredibly blue skies that only autumn can produce.

She was usually up at dawn, but this Saturday her 'rounds' were delegated to one of her wardens. She'd have to remember to ask him about the magpie situation. Magpies would play havoc in the spring, with their nasty habit of taking young chicks from the nest.

She sighed and glanced below into the garden. Already vans and trucks were pulled up in the driveway. From the biggest, a bright red-and-white-striped marquee was being extracted, with the usual difficulty, by a horde of amiably cursing men. Another truck bore the name of a local reputable catering company. Of course, many of the local men and women would bring home-made cakes, scones and toffee apples, and the baker had, ever since moving to Upper Rousham five years ago, provided a good range of crusty rolls and iced buns for the crowd's delectation. Still, one could never have enough good food.

At the annual pre-fete meeting the villagers had all jealously staked their claims, and already Keira could see Maud Kennedy marking out her skittles run while her husband, a dedicated hoopla enthusiast, was setting up by her side. Soon, Keira knew, other locals would come to set up yet more traditional village fete attractions. She'd forgotten who was to play Aunt Sally, and who she could expect to see in the fancy-dress competition, of which she was the judge.

She took a leisurely shower, then donned a warm orange, cream and black outfit that went well with her raven hair and her fast-disappearing tan. When she emerged into the breakfast room, Lucas was already at the table, sipping tea and studying the newspapers. He looked up and his eyes warmed. Her hair was caught back in a very elegant chignon, and she'd added golden hoop earrings and a chunky gold necklace that went well with the V-neckline of her orange blouse. Her green-grey eyes sparkled.

'So, what's the form?' Lucas asked, determined to be positive after the rather depressing visit to his doctor.

Since moving to the area, he had of course attended all the Autumn Fayres, but strictly as a guest. This year, he supposed, he would be playing Michael Westcombe's old role of official host.

'Oh, it pretty much muddles along at its own pace,' Keira said, reading his mind, and anxious to reassure him. 'Mrs Reversham does all the announcing, and nobody can understand her if she's forgotten to put her teeth in, so somebody reminds her. Then a timetable of events is read out and promptly forgotten. Groups range around, trying to pull unsuspecting people into Madame Strange's Fortune-Telling Tent, or whatever, and nearly every year two men turn up dressed as knights and have an impromptu joust. They usually wreck something or other, and the gardeners get cross. The only really important thing you have to remember is, if it starts to rain and you're standing in the doorway to the marquee, you'll get trampled. So shift yourself. Fast!'

Lucas laughed, appreciating the utterly British picture she'd painted. 'But aren't I supposed to be judging something or other?'

'The knobbly knees. Don't worry, some earnest matron will grab you by the scruff of the neck and cart you off when the time comes.'

'Can't wait!'

Bessie coughed from the doorway. 'The police, Keira.'

Lucas gave a start, and Keira shot Bessie an admonishing look. Her housekeeper had a startling sense of humour sometimes. If you didn't know about it, it could catch you unawares. 'Don't worry, Lucas,' Keira soothed. 'It's just the local constable. He'll want to know if we're using Dingle field for a car park again, and what we want to do about traffic control. Tell him we'll go with last year's arrangements again, Bessie. They seemed to work well enough.'

Bessie retired, hiding a smirk as Lucas mock-frowned at her. 'I think we'd better have a good breakfast,' he said heartily, helping himself to sausage and eggs from the silver trays on the table. 'I have a feeling that with Bessie in a spry mood, and a horde of guests awaiting us, we're going to need it!'

Keira watched him eat with a fond smile, but stuck to just a cup of coffee. She knew how these days went. The caterers cajoled her into trying their canapes, the WI buttonholed her to try their latest shortbread recipes, the candyfloss man bowed his head and wept if she passed him by, and the appropriately named Mrs Candyman's toffees were irresistible.

'At least the weather looks like holding for once,' Lucas commented. 'I remember the first time I came to one of these shindigs, it rained cats and dogs all day. And still everyone seemed to have a good time.'

'I remember. I set up a "Best Drowned Rat" competition and everybody entered!'

Lucas snorted. 'I thought I should have won that.'

'Diddums.' Keira stuck her tongue out at him, glad to see him laugh. If only he didn't look so distressingly ill . . .

Lucas was still laughing when Keira, biting the bullet, stepped out into the grounds to oversee things. The gardeners would have her guts for garters if she let the marquee people ruin the lawn . . .

* * *

Fane followed the line of traffic to the turn-off for the village, surprised by the amount there was. He hadn't thought a village fete, particularly one held in October, would be so popular.

Fane hadn't been idle the past few days. He'd been busy scouting the area, and was well aware of its potential. His father's land was ideally situated: near Oxford and within easy reach of the motorway. London was just over an hour away. Prime country-residence land, if he could get planning permission. He'd checked out in detail the plot of land his father had told him was to be his, and, although the area was too rural to think of a housing estate, a few large, comfortable houses dotted here and there in acres of gardens would be many a rich man's retirement dream.

He already had separate appointments made to wine and dine the local councillors. He'd need their help soon to get planning permission. He intended to present his father with all the relevant details too, and try to get him interested. He didn't like the look of his father at all, and it was obvious inactivity and retirement were wearing him down. A few simple building projects would be just what he needed to pique his interest, and, more importantly, give father and son a chance to get to know each other all over again. And a few scattered houses weren't going to upset the Westcombe Nature Reserve one iota, so he wouldn't be stepping on his darling stepmother's toes.

He smiled grimly and wondered, with pleasure, how long it would take Keira to hear about it all.

A bobby at the head of the road directed him into a field, and he parked his Jag beside a large oak. Locking the door behind him, he glanced at his watch and saw that it was still only half past one. He was dressed in warm corduroy slacks in navy blue, which hugged his powerful thighs, and a heavy-knit blue and white pullover. He looked devastating, and many female eyes followed his progress across the field.

Impervious to their collective gaze, he emerged near the church, and for a moment stood staring at it thoughtfully. Gooseflesh rose on his arms as he recalled the day he had stepped inside and met a witch. A beautiful, conniving, fascinating witch.

Just then he heard the sound of heavy clip-clopping and looked up the road, away from the centre of the village and towards the entrance to a large farmyard.

His eyes widened at a sight so picturesque it made him blink. Aidan was leading two matching black horses. Both had four white feet, and the 'feathers' — the loose white hair that covered the foot — were pristine, newly washed and combed. The horseshoes were highly polished and glinted in the sun as each horse lifted its foot. Their manes were intricately plaited, with each plait having been finished off by a tiny red ribbon bow. They wore full harness, which was festooned with horse brasses, the kind he usually only saw decorating pseudo-country inn walls. Fane had never seen them on live animals before.

Each horse looked resplendent. No doubt they were on their way to the fete, to be admired and petted, and fed carrots and sugar-lumps by an adoring crowd. And why not? Fane thought, watching them approach with appreciative eyes. Their black coats shone like ebony in the mellow autumn sun. Their owner obviously knew how to show them. Then he realized that, technically, Keira probably owned them, but he'd bet his last pound that *she'd* had nothing to do with the grooming of the animals.

His eyes moved thoughtfully to the man leading them. He moved a lot like them, Fane noticed, with a heavy but graceful tread. His own head was hanging and looking at the ground, just like the big bobbing heads of the horses.

Suddenly aware of a presence near him, Aidan lifted his head quickly. His eyes narrowed as all his senses came to full alert. Although he'd never met Fane Harwood before, Aidan knew instinctively who he was.

For his part, when Fane felt those hazel eyes run over him, he found himself straightening up, his backbone stiffening automatically. But it was not antagonism that had his senses sharpening. He felt none of the usual macho challenge emanating from the horse man.

And yet Fane had the strangest feeling that he *knew* him from somewhere. In a matter of a few seconds his quick and agile brain had searched his memory and reassured him that they'd never actually met, and yet the feeling of recognition remained.

Aidan nodded. 'Good afternoon,' he said simply.

Fane nodded back. 'Yes, it looks like it. Must be good news for those fine fellows.' He nodded at the horses, who were looking at him with indifferent eyes.

Aidan smiled. 'Oh, they wouldn't mind getting wet.'

Fane's eyes sharpened. There was something odd about the man's pronunciation. If he hadn't known better, he might have thought he was slightly drunk, for the words were oddly slurred. But there was nothing in the keen hazel eyes to hint that he was inebriated, and there was no tell-tale smell of alcohol wafting about.

Besides, Fane knew that this man would never get drunk. He didn't know how he knew it. He just knew that he did.

'What kind of horses are they?' he asked, curious not only about the animals but about the man.

'Clydesdales,' Aidan said simply. And waited.

Fane didn't nod. He wasn't about to pretend knowledge he didn't have. And a moment later he was glad.

The older man looked at him assessingly for a moment, then nodded. He never so much as lifted the corner of his lips in a smile, but Fane got the impression that the horse man appreciated the reason behind his silence, and approved.

'There are four main kinds of draught horses,' Aidan said, watching him carefully for signs of boredom and finding none. 'There's Shires, Clydesdales, Percherons and Suffolk Punch. Different counties prefer different horses — the eastern counties favour Percherons; in Lincoln and Cambridge it's Shires. Suffolk, obviously, has plenty of Suffolk Punches.'

'Which do you prefer?' he asked, genuinely interested.

Aidan smiled. 'Lady . . . Penda . . . has all four on her farm.'

Fane noticed the hesitation over Keira's name, and wondered at its cause. Habit would have had him calling her Lady Westcombe, he was sure. Now, etiquette might dictate that she be called Lady Harwood. It was intriguing that this man had chosen to call her by her more ancient and villager-preferred title. He wondered what motivated it.

'She likes to play all the options, I've noticed,' Fane said carefully, and immediately saw the shutters come down.

'You need at least four horses for every hundred acres. There are twenty times more than that on the home farm alone,' Aidan explained, his voice a little cooler now.

Fane nodded. So it was not Keira he disapproved of. That only left her new husband.

'I'm Lucas Harwood's son,' Fane said. He didn't say it to discomfit the stranger, but out of a sense of fairness. He wanted the horse man to know exactly who he was, before he could say anything potentially embarrassing. For both of them.

To his surprise, Aidan merely nodded. 'I know,' he said. Fane had the weirdest feeling that the horse man had once again correctly read him, and had realized *why* Fane had introduced himself. And, again, was quietly approving.

Fane was glad. Was it just his imagination, or were they connecting somehow? 'Have we met before?' he finally asked, his eyes narrowing.

Aidan smiled. There was something in that smile, Fane saw at once. Irony. A touch of . . . not bitterness, exactly, but something in that area. 'No,' Aidan said. Firmly. And truthfully.

Fane nodded. 'No,' he agreed. 'But—'

Behind them, an impatient motorist blasted his horn and one horse shifted nervously to the side. Instantly Aidan turned with the horse, his hand tightening on the bridle.

'There — easy, Mandrake. Easy, old son.'

His voice had dropped an octave into a deep, bass croon. The animal seemed to settle at once.

'It must be hard to persuade them to do something if they don't want to do it,' Fane said to the back of his head.

Aidan walked the animals to the side of the road and waved the car on. 'Silly idiot,' Fane muttered. 'Don't you get sick of people's ignorance?'

Aidan said nothing, but gave the horse a reassuring pat. Fane watched him, his frown deepening. And then, suddenly, he understood why the horse man talked the way he did. His own eyes became shuttered now, and he said nothing until Aidan was once again looking his way. Then he nodded at the horses. 'They trust you.'

Aidan nodded. 'Aye,' he agreed simply.

Fane smiled. He remembered now that someone had said Keira's head horse man came from Yorkshire. Without another word, Fane fell into step beside him as Aidan led the horses off. From time to time he was aware of Aidan shooting him an assessing glance.

What Aidan saw was a handsome, well-groomed man. A confident, rich man. A powerful man.

All in all, Aidan was pleased. But he was also wary. For some reason Fane Harwood had it in for Keira. And Aidan wanted to know why. And what he should do about it, if anything.

* * *

Keira, from a little wooden podium, glanced around at the assembled crowd. The sun was still shining, not with much heat, perhaps, but with a cheerful light. The crowd directly in front of her was itself circled by a larger crowd, clapping and cheering as each contestant did a twirl.

She smiled as a small child of about four took his turn. He'd got two cardboard pieces tied front and back around him in the shape of a beer bottle. His mother had painted a fairly good picture of a local beer label onto the front, and on his head was a gold-foil cap in the shape of a bottle top.

There were the usual witches, wizards, tarts and vicars, and extremely ugly men dressed in extremely feminine clothing, but, for sheer innovation, Keira came down off the podium and donated the small silver cup to a ten-year-old got up as a heron. She was relieved to see the 'feathers' weren't real. The youngster blushed and stammered, then ran off with a look of glee on his face, to show the cup proudly off to his mum.

Leaning against a cherry tree in full copper colour, Fane watched the young lad's beaming face and laughed softly. The fancy-dress crowd clapped gamely, and good-naturedly began to disperse.

Fane watched Keira like a cat watched a mousehole.

'I don't know what we're going to do about the beautiful ankles competition.' A woman dressed in a hat that would not disgrace Ascot suddenly appeared at his side, startling him for a moment, until he realized that she was talking across him to a woman minding the White Elephant stall.

'Why, Flo? What's happened to Ernie?'

'He's passed out in the beer tent,' the tetchy Flo said, rearranging her hat. It was some feat, and Fane watched her with amused eyes.

'Is he, indeed?' said the White Elephant lady. 'Wait till Cecilia hears about that.'

'Thing is, he *always* does the ankles competition.'

Fane, unable to withstand it any longer, coughed discreetly. 'Excuse me, ladies, perhaps I can help?'

Flo blinked and tilted her head back to look at him through a plume of pink and purple feathers. 'Eh?' she said, somewhat inelegantly.

Fane gave a half-bow. 'I don't like to flatter myself, you understand,' he began modestly, getting into the spirit of the thing, 'but I consider myself as good a judge of feminine ankles as the next man.'

The White Elephant woman ran a judicious eye over him. Casually but elegantly dressed. And he was wearing good-quality boots. Her mother had always told her you could judge a man by his footwear. 'Well, I don't see why not,' she said at last, catching her friend's eye.

Flo waved a hand vaguely towards the east. 'You'd better get yourself over to the gazebo. The vicar's in an awful twitter, since he thinks he'll have to judge, and, well, he doesn't think it quite proper.'

Fane bit back laughter with an effort. 'In that case, we really must spare his blushes, then, mustn't we?'

He was beginning to see why the fete was so popular. It was so unreservedly Old English.

He wandered over to the gazebo, which turned out to be a white wooden affair with a pretty domed top. Its back was facing the pretty ankles competition, and a red-leaved creeper was draped lovingly around it.

The vicar was looking at a line of a white awning with the nervousness of a gazelle watching a leopard. Two wooden stakes about seven feet apart could hold the material up to well above head-height, but there was only a foot-high gap at the bottom. There, lined up behind it, was a row of feminine feet.

Fane approached the hand-wringing reverend and introduced himself. 'Hello, there. I've been roped in to judge the lovely ankles competition.'

The vicar fell on him like a grateful sack of coal. 'Oh, wonderful, Mr . . . er . . . wonderful! Well, there they are,' he said, rather unnecessarily, and beat a rapid, undignified retreat. Fane watched him go with an amused look, then turned back to the task in hand.

The line-up was varied. Three of the ladies were obviously of advancing years. It was not their stockinged legs that gave them away so much as their flat, sensible, lace-up shoes. Nevertheless, the flat-shoe brigade did indeed have fine ankles. There was a rather racy pair of red high-heels at the end, and several more modestly heeled shoes towards the middle. Fane rubbed his hands. It was a rotten job, but somebody had to do it.

'Right, then, my lovely anonymous ladies,' he began, and heard several titters and giggles emerge from behind the canvas. 'No doubt you're aware that I am not the vicar.' More giggles. 'But I can assure you of a fully unbiased decision. As a stranger to these parts, I can't even pretend to guess at your identities.'

Behind the awning, Mrs Sylvia Matthews — one of the sensible-shoe wearers — gave Miss Deborah Knight — of the racy red high-heels — a smug look. No doubt Deborah had been expecting the drunk Ernie to guess her identity. Mrs Matthews wouldn't have put it past the minx to promise that Ernie Feathershaw a kiss if he picked her!

In the middle of the group, Keira closed her eyes briefly and prayed she was mistaken about the owner of that voice. But she knew she wasn't, of course. Damn him, what was he doing here? A little squeak from the very timid Miss Cruickshank, who was standing at the very beginning of the row, had her eyes coming wide open as all the ladies turned to look at her questioningly. Miss Cruickshank, seventy if she was a day, was blushing a very becoming schoolgirl pink.

Keira's eyes, along with everyone else's, were drawn to the ground, where a strong, finely boned but distinctly *masculine* hand was caressing the old lady's ankle.

Keira opened her mouth crossly, about to tell him he was supposed to judge by sight only, and then closed it again. If she'd recognized *his* voice so easily, he was as certain to recognize *hers*. And she'd much rather he had no idea she was behind here, thank you very much!

Michelle the barmaid was next, and she gave a nice little, 'Cor, thanks, darling, I needed that,' as Fane ran a hand over the back of her heel.

In front, Fane grinned. 'You're welcome, I'm sure.'

He hoped there were no jealous husbands nearby.

Keira gritted her teeth as her turn slowly approached. By now, the rest of the women were having a huge amount of fun. The stranger was far better at this than Ernie Feathershaw!

Sylvia Matthews held her breath when her turn came, and then let it out in a hugely audible sigh, making Deborah on the end roll her eyes in mock disgust.

Keira felt her heartbeat pick up as the woman next to her gave a little shriek. 'What smooth fingertips you 'ave, dearie,' she said, nudging her next-door neighbour and grinning widely. She was the mother of four strapping lads.

'"All the better to feel your ankles with, my dear," said the Big Bad Wolf,' Fane shot back, and gave a very convincing growl. Keira wished it wasn't her turn next. The sound of that throaty growl was echoing about inside her eardrums, doing strange things to her sense of balance.

Fane moved on and looked at the next set of feet. They were shod in good-quality but seasons-old black leather pumps, with a modest heel. They were just the sort of thing Keira would wear . . . From his kneeling position in front of the white awning, he tried to stare through it, but failed. He couldn't even make out the outline of a shape.

He reached forward slowly, his fingertips connecting with the round nobble at the side of her ankle. She'd have hardly considered it an erogenous zone, but the heat from his fingers seemed to shoot through her bones and race upwards, making her thighs tremble. Keira dragged her breath in, very much aware that all the women were watching her, expecting her to play along in the spirit of the thing.

Knowing that if she spoke she'd be lost, Keira desperately put her finger up to her lips to signal to the others to keep quiet. There were more conspiratorial giggles. Evidently they thought that she was being a sport, keeping her identity a secret. After all, if the judge knew she was the lady of the manor, it would give her an unfair advantage over the others. If they only knew, Keira thought desperately.

Fane leaned forward a little, the shape of his head nudging against the awning. Keira looked down at its rounded shape, and imagined his dark head. He'd be kneeling. She wanted . . .

She looked straight ahead and gritted her teeth as his palm flattened against her foot, his fingers coming around to curl over the back of her heel. Keira only managed to keep still with the greatest of effort. She hoped her face wasn't as flushed as it felt. Damn him, why didn't he move on?

'Hmm, now that's an interesting piece of ankle flesh,' Fane murmured. 'A bit well-padded, perhaps . . .'

There were shrieks of laughter from the others. 'Ere, luv, he's saying you got fat ankles. Give him a thump,' Michelle chortled.

Keira gritted her teeth and smiled through them gamely.

Fane, aware of the determined silence, suddenly grinned. He was now convinced of the identity of the ankle. 'Hmm, perhaps I'd better check the other one, just to make sure.'

Keira could have screamed aloud as he transferred his hand to her other foot. There, his index finger traced the contours of her foot, then his palm cheekily went to the back of her leg and cupped the lower half of her calf. Keira's knees promptly turned to jelly. She took a deep breath.

'Hmm,' Fane said noncommittally, and moved on to the next in line. Keira just managed to resist the urge to stamp her feet in sheer frustration. She could still feel the warm impression of his skin on hers, and her bones still tingled where his fingertips had pressed.

The red high-heels on the end nearly broke one of his fingers through too much horseplay, but Fane was wise enough to pull his hand away the moment Deborah started prancing about. 'Now, now,' he said, and wagged an admonishing finger under the awning. Deborah laughed and apologized, while Keira firmly told herself it was all in good fun, and what did it matter if Fane and Deborah flirted together? It was hardly any of her business.

Damn them!

'Well, ladies, it's a very hard decision to make, and no mistake,' he said, rising thoughtfully and slowly walking back along the line. He hesitated by Keira's nervously shifting feet, and grinned. Then he shook his head and moved on. 'But I think, on the whole . . .' he reached down and tapped a sensibly-shod foot '. . . that this lovely lady is the winner.'

Sylvia Matthews gave a short cry of triumph and stepped from behind the awning, along with all the other ladies — minus one.

Sylvia, a buxom lady with grey curly hair and red-veined cheeks, looked at Fane with an appreciative eye. He was so dark and hawk-faced that he reminded her of one of those matinee idols back in the forties. When men had really looked like men.

Fane glanced around, found that the cowardly vicar had returned, bearing a potted plant as first prize, and handed it over to Sylvia with a bow. Then his dark eyes swept over the rest, saw that Keira was missing, and he smiled knowingly.

He managed to extricate himself from the ladies and moved off around the awning to look at it thoughtfully.

Just then the loudspeaker announced that the pantomime was about to begin, and his area of the garden emptied rapidly.

Fane continued to look around. That was a very clever disappearing trick she'd pulled. He would swear she hadn't gone off to the left or right, or he'd have seen her. And she hadn't gone past him. Which left . . .

His eyes narrowed on the back of the gazebo. It was a full-backed structure, and the front of it probably looked out over the lake or something. Slowly, silently, he made his way around it.

Inside, Keira was sitting on the padded bench that ran around it in a fixed semi-circle. She looked up warily but without any real surprise as his tall figure suddenly appeared in the narrow entryway, blocking out the light.

'So this is where you slunk off to,' Fane said, leaning against the doorjamb and crossing his arms across his chest.

'I like a good slink now and then,' Keira agreed drolly, her voice an amused drawl.

Fane laughed, but then his face slowly became serious. 'I just wanted you to know that all that back there,' he nodded his head towards the pretty ankles competition, 'it was just a bit of fun. Nothing more. I wouldn't want you to think I meant anything by it.'

His voice was rather tense, and Keira glanced at him quickly, puzzled. Then, as she understood the reason for his unease, her lips twisted into a totally unamused smile. 'There was no need for you to worry, Fane,' she said coldly. 'I wasn't going to go crying to Lucas about it.'

Fane felt the furious heat begin to burn in his bloodstream. Her confidence was so palpable he wanted to smash it! 'How very magnanimous of you,' he gritted. 'Of course, it was totally out of line for me to think that a woman like you could actually pass up the opportunity to score a few points with her husband. Especially if it meant doing his son down into the bargain.'

Keira's eyes narrowed ominously. 'A woman like me, Fane?' she said softly, but with an undercurrent of steel in her tone now. Did he really think she'd try and turn Lucas against his own son by claiming that he'd bothered her? Even if he *had* bothered her, she thought wryly, the memory of his hands on her feet still making her yearn to shift restlessly on the seat.

Fane laughed harshly. 'Oh, never doubt I know all about women like you, My Lady,' he said grimly. 'I should do! I was engaged to one once.'

Keira felt a painful fist begin to clench deep in her stomach. She swallowed hard. 'I didn't know you'd ever been serious about anyone,' she said quietly. It had always been far easier to see him as a fancy-free and heartless ladies' man.

Fane's lips twisted grimly. 'Perhaps I only thought I was serious,' he said, forcing himself to shrug nonchalantly. 'The point is, she was serious, all right. Seriously dedicated to marrying a rich man. She was beautiful, too, like you. And she was a first-class actress.'

The implication was so insultingly clear that Keira only just managed to stop herself from laughing out loud. She, a good actress? If only!

'It sounds as if she broke your heart,' she said, determined to steer the conversation away from her own non-existent talents. And attack really was the best form of defence, she realized the next moment, as she watched him pale and straighten upright into a stiff, defensive posture.

'Did she hell!' Fane snarled. 'The moment I caught on, I sent her packing.' His face, for a moment, looked briefly satisfied, and then it turned back to the hard, mocking smile she knew so well. 'Not that that worried her unduly, I don't suppose,' he drawled. 'There are plenty of rich and more gullible men around, after all.'

Keira's eyes narrowed to slits. 'Like Lucas, you mean?' She spoke the words for him through lips gone stiff with outrage.

'You said it,' he agreed tersely. 'I'm glad to hear you admit it, at last.'

But he wasn't glad. He wasn't glad at all.

'I admit to nothing of the sort,' Keira snapped, her voice as cold and calm as she herself felt upset and jumpy. 'You don't know your father very well, do you, Fane?' she said quietly. 'Nobody could pull the wool over his eyes. And shall I tell you something else?' she said, her chin angling upwards, her eyes spitting defiance now. 'I don't regret marrying him for one second. And I never will.'

'Is that so?' he said, and his voice was soft with menace and something else now, as he added quietly, 'You never know when to back down, do you?'

Keira leaned back against the white wooden boards, her hair contrasting against it so starkly that it took his breath away. 'I never back down,' Keira said, her voice as hard as nails. Inside, she was quivering like the final leaf on an aspen. Perhaps Fane was right after all, she thought with semi-hysterical ruefulness. She was something of an actress after all.

Fane smiled grimly. 'Perhaps it's time you were taught how,' he said, even more softly than before.

'By you?' Keira shot back. 'I don't think so.' She'd die rather than let him guess how much he affected her.

Goaded beyond endurance, Fane pushed away from the doorframe and his hands came to his sides. They were clenching and unclenching into fists, she noticed absently.

'What's the matter, puss-puss?' Fane crooned. 'Is your fur all ruffled the wrong way because I chose somebody else's ankles?'

Before she knew what he was about, he'd hunkered down and had grasped one foot, slipping off the shoe and resting it against his thigh.

Her whole leg twitched, and she dragged in a deep, raspy breath before she could stop herself.

Fane laughed.

So she wasn't *quite* the super-cool ice queen after all.

Keira saw the confidence in his eyes and her own blood began to boil. Two could play at this game.

'Oh, that's all right,' she said airily. 'I wouldn't expect a man of your limited calibre to show much taste.' And deliberately clenched her toes.

Her big toe immediately dug into the major thigh muscle just above his groin, and she had the immense satisfaction of seeing his pupils dilate in shock.

Quickly he put his hand down on the dusty wooden floor to steady himself, and he paled. Quite spectacularly.

Keira raised one eyebrow.

Fane stared back at her.

His jaw was clenched so tight that her own teeth started to ache in sympathy. A little pulse ticked in his right temple. His eyes began to resemble thunderclouds.

This, a voice screamed at the back of her head, is dangerous! Stop it! But it was too late for all that. Now that she'd batted the ball back into his court, it was pointless to wish that she hadn't.

With a thundering heart and bated breath, she could only wait and see what he did next.

With his free hand, Fane curled his fingers around her foot and slowly, inexorably, pulled it closer to him. She felt her bottom shift to the very edge of the bench as he pulled on her limb with insistent strength.

Then he pressed her foot firmly against his loins. Underneath her sensitive arch, she felt his manhood stir into hard and throbbing life.

Her mouth went dry.

Fane slowly raised one eyebrow. And yet the jaunty, challenging gesture was totally at odds with the hot, desperate, almost pleading look in his eyes.

At the same time as all of that, he looked, Keira thought with infinite sadness, as if he wanted to kill her. It was not the look she wanted to see on his face. No.

Not the look at all . . .

She almost groaned aloud.

She'd brought all this on her own head. If she'd just allowed him to be his own insufferable self, without feeling the need to beat him at his own game, she wouldn't be in this mess now.

With her heart thumping.

With her mouth as dry as desert sand.

With her foot itching to . . .

'Lady Penda! Cooee!'

The voice was bright and breezy and belonged to Mrs Jones, the vicar's wife. 'We need you for the prize draw. Cooee!'

Keira shot up with a start. She fumbled into her shoe and all but staggered across the floor to the opening. Once outside she had time to take in one gigantic gulp of air, plaster a no doubt vapid smile onto her face, and set off after Mrs Jones.

Inside, Fane still stared numbly at the empty seat in front of him, a haggard expression on his face. His whole body felt as if it wanted to burst. Losing all strength in his upper body, he leaned slowly forward, hanging his head and taking deep, shuddering breaths.

And then he began to laugh. It was a desperate kind of laughter. The laugh of a man when the joke had been on him . . .

CHAPTER 8

Colin Rattigan looked up as his secretary tapped discreetly on the door. In the august offices of the old and established Woodstock law firm such things as intercoms were anathema. Most of their clients still preferred the old-fashioned courtesies and the personal touch, but Colin would be glad when the twentieth century finally caught up with them.

'Yes, Frances?' he murmured, glancing up from the property dispute he was handling for one of their more bloody-minded clients, his eyes puffed from lack of sleep.

'A lady to see you, sir,' Frances said, looking slightly ruffled. She'd been with the firm twenty years, and looked it. 'I know she doesn't have an appointment, sir, but she insisted that you'd see her.'

In the life of a solicitor, clients sometimes came to the office in very urgent need, a fact that Frances deplored. In her opinion, *nice* solicitors had nothing to do with the criminal class. Not that the imperious woman outside *looked* like a criminal, Frances supposed, but nowadays you never could tell.

Sensing the reason for his secretary's unease, Colin smiled wryly. Frances disliked any disturbance to the unruffled routine of office life.

'I see,' Colin said mildly. 'Does the lady have a name?'

'Mrs Goulder.'

Colin's face suddenly took on that pinched, upset look that brought all of Frances's maternal instincts to the fore. 'You'd better show her in. Oh, and, Frances, if my eleven o'clock appointment arrives, tell him there's been a slight emergency, and would he mind waiting? If not, perhaps you could reschedule him?'

Frances nodded stiffly, and made her way back to the waiting room. 'Mr Rattigan will see you now . . . madame.' She added the last word dubiously.

Jennifer smiled at her with genuine amusement, and followed the stiff-backed, grey-haired figure into a spacious, rather handsome office. Through the large window, the picturesque panorama of Woodstock glowed in an autumn sun. Behind banks of trees, the rooftops of Blenheim Palace could just be seen.

'Mr Rattigan,' Jennifer murmured, well aware of the secretary's flapping ears as she headed back to the door. She glanced around at the wood-panelled room, the few rather good portraits and the potted plants.

'Please, sit down,' Colin said, deliberately not mentioning her name again. With a bit of luck, Frances wouldn't remember it. The less Frances knew of this visit the better. In fact, the less anyone knew of it the better.

Once the door was firmly shut, Colin gave his visitor as angry a stare as he dared. 'Don't you think it would have been more discreet to have met elsewhere?' he asked, his voice frigid with disapproval.

Jennifer folded her hands over her cashmere coat of autumn brown and gold and smiled at him placidly. 'But I wanted to see your place of work, Mr Rattigan,' she said sweetly. 'Just so that I could get a feel for myself of all that you stand to lose.'

The words were so silkily injected into the conversation that for a second or two Colin didn't realize their meaning. Then a slow, ugly flush spread over his face.

Jennifer nodded and smiled. 'That's better. Now, about this will of Father's. You have it?' she asked imperiously.

'It's in my safe at home,' Colin said, feeling just a little pleased to have outmanoeuvred her, even in so small a thing.

Jennifer's eyes turned to ice. 'Then I hope you can remember its contents by heart,' she snapped. 'I want to know where every penny goes, down to the smallest bequest to the lowliest servant. And I want to know, to the last inch of acreage, how that land is dished out.'

Colin, in fact, would have had no trouble reciting the will, for it had been burning a hole in his memory ever since he'd drafted the damned thing. But before they got into all that, he wanted to do a little fishing of his own.

'You know Lucas's land is valuable only as farmland?' he said, trying to wheedle some much-needed information out of this woman. At the moment, he was still stumbling about in the dark. 'It's prime green-belt country, and although Lucas, or your brother, for that matter, might be able to obtain planning permission for the occasional house — built to fit in with the local surroundings, of course — it's almost certain that the authorities won't permit any large-scale building on it. The rural area it's situated in is already suffering from low employment, and—'

'I'm well aware of all that,' Jennifer snapped, clearly not interested in big business. 'But there's still a pretty profit to be made nevertheless.' In truth, Jennifer was just as anxious to stop Keira Westcombe getting her hands on anything of her father's as she was to make money from the inheritance for herself. 'Believe me, the satisfaction of seeing the Westcombe woman's face when she realizes that marrying my father got her nothing at all will be well worth any amount of money.' Well . . . almost any amount, she amended silently.

Colin watched her beautiful face crease into a spiteful smile, and mentally nodded his head. So, that was what it was all about. Spite and revenge.

He felt a cold trickle of unease run down his spine. This was not looking good. Such a woman as this one could raise no end of trouble for everyone concerned. Not least himself.

Miserably, he began to outline the terms of the will, as Jennifer listened with growing appreciation. So, she had not been cut out of his will altogether after all. After that misunderstanding about power of attorney she'd feared the worst . . . Bless Dad, she thought, with a great surge of relief. But when Colin, somewhat nervously, outlined the cash lump sum and the parcel of land to be left to his widow, Jennifer's hands tightened on her alligator-skin handbag.

'That woman will never have one penny of what should be mine,' Jennifer hissed, when the solicitor's faltering voice had come to an end.

Colin coughed nervously into his hand. 'With respect, Mrs Goulder, I don't see how you can prevent it.' Jennifer, dragged back from her vengeful thoughts by the timid little mouse in front of her, raised one perfectly plucked eyebrow and smiled coolly.

'Tell me, Mr Rattigan, when a new will is made, exactly what happens?'

Colin felt the cold trickle down his back turn to a torrent. He'd always known, ever since this woman had told him about buying up his gambling debts, that this moment would come. He felt his hands begin to shake and he hastily removed them from their position lying on the desk in front of them and dropped them into his lap, out of sight.

'Well . . .' He grappled with his panic, and, to some extent, succeeded. 'A new will instantly invalidates any other wills a testator may have made, of course . . .'

'Yes, yes, I understand *that,'* Jennifer said impatiently. 'I meant more specifically, what happens? You have to give a copy of the will to my father, I suppose?'

'Of course.'

'And you keep a copy here, in the office.'

'Naturally.'

Jennifer felt herself tense now. So many things depended on the next answer. 'And is a third copy lodged with another authority? I had heard that copies of wills are automatically lodged in some place or other. Somerset House, or something?'

Colin smiled. 'No. Wills are not, nowadays, automatically lodged anywhere else, unless the client specifically asks for them to be. Then they have to pay a fee—'

'Has my father asked for the will to be registered somewhere else?' she interrupted hastily.

Colin was beginning to get a sick feeling in the pit of his stomach. 'No,' he admitted miserably.

Jennifer slowly let out her breath in relief, and began to smile in earnest. 'So, at the moment, the only copy of his latest will is the one you have?'

Colin swallowed hard and nodded.

'And the next step is to get my father to sign it, and two witnesses to say he's signed it?'

'Of course. But he'll be expecting to sign two copies. One for himself and one for me.'

Jennifer waved that away. 'Fine, we can easily destroy them.'

'That's illegal,' Colin said automatically, but without much hope. It was obvious now what she had in mind. She wanted the old will to stand, and for that, all traces of the new will had to be destroyed. Colin knew that Lucas's marriage would instantly ensure that the widow got at least half his estate, but he was not about to say so now — he didn't know what extreme lengths Jennifer might go to in order to have her way.

Jennifer ignored the pathetic reminder. What did she care what was legal or not?

'Before you take the will to the Heronry for my father to sign, I want you to call me first and wait. Two men will call around here to the office and go with you. When you get there, I want you to tell my father that the two men are law clerks, and that you want them to be the witnesses.'

Colin paled and immediately began to protest. 'But why on earth should I do that? There are plenty of people at the Heronry available to act as witnesses, and Lucas knows it. He'll be suspicious!'

Jennifer gave him a gimlet-eyed look. 'You don't have much backbone, Rattigan, do you?' she asked disgustedly. 'Tell him . . . oh, tell him you thought he might want to add a codicil leaving something to one of the servants, and that if they signed as witnesses, they couldn't then inherit anything. That's right, isn't it?'

Colin nodded mutely.

'Well, then. Lucas will think you're just being your overly officious self.'

Colin flushed at that, and decided not to tell her that Lucas had indeed intimated that he might want to make a codicil. Why should he volunteer information to this cold-hearted bitch? Instead, he tried a different tactic. 'If these men of yours sign a document using a false name, then . . .'

'They won't,' Jennifer said shortly.

'But don't you see? If anybody calls the validity of the old will into doubt — and Lady Penda will almost certainly do so — those men will be forced to testify that they witnessed the signing.'

'And how will anybody find them?' Jennifer said silkily. 'If a couple of the gardeners acted as witnesses, Lady Penda,' she spat out the title, 'could easily lay her hands on them. But two anonymous law clerks?'

Colin by now was sweating. This woman was obsessed. 'But don't you see? The police will check our records and see we have no law clerks here by whatever names they're going to sign. I'll be disbarred . . .'

Jennifer sighed in frustration. 'Colin, Colin,' she chided. 'Use your head. If you get Lucas alone when he signs the will, who's to know the will was ever signed? All you have to say is that Lucas never got around to signing the new will. That he'd begun to have doubts about it.'

Colin, in spite of everything, had to laugh. 'And do you really think they'll believe *that*?'

This time it was Jennifer's turn to laugh. 'What does it matter what they believe?' she asked. 'As a solicitor, you above all others should know that it's not what the authorities believe that matters, but what they can prove.'

Colin looked at her in despair. 'But word will get around. The rumours alone will kill me. If people think they can't trust me . . .'

'And what would people think if it got around that you can't even manage your own monetary affairs, Colin?' she purred. 'What would it do to your precious reputation if people knew they were handing over their personal and financial affairs to a man who's a gambling addict?'

Colin opened his mouth, then shut it again.

Jennifer nodded, satisfied, and rose slowly, elegantly, to her well-shod feet. 'It's been so nice visiting you like this, Mr Rattigan,' she said with mock-graciousness, and walked to the door. 'And don't forget. Call me an hour before you're due to take the will to my father.'

Colin watched her speechlessly as she left his office. Then he took a deep, shuddering breath, close to tears.

For an hour or so after she'd gone he paced his office, but he could see no other way out. He was trapped. They might get away with destroying the new will, but Lady Penda would easily be able to get her fair share through the court, and then . . . He shuddered to think what Jennifer would do. No, all he could do was go along with her insane plot for now, and hope another solution presented itself. It had to.

It was a forlorn hope, but a drowning man would always clutch at straws.

Then, with a heart as heavy as lead, he reached for the phone and dialled Lucas Harwood's number.

* * *

Lucas was in his study, a sunny parlour Keira had had converted to his own private hidey-hole, when the telephone on the desk rang. He reached for the receiver with a hand that had begun to tremble intermittently, and was still frowning at his own recalcitrant limb when he recognized the voice of his solicitor on the other end, informing him that the new will was ready for signing.

'Splendid,' Lucas said, swivelling in the chair to look out across the gardens. 'Bring it round in a couple of weeks, then. Say a fortnight tomorrow?' He added a determinedly cheerful goodbye and hung up, his eyes narrowing thoughtfully. Although the garden, or rather the small part of it that he could see from his window, was rife with autumn dahlias, chrysanthemums, Michaelmas daisies and a huge bank of berry-bearing shrubs, Lucas was hardly aware of the colourful scene.

The call from his solicitor had given him something much more urgent to think about. He'd told Rattigan he might need to add a codicil to that will. Now he could put it off no longer. He needed to find his eldest son. If he still lived . . .

Lucas sighed, feeling suddenly ten years older and as ill as it was possible to be without being dead.

He reached for the telephone book and began to scan the list for discreet private detectives. If he was to leave *all* his children a fair share of his inheritance, he had little time left to lose. He made the call briskly and efficiently and set the whole thing in motion. Only then was he able to relax.

His eldest son . . . He hadn't seen him since he was six years old. When Alice had taken him away.

* * *

Blaise lifted the cover off the canvas and very carefully checked that it was fully dry.

It was.

She stood back and checked the painting, then stood back a bit more, then a bit more, stopping to check it from every distance.

It was good. *Really* good. She felt a distinct thrill of creation, of pride, of achievement. At last she'd painted something really decent. With this one canvas she had stepped from merely dabbling at being an artist to *being* an artist.

It was a heady feeling. One of those rare moments in life that she knew she would never forget.

The painting had captured everything she could have hoped — the first touch of autumn colour, subtle but beautiful, the majesty and strength of the horses. But, most of all, she'd captured the relationship between man and horse. The osmosis, almost, of the man behind the plough and the animals pulling it. It was earthy, yet magical. Mundane, yet significant.

Behind the man rose a following flock of white seagulls, hungry and intense. Above him was a stormy sky. The connection between man, horse, the land and nature itself was clear at first glance.

And Aidan looked so very like . . . Aidan. Attractive, not just handsome. The figure of the ploughman held it all together. It was a celebration of mankind, as well as of nature.

She just had to show it to him.

Carefully, she covered it again and left the house, counting down the cottages until she came to his.

It had not been hard, in Upper Rousham, to find out where he lived. She only hoped she would catch him in.

As she approached, she felt her steps slowing, her eyes widening. In a village of pretty cottages all with pretty cottage gardens, Aidan's was by far the loveliest. She shouldn't have been surprised by his green fingers, of course. She was beginning to suspect that every living thing responded to Aidan's touch with affinity.

The cottage was similar to hers, but his had a wooden porch rife with honeysuckle. One or two hardy flowers still clung to the stems, but the leaves were already turning a delicate lemon.

The garden was still bursting with colour, even now, on the first day of November. Of course, it had been unseasonably mild.

Snapdragons. Roses. Dahlias. Chrysanthemums. And not just flowers. Bushes lined the walled garden, hanging heavy with — no, her eyes were not playing tricks on her — *pink* berries. She would learn later from Aidan that the bushes were spindle bushes, a hardy native. Creepers in flaming scarlet climbed the mellow Cotswold stone walls. A delicate dwarf maple was bursting with copper colour. A weeping silver birch in one corner was the most beautiful thing she'd ever seen.

Aidan watched her standing, transfixed, in the gateway. He'd seen her pass the window and was already on his feet and at the door, looking out, before she'd even reached the gate, trying to deny to himself the sudden leap in his pulse at the sight of her. She could have been on her way to the shops. Or the church. But he knew she wasn't. He just *knew* that she was coming to see him.

Now he watched her round-as-saucer-eyes and smiled.

'Like it?' he asked, stepping out from the porch and watching her jump.

Blaise laughed. 'Sorry. I didn't mean to gawp. But it's lovely. I always thought of summer as being the time to paint idealized rural scenes, but this has so much more . . . *atmosphere.'*

'The leaves are dropping.'

'I know,' Blaise said, slowly walking forward, getting nearer and nearer, unknowingly bringing a breath of warmth with her. 'That's what gives it such a new . . . slant. You can see that everything is on its last legs — a frost has blackened the odd petal; the leaves are beginning to settle on the lawn. You can almost see winter, like a ghost, waiting in the background, and yet still the flowers are so full of colour. It's like they're defying time. Oh, Aidan, I have to paint it. Can I?'

Aidan smiled. He couldn't help it. But he wasn't smiling at her enthusiasm, but at his own. He was almost wilting with relief that she'd just come up with the perfect excuse to carry on seeing him.

He was not into lying to himself. He knew that with the ploughing painting finished, he'd missed her presence at the side of the field. He'd missed her mismatching brightly coloured clothes. The way the wind ruffled her already ruffled hair.

And more than that.

Without her, he would still be . . . anonymous. She'd brought a definition and shape to his life that was totally new. It worried him, but it also thrilled and terrified him.

'Of course you can paint it,' he found himself saying, his heart jumping in before his head had a chance to spoil it all. 'But you'll have to take your chances with the weather. And if we get a really hard frost . . .'

Blaise came to a stop in front of him and looked around, nodding. 'I'll be quick. And I'll take lots of photos for backup. Can I come round tomorrow, with a camera?'

Aidan nodded. 'Stay for lunch. I'll cook something,' he offered, and then wondered what the hell he thought he was doing.

Blaise, however, gave him no chance to change his mind. 'I'd love to, thanks,' she said, so quickly she almost tripped over her own tongue. Then she suddenly looked away in rather guilty shyness.

Aidan saw the downy softness of her cheek as she turned, and dragged his breath in roughly. Then, casting around desperately for something less threatening, he glanced at the canvas she was carrying. 'That it, then? The finished thing?'

Blaise nodded, barely noticing now how oddly he pronounced words. She was becoming as used to his voice as she was to his face.

And she liked his face. Very much.

'Yes. I promised you that you could see it when it was finished. Well, here it is.'

Aidan stood back and ushered her inside. Blaise followed him into a small but comfortable living room where a real fire danced hypnotically in the grate. The furniture was plain and simple, the curtains unfussy, the carpet a hardwearing weave. But, for all that, the place had the feel of a real home.

She put the canvas onto a side table, standing it against the wall, then whipped the covering away.

'Tah-dah!' she said with a little flourish, looking at the canvas yet again, just to make sure she hadn't missed anything.

She hadn't.

The silence lengthened and at last Blaise looked over her shoulder, a tiny anxious frown fiddling with her golden brows.

But she needn't have worried. Aidan was staring at the painting with an expression on his face that, though hard to define, appealed to her.

'You've captured . . . everything,' he said at last. Although he'd seen enough of the painting to know its general composition, he had never expected the finished thing to be so . . . powerful.

'I'm glad you think so. I'm going to take it in to one of the premier galleries in Woodstock tomorrow,' she said firmly, making the decision on the spur of the moment.

'So soon?'

Blaise laughed, but with just a touch of pain. 'I have to. If I don't . . . I probably won't be able to part with it. And I need to start earning a living. Besides, I have to be professional about it.' One of the things she'd promised herself in her new life was a proper career. And proper careers didn't grow on trees. You had to make them.

Aidan looked at her for a long, long time, then slowly nodded. 'I'll buy it,' he said at last.

Blaise stared at him. Then she frowned. 'I don't think . . . I mean . . . I can't . . .' She stumbled to a halt, wondering how she could possibly put this without sounding like a right pig. 'I have to begin building up a reputation, Aidan,' she tried to explain softly. 'I have to go through the channels. I can't just keep selling privately to friends and family. This painting is worth more than that.'

'That's all right,' Aidan said, understanding at once, and approving of her spirit. 'Just tell me which gallery has taken it, and I'll buy it from them.'

Blaise rubbed her cheek with her fingertips, wondering how she'd wandered into such a minefield so quickly. 'But the gallery will put a price on it only after their expert has assessed it and . . . well, with their commission to think of as well . . .' She turned back to the painting and Aidan swiftly moved around her in order to get her profile in view. 'It might be pricey. I think it really is a good picture. Even by an unknown artist like myself it'll be . . .'

But she couldn't say it. So Aidan said it for her. 'Too expensive?'

Blaise nodded miserably.

Aidan stepped closer and lifted her despondent chin with his knuckles.

Blaise's wide blue eyes opened even wider.

'It doesn't matter,' Aidan said. 'I want the painting. I have money saved. I think in years to come you're going to be famous, Blaise Clayton. And if I want a Clayton original, I'm only going to be able to afford it if I get in on a good thing right at the very beginning. That painting's *mine*,' he said, and slowly lowered his head.

Blaise's heartbeat leapt as her eyes feathered closed and his lips touched hers.

Aidan felt her sweet lips part beneath his as his arms came around her, pulling her near to him. He felt so close to her in that instant it felt as if he could almost absorb her physically into himself. He felt as if he needed to.

Even though his Yorkshire common sense would insist that it was impossible, his heart was telling him that it wasn't.

He loved her.

He'd hadn't known her long. They'd shared little more than a picnic and a drink in the pub.

But, before Blaise, both would have been impossible for him.

He held her even tighter, but was careful not to crush her. Beneath his lips he felt her tongue press against his, and he shuddered.

He could smell her perfume — lily-of-the-valley — teasing his nose. It was so like Blaise: fresh and simple and lovely.

'Blaise,' he said quietly, the feel of her name strange on his tongue. He wondered what it sounded like — her name. No matter. 'Blaise,' he said again. It felt wonderful against the inside of his lips.

Blaise had never heard her name spoken like it before. She opened her eyes, her mouth still tingling from his touch, and found his eyes boring into hers. She was still pressed tightly against him, and wanted never to move.

When his hands slackened, she reached behind herself to press his hands more firmly into the small of her back again.

'Don't let go,' she said, her eyes dazzlingly blue.

Aidan, defeated, swooped to kiss her again. It felt so good, holding her in his arms. So right. So wonderfully . . . filling.

He hadn't realized until now just how empty his life had always been.

'Blaise,' he said again. 'Oh, Blaise . . .'

CHAPTER 9

In the tiny cubby-hole that pretended to be her office at the animal hospital, Keira turned the page of the document she was studying and gasped. A full-size picture of a swallowtail butterfly filled her eyes with its dazzling beauty. Pale lemon and powder-blue, with a red spot, it had to be one of Britain's most lovely butterflies — and it was all but extinct, except in isolated parts of East Anglia. In the Norfolk Broads the old-time farming methods had led to the boom in swallowtails. Now the modern farming calendar meant they were all but gone.

She walked to the huge detailed map of her property that covered one entire wall of her office and ran her eyes across the marsh. It was not a canal system, true, but if she were to bone up on what the swallowtail needed, what was to prevent her starting up her own colony in Oxfordshire? Once she'd acquired the eggs, the animal hospital already had incubators in place that could be modified . . .

Fane parked the car outside the hospital, which was obviously a converted barn, and began to walk towards the main door. It was time to take his stepmother up on her offer to show him around. Besides, after that bombshell at the fete, he needed to get their relationship back on an even keel. Or at least as even as possible, under the circumstances.

He opened the door and walked in. The place had the hushed but competent quiet that places of research and medical treatment often had. He began to follow the nameplates on the doors, passing surgery, the nurses' office and the X-ray room, making for a door that was slightly ajar at the end of the corridor.

In her office, the telephone rang, interrupting Keira's growing excitement. Perhaps she could start off a modest endangered species sanctuary? With the much-needed addition of Lucas's land, the possibilities were there. Who did she know who could put her in touch with . . . ? She picked up the phone, her mind only half concentrating on the voice on the other end.

'Hello?'

Fane had reached the door, and the sound of her voice momentarily made his hand freeze on the handle.

'Yes, this is Lady . . . Billy, is that you?' Suddenly all thoughts of butterflies fled as she recognized the whispering voice on the other end.

Fane, about to walk in and cheerfully announce himself, suddenly changed his mind. There was something almost furtive in the way Keira's voice had changed. His heart lurched slightly in his chest. Just who was this Billy?

Keira listened to the all-but-whispering voice at the other end of the line. 'Yes, I can't talk for long. They're riding out tomorrow morning.' The voice was so low Keira could hardly hear it. Wilhelmina Morton, Billy to all her friends, was an earl's daughter who 'worked' as a social secretary for her father, who was Master of the Hunt of a local fox-hunting team. Keira had met her years ago at one of those awful Deb of the Year dos. Keira had quickly realized that Billy, a gentle-souled girl, disapproved of her father's fox-hunting. And, although Keira had asked nothing of her, Billy herself had insisted on donating to the reserve's charity fund, in spite of her father's rabid disapproval of it. And, again, it had been Billy who had made the first move in making herself a 'spy' for Keira.

Not that Keira really needed one. She was not one of those fanatics who sabotaged fox hunts with aniseed or violence. And many fox hunters were perfectly nice and respectable people, if a little misguided, in Keira's opinion. Nevertheless, she did like to know when a hunt was on in her immediate area. Her father had let the Hunt use Westcombe lands only because of his sense of tradition. Michael had never ridden to hounds himself, and his relationship with Lord Morton had hardly been chummy, but when he'd died, and Keira had written to the Master of the Hunt, stating that Westcombe land was now off-limits to the Hunt, Lord Morton had not taken it well.

At first he'd tried to charm her out of it. Keira could still remember, with shudders, the day he'd come to the house, offering condolences over her father's death and asking her to reconsider her decision to ban the Hunt from her land.

Morton was a thin, sharp-faced man, whose face wasn't suited to smiling. Even insincere smiling. Keira could almost hear him now. 'M'dear, I know how much of a shock this is to you, but really, you know, your father wouldn't approve. Indeed he wouldn't. He knew his duty as a major landowner. Why don't you think about it a little more, hmm?' he'd asked, and even — and here Keira had had to smile — patted her knee. She might have been two, instead of twenty.

When she'd finally made it clear to him that she was not to be cajoled, patronized or sweet-talked into seeing things his way, Morton had become nasty. Threats had been voiced in very roundabout ways. He'd made it clear that 'we landowners' had to stick together. That 'we scratch each other's backs'. And that if one stopped . . . well, 'things could become very sticky'. Agricultural suppliers might start letting her down. The local councillors, who were all such good friends of Lord Morton, might stop seeing it her way when it came to asking permission for the odd building job.

Of course, she'd very sweetly pointed out that since she was turning the farms to organic production, his agricultural suppliers would not be the same as hers, and so it would have no influence over her in the slightest. She'd then gone on to tell him that local councillors were not the ultimate authorities, and quoted him a few of the 'friends in high places' that the Westcombes knew.

How she had kept her temper, she didn't know. But a voice had warned her that Lord Morton *wanted* her to act like a screeching hysterical female. Acting like a level-headed businesswoman who didn't find him in the least attractive or intimidating had totally nonplussed him.

He'd left in a huff and had never so much as spoken to her from that day to this. Since they met quite often at local 'high society' bashes, Keira had always found this rather amusing. Not to mention convenient. Not having to make conversation with Lord Morton was definitely a bonus.

But it did place Billy in a rather precarious position, and Keira found herself hunching almost involuntarily over the phone. No one knew about Billy's 'warning' phone calls, and she'd rather keep it that way. She dreaded to think what scorn her father would pour on her poor head if he ever found out.

In the doorway, Fane watched the protective movement and felt his teeth begin to grind together. Secret phone calls now, was it?

'Are you sure you're being careful?' Keira said quietly, anxiously.

In the doorway, Fane's teeth began to grind. Why should this Billy person be careful? Unless he was married.

'Of course,' Billy's voice came soft and confident. 'They've planned the first hunt of the season to start on Mr Hardy's land.'

At this, Keira sat up more alertly. Hardy land bordered some of her land on the east. But he was mostly Lucas's neighbour. Or he used to be. Now that Lucas had promised her she could use the land for her reserve, Hardy was much more on her doorstep, so to speak, than he had ever been before.

'I see,' she said thoughtfully.

'But he wouldn't trespass onto Mr Harwood's land . . . I mean, your husband's land,' Billy's anxious, rasping voice had her spine stiffening. 'Especially not now.'

Now that she was married to Lucas, Billy meant. Keira could well imagine Morton's face when Lucas had told him the Hunt was no longer welcome on his land, either. At first, playing the new country squire to the hilt, Lucas had been keen to 'play the game' with the local hunt. It was only after a year or so that Keira had been able to persuade Lucas that the cruelty was real, and that no amount of 'tradition' could excuse it. No doubt Morton knew who he had to thank for losing yet more land on which to play.

'Right. I understand.'

'They'll be out tonight, won't they?' Billy said obliquely, but Keira understood at once.

'Oh yes,' she said, on a wavering sigh that Fane, still eavesdropping in the open doorway, misunderstood completely. 'Tonight's the night.'

Fane spun around and quickly headed back for the main door. Luckily the hospital was still as quiet as ever, and nobody saw him leave. The truth was, he didn't trust himself to stay. After listening to Keira make a secret rendezvous for tonight with her married lover, Fane didn't think he could face her without throttling her.

In the office, unaware that she'd had a secret visitor, Keira said goodbye to her friend. 'Well, thanks for letting me know, Billy.' She hung up thoughtfully and glanced at the map on the wall. She'd have to make up another one now, one that included Lucas's land.

She rose and pulled forward a sheet of paper, making a very rough sketch of Hardy land and how it adjoined her own. She frowned as she came to the far north-east border. Wasn't there a big network of fox holes in that corner? Foxes, when hunted, tended to bolt down holes. That was why some of the more unscrupulous members of the Hunt would go around the night before the hunt blocking up escape routes. Keira wondered what the majority of the Hunt would say if they knew about it. Perhaps it was time she took some photographic evidence and presented it to the more fair-minded members of the Hunt? Well, as fair-minded as fox hunters could be. She'd look into the feasibility of buying some night-film for her camera.

Keira put that thought aside for future reference and wondered about the fox-hole network instead. It was so very close to the border. Only one field away, in fact. And would Morton be arrogant enough to ignore a 'Keep Out' sign? Especially if his hounds got the scent, and the bolthole was so temptingly close to Hardy land? It was a particularly deserted piece of ground. There was no road for miles. No village nearby. Keira smiled grimly. Yes, Morton might just risk it.

What were the chances of 'Charlie', as they so infantilely liked to call the fox, making a bolt for a well-known hole network?

Good, Keira thought, who knew more about foxes than even Morton's breeder. She nodded thoughtfully. But that was tomorrow. She pushed the speculation aside, and got back to the plight of the swallowtails.

* * *

In his car, driving with careful ferocity away from the village, Fane hoped Keira was happy, thinking fond thoughts of her lover. Because tonight she'd be far from happy. He'd make sure of *that*. He smiled wolfishly, even as a curious pain persisted in gnawing away at the region of his heart.

* * *

That night, Keira kissed Lucas goodnight at about eleven and went slowly upstairs. She didn't, however, get undressed, but paced about silently, listening to the house quieten and settle. For the next two hours she read the latest research on pollution created by farmers, who were a much bigger culprit when it came to polluting rivers than giant industrial complexes, and made copious notes.

It was nearly two o'clock in the morning when she rose from her fireside chair, crept downstairs into the small hall off the main hall and donned a sturdy pair of wellingtons. From the coat cupboard she selected one of her father's old coats — a heavy black serge garment that came almost to her ankles — and let herself out.

Although England was in the grip of one of those increasingly common mild autumns, the night air was still chilly.

She made a short detour to the well-equipped garden shed and selected a sturdy shovel. Just in case the nasty suspicions crowding her mind should prove to be justified.

The moon was full as she set off, which would make her task easier. She walked on the grass, just in case the sound of her footsteps on the gravel should disturb Lucas or any of the others. Her husband was looking more and more tired recently, and she was getting worried about him. But the stubborn ninny wouldn't go and see her doctor. Loath as she was to even contemplate it, she was beginning to wonder if she shouldn't tackle Fane and ask him to have a word with his father about it.

The same moon that aided her, however, also aided Fane. From his car, parked discreetly behind a large beech, with an excellent view of the house, he'd been waiting for what seemed like hours.

In fact, it was hours, he realized as he glanced at his watch. He had expected her to be setting off long before this. Then he saw her. If it hadn't been for the strong moonlight he'd have missed her totally, for she was dressed in some long black outfit that all but hid her.

He slipped out of the car and closed the door as quietly as he could, nevertheless wincing at the slight 'click' it made. Feeling slightly ridiculous, but at the same time fired with angry passion, he began to shadow her, across the lane and over the stile.

Whoever this Billy was, he obviously lived in a neighbouring village. What a perfect alibi she had with this nature reserve of hers, he thought with a savage smile. If anybody caught her sneaking off to see her lover, she could always claim she was out and about counting bats, or whatever the hell it was she was supposed to do.

Grimly, Keira tried to push all thoughts of Fane from her mind as she walked carefully across the fields. In the dark, the progress was, of necessity, slow. But, even having to be careful not to turn or twist her ankle, it still wasn't an easy matter to forget Fane Harwood! The damned man had a habit of popping into her mind at the most inconvenient of times.

For instance, yesterday she'd been watching Steven Firth, the resident vet, operating on a badger that had been run over by a car. Fortunately all the locals now knew about the hospital, which had a complex right at the end of the village, and any injured wildlife they came across was very promptly ferried there. But, right in the middle of a tricky bit of surgery, Fane's handsome face had popped into her mind. He'd been wearing that particular rage-inducing mocking smile. She could almost hear his voice, drifting over her shoulder. *How sweet. Playing Florence Nightingale to Mrs Tiggywinkle.*

'Mrs Tiggywinkle was a hedgehog,' she snorted out loud, then promptly felt like a right fool. The man was really getting to her if she was holding imaginary conversations with him at two o'clock in the morning!

Behind her, Fane kept back a good few hundred yards. After all, it was not as if he could lose her in the middle of fields, was it?

He paused, stilling his footsteps to cock his head. He could have sworn she'd said something just then. It had seemed to him he'd heard her voice float across the eerily silent night air. But who would she be talking to here, in the middle of nowhere? He shook his head, told himself not to start imagining things, and carefully set off again.

He didn't know it, but ahead of him was a good three-mile walk.

Keira, still blissfully unaware of her avenging shadow, didn't mind the walk at all. In the woods to her right, a tawny owl cried out his hunting call. She could hear shuffling in the undergrowth. Probably badgers, or even roosting birds. She passed the river, which was like a ribbon of black silk in the night, and heard the plop of a disturbed river vole. She knew that the resident barn owls would be out hunting, too, but she didn't see any that night.

As she approached the far north-east corner of Lucas's land, she began to slow down her pace. She didn't know it, but this manoeuvre took Fane off guard, and he rounded a hedge and found himself not ten yards behind her. Instinctively, he crouched.

He took a quick look around for any male figure emerging from the darkness to join her, but saw only the restlessly moving shapes of cattle in the next field.

What she did next took him totally by surprise.

Keira made straight for one of her recently replanted large, mixed hedges, and began to walk, doubled over, alongside it. It provided excellent cover, and she was glad that she'd had the foresight to think of it. For, in the glaring light of the full moon, her profile would have been plainly visible to the man who was busy at work in the open field.

Keira heard him long before she saw him. The sound of a shovel in the earth, a small grunt of effort, some heavy breathing. She crouched by the hedge and watched as the man filled in the fox holes with earth, branches, even bricks, which he'd carried over on a dilapidated wheelbarrow.

Fane, too, heard him. He'd taken up a similar half-crouching walk behind her, and he was about to step out and yell to Billy that he had company — the lady's stepson, no less — when he realized that they were hardly acting like a couple planning a moonlight serenade. He'd been so anxious to catch them out, so fired up to tear into them, that he'd already taken a deep breath, ready to breathe fire, before his brain rather belatedly told him that he wasn't using it enough.

Now that he came to think about it . . . wasn't Billy *digging*?

While Fane hesitated, wondering just what the hell was going on, Keira, who knew precisely what was happening, dithered. She could, she supposed, confront him here and now. She didn't for one moment think the man would actually attack her. She could simply demand that he leave her land and in the morning report him to the police. She knew his name. She made it her business to know all the members of the Hunt.

But she had a much better idea.

So she waited while Jim Craig, an estate agent from Oxford, sweated and toiled in the night, doing more physical labour than he'd ever dream of doing legitimately in his own garden, unaware that he was being watched by two very different pairs of eyes.

Fane was totally nonplussed. He had no idea what the man was doing in the middle of the night digging in a field, and he had even less idea what Keira was doing, secretly watching him. Whatever he'd expected to happen tonight, this had definitely not featured in his list of possibilities.

It was nearly four o'clock in the morning before Jim Craig had finished, for the network was a large one, and had several holes.

All last year, Keira and one of her rangers had watched a vixen raise four energetic cubs here. The vixen, the dog fox, or any of the cubs, if chased, would head for home in an instinctive desire for safety.

Jim straightened at last, grunting at the effort but no doubt feeling pleased with himself, and surveyed his handiwork for a while. Then he slung his shovel into the old wheelbarrow and trundled noisily off. Keira waited another quarter of an hour to make absolutely sure he was well away and out of earshot, then rose from behind the hedge and approached the earth.

Once there she looked at the neatly blocked holes and sighed. It would take her the rest of the night to undo the damage. With grim lips, she set to. As she began to dig, she couldn't help but laugh.

What would Fane say if he could see her now?

Fane slowly emerged from the hedge and walked up behind her. Because she was already industriously digging away, she neither heard him nor sensed him.

'What the devil are you up to?'

The deep-timbred voice, coming from just behind her right ear, made her yelp and spin around. Since she was still holding the spade in her hand, Fane had to nip nimbly back on his heels to avoid getting the blade dug into his ribs.

Keira gaped at his moon-silvered outline, her heart racing. 'You damn near scared me to death!' she yelled. Then, as she got over the initial shock, her eyes narrowed suspiciously. 'And just what, may I ask, are *you* doing here?'

'Following you — what else?' he said, so matter-of-factly that Keira could only gape at him like an idiot.

Fane glanced at the mound of earth, for the first time seeing it clearly. He nodded at it. 'What's going on, exactly?'

Keira blinked, trying to rearrange her thoughts, which seemed to have scattered themselves rather widely. 'What? Er . . . oh, he was a member of the local fox hunt. They're riding tomorrow.'

Fane already knew that, had spoken to the Master of the Hunt himself, but he was hardly about to say so now. Instead he looked at the neatly piled mounds of earth, brick and wood. 'I still don't understand. What's with all this moonlit flitting around?'

Keira smiled wryly. 'He was filling in fox holes. So that the foxes would have no escape routes tomorrow.'

In the moonlight she saw his face stiffen in disapproval, and couldn't help but feel a thrill of joy.

Then Fane glanced at the shovel in her hand, and his head tilted as he observed her face more closely. He looked . . . strange.

'And you're out here to unblock them, is that it?' he asked, his voice as strange as the look on his face. It was an odd mixture of chagrin and relief and something else. Something far more . . . wonderful. But then his eyes became shuttered again, and she wondered if she had imagined it after all.

'Of course,' Keira said, slightly puzzled, then looked at him suspiciously. 'What else did you think I was up to at this time of night?'

Fane held out his hand for the shovel, and after a moment's hesitation Keira handed it to him.

As he began to dig, with far more expertise than she'd been able to manage, Keira watched him eagerly, admiring the steady flowing rhythm of his movements, the rippling of muscle across his back, the evenness of his breathing during the hard labour. She could watch him all night . . .

She gave herself a mental shake, and bent to help out. They had little time left to undo the damage; she couldn't spend it mooning over Fane Harwood's muscular body. Much as she might like to!

'Who's Billy?' Fane asked, half an hour later, as he paused to take a breather. He leaned on the spade handle, his eyes following her movements lovingly as the sky began to turn dusky pink.

Keira, who'd been moving the wood and bricks under the hedge, paused in surprise, panting slightly at the exertion.

'Billy?' she said, for a moment totally lost. Then, 'Oh, Billy! The Honourable Wilhelmina Morton to you or me,' she laughed. 'She's my spy in the fox-hunting camp.' Then, with growing curiosity, 'Why?' she asked, reaching down for the last brick.

Looking at her standing there with a brick in her hand, Fane didn't think it prudent to tell her why he'd wanted to know.

'Oh. Nothing.'

* * *

Fane grunted as the alarm went off. Back in his Woodstock flat, he glanced, bleary-eyed, at the small luminous dial and groaned. Six-thirty! He'd had barely an hour's sleep. He swung his legs to the floor and, naked, padded to the bathroom. There he had a brisk shower, slipped into a terrycloth bath gown, had a wet shave and brushed his teeth. In the kitchen he made himself a tomato and cheese omelette, and ate his breakfast while mentally going over the unexpected twists and turns of the night.

He had to admit he was relieved there was no secret lover. And he also had to admit that Keira's dedication to her wildlife reserve went much deeper than he'd ever thought. She'd worked like a Trojan clearing those fox holes, and if he hadn't been there to help he had no doubts at all that she'd still be there now, digging out those damned holes.

But he couldn't let it totally blind him to the facts. She'd still married his father for money, and it was still up to him to see that she didn't do any more harm.

Besides, he had other things to think about. He might be on holiday, but he was and always would be a businessman. As was Lucas, at heart. He should never have retired. The last time he'd seen his father he'd seemed depressed. It was time he got the old man's juices flowing again. And that meant a building project or two, whether Keira approved or not! If all went well today, he'd have his introduction to the local council. He'd need them on his side if he and Lucas were to build the odd des res or two.

He pushed the half-eaten omelette away and went to his wardrobe. There he removed the scarlet garment he'd purchased only yesterday, in one of those 'quaint little tailor shops' Oxford could still produce, even in this modern day and age. It looked as ridiculous and gaudy to him today as it had done yesterday. He withdrew the rest of the riding outfit, holding it out at arm's length with a wry twist of his lips. Then he shrugged. Oh well. When in Rome . . .

Besides, after the activities of the last few hours, he was anxious to discover for himself if all the hard work they'd done had been necessary. Or if the Hunt was not the big bad bogey Keira assumed it was.

He left the Woodstock flat, glad that it was still early. Any of his neighbours seeing him done up in such scarlet finery would have been bound to make some sort of comment! He drove to Lord Morton's stately pile in record time, the roads being mostly deserted.

It was the first Hunt of the season. Although Fane could ride a horse reasonably well — he'd learned at a London riding school — he had spent most of his time in the saddle on the bridleways of New York parks.

When he arrived, there was already quite a gang, and Fane was relieved to see that all the men — and women, for that matter — were dressed in similar fawn riding breeches and scarlet jackets. He retrieved his black, velvet-covered riding hat from the back seat.

He hadn't brought a whip, however.

Lord Morton, standing beside a big roan, watched his approach with speculative eyes.

Lord Morton wasn't averse to making money, and had some land of his own that he wouldn't mind selling off to a developer, if he could find a way to wangle it around the 'green-belt' laws. It was easier to appease his conscience, too, when he could claim that the developer was really 'one of them'. *Had him on the hunt, you know. A good chap, who can be trusted to build a decent house.*

'Mr Harwood, so glad you could make it,' Morton gushed heartily. 'I see Jackson fitted you out splendidly. Let me introduce you to . . .' The next five minutes were taken up with the social nitty-gritty. As a millionaire, Fane was the centre of attention. Most of the Hunt members had pedigrees going back generations, but most were also cash poor. Trust old Morton to land a prize fish! Of course, half of them suspected he'd fall off his horse, not know what the Stirrup Cup was for, and all sorts of other embarrassing gaffes, but they were prepared for that.

It came as something of a surprise, then, when Fane mounted the horse Morton had selected for him with fluid ease. The horse, a huge but gentle-natured hunter, had a coat the colour of chestnuts and a white blaze down her nose, together with white markings on all four feet. She snorted contentedly.

Fane had done a little research on the etiquette of fox-hunting. Consequently, he knew all about the calls they used — there were more than just the trite 'tallyho' — and knew who the Whipper-In was, and what he did. So he did not disgrace Morton, or commit any social gaffes. He'd even earned himself enough Brownie points before they'd started off for Mrs Campbell-Smythe, a local councillor, to invite him over for afternoon tea to meet the rest of 'the gang'.

It was arranged under the guise of a charity tea in aid of something or other. But both of them knew it was to introduce him to people who had the local community's best interests at heart. And, of course, they would be only too happy to make themselves a lot of money into the bargain. How his father would appreciate all this upper-crust hypocrisy, Fane thought, smothering his grin.

When they finally set off, the group of hounds looked surprisingly large to Fane. There must have been at least forty of them. He hadn't expected so many.

He nudged his horse gently with his knees, and she responded gamely with a prick of her ears and a spurt of speed. Coming alongside Mrs Campbell-Smythe, he smiled and began to talk about how lovely the autumn countryside was. And how well half-timber houses would fit in with the landscape . . .

He wondered, with another smothered grin, what Keira would do if she could see him now.

* * *

Keira hadn't bothered going to bed that night. But even though it would have saved time for her to stay out on the site, she wanted Lucas to feel that everything was 'normal', so she returned to have breakfast with him as usual. She chatted brightly and insisted he eat his egg, worried about his lack of appetite, and talked about swallowtail butterflies. She decided it best not to mention that Fane had been following her about.

But Lucas was obviously distracted and worried about something, nevertheless, and when he left to go to his study, saying he was expecting a phone call, she watched him go with troubled eyes.

Then Keira made her way to her own study, grabbed a pair of binoculars, and hesitated. Eventually she walked over to the gun cabinet, retrieved the key from a secret hiding place, and withdrew a shotgun. It had been her father's, and was a man's gun, but she handled it competently, breaking it in the middle to reassure herself it was not loaded. Then she grabbed a pack of cartridge cases and walked back into the hall. There she re-donned the heavy black coat and put the cartridges in her pocket.

Outside, she ran into Steven Firth.

The vet was a handsome man in his early thirties, with a great shock of pastel-fair blond hair and piercing blue eyes. When he'd accepted the challenge of setting up, organizing and running his own wildlife hospital for the Westcombe Nature Reserve, he'd sent the local female population into a spin from which it was yet to recover. For Steven was still a bachelor, and very much every mother's favourite prospect for a son-in-law. Now he looked Keira up and down, his eyes widening on the shotgun.

'Steven,' Keira smiled, always glad to see him. He'd done a marvellous job over the years — much better than she'd ever imagined. Now the RSPCA brought wildlife cases to *them* to house, and she was very well aware that both the fame and respect that was growing for the Westcombe Nature Reserve had a lot to do with the success of the animal hospital. It was truly a team effort, and it was paying off. 'Something wrong?'

'No, I just came to tell you we've had a buzzard brought in.'

Keira paused, the fox hunt momentarily forgotten. 'Male or female?'

'Female. She's only got one very clean fracture of a wing. Surprising, really, since it was due to a pellet wound.'

'Shot by a gamekeeper?' Keira asked sadly, and was not surprised when Steven nodded grimly.

''Fraid so. I can't see any reason why she shouldn't fully recover, but the RSPB won't release her back where they found her, and . . .'

'You wanted to know if we could have her?' Keira said. Naturally she yearned to say yes right away. It was an instinctive reaction, but she knew, after years of experience, that it wasn't always feasible to take every wounded creature and protect it. 'I know they need a wide territory. And I think they need fairly open ground to hunt. I'm not sure the reserve is big enough. Let me ring up Jonny Blunt. He'll know whether or not we can accommodate her. If not, give me a day or two and I'll find somebody who'll take her, even if we can't. But it would be nice if we could have her. Perhaps introduce a male . . .' But then, she thought forlornly, where would the grown chicks go in this, one of the most heavily farmed counties in England?

She noticed Steven's eyes fall once again to the shotgun, and his eyebrows rose questioningly.

'It's nothing to worry about,' she said, and hoped she was right. 'It's . . . just a precaution.'

She didn't like to say more. Just because Jim Craig had blocked off the fox holes, it didn't mean that the Hunt *would* trespass on her land. It depended on the fox. And she didn't want any unnecessary unpleasantness if it could be avoided. She had to live with these people, after all.

Steven watched her go, his blue eyes hungrily following her figure as she crossed the lawn and headed for the gates. Then he sighed, and set off in the opposite direction, back towards the hospital.

The hounds began to bay at just past ten o'clock. They'd picked up a scent, or so one of the more experienced members of the Hunt had informed Fane, over an hour ago. Now, after an admittedly thrilling cross-country ride across ditches, fences and undulating fields, the dogs' excitement was beginning to become infectious.

'Charlie!' somebody yelled, and Fane turned, following the pointing fingers, to watch a ginger streak pelting low across the field away to his right. *Run,* Fane thought, as he watched the hounds go after it. *Run, you poor bugger.*

He saw Morton glance grimly at one of the others, who nodded to the hedge and said something. But over the baying of the pursuing hounds, the excited chatter of the hunters and the pounding of the hooves, Fane didn't catch what it was.

But the area looked strangely familiar . . .

Soon they were all streaking off after the fox, the Hunt closer together now. They'd strung out a bit during the slow period, but now every man and woman was concentrated on the chase.

The dogs disappeared over a rise in the hill. Morton, who was about three or four back, gave the order, and, as one, the riders crested the hill together.

What happened next was sudden.

The whole Hunt was stunned by the sound of a loud bang. Everyone recognized it, for the sound of a shotgun going off was hardly unknown in the countryside. Reactions were instinctive. Everyone began reigning in like mad. The dogs skidded to a halt too, but began to bay restlessly. They were well on the scent now, and were loath to give it up.

Fane nudged his horse around to the front to see what the hold-up was.

The hold-up was Keira Westcombe.

She was dressed in the same ridiculously long, baggy black coat. Her hair was held back in a loose ponytail, and the growing wind had whipped her cheeks into a becoming rosy colour. She stood with her legs slightly apart on the top of the small mound of earth they had cleared. But it was not the backdrop, nor her dress sense, that captured Fane's glance. It was the shotgun she was holding.

She'd said nothing last night about shotguns!

Suddenly aware of the sensation of familiar eyes upon her, Keira swung in his direction. He saw her eyes widen in stunned surprise.

For a second, Keira stared at him. Then her eyes darkened to a storm-tossed sea-green. The treacherous, conniving, deceitful, despicable . . . Oooh! All last night, as they'd worked and chatted side by side, he'd known he was going to be riding in this very hunt. And he hadn't said a word! Not a single chirrup!

For a moment she wanted to walk across the few feet separating them and . . .

But she really shouldn't feel so surprised. So . . . betrayed. She forced herself to smile. It was a grim smile, and for some reason it hurt him.

'I might have expected you to be in on this,' she said. She broke the gun, ejected the cartridges and competently put two more in place. Then, instead of leaving it safely broken, she snapped it into place in a way that made Lord Morton pale.

'Be careful with that thing,' he snapped.

Beside him, as if catching his nervousness, several horses began to prance, and had to be checked by their riders. Suddenly Fane became aware that some of the members of the Hunt were looking at each other with more furtiveness than seemed called for. And he knew the reason, of course. Just as Keira had predicted, they were trespassing. Obviously some of the Hunt members were aware of it.

'That gun's loaded,' Morton said, and Fane glanced back at her.

'Yes,' she said calmly. 'It is.'

Fane's eyes narrowed, even as his heart leapt. She was so cool. So . . . sexy. He took a hasty, inelegant breath and willed his body to remain unaffected.

It was not a successful effort on his part. He could feel his loins hardening uncomfortably, and his blood began to heat. It was as if she was holding him over a low flame.

Keira, unaware of the chaos she was causing in him, smiled grimly at Morton. 'You have a minute to call off your hounds, before I start shooting them,' Keira said, her voice calm and level and shockingly clear.

Fane's eyes went immediately to the hounds, who were all congregated around one of the holes. Some pawed at the earth, others bayed mournfully.

At her words, the Master of Hounds, a short, red-faced man, gave a half-yelp of outrage. He hastily nudged his horse, a handsome grey, to the front. 'You can't do that!'

Keira knew that she couldn't too. It wasn't in her to hurt any animal just for the sake of it — and it was hardly the hounds' fault that they'd been bred for this purpose. 'I can do it,' she lied clearly, her voice rising a challenging octave, 'and I will. You now have less than one minute to call them off.'

Fane fought back the insane urge to give her a slow hand-clap. She was magnificent! He turned to look at Morton. 'What were those holes doing blocked up in the first place?' he asked, his cold voice cracking across the taut silence like a whip.

Morton, who'd been intent on trying to stare Keira down, suddenly blinked, and looked across at his 'star' guest.

'Eh? What?'

Fane nodded at the earth. 'I thought it was a fallacy that hunters blocked fox holes,' he pointed out.

Beside him, one of the women looked away in embarrassment. Obviously she had thought so too.

Keira nodded back to the dogs. 'You have thirty seconds.' To carry through the bluff, she crooked her elbow and rested the barrel of the gun against it, lining the sights up with a group of dogs that were digging frantically at the entrance to one of the holes.

'I'll have you arrested,' the Master of Hounds squeaked.

'No, you won't,' Keira said, a fine sweat breaking out on her forehead. If the man didn't call off the dogs soon she'd have to back down. And in front of Morton, too. 'This is my property. You were told to keep off it. As the landowner, I'm entitled to shoot any dogs doing damage to my stock.'

'A fox isn't stock,' Morton snarled, in an attempt to keep everyone's attention off Keira's statement about trespassing.

'You now have ten seconds,' Keira said, and raised the gun just slightly. The Master of Hounds was taking no chances and blew the horn, making the dogs jump. Several of the other hunters began to help him chivvy them away.

'Look here, Harwood,' Morton turned to Fane, 'this is your father's land. Tell the woman to stand back.'

Fane glanced at Keira and smiled. It was a slow, rather devastating smile. 'When she has a loaded shotgun?' he drawled. 'I don't think I dare chance my arm. The lady would be only too pleased, I think, to let me have it with both barrels.'

Keira smiled at him sweetly.

Morton went red. Then white.

'If you don't get off my land,' Keira said, her voice like buckshot now, 'I shall have all of you up for trespassing. Just think of it. Court appearances. The local papers out to snap pictures . . .' The mention of the press had several of the hunters looking at her aghast.

Finally, one — a retired judge, of all things — spoke up. 'I say . . . er . . . Lady Penda, we had no idea we were on your land. I thought we were still on Hardy property.'

Which, Keira thought fairly, was probably true. 'Well, you're not, and I'm asking you to leave.'

More than half of them very quickly did as she asked, turning their horses and galloping away, glad to get away with it so lightly. The Master of the Hounds and some others ran the dogs off, leaving only Morton, herself and Fane staring each other down.

'I won't forget this,' Morton hissed, his face full of venom.

'Neither will I,' Keira said coldly.

Morton wheeled his horse away. 'You coming, Harwood?'

Fane smiled wryly. 'In a minute. I have things to say to Mrs . . . to Lady Penda first.'

Keira smiled as he stumbled over her name. He still couldn't bring himself to call her Mrs Harwood. Now that relief was washing over her, she felt so euphoric she just couldn't resist a little dig. 'My stepson no doubt wishes to apologize for this . . . misunderstanding,' she purred, and watched as Fane's head whipped around, his eyes narrowing.

Stepson! Damn her impudence!

Morton grunted and cantered off. Fane slowly dismounted. Keira felt herself tense as he walked towards her, keeping eye contact to the last second, and only then walking past her to stand beside the fox hole. Behind him he heard Keira unloading the gun.

'The fox is in there, huh?' he asked, thinking how scared it must be.

'It is.' Keira told him briefly about the family that had been raised there. 'That was a young fox, one of the cubs. A vixen, I think.'

Fane grimaced, then looked up at her. 'So all our hard work wasn't in vain, then?' he asked simply.

Keira gave a rather inelegant snort. 'I just don't understand you,' she said, carefully laying the now broken shotgun onto the ground. She turned to face him, arms akimbo. 'Just what were you doing, riding with the Hunt?'

'It's a free country, Keira,' he pointed out reasonably. His hands reached out and settled on her shoulders. She tried to rear back, but without much success. His grip was one of steel.

'What do you think you're doing?' she squawked.

'If you're anything like me,' he murmured, his voice lowering a seductive octave, 'your shoulder muscles must be killing you.'

His hands began to squeeze, in and out. His crafty fingers found knotted muscles and caressed them into quivering ease. Keira closed her eyes briefly. She couldn't help it. It felt so good.

But she couldn't afford this luxury. She had to remember just who she was dealing with! 'I suppose you expect to get something out of all this?' she forced herself to say coldly, opening her eyes but making no move to shrug off his caressing hands. She didn't quite have the willpower for that. Yet. 'Toadying up to the Mortons of this world, I mean,' she added hastily, as he looked at her with a rather mischievous twinkle in his eye at her choice of words.

Fane shrugged. 'Morton asked me.' He was not about to tell her *why* he was cultivating the peer, of course. Although he admired her stand, he wouldn't let her bluff *him* out of what he wanted. 'Shoot the dogs indeed,' he said, his eyes glittering. 'As if!'

She really was a marvellous actress. Standing there with the gun aimed, her voice as hard as diamonds. No wonder the Master of Hounds had believed her. She'd almost chilled his own blood. Damn her, she *had* been magnificent!

Suddenly he dragged her against him.

Keira gave a short cry, and then his lips were on hers. Hard and yet soft. Hungry and yet generous. She could smell him: the subtle blend of soap and aftershave, and an animal scent that was totally Fane. His body heat ignited her own. She felt the hard, long length of him pressed against her, and when his hands splayed against her back she felt her knees buckle.

She wanted him so much it hurt.

But then she began to struggle. She simply *couldn't* surrender. He wanted to destroy all that she'd worked for. And there was Lucas . . . Even though it was no real marriage, he *was* still her husband. Oh, all the reasons were there, but her heart wasn't listening — it just didn't want to know.

Fane held the kiss for as long as his breath lasted and then he pushed her away, stunned by the depth of a kiss that had seemed intent on sucking his soul from him.

His eyes glittered. He wanted to kiss her again . . .

Keira wiped the back of her hand insultingly across her mouth, and watched his eyes darken. She had to get him to back off. If he reached for her again, she knew she wouldn't be able to struggle a second time. Not when her whole body was crying out for him . . . But what weapon could keep him away? Already his eyes were triumphant. So she blurted out the first thing that came into her head. And it was a doozy.

'That was not a very appropriate kiss to give to your mother,' she snapped, her voice thick and harsh.

Fane reeled back as if she'd kicked him. His eyes rounded.

'You bitch!' he snarled. With feeling.

Keira watched him fling away and remount, and took a deep, shaky breath. If he'd even halfway guessed how close he'd come to defeating her . . .

When he looked back at her she forced herself to smile archly. 'Why don't you come to dinner one Sunday? We'd be glad to have you. Your father and I.'

Fane stared at her for a long, long second. Then he smiled. 'Thank you. I'd love to come. Mother.'

The word hit her like a blow. She knew she must have gone white, because he laughed. It was a cruel and delighted laugh. And it made her loins ache . . .

For one insane moment of overwhelming passion she wanted to frighten the horse, make her rear back and deposit Fane on the ground at her feet, so that she could throw herself onto his supine body and kick and punch and kiss and touch and strip him naked and take him . . .

Fane gave her one more loathing, longing glance, then turned and rode away.

Keira watched him go, her heart and body still aching.

'Oh, Fane . . .' she whispered, through the helpless tears that crowded her eyes. 'Oh, Fane . . . what are we going to do?'

CHAPTER 10

Lucas watched his wife finish the last of her tea, and smiled as she glanced up at him. 'And what's on the agenda today?' he asked, his voice gentle with affection and real interest.

'Buzzards, I think,' Keira said, her eyes softening into a familiar look of worry as she glanced across at him. 'Why don't you come down to the hospital with me and see this new female we've just had brought in? She's magnificent.'

Lucas smiled, knowing that she was genuinely worried about him. And he wasn't surprised. This morning, looking in the shaving mirror, his own haggard reflection had made even himself wince.

'I'd love to, but I can't today, my dear. The Rat is coming with the new will for me to sign.'

'The Rat?' Keira echoed, amused. 'Is that any way to talk about your solicitor?'

Lucas grinned. 'It's *just* the way to talk about *any* lawyer,' he chortled. 'But when a man with a name like Rattigan goes into the law . . . well, he's just asking for it. What else can the man expect?'

Keira, still chuckling over that one, told him about her latest idea for butterflies, then, knowing how he'd appreciate it, went on to give him the more hilarious highlights of her run-in with the local hunt.

Lucas let himself be cheered up, and, when she finally left to start the day's chores, he sincerely hoped she was feeling a little less worried about him. He hadn't really considered how unfair it was on Keira, to go and die on her within months of their marriage, and now he was feeling guilty about it.

He sighed and left the breakfast room, heading for the refuge of his study. He'd brought his own huge walnut desk from Green Acres, one of the few pieces he *had* brought to his new home, and the room was fast becoming his favourite domain. More and more he was spending his days snoozing away beside the real log fire that Bessie, with her usual kind-hearted consideration, always made up for him in there.

Now, he walked wearily to the desk and sat down, his feet shuffling along the carpet, barely leaving the floor. He felt so tired he wanted nothing more than to go back to bed and stay there.

But he didn't dare. He had things to do.

Keira, bless her, *had* cheered him up no end, chattering about her butterflies and buzzards, and regaling him with how she had put one over on that ass, Morton. Now he chuckled again, wishing he'd been there.

There was no doubt about it — he couldn't bring himself to regret marrying the Lady of the Stones. She was as spirited, dedicated, kind-natured and full of fun as she was beautiful. If he'd been even twenty years younger . . . Ah well, no point in thinking of that now. If only she and Fane could settle their differences . . .

He glanced up as a shadow crossed the window, and he turned to watch his wife setting off for her transport meeting.

Since the buses had been privatised, and the new profit-at-any-cost philosophy meant that most rural areas were now delegated as no-go areas to the bus companies, the village was starved of public transport. Keira had solved that problem by buying a coach and hiring a qualified driver. Now, the coach ran regularly to Oxford, Banbury, Bicester, Kidlington and Woodstock. Old age pensioners went free, of course.

Lucas knew that she was considering a plan to ask Aidan Shaw, her horse man, if they might be able to set up a horse-and-wagon run next summer, so that tourist visitors to the Heronry and the gardens could have the option of taking a horse-drawn tour of the village and surrounding area.

The businessman still alive and well in Lucas thought it was a splendid idea — tourists loved that sort of thing — and if she charged a reasonable fee, it should swell the coffers of the reserve's trust fund admirably.

But, much as he looked forward to seeing her lovely face first thing in the morning over the breakfast table, and much as he loved to discuss with her the everyday running of her empire, he was, for today at least, glad to see her go.

The Rat was due at any minute, and he couldn't relax until the important business of the new will had been settled once and for all.

The phone rang, making him jump. He scowled, angry at the state of his nerves, and snatched up the receiver. 'Yes?' he barked, with more bite than normal.

'Lucas?' Leslie Coldheath's voice sounded just slightly amused. 'Caught you at a bad time, did I?'

Lucas grunted at his doctor and long-time friend. 'As it happens, you did. What's up?'

Leslie hesitated. He had grave news, and had hoped to go about this gently. 'I was wondering if I might come up and see you sometime soon?'

Although the doctor's voice was bland, Lucas felt his hand shake, knocking the receiver against his ear. He took a shaky breath and leaned slowly back in the chair. 'That's the first time I've ever heard you volunteer to come to me, Les,' he said slowly, forcing his voice to take on a jocular tone. 'I thought it took crowbars to prise you fellows away from Harley Street. What's going on?' he added, his voice just a little gruff now.

Leslie coughed. 'I've had those test results back.' Normally a terminally ill patient would have little need for tests, but Leslie had wanted to keep a close eye on the disease's progress in Lucas. He knew a man of Lucas's immense wealth had a lot of things to clear up, and Lucas himself had asked Leslie to give him plenty of warning when time became . . . really short. The only way to do that was to monitor him closely. Now he was glad that he had, for the latest tests had picked up an alarming deterioration. It wasn't unknown in cases like Lucas's, but still, Leslie had confidently expected that his old friend would have months left. But now . . . He coughed again, trying his best to work up to it. 'As you know, the last time you were here we took blood, urine and a complete—'

'Don't waffle!' Lucas snapped. Then he sighed. 'I don't . . . Just get on with it, Les.'

Leslie sighed. 'It's bad, Lucas. I think that we really should consider booking you into St Bernadette's. It's on a lovely site, and I can guarantee you a room with a view. Just for a few days.'

Lucas heard the lie behind the mild words and smiled. Just for a few days?

'I don't think so, Les,' he said softly. He knew, as surely as if his old friend had come right out and said it, that if he went into hospital he'd never come out again.

Les sighed. 'Lucas, I really do think . . .'

'Les, don't think for me, all right?' Lucas said, a stronger, calmer tone coming into his voice, now that the first wave of frightening shock had worn off a little. 'I want to stay at home.'

He looked around the study, with its higgledy-piggledy books and worn leather armchairs. At the fire crackling merrily in the grate. Funny, he'd lived in Green Acres for years, and had never thought of it as home. Now, after just two months at the Heronry, it felt as if he'd lived here all his life.

Unconsciously he smoothed a hand over his big desk. It had been the first item of furniture he'd bought for his office when he'd first set up Danelink, and after his retirement he'd moved it from office to home. It had seen him through so many years of his life. His hands curled around the rounded edge, his knuckles white with tension.

'All right,' Les sighed. 'But I'm going to courier down some pills. I want you to take one every four hours. Promise me.'

'Scout's honour, Les. And . . . thanks.'

Les muttered something and hung up.

Lucas slowly replaced the receiver. So that was that. Both men knew they would never speak to one another again. Funny, but now that the time had almost come . . .

'Mr Rattigan for you, Lucas.' Bessie's cheerful voice broke into his rather morbid thoughts and he started.

'What? Oh, splendid. Please show him in, Bessie.'

Colin walked in, his face all confident smiles, belying the sick feeling in his stomach. Lucas nodded to Bessie, who discreetly withdrew, and then glanced at the Rat. He silently indicated the chair opposite the desk.

'I've . . . er . . . brought some junior law clerks with me.' Colin leapt in with both feet as he fumbled in his briefcase for the documents. 'I thought, later on, you might want to leave a small bequest to one or other of the servants, and, as you know, a witness to a will can't then be a recipient of any bequest. This way, you're free to add any little codicil you like and not have to worry.

'Besides, it never hurts to have professionals sign a will as witnesses, especially in a case such as yours. Very wealthy men, I mean,' Colin gushed on, knowing that he was babbling, but unable to stop himself. He was very conscious that he was sweating now, and hoped the other man couldn't tell. 'When you're dealing in multi-millions, it's always best to dot every "i" and cross every "t",' he added fatuously.

Colin, finally managing to extricate the bulky documents from the briefcase, at last plucked up the courage to look across at his client.

Lucas would rather have had more time to recover from Les's phone call. But then he'd probably only have brooded over it. This was far better therapy for him than that. In a way, he owed the Rat a favour. His timing was impeccable.

But he wondered what had made the man so nervous. He was gabbling on like a clockwork doll that had been wound too tight. And . . . yes, the man was sweating like a pig. Lucas could see tiny beads of sweat on his forehead and upper lip.

'Are you all right, Colin?' he asked. 'You look a little . . . hot and bothered.'

Colin swallowed hard. 'Hmm? Oh, that. Well, I've got a touch of flu. But I'm long past the contagious stage, I'm glad to say,' he added hastily, as Lucas frowned. 'No need to worry about catching it!'

Lucas suddenly realized that catching flu was the least of his worries, and couldn't help but grin.

Colin saw the old man smile and relaxed a little. Things would be all right. All he had to do was keep his head, play his part and get himself out of this mess as best he could.

'Well, Mr Harwood,' Colin turned the copies of the new will to face his client. 'If you'd like to read one copy through, and satisfy yourself it's all in order . . .'

He tried to keep his voice calm and level, and supposed he must have succeeded as Lucas pulled the top copy closer to him and reached into the desk drawer for a pair of reading glasses.

He'd left the two men Jennifer Goulder had sent round to his office waiting in the hall. He had to admit they *looked* alright. Both were dressed in suits and were well groomed. They could easily pass for law clerks, although what their true professions were he shuddered to think.

As Lucas carefully read the will through, Colin knew he really must do some serious thinking. The will of a rich man was usually long and complicated, which meant that Colin, for better or worse, had plenty of time in which to do it.

He couldn't keep his head buried in the sand much longer. He had to face facts. Jennifer Goulder intended to destroy all evidence of the new will in the mistaken belief that her father's old will — the will in which she inherited a greater share of her father's wealth, since Keira Westcombe, naturally, was not even mentioned — would then stand as Lucas Harwood's last will and testament.

Of course, as a solicitor, Colin knew that no such thing would happen. To begin with, Lucas's marriage, by law, automatically made void any old will previously in existence. It was a circumstance that some well-informed members of the public might know, but the majority, Colin suspected, were probably in ignorance of it. And although he knew that Jennifer Goulder was married to an Oxford don, he was obviously not a professor of law. But then, academics and their spouses were often far more ignorant of basic day-to-day facts of life than, say, your average secretary.

The question was, what should he do about it? If he told her that by destroying the new will Lucas would then legally die intestate, who knew what other, even more crazy schemes she might cook up next? Colin was well aware that in most circumstances if a person died intestate the bulk of the inheritance went automatically to the spouse. Or at least a sizeable chunk of it did. The rest would then be distributed to the remaining children or immediate family.

And that would not suit Jennifer Goulder at all. No doubt she'd blame him, Colin, for it all. And then he'd be in even worse trouble.

But he still had a little time, he tried to console himself. After all, Jennifer couldn't make her move until after her father's death, and surely the old man wasn't going to peg out any time soon?

But when Colin looked at the old tycoon carefully reading the legal papers, he began to wonder. Lucas already looked like death warmed up.

Colin, for the first time, began to seriously consider the possibility of leaving the country. He'd have to go somewhere where there was no extradition treaty with the United Kingdom, just in case Lady Penda or Jennifer Goulder ever brought criminal charges against him. And the likelihood of that had to be high.

But he had no money. And he'd never be able to practise law again.

But prison was worse. Far worse. If only . . .

Lucas, having read the last page, slowly leaned back in his chair and fiddled thoughtfully with a pen.

Colin felt the sweat begin to trickle under his armpits now. He cleared his throat. 'Er . . . everything's in order, I trust?'

Lucas blinked. 'Hmm? What? Oh, oh, yes, everything's just as we discussed.' He leaned forward, his pen poised over the dotted line but, tormentingly, remained still.

'I'd better call the witnesses in,' Colin said quickly, half rising to his feet, but Lucas made a swift movement with his hand.

'Not just yet. I wanted to discuss something with you first.'

Colin retook his seat and gave a deep shaky breath. Fleeing to far and sunny climes was suddenly looking a lot more appealing than before. He could almost hear the clank of prison doors behind him.

Lucas looked at him thoughtfully, a small frown tugging at his brows. Really, the solicitor didn't look well.

'Sorry to keep you, Colin, but I just wanted your advice on any codicil I might want to make. How's the best way of going about it?'

'Calling me, of course,' Colin said hastily. 'Just tell me what you want done, and I'll get onto it and bring a paper over for you to sign.'

Lucas sighed. He could just guess how long that might take. Red tape had a timetable all its own, and right now he couldn't afford to waste even a precious minute. 'But I could do it myself?' he said, a trifle impatiently now. 'Just write it down in my own hand, stating what I want done, and sign it?'

Colin was beginning to get alarmed now. 'Well, I don't recommend it. There could be so many problems afterwards . . . Suppose we had trouble reading your writing, for instance?' He gabbled the first thing that came into his head, thinking in horror of what Jennifer might do if there were any last-minute surprises.

'I could always type it out as well, and sign both copies,' Lucas said, a little amused now at the aghast look on the lawyer's face.

'It would have to be witnessed,' Colin said, trying to put as many obstacles in front of him as possible.

'All right. I can always get a couple of the gardening lads in.'

Colin swallowed hard. 'Might I ask exactly what sort of codicil you had in mind?'

Lucas looked at him, rather surprised. 'It's personal,' he said shortly. 'Besides . . . I don't know yet if I *will* be making any changes.' It all depended on what the private investigators he'd hired had to tell him.

'Oh, I see. Well, in that case . . .' Colin subsided reluctantly. 'But I really do urge you to call me in if you do wish to make a codicil. The law can be very hazardous to someone who's not used to its workings. If you write your own codicil you might inadvertently make a mistake in the wording that would result in your wishes not being carried out as you might have meant them to be.'

Lucas waved a hand in the air, his amusement turning to speculation. Really, the Rat was behaving like a cat on a hot tin roof. That flu must be giving him more trouble than he realized. 'I'm pretty sure that I can word a codicil clearly and precisely, Colin. Please don't worry about it. Now . . .' He bent over the will, and Colin, realizing he could do or say nothing more, hastily crossed the floor to the hall and beckoned the two 'law clerks' in.

They watched, stone-faced, as Lucas signed his name to the original, and both walked forward to sign their own names as witnesses.

'And the copy,' Colin said, his voice little more than a croak. He watched, dry-mouthed, as Lucas signed with a flourish.

The two witnesses, neither of whom had said a word, did likewise.

'There you go,' Lucas said, handing the copy back to him. 'You keep this, I take it?'

Colin nodded at the two men, who left as quietly as they had come. Lucas, he'd noticed with some relief, had hardly even glanced at them. Only the housekeeper, who'd let them in, even knew of their existence.

Colin felt his tense shoulders relax slightly as the men left, then he glanced down at the copy Lucas had handed him and the tension flooded right back in. He glanced at the original longingly. 'I can keep both, if you like. Often it's safer . . .'

But Lucas was already picking it up and shaking his head. 'No need, Colin. If a copy is with you then that's surely safe enough.'

Jennifer had instructed Colin to get both copies if he could, but if not, he was to watch carefully where her father put his own copy.

Colin did just that.

Lucas lifted a key from a small 'hidden' drawer cunningly tucked away in the top of the desk, a tiny, flat drawer that looked like part of the desk's round-edged top. He bent down to unlock the sturdy bottom drawer. He placed the will inside, relocked it, and returned the key to its original location.

Colin made a careful note of it, but he had no doubt that Jennifer was already well acquainted with her father's desk.

'Right, I think that's it, then,' Lucas said, with a final sigh of satisfaction.

Colin gathered his copy and stuffed it back into his briefcase. He'd have to look up a list of countries that would suit his purposes. Somewhere not too hot, nor too out of the way. He was not the beach-bum type. He wondered if he should get himself a false passport. But then, he wasn't even sure if he *could* get himself a false passport. As far as he knew, he'd never defended any forgers.

Really, he thought miserably, for a solicitor, I really am singularly ill-equipped to know just how to go about 'disappearing'.

He said a rather distracted goodbye to his client, and Lucas watched him go, his face a mixture of sympathy and mild puzzlement.

'There's something eating at the Rat,' Lucas murmured out loud, then glanced down at the locked drawer of his desk and shrugged.

He leaned back wearily into his chair and then looked towards the window as he heard the solicitor's car pull away. He tried to rise, found he just didn't have the strength, and sighed. Perhaps Les was right. He should think about booking himself into a hospice. Although he wanted to die at home, and not in some soulless institution, he hadn't really thought about what it might all mean to Keira.

She'd have to nurse him, he supposed, with a twinge of guilt and fear. Right now, he didn't feel as if he had enough energy left to lift a cup of tea on his own.

He smiled grimly at the thought, telling himself sternly not to get maudlin. He was not down and out quite yet.

He'd just sit quietly and take it easy. Get his breath back into working order . . .

An hour later the phone rang and he awoke with a start. He was still sitting in the hard-backed chair, but he'd slumped forward and had slept with his head pillowed against his folded arms on the desk. He rubbed his eyes wearily and blinked, trying to focus his mind.

The ringing sound persisted.

Of course. The phone.

Lucas reached for it and lifted the receiver. He was pleased to see that he'd got some of his strength back at last. If he could lift a phone, he could lift a teacup. In fact, he quite felt like a cup of tea. Bessie probably had some sort of cake on the go, too. Her coffee and walnut was delicious.

'Hello, can I speak to Mr Lucas Harwood, please?' A polite but firm male voice spoke into his ear, interrupting his pleasant reverie.

Lucas cleared his throat, marshalling his thoughts together. He hoped whatever pills Leslie Coldheath was sending down would give him a little more pep.

'Er . . . yes, speaking,' he slurred, straightening back against the chair and rubbing his eyes again. They felt as if they'd been coated in gritty sand. 'This is Lucas Harwood,' he added, more crisply.

'Mr Harwood, this is Chris Hewitt. Of Hewitt and Palmer, Private Investigations?'

Lucas blinked, the last of the fog clearing from his mind. 'Oh, yes, Mr Hewitt. Any news?'

'Yes, sir. We've located your first wife. That is, we've traced her life since your divorce. I'm sorry to say that Mrs Alice Harwood died eight years ago, in a small village in West Yorkshire. The cause of death was a heart attack.'

Lucas sighed. That was hard news. Alice, with the lovely brown hair and eyes like a doe. Of course, she had refused to have anything to do with him after the divorce, but he'd often thought of her with fondness and regrets.

She'd told him then that she intended to disappear out of his life, and she had. Oh, he'd wanted to argue with her, to at least keep some visitation rights to his son, but she'd been so furious and so adamant that he'd given in. He should never have let her have her way, of course; he knew that now. And if he had it to do it all over again, he'd never have let her take his son out of his life for ever. But back then things had been different. The mother always knew best. And he himself had been racked with guilt. For he suspected, deep in his heart, that he *had* been afraid that Alice was right when she'd said that he didn't love his son just because he was . . . how had she put it? Damaged goods.

Yes. Perhaps she'd known him better than he knew himself. Back then he'd been the relatively young lion still. He'd expected his firstborn, his pride and joy and heir to all his empire, to be . . . perfect. And, of course, his son was not that. As if that was the poor boy's fault, Lucas thought with a pang. And so, proud, stupid and stubborn man that he was, he had angrily told himself that if his wife wanted to walk out of his life and take their boy with her then he had no right to keep them.

Oh, yes, he had regrets. Too late now to do anything about them. But . . .

He looked down at the locked drawer and thought of the will within it. Perhaps not quite so late as all that, after all . . .

'Mr Harwood? I'm sorry, sir, did you hear what I said?' The voice of the private investigator over the line abruptly interrupted his thoughts.

'Yes. Er, yes. I see,' Lucas said hastily. 'Alice is . . . gone. But what about the boy? My son?' he asked, coming right down to the nitty-gritty.

For a moment there was a long, slightly puzzled pause.
'Are you there?' Lucas snapped.

'Yes, sir. I . . . well, I thought it possible that you already knew where your eldest son was living.'

Lucas frowned. What was the man gibbering on about? 'If I'd known where my firstborn was living, Mr Hewitt,' he said with restrained impatience, 'I'd hardly have hired your firm to find out, would I? As I told you, his mother severed all contact with me years ago, and I . . .' Never could bring myself to make the first move to get back in touch, he thought sadly. Coward that he was.

Reacting to the testiness in his client's voice, Mr Hewitt very promptly gave him the details on his firstborn son — a brief but comprehensive run-down on his life since his mother had taken him away at the age of six, starting with the special schools he'd attended and going right through to his present employment and, last of all, his current address.

But long before the private investigator had got to that part Lucas had stopped jotting down the details. For it was all beginning to sound so familiar. So outlandishly, so *fantastically* familiar . . .

He stared down at the pad in front of him, his heart thumping sickeningly in his breast.

At last, when the businesslike voice at the other end had finished relating all the details, Lucas sat immobile.

Dark spots danced before his eyes. The breath rattled in his throat.

'Mr Harwood?' The enquiring voice made him blink. 'Mr Harwood, are you all right, sir?'

'Er . . . yes. Yes, I'm fine. Are you sure? I mean *really* sure about all of this?'

'Quite sure, Mr Harwood. We can send you the documentation if you like.'

'No!' Lucas said quickly, and then wondered why. 'I mean, that won't be necessary. Just send me your bill.'

The other man thanked him, promised to do just that, and rang off.

Lucas slowly fumbled the receiver back into place, his hands shaking wildly.

It didn't make sense. He'd expected the PI's report on his son to name some faceless man, living in some other part of the country, perhaps happily married with a family of his own by now. A stranger, in other words. Not . . .

'It doesn't make sense,' Lucas said, his voice old and cracked and little more than a whisper now.

He didn't doubt the investigator's report. But . . . 'Why?' Lucas said, his voice puzzled and full of hurt and pain. 'Why, boy? Why have you done this?'

CHAPTER 11

Blaise checked her appearance in the small kitchen mirror one last time.

She was wearing her best 'casual' outfit: a mock-velvet wraparound skirt of palest lilac. Lemon stylized poppies marched over the material, swirling and rippling as she walked. She'd donned, for the first time that season, the caramel-coloured soft leather boots that had been one of the greatest finds of her jumble-sale rummaging two years previously. A pale caramel blouse completed the look.

She smoothed her curls with one hand, saw them bounce immediately back into their usual haphazard mop and smiled wryly. She didn't look much like a femme fatale. But she felt like one.

For she'd awoken that morning determined to seduce Aidan Shaw!

She'd been painting his cottage and garden now for five days. She couldn't hope for the frosts to keep away for ever, and had captured the garden first, with a burst of speed that had surprised and satisfied her. Now, with only the cottage to do, she could afford a little time to relax and . . . well . . . net her man, so to speak.

'Yeah, right,' she said, looking at her gypsy-like appearance.

Keats mewed as if in agreement and leapt lithely onto the sideboard to purr and push her head against Blaise's ribs. Absently, she reached down and stroked the cat from nose to tail-tip. Purring reverberated around the room, sensuous and rich.

Blaise laughed. 'I wish I could do that,' she told the cat. How could Aidan resist her if she could make a vibration like that against his ear?

'Let's just hope that Aidan *wants* to be seduced, hmm?' she said with a smile, and gave the cat one last ear-rub.

Then she grabbed her only coat — which tended to spoil her look somewhat, since it was brown and rather shabby — and collected her canvas, easel and other paraphernalia.

Once outside, she set off the few hundred yards up the road, glancing automatically to look towards the Penda Stones.

Funny, but she still hadn't explored them close up. That first day she'd set off to do so Aidan had distracted her! Her pace slowed as she looked at the stones thoughtfully. Once the autumn cottage and garden painting was finished, it would be more or less winter. The perfect time to paint the ancient monument.

With a blood-red sun setting or rising behind it, her little artist's voice piped up. With the intricate skeletal branches of the silver birches that stood on its west side as a backdrop, it would be a striking painting. Perhaps Blaise might try a more primitive style of painting to go with it, to echo and complement the stones, which had been raised in more primitive times.

She'd have to see, when the time came.

Already she was thinking, feeling and acting like an artist. She shivered, but pleasurably. For too long she'd stagnated — now was the time to surge forward with . . . well, a braveish heart, anyway. Her lips lifted into a gentle smile.

She'd have to at least attempt to capture the sensation of time. Of time as something both meaningless and yet powerful. Time, to the stones, meant so much less than it did to humans, with their few paltry years of life on earth.

Those stones, she thought, looking at them and coming to a complete stop on the pavement, had been there thousands of years. And would still be there thousands of years from now.

They had power, those stones.

She shivered again, but still not with foreboding. There was something . . . not comforting, exactly, about the stone circle, that stood so silent and grey and constant, but something . . . reassuring.

She shook her head, glancing around to see if anybody had noticed her daydreaming about in the middle of the village like a right dope.

There was the usual line of customers streaming to and from the baker's, of course, and over by the telephone a few old ladies waited for the bus. One of them waved, then the other two, noticing the wave, turned and did the same.

Blaise waved back vigorously. She recognized all three.

She'd held an 'open house' last week, to show off her one and only painting before taking it to the gallery. She'd merely had to spread the word that anyone was welcome to drop in, any time from nine to five, to see the painting, have a cup of tea, a piece of cake and, of course, a chat. The cake she'd rather wisely bought from the baker. She didn't think she was up to baking her own fruit cake quite yet.

The one good thing about village life, she thought as she turned once more for Aidan's place, was that you didn't have to spend money on advertising. She'd simply told the first person she'd seen about the showing and the next day, in dribs and drabs, the whole village had shown up.

It had been a very satisfying day for Blaise. All of her guests had loved the painting, in varying ways. The old farm workers, some of whom still remembered working with the horses from days gone by, had commented on her skill in capturing the horses. The gardeners who'd come up from the big house had admired the way she'd captured the blackberry hedges and the ferns and the woodlands. Most of the ladies had taken one look at it and commented on how handsome Aidan Shaw was, and why hadn't they noticed it before?

Blaise had promptly given the game away by blushing fit to put a beetroot to shame, and now, she knew, talk was rife about where the new 'artist lady's' heart lay. She could only hope that Aidan hadn't got to hear about it yet.

And then she wondered. Perhaps it would help pave the way if he *had*?

She shrugged and turned in at his gate, looking up at the garden and cottage she now knew as intimately as only a painter could know her subject.

She was wise enough to know that her painting of Aidan had been her ticket towards total acceptance by the villagers. Before, she'd been the new girl. The city girl from Birmingham, with the Brummie accent and a cack-handed way with lighting fires. After the painting — which had so faithfully depicted the rural scene — she had somehow been transformed into one of them.

And the feeling was still precious to her. No doubt, as the years went by, she'd begin to take it for granted. But right now she was still revelling in the feeling of belonging.

She'd just set up the easel in the garden and was securely placing the canvas on it when the door to the cottage opened. She looked up, a radiant smile on her face, expecting Aidan, with his usual cup of steaming tea and welcoming smile.

The last five days had been perfect, as far as Blaise was concerned. Ever since they'd first kissed Aidan had been a little aloof, it was true, but he'd always been glad to see her, of that she was sure. He would wait for her arrival, his eyes taking on that glow that warmed her whenever she saw it, then he'd give her tea and toast and point out some little thing in the garden that she might have missed — a spider's web covered with dew, over in the privet hedges, the remains of a martin's nest under the gutter.

Then he'd set off for the farm. He never locked the door — Blaise doubted that many in Upper Rousham did — and she now used his cottage almost like her own, going inside for cups of tea whenever the chill got to her.

Yesterday she'd even taken the liberty of preparing a casserole, and when he'd returned from the farm, dirty but glowing with tired health, he'd taken one sniff, glanced at the table which she'd set with care, at the centrepiece of hardy carnations, the very last of the year, and had looked pleased.

She'd been worried all that day about how he'd take it. She'd half feared he'd resent her intrusion, perhaps become cold and distant because she'd 'invaded his space'. She'd spent the afternoon, even as she'd peeled potatoes and diced swedes, dreading that he'd come home and give her a lecture on taking things for granted.

Instead he'd said how good it smelt, and had opened a bottle of Michelle's delicious elderflower champagne to go with the meal.

Blaise could still remember that moment. He'd reached into a cupboard and turned, and there was the bottle in his hand. And Blaise had known instantly that he must have bought the bottle recently, just for her. Yes, all things considered, Blaise was most content with the way things were going.

It had been the elderflower champagne that had been the catalyst for this morning's resolution. Whereas before she'd been too cowardly to attempt it, she now felt confident enough to seduce a man who had, after all, bought her elderflower champagne.

Now, as she looked up at the door, her bright smile suddenly faltered, for the man stepping unsteadily out onto the porch step was definitely not Aidan.

Blaise straightened, her hands coming down to her sides as she watched the old man reach for the wall to steady himself. He looked grey of face, even from a distance, and Blaise took an instinctive step towards him, ready to help, before checking herself. He might not appreciate the gesture, after all.

She hesitated, wondering who he could be. As far as she knew he was the first visitor, besides herself, that Aidan had had since she'd first moved to the village.

At first she'd been slightly puzzled by Aidan's reclusivity. Now she took it for granted. Besides, it was nice to have him all to herself.

Behind the old man, Blaise saw Aidan appear, his tanned face looking full of health and masculine vitality. The contrast between the two men made her wince.

She suddenly wondered if the old man was his father, and promptly realized that she knew so little about Aidan and his background. She knew his mother was dead because he'd told her, but, try as she might, she could recall nothing that Aidan might have said about having a father still living.

The old man began to walk, stiffly and slowly, up the paved path. Blaise hastily picked up her easel and canvas and stepped out of the way onto the lawn.

Aidan, she saw, was still standing in the porch, watching the old man leave.

Her movement must have caught the stranger's eye, for he looked up suddenly. Blaise met the pale blue eyes and smiled, a touch unsure of herself.

But the old man smiled back instantly, and when he did so his watery eyes twinkled. It was the only sign of life she could see in his face, and she smiled back even more brightly.

The old man shuffled slowly towards her, and Blaise saw that he barely lifted his feet. When he was at last level with her, he glanced at the canvas, then back at Blaise.

For a moment he hesitated, and then he looked back at Aidan, still standing silently in the doorway. When the blue eyes turned back to Blaise they looked warmer, somehow.

'Good morning,' he said, his voice as desiccated as autumn leaves.

'Hello,' Blaise said, and glanced around at the pale lemon sunlight. 'It's a really lovely day.'

The old man nodded. 'Just right for painting, I imagine?'

'Perfect!' she agreed, and their eyes met in one of those rare moments of understanding. She felt, in that instant, that this old man, a perfect stranger to her, understood her passion for art. A passion that only talent could demand. She knew instinctively that he understood why she was here, on this cold November day, in a rush to capture on canvas the fading glory of a garden.

She did it because she could.

The old man smiled, but it was so much more than just a polite smile. It looked strangely . . . happy. As if she'd said something, or done something, to please him. Puzzled, she watched him walk to the gate and open it. When he turned to shut it, he looked up at the man still standing silently in the porch.

He nodded. It was stiff, dignified and yet . . .

Blaise's head swivelled to catch Aidan's expression, and she was just in time to see him nod back. It was a grave nod. One that carried weight. The skin on her forearms began to prickle. Something . . . momentous had happened between these two men. She just knew it. But when she turned back the old man was already moving off, with the same painful slowness, back down the village lane.

She heard Aidan coming up behind her.

'Shouldn't someone be giving him a lift in a car?' she said, the concern plain in her voice.

When she turned to look at him questioningly, he tensed. 'What?'

'I said, surely someone should bring a car out for him. He can hardly walk.'

Aidan shook his head. 'I doubt he'd accept a lift. Besides, the Heronry isn't far.'

Blaise blinked. 'I didn't know Keira had guests.'

Aidan looked at her for a long moment, then smiled gently.

'That was Mr Harwood. Lucas Harwood.'

For a moment Blaise didn't make the connection, and then Aidan saw the moment the truth hit her in the widening of her blue eyes.

'You mean . . . that was Keira's husband?'

Aidan nodded.

Blaise blinked and took a deep breath. 'I see,' she said slowly.

Aidan smiled again, this time a harder smile. 'Do you? I wonder.'

Blaise glanced up, sensing a rebuke in those few words. 'I see why his daughter is making such a bitch of herself,' she said, a touch angrily. 'Everyone in the village is talking about it. And I can see why the rumours are going around that Mr Harwood's son — Fane, is it? — is manoeuvring to get his father's land. Everyone's talking about that, too. Apparently he's getting well in with the people who can influence planning permissions.'

Aidan frowned, looking suddenly distracted. 'Is he?' His eyes narrowed as they swivelled to watch Lucas Harwood turn in at the gates of the big house and disappear. Once again, Blaise noticed, he looked tense. Standing right beside him, she felt as if she were next to a crossbow, the tension wire strung tight and ready to release an arrow.

But where was it aimed? That was what she couldn't tell.

'And what do the villagers think about Keira's choice of a husband?' Aidan asked, the words once again running into one another in a way that Blaise was beginning to accept as normal for him.

'It's mixed,' she acknowledged, giving herself time to get her bearings back. 'Some think it was a mistake — a young woman like Keira marrying someone so much older than herself. Others seem to think it was a marriage of convenience, and that Keira was merely doing her duty as Lady Penda to secure more land and keep the village prosperous.'

Aidan glanced down at her. 'And what do you think?'

Blaise looked back up the now deserted lane, and sighed. Aidan quickly stepped to one side to watch her profile. 'I think that I can't make up my mind which explanation I would find more patronizing, if I was her.'

She turned to look at Aidan, and there was a distinct light of battle in her eyes. 'I can't pretend to know Lady

Keira well. But I've got eyes in my head, and I know a bit about the world, for all I'm supposed to be a woolly-headed artist. She's taken something that could have been a millstone around her neck — a huge house and garden that must need masses of upkeep — and turned it into a viable business. She's taken over-farmed land and returned it to the rich, life-filled ecosystem it used to be. And made it pay. She's kept the village alive, and she gives the people living here as much or as little help as they need. All of this says to me that she's compassionate, intelligent and principled. And I think if she married Lucas Harwood, she did so for reasons that are absolutely none of my business. Or anyone else's.'

And, having got that lot off her chest, she waited, feeling suddenly stricken.

She had no idea whether what she'd just said was what Aidan had wanted to hear or not. She had no idea why Lucas Harwood had been calling on him, or what business the two men had together.

She could feel his eyes searching hers. And then, just when she'd thought she'd lost him, she felt the tension drain away from him. He smiled, and it was the warmest thing Blaise could ever remember. She was convinced she could feel the heat of it warming her right through her shabby brown coat.

'That was quite some speech,' Aidan laughed. 'Fancy a cup of tea?'

Blaise laughed too. 'I'd love one.'

Together they went inside, Aidan heading for the kettle. Blaise pulled out a kitchen chair and glanced idly at a thick brown envelope lying on the table.

It hadn't been posted, she realized vaguely. No stamp.

Aidan retrieved two mugs and took them to the table. Then his eyes fell on the envelope and his face suddenly took on a curiously blank expression. His eyes flickered uneasily. Blaise, about to ask him something light and frivolous, found the words dying in her throat.

Without a word, Aidan picked up the envelope and took it into the other room, leaving Blaise feeling slightly chilled. There was something in that innocuous, plain brown envelope that was worrying him. She could tell.

When he came back, however, he was once again his usual smiling self. 'Do you want to risk some out-of-date biscuits with that?'

Blaise grinned. 'You know me. I always live dangerously.'

But she wondered what that envelope contained that had made him look so . . . strange.

It made her feel distinctly nervous. Which was absurd. Wasn't it?

* * *

Lucas closed the great hall door behind him and leaned against it wearily. He glanced at the stairs — which seemed to climb up for ever — and sighed, heading towards them with painful slowness. It was no good; he'd have to take some more of those pills Les had sent him. He climbed the stairs with infinite patience and trudged to his bedroom, leaving his stick propped up against the oak wardrobe.

He pulled the covers back from the bed, slipped off his shoes and, too tired even to undress, pulled the covers over him. He shivered, then rather reluctantly reached for the bell-rope. He, like Keira, disliked using the old-fashioned device. A minute later, though, Bessie faithfully tapped timidly on the door. She'd never had a summons to Lucas's room before. When Lucas called for her to come in, she did so, her round face creasing into a worried frown when he asked her for a hot water bottle.

Bessie hurried back to the kitchen and prepared two, then tapped on the window as one of the gardeners, wheeling a barrow full of muck, passed by on the way to the greenhouse.

He looked up as Bessie opened the window and leaned out. 'Do you know where Keira is?' she asked anxiously.

'I reckon she's at the hospital. Steven Firth called in to say they were going to fly the buzzard today.'

Bessie nodded and withdrew and went straight to the telephone. She knew the number for the animal hospital off by heart. When she returned to Lucas's room, she tucked the hot water bottles around him, her lips firmed into a tight, grim line. She didn't like the look of Mr Lucas, and no mistake.

Lucas was grateful to her for not commenting on his still fully dressed state. 'Thanks, Bessie,' he murmured quietly.

With the warmth of the bottles around him, Lucas stopped shivering. The last of his unfinished business was settled; he felt peacefully drowsy now.

He'd done the right thing. The codicil had been made out in his own carefully readable handwriting, and signed, and he'd got two of the gardeners to witness it. He'd have to remember to write and tell the Rat about the codicil and its conditions. But his copy of the will, with its new codicil, was safe enough.

Yes, he'd done the right thing. No matter what the lad had said.

If only he didn't feel so damned tired . . .

Outside, a wood pigeon settled in a towering horse chestnut tree and began his throaty call. It was a lovely, haunting, peaceful sound.

Lucas sighed, and fell asleep.

* * *

Blaise watched Aidan put another log on the fire, and leaned back against the settee. When he returned to his favourite armchair, she saw him glance at his watch. 'Lunch hour's nearly over,' he said, but settled back more firmly in the chair, obviously in no great hurry to rouse himself.

'I thought when winter was approaching you farmers had less to do?'

Aidan smiled. 'We do.'

Blaise nodded, and then very casually crossed her legs. The wraparound skirt obligingly fell apart, revealing her knees and thighs. She wore no tights. Again very casually, she began to gently swing her booted leg.

When she glanced his way, she was very gratified to see that his eyes were dragged, time and time again, to her creamy thighs. The firelight danced across her flesh, playing shadows against her skin.

'You don't mind if I take these boots off, do you?' she asked innocently. 'Otherwise I won't feel the benefit of them when I go back outside.'

'Hmm? Oh, no. Er, no.' Aidan licked his lips, which felt oddly dry. 'Go ahead.'

Blaise lifted one leg, reached for the top piece of leather, and gave a very ineffectual pull. She shifted ostentatiously in her seat and gave another ineffectual tug. 'Damn,' she said softly, and glanced at him. 'Aidan, would you mind?'

Aidan started, gave her a long, lingering look, then got to his feet. With his eyes still on hers, he knelt down on one knee, his face slowly coming down on a level with hers. Her heart leapt. His position was so suggestive she could feel her breasts tighten. Somewhere, deep inside her, liquid warmth began to roil, like the rising twist of plant roots.

Aidan reached for her boot, his palm cupping her heel and pulling.

The boot slid off easily.

Blaise licked her own lips, which felt as dry as the Sahara on a bad day, and re-crossed her legs. The wraparound skirt fell open, revealing her best pair of panties — a pinky-peach pair with a lace trim.

Aidan's eyes fell to them and darkened. He reached for her other boot and pulled it free. This time his hand stayed on her newly exposed calf. The boots were fur-lined, and her skin felt deliciously warm.

He looked at his hand, square and large and brown, with blunt fingernails that had trapped just a little dirt, and grimaced. It was inevitable, of course, in his job, that he accumulated some dirt, but, as Blaise followed his line of sight, the vision of his strong hands on her pristine pale flesh made her shudder with longing.

He was so . . . primeval, in a way that was of the earth, not of violence. She could imagine those hands soothing skittish horses. She could imagine those hands sowing corn that would grow and feed people. She could imagine those hands on the plough, as she'd painted him. She moved her leg slowly, rubbing it against his palm. She could feel the hardened calluses that hard labour had put on his skin and she drew in a ragged little breath of pleasure.

Aidan didn't hear it, but he felt the ripple of it vibrate in her skin and looked up curiously.

Her eyes were as blue as cornflowers.

'Blaise—' he said, but she quickly leaned forward, putting one finger against his lips. She didn't know what he'd been about to say, but she instinctively knew she didn't want to hear it. The aloof look was struggling to come back into his eyes, and she knew she had to defeat it now — quickly — before it was too late.

She didn't know why he was fighting what was between them. She only knew that now, at this moment in time, she had to be stronger than he was. Then, forever after, she need never be stronger again. It was both a heady feeling and a gentle one.

Slowly, with fingers that trembled, Blaise reached for the first button at the top of her blouse and undid it. Aidan's eyes fell to her exposed throat. Sliding her hand smoothly across his cheek, she revelled in the hard-softness of his skin, then rubbed her palm up to his temple, running her fingers through hair that felt clean and thick and cool against her skin.

Cupping her palm firmly around the back of his skull, she applied a little pressure. Just enough to bring his lips to the pale skin of her throat. As his lips touched her there, she moaned.

Again, Aidan didn't hear it, but felt the tremors of it against his lips.

Gently she pushed his head away again, and reached to undo the next button. She was wearing no bra. Again, holding his eyes with her own, she reached out and pulled him to her.

His lips kissed the valley at the top of her breasts, and she dragged in a single, ragged breath.

She pushed him back, and his big body rocked smoothly on his bent knee. She could feel the power of him in his every sinew and closed her eyes, her head falling back a little.

She undid the remaining buttons, and the two parts of the blouse fell slowly apart to reveal a generous cleavage.

Now, Aidan thought, dazed and dizzy, her eyes looked like the colour of woodsmoke.

He felt her fingers on his scalp, felt the pressure of her hand pulling him forward, and moaned, just a little. When his lips pressed against her, he flicked out his tongue, laving the hot valley of her sternum, his nose nudging into one hot mound.

Blaise lifted one shoulder and shrugged it out of the material. Aidan, like a willing slave, obediently followed the line of exposed flesh with his lips, kissing a blazing trail along the top of her breast and up to the tender indentations in her shoulder. He moved closer and Blaise's legs fell apart, to allow him to press against the sofa seat between them. He fell onto both knees now, stretching up and forward, to kiss the very top of her shoulder, to continue the trail of moist kisses all the way along her shoulder blades to the gentle curve of her neck.

The taste of her skin reminded him of strawberries.

He kissed the cords of her neck and then higher, nipping the lobe of one ear. When his tongue flicked inside to trace the whorls and contours of her ear, she cried out.

With a convulsive movement, she shed the rest of the blouse and clasped his head in both her hands, dragging his head back an inch. His breath feathered against her face, and when he opened his eyes they were both glazed and piercing. Hazel, with flecks of green that seemed to glow like emerald chips.

Slowly, she pulled his head down to where one pink, quivering tip on her breast tightened in an ever-growing ache of want. She needed those lips on her there so much it almost hurt her.

But it was a hurt she wanted him to inflict on her for ever.

And then, for one instant, she felt the downward motion stop. His head refused to bend to her command and her eyes flew open.

'Aidan!'

Aidan stared at her. She was so beautiful, with her face flushed and her eyes glowing. She might love him, Aidan thought, but she didn't *know* him. What would she say, right now, if he told her that he'd never touched a woman like this before in his life?

And then, in a flash of blinding self-knowledge, he realized that it wouldn't matter.

It didn't matter to him, and it wouldn't matter to her.

With a sound that was part-groan, part-snarl, part-plea, he swooped. His mouth found her breast and his tongue pressed hard against the button of flesh that seemed to pulsate against his lips. Blaise gave a great cry and arched instinctively, the movement thrusting her even closer against him. She whimpered as he sucked on her hard, and her hands fluttered uselessly against her sides.

When his lips moved across to her other breast, which was aching for its own turn, her hands curled around the arm-rests in white-knuckled strength. Her back arched again, and a rumbling sound — very much like a purr — echoed around the room.

Aidan tugged on the band of the skirt and it fell away easily. Then he moved back to sit on his heels, and his hands reached down to cup the backs of her calves. His fingers feathered up to her knees.

As he lifted one long, silky leg, Blaise fell back onto the sofa, her body slipping down onto the cushions as he raised her leg higher. Then he darted forward and planted a single kiss on the tender skin at the back of her knee. Her foot jerked in helpless reaction.

Watching her, noting every expression that crossed her face, he put her foot back on the carpet beside his own thigh and lifted the other leg. Again he kissed the back of that knee and again she gave a sharp little moan.

Tiny tremors of desire raced up from her knees to lodge in the junction of her thighs, filling her with moist, hot need.

Slowly, Aidan leaned forward, holding her legs apart, and kissed the white trembling skin of one inner thigh.

Blaise sighed, and slid even further down the sofa. Aidan's lips moved upwards, planting tiny, sucking kisses against her thigh. When his lips touched lace, he moved across it to flick against the silk.

Blaise nearly leapt off the sofa, but Aidan was ready and held her firmly, before pressing his tongue hard against her. The material was cool, but the heat beneath it seemed to scorch his tongue. He delved deeper, pressing against the very core of her, and Blaise almost screamed in ecstasy.

Unable to bear it any longer, she reached down and lifted her bottom, pulling on the silk and thrusting it away from her.

Aidan pulled the silken garment down her legs, loving the way her skin shivered with its passing. Once again he could only marvel at the naturalness of her beauty, the golden triangle of hair, the shivering anticipation of white skin.

With a final moan, Blaise slithered off the sofa altogether, falling into his arms and forcing him backwards. Aidan collapsed onto the rug in front of the hearth, easily taking her weight on top of him.

Blaise feverishly began to unbutton his shirt, her hands pushing inside the flaps to run over his chest, which was lightly matted with dark silky hairs. Her fingers reached for one taut, male nipple and tweaked it.

Aidan moaned as she dipped her golden head and bit one hard button of flesh. Her teeth were gentle, but firm, and as she pressed the tip of her tongue against the hardness in her mouth, she felt his body tremble. She moved back, sitting on his knees now, as if scared he might attempt to bolt and determined he'd not get away from her.

Not now.

Her gaze lingered on his exposed chest, her artist's eye adoring the symmetry of his muscles as her hands fumbled with his belt.

Aidan closed his eyes, then quickly opened them again to look at her, just in case she was saying something.

But Blaise was too intensely concentrated on stripping him as naked as herself to even think about something as mundane as words, and when at last he was naked and free, strong and hard and proud, she sat back on his knees once more and simply feasted her eyes on him.

She was taking deep, gulping breaths. Every atom of her being seemed ultra-sensitive.

Then, rising to her own knees before him, as he had once been on his knees before her, she positioned herself over him.

His eyes widened as he realized her intent and he half rose, his eyes suddenly full of doubt.

'Blaise, I'm cheating you,' he said, but once again she quickly put her finger over his lips and firmly pushed him back against the rug. As she did so, she lowered herself firmly onto him and threw her head back with a short, sharp cry of triumph.

He filled her so perfectly.

Aidan felt the hot tightness of her surround him, and as he thrashed his head from side to side, he moaned, and felt it echo in his head . . . *heard* it echo in his head . . . and moaned again.

His hands came out either side of him to clench great handfuls of the rug.

Blaise began to move up and down, the friction of the movements sending great shudders of passion throughout her body. Her mouth fell open on a groan of ultimate fulfilment.

Aidan opened his eyes, feasting on the sight of her face racked with ecstasy.

He didn't think he could hold on, then knew he'd hold on for ever, and his head thrashed once more from side to side as she moved, ever quicker, her healthy young body contracting and squeezing with uncontrollable pleasure.

Then, when Aidan thought he could stand it no more, he felt her body give a great shuddering leap, and then collapse against him; instantly his own back arched high off the floor as he was catapulted into a place he'd never been before.

He screamed, but didn't know it, and his hands slowly released the rug, leaving it heaped in bunches either side of their sweating, shuddering, united bodies.

Blaise slowly became aware of the crackle of the fire. Beneath her ear, the thundering of his heart slowly lessened, and her own ragged breathing turned to a satiated, satisfied sigh. Gently she nipped his nearest nipple, felt him shudder, and smiled.

Now he could say whatever it was he'd wanted to say to her. Some kind of nonsense about cheating her?

Now it wouldn't matter what he said.

She was right about that, of course.

But Aidan didn't know it.

Not then.

CHAPTER 12

Keira moved towards the fire, drawn to the flames and their flickering promise of warmth, and held her icy hands out to the blazing heat. She still felt numb, but she knew that the kind and compassionate cotton-wool feeling of shock wouldn't last for much longer.

Bessie put a tray of steaming tea down on the table and looked at her with anxious eyes. 'Would you like a drop of brandy in with it, Keira, luv?'

Keira shook her head, still staring into the flames. Bessie poured a cup of tea and put it on the mantelpiece in front of her. Keira made no move to retrieve it.

'I'll have to call Fane. And Jennifer,' she said, her voice dull and flat.

Bessie bit her lip. 'I'll call Mrs Goulder,' she said firmly. She didn't want Keira speaking to that cat, not now. Then she immediately felt guilty. The woman *was* Lucas's daughter, after all. 'I'll break it to her as gently as I can,' Bessie added, but when Keira made no reply she quietly withdrew from the drawing room and walked with a heavy heart towards the hall telephone.

Keira at last turned away from the fire and stared at the telephone for a long, anxious moment. Then she walked towards it on legs that felt curiously leaden. When she looked down at them, her feet seemed to be very far away.

She reached for the phone and lifted it, the receiver trembling wildly in her hand. For a brief instant of panic she couldn't remember the number of the flat Fane had rented. Then her embattled mind reminded her it was a Woodstock code, and with that her memory, rather reluctantly, came up with the rest of the number. She dialled it, and listened to the hypnotic burr-burr on the other end of the line. When he answered, it took her a moment to realize.

'Hello? Hello? This is Fane Harwood speaking.'

'Fane,' Keira said at last. Her voice sounded faraway, even to her own ears, and she took a deep, determined breath. The added oxygen helped a little. But not much.

In his flat, Fane felt an icy trickle creep up his back.

'Are you all right? You sound . . . odd.'

Keira closed her eyes briefly, then opened them again.

'Fane, I want you to come round to the house. Immediately.'

Fane's hand clutched the receiver a bit tighter. 'Why?' he asked abruptly.

Keira heard the hardness and suspicion in his voice, and felt her heart crack. She gave a compulsive sob, and then bit her lip hard, trying to strangle it. She hoped he hadn't heard, or, if he had, would put it down to some sort of telephonic blip.

He didn't.

'Keira! Keira, are you crying?' His voice was urgent now, all trace of hostility gone. 'What's wrong? What's the matter?'

If anything had happened to her, he'd . . .

'It's Lucas, Fane. Your father,' she added, then could have kicked herself. She was handling this all wrong. 'I think you should come at once.'

In his lonely flat, Fane blinked. He remembered the last time he'd seen his father, two days previously. They'd had a game of chess, which, unusually, Fane had won. His father was a masterful player, but that day he'd seemed to have something else on his mind. And, try as he might, he hadn't been able to interest his father in the new building projects he was planning, or indeed in anything else. He'd seemed so . . . tired. Even when Fane had asked him if he was interested in coming into Harwood Construction as a consultant, although Fane could see his father had been genuinely gratified and pleased to be asked, he'd still, nevertheless, been vague about accepting the offer.

And Fane could still remember how ill he'd looked.

'What's happened?' he asked, his voice more curt than he'd meant.

Keira didn't want to tell him over the telephone, but she could hear the tension in his voice. Was it fair to make him drive to the house in the agony of suspense? She didn't know. She couldn't seem to think what was the best thing to do.

'Keira!' he all but roared in her ear.

'I'm sorry, Fane,' she said, and then thought, appalled, how inadequate that sounded. 'He's . . .' But her throat constricted, refusing to say the word 'dead'.

Instead, she swallowed hard and whispered, 'He's . . . passed away, Fane.'

For a moment there was a profound silence on the other end of the line, and then Fane drew in a deep, ragged breath. Then he said, quite calmly, 'I'm on my way,' and hung up.

For a long moment Keira stood by the table, the receiver held loosely in her hand. Then she slowly hung up and went back to the fire.

But no matter how long she held her hands over the leaping flames, they still felt icy.

Upstairs, Max Phelps, Keira's family doctor, rang the number Bessie had just given him of Lucas Harwood's own doctor in Harley Street. Les Coldheath took the call immediately, and the two doctors conferred.

Finally, satisfied, Max hung up and glanced down at the old man lying peacefully in the bed. He could now write out the death certificate with a clear mind. But what should he tell Keira? Max had been the Westcombe family's doctor for nearly thirty years. He'd seen Michael Westcombe through his final days, and had comforted his daughter the best he could.

Now he had to tell her that her husband had known all along that he was dying, even when he'd married her. He wasn't sure, but he suspected that Keira might have known nothing about it.

He sighed, pulled the sheet respectfully up to cover the old man's peaceful face, and left the room.

Downstairs, he found Keira in her favourite drawing room with a tall, handsome blond man, solicitously pouring her a fresh cup of tea. It took a moment for Max to place him, then he smiled. Of course. The vet.

Word travelled fast in a village. Max knew that in the next few days practically the entire population of Upper Rousham would call to pay their respects, bringing cakes and flowers — or perhaps evergreen wreaths. He could only hope that Keira was up to it. At the moment she looked pale and lifeless. Still in shock, he thought professionally, and reached into his bag to retrieve a mild sedative.

When Fane pulled up in front of the house, Bessie was already waiting for him at the door, her round face full of calm sympathy.

'He's upstairs, in his room, Fane,' she said quietly. 'Would you like me to show you?'

Fane shook his head without speaking, and mounted the stairs two at a time. His face was set in a tight, hard line.

Bessie watched him go, glanced at the closed drawing-room door and sighed. She retreated to the kitchen, where her husband was at the table, nursing a mug of tea he wasn't drinking.

'How are they?' Sid asked.

Bessie mutely shook her head.

Upstairs, Fane pulled back the sheet covering his father's face and sighed. He'd known Lucas was looking ill. Why hadn't he insisted he see a doctor? He thought back to their last chess game and how distracted he'd been. His lips tightened and he felt an ache in the back of his throat. Oh, Dad! He hadn't exactly been a pillar of support for him, had he? Quarrelling with Keira all the time. Being so obviously opposed to his marriage. No wonder he'd looked tired and ill.

Fane shook his head. 'I'm sorry, Dad,' he said, his voice hoarse, and slowly turned away.

As he closed the door, though, he realized that at least they had got back together again. At least they'd healed the terrible breach between them. That was some comfort.

He moved down the stairs, his hand firmly on the hand-rail, and glanced around the big hall and the rows of shut doors. Nevertheless, he unerringly made his way straight to the door that led to Keira.

When he quietly pushed open the salon door, he saw a grey-haired man offering her a cloudy white drink. Beside her, a tall, handsome blond man hovered, looking at her with anxious, tender eyes.

Fane felt a wave of rage hit him, and he shut the door behind him with a vicious thud.

Everyone jumped and looked up.

It was only then, when the old man who was obviously a doctor moved away from the woman in front of him, that Fane first saw her properly.

Her eyes were wide and dark with shock and suffering. She was as pale as the liquid in the glass she held. She was sitting in a peculiarly stiff-jointed way that Fane instantly recognized. Wasn't he walking just as rigidly, like an unco-ordinated automaton?

He walked slowly forward, going, as she had gone, straight to the fire. He too felt viciously cold.

'Fane,' Keira said. 'Oh, Fane, I'm so sorry.'

Fane didn't look at her — he couldn't. He'd wanted to find a hard-hearted witch, playing the mourning widow. He'd wanted to see her inwardly gloating over having got what she wanted. Instead, he saw a woman in obvious distress.

He stared into the flames and said nothing.

'Max, this is Fane Harwood. Lucas's son.'

Fane glanced at the older man and gave a curt nod. 'What happened?'

Max opened his mouth, hesitated, then glanced at Keira. Fane stiffened, sensing immediately that there were things here that he didn't know about, and, straightening up, he leaned one arm along the fireplace and faced him squarely. 'Doctor?' His voice was a demand.

Max sighed, and, as gently as he could, explained about Lucas's condition and what Les Coldheath had told him.

When he'd finished, both Keira and Fane were staring at him in disbelief.

'You're telling me . . . he knew?' Fane said at last.

'And he didn't tell us?' Keira added, her breath catching. Oh, Lucas! Lucas, why?

Max saw that she was still cradling the sedative in her hand. 'Drink it, Keira,' he said softly. 'It'll help you to . . . well . . . it'll help.'

Keira stared down into the glass vaguely.

Steven Firth shifted restlessly by her side. 'You really should do what the doctor says, Keira,' he said, appalled by the stricken look on her face. 'You need to rest.'

'Leave her be,' Fane snarled. There was no other word for the sound that left his lips. Steven jerked, surprised by the animosity, but Max, perhaps more used to the varied processes of grief, merely gave him a long, thoughtful look.

'Who are you, anyway?' Fane demanded. He knew he was acting like an idiot, but the sight of the handsome man, obviously so damned smitten with Keira, was making him itch to take him by the scruff of the neck and forcibly throw him out.

'Steven Firth,' Keira made the introduction hastily. 'He's the vet who runs the animal hospital,' she added, sensing the simmering tension between the two men and anxious to defuse it. 'Steven,' she added, turning to him, 'don't worry. I'll be all right. Really. You should get back to the hospital.'

Steven glanced at her, opened his mouth to say something more, then decided against it. He glanced at Fane, remembered that the man had just lost his father, and nodded.

'All right.' He left silently.

Max nodded yet again at the drink in her hand. 'Drink up, Keira,' he insisted once more.

Eventually, because it was less trouble rather than because she really wanted to, Keira drank the bitter-tasting liquid in three quick gulps.

Max nodded, satisfied, and took the empty glass away from her. 'I'll see to all the paperwork,' he said. 'And I expect Bessie and Sid will help with all the other . . . arrangements.'

'I'll see to that,' Fane said curtly.

Max nodded, glad to have someone capable there to help Keira when she needed it most, and quietly left. There was nothing more he could do there.

When they were alone, the room fell totally silent for a long couple of minutes. Then Keira took a deep, shuddering breath.

Fane moved away from the fireplace and went to sit in the chair opposite her. He leaned forward, dangling his hands loosely between his knees. He was dressed casually, in black slacks and a black-and-white sweater. His hair was mussed, as if he'd forgotten to brush it. As he probably had. He looked tired. Lost. And Keira's own bruised heart cried out to him. But when he lifted his head at last to look at her, his face was grim.

'You really did love him, didn't you?' he said at last, such a wealth of relief and anger and . . . something else in his voice that Keira rocked back in her chair.

Yes, she'd loved him. Like her dearest friend and ally. A second father. A favourite uncle, who was always on her side. But how could she say that now? It would sound so . . . callous.

Fane watched her battle against tears, and felt a heaviness settle firmly on his shoulders. She'd really cared about Lucas, after all.

But Keira couldn't bring herself to simply lie. She knew, deep in her heart, what he was asking, and no matter how ugly it might make her seem, she couldn't lie to him.

'Yes and no,' she said at last, and watched him rear back. For a second his eyes blazed accusingly into hers. She held his gaze steadily, patiently, and then she saw the dark fire in his irises begin to bank, like embers in a fire starved of oxygen.

'Tell me,' he said simply. At last willing to listen before judging her.

'I did love him,' she said softly, 'but not in the way that I think you mean. Not in the way a wife is supposed to love her husband. I loved Lucas in a way that . . . well . . . suited us both. He was the best friend I had,' she said, with a quiet, simple dignity that was unmistakably sincere.

Fane felt a massive wave of relief hit him, followed by an equally massive wave of guilt for feeling it.

'Your father and I . . . had an arrangement,' Keira said. She was determined not to bring Jennifer's treachery into this, but she could at least *try* and explain how it was. 'He admired what I was doing. And he was lonely. I was honoured to marry him. But . . .'

Fane stiffened, expecting a body-blow. 'But?' he said, his voice gruff.

Keira looked down at her cold, folded hands. 'Your father slept in another wing of the house.'

She said nothing more than that. But it was enough. Fane felt a thaw begin somewhere deep in his soul. But . . . oh, hell, what a mess it all was! Keira was now his father's widow.

He ran a tired hand over his eyes. He felt the distance between them like a physical chasm. And it hurt. Right now, more than anything in the world, he just wanted to take her in his arms and hold her. To somehow magically make it all better. But he couldn't. There was still so very much between them. But . . . it didn't have to *stay* that way, did it?

'I think we should call a truce,' he said at last, and, when she lifted her head quickly to look at him, smiled wanly. 'Don't you? Under the circumstances?'

For a long, long moment Keira looked at him, a mixture of emotions fighting to battle free of the numbing shock. He'd been through so much, and yet he looked so strong. She wanted more, much more than just a mere tactical truce between them, but she was in no fit state to deal with the rest of her personal baggage just then. And surely neither was he.

She nodded wearily. 'Yes, all right,' she agreed sadly. 'A truce.'

* * *

Aidan fumbled with his black tie. He so seldom wore one, it looked misshapen and clumsy at his throat, but it was the best he could do. He closed the door behind him and glanced up at the dull, leaden sky. It looked set for rain.

He set off up the road towards the small church, falling into line with a little cortège of respectful, similarly black-clad mourners. The ladies of the village had dug out old-fashioned hats that hadn't seen the light of day since the last funeral. Everyone spoke in hushed tones.

Ahead, the tiny village church rang to the peal of a solitary bell.

Inside, the heaters were on full blast, but still Aidan shivered. He saw Blaise seated in one of the back pews and went instinctively to join her. It didn't take long for the church to fill.

Aidan felt her hand slip into his, and he folded his fingers over hers. Slowly, little by little, the warmth and strength of their hand clasp rose to warm his heavy heart.

The vicar approached the pulpit with a sadness of spirit. Not many weeks ago he'd stepped into this very church to marry Keira to her husband. Now he had to try and find words of comfort to offer her in her widowhood.

She looked curiously alone in the front pew, even though she had Bessie and Sid either side of her. She was wearing a simple calf-length black dress, black shoes and a warm black coat. With her raven hair pulled back into a dignified chignon, her face looked almost supernaturally pale.

The congregation rose to sing the first hymn.

Aidan would go out into the churchyard to say a proper goodbye, but he would not go up to the big house afterwards to join the wake. He still felt, in spite of what the old man had said to him, that he didn't belong there.

* * *

In the huge library an hour later, Bessie moved silently around the quiet room, offering tea or cognac to the small group of people gathered there.

Keira was sitting in a huge armchair facing the round oak table, her eyes fixed not on the lawyer who was preparing to read Lucas's final will and testament but on her hands in her lap.

Would they ever feel warm again?

Out of the corner of her eye she saw Fane take a seat over by the fireplace, and was glad of his presence. Just the sight of him made her feel stronger. He'd been a pillar of strength since Lucas had died, making all the arrangements, and bringing some sanity back into her world with just the sound of his voice or the touch of his eyes upon her.

Now she glanced up and met his steady gaze. She smiled — a wan, rather weary smile. Just this last hurdle to go and then . . .

What?

Across the room, Jennifer saw the look pass between her brother and her father's widow and felt like screaming her frustration. What had got into Fane recently? Why wasn't he as violently angry about Lucas's death as she was?

It was Keira's fault he was dead. A woman her age marrying a man of her father's. It was as plain as a pikestaff to anyone with any brains that she'd killed him, almost as surely as if she'd held a gun to his head.

Colin Rattigan put his empty briefcase onto the oak table and coughed nervously. The solicitor was looking particularly ill at ease as he took a seat. His hands, Jennifer noticed with scorn, were shaking as he folded them in front of him.

Jennifer smiled — a complacent, cat-with-the-cream smile. 'Now things will get interesting,' she murmured. She turned to glance vaguely at her husband, rising from the settee where she was sitting. 'I won't be a moment, darling,' she said softly.

With everyone busy in here, now was the perfect opportunity to slip out . . .

Patrick watched his wife silently leave the room, a worried look on his face. He knew she had taken her father's death hard — much harder than a stranger might expect, given their rather turbulent history. And she had been looking at Keira Westcombe — no, Keira Harwood — with such desperate loathing that it filled him with a dreadful tension.

He frowned, wondering where Jennifer was going. Just to the bathroom to freshen up, surely? Why, then, did he feel so uneasy? Probably because he knew his wife well. She was not the kind of woman to take any defeat in her stride. And the marriage of her father to a much younger woman was surely that, in her eyes at least.

Patrick shifted uncomfortably on the sofa. He was worried about Jennifer — he knew what desperate folly she was capable of. She would always act first, and then, later, wonder why the consequences were so hard to take.

Out in the hall, Jennifer cast a quick look around, but, as she'd expected, the place was deserted. And no one would miss her for a while yet. Etiquette demanded that the widow not be in too much of an indecent haste to hear how much she was getting.

She moved across the hall, impatiently opening doors, and then, finally, the one that led to what was obviously her father's study. She recognized his big old desk at once, and the books, and one of his favourite portraits he'd brought with him from Green Acres. She carefully closed the door behind her with a slight 'click' and looked around, breathing a sigh of relief at its emptiness.

This was a really big gamble, she knew, and she could feel her heart thud sickeningly in her chest. If the merry widow had found her father's copy of the will, then all was lost. But she calculated that the chances were good to middling that Keira wouldn't have discovered the secret drawer in the desk and the key it contained. Besides, with any luck she'd have assumed that Rattigan would bring a copy with him, and so wouldn't even have looked for Lucas's copy.

She walked quickly to her father's desk, expertly retrieved the key, and opened the bottom drawer.

There were papers in there; deeds, life assurance policies, but . . . no will.

Jennifer gave a sob of rage and anguished defeat. She slammed the drawer shut viciously, then winced as the sound echoed around the room. More circumspectly now, she locked the drawer and put the key back in its hiding place. The last thing she needed was to get caught. Especially when Fane was acting so damned oddly.

She walked to the door, opened it a crack and peeked through, saw the hall was empty, and emerged. She walked with determined calm back to the library. She'd only been gone a minute. Everyone looked up briefly as she came in.

Keira looked away first, and Jennifer felt a bitter smile twist her lips. Yes, she could look guilty. She could afford to play the magnanimous grieving widow, couldn't she? The high-and-mighty Lady Keira Westcombe had got what she wanted, just as she always did.

Unless . . .

It was not in Jennifer to admit defeat so easily. She made her way to the solicitor, stopping to murmur a word or two here and there to one of the villagers, in an attempt not to make it look too obvious. And only Patrick, who was watching her and knew her so well, could sense the tension in her.

'Colin,' Jennifer murmured, making the solicitor jump a little and look up at her, the alarm obvious in his eyes to anyone looking.

'Mrs Goulder,' Colin said, licking his lips nervously. He felt like a rabbit confronted by a stoat.

'I want you to go across to the widow and ask her if she knows where her husband's copy of the will is,' Jennifer said quietly.

Colin blanched a little. 'You mean it's not there?' he asked, in a shocked and genuinely appalled whisper. He'd always assumed that the will would stay just where Lucas had put it, and that Jennifer would get it back. He'd watched her slip away and known what she was up to, all right. But now . . . This cast a whole new light on the venture.

'No,' Jennifer gritted, the word whistling past her clamped teeth. 'So go and see if she has it!'

Colin couldn't see the point. Who else would have it? It was obvious that Jennifer Goulder was just clutching at straws. Nevertheless he was so cowed by her, and he was already in such an invidious position, that he found himself getting up and walking across to the widow. Keira was talking to the vicar over by the big, diamond-paned windows, unaware of the avalanche about to bury her.

The vicar, seeing the solicitor approach, very tactfully moved away. 'Good afternoon, Mrs Harwood,' Colin said, shaking her hand formally.

'Are you ready to start?' Keira asked.

Colin coughed. 'I was just wondering if you had your husband's copy of the will?'

Keira frowned and shook her head. 'No. I didn't think I'd need it. I imagine it's in his study somewhere,' she said calmly. 'Do you want me to go and see if I can find it?'

Colin, expecting the exact opposite answer, found himself staring at her like a stunned mullet. But her eyes were wide and guileless, and besides, why should she lie about it? But if the widow didn't have it, and Jennifer hadn't found it, then where the hell was it?

'Mr Rattigan?' Keira said a touch sharply, wondering why the solicitor looked so sick all of a sudden.

Fane, sitting by the fireplace and moodily sipping a brandy, just caught the sharpness of her tone and turned to look at her, surprised. He didn't recognize the man she was talking to. Curious, he began to move towards them.

Jennifer, too, sensing that something was amiss, began to do the same.

'Keira?' Fane's voice, even questioning and curious, was like a soothing balm on her stretched nerves. She turned towards him, relieved to see him. His closeness felt so overwhelmingly . . . *welcome.*

'Fane, this is Mr Rattigan. Lucas's solicitor.'

Behind him, Fane saw his sister draw up close. No doubt her ears were flapping, he thought with an inner smile. Fane had no illusions about Jennifer. She was a complicated, greedy, passionate woman. Trust her to be in the thick of things.

Fane nodded briefly at the solicitor. 'You want to get things started?' He, too, assumed that all the solicitor wanted was to get things moving along.

Colin shifted uncomfortably. 'In just a moment,' he said, then smiled rather unconvincingly and moved away. Jennifer went with him.

Fane watched him go, a small frown tugging at his brows. 'What was all that about?' he asked quietly.

Keira shrugged one black-clad shoulder. 'I'm not sure. He asked me if I had a copy of Lucas's will.'

Fane glanced at her, obviously surprised. 'And don't you?'

Again Keira shrugged. 'I haven't the faintest idea where it is. I honestly never gave it a thought.'

Fane glanced once more towards the solicitor, who was now deep in earnest conversation with his sister.

'Well, I don't suppose it matters,' he said. 'He'll have his own copy.'

But there was something about the man that worried Fane. He looked pale, and sick to the stomach. And a nervous tic was pulsing just beside his rather weak chin. And, for some reason, the fact that he and his sister obviously had so much to talk about made him feel suddenly uneasy.

Colin was feeling more than uneasy. He was feeling downright panic-stricken. 'But I can't say that the will was never signed,' he was saying, aghast, to Jennifer, who was looking wild-eyed with unexpected triumph.

She had hardly been able to believe her luck when she'd heard that Keira didn't have the will. And although she knew everything would fall through if the house was searched and the widow came up with it, she was willing to take the gamble. Her father had been a crafty man. He might have had it put in one of his safety deposit boxes, or even posted it off to another solicitor. But any delay was a spoke in Keira Westcombe's wheels, and if Jennifer could make life difficult for her, she would.

'And why not?' she asked archly, giving Colin Rattigan a scornful glance. 'Nobody saw your "witnesses" sign the will did they?'

Colin ran a harassed hand through his hair. 'Look, I don't think you fully understand what's—'

Jennifer stiffened, giving him sudden warning. He turned, just in time to see Keira and Fane move up beside him.

'Mr Rattigan, I think it's time the will was read,' Fane said, his voice hard and level. Whatever the hell was going on, he wanted it broken up.

Colin gave him an agonized look. Before he could say anything Jennifer broke in, her voice rich with spiteful victory. 'I'm afraid that won't be possible,' she purred. 'The will seems to have gone missing.'

For a second Keira didn't think she had heard correctly. Fane immediately shot a glance at the solicitor, who was looking even more sick, and then, with narrowing eyes, towards Keira.

But Keira was looking round-eyed with what seemed like genuine shock. After a stunned moment, she blinked, and said quietly, 'I'm sorry?'

Colin glanced at Jennifer, wishing he knew what madness she was going to pull next. Then he glanced at Fane, saw the hardness in the eyes, and felt even more sick. The moment he was out of this house he was going to board the first plane out of the country. He didn't care where. He didn't care if he had to use his own passport. He'd worry about disappearing once he was well away from this whole, insane family. But first he had to get out with his skin intact.

He licked bone-dry lips and cleared his throat. 'I'm sorry, Mrs Harwood, but I'm afraid that's true.'

Keira glanced at him blankly. 'But don't you have a copy?'

Colin shook his head. 'I'm afraid not.'

'But surely it's common practice, when getting a client to sign a will, for a solicitor to retain a copy for the office files?' Fane said.

They'd all four been talking in unconsciously quiet tones. Around them, the vicar was still preaching a quiet sermon to a group of people in one corner, and Bessie still patiently circulated with drinks. Only the four people towards the large book-lined wall were impervious to it all.

'Naturally, that's the usual course of events,' Colin said, trying to meet Fane's suspicious look with a level glance. 'But your father was quite insistent on keeping *all* the copies. I tried to tell him that was most unwise, but he insisted.' With his peripheral vision he saw Jennifer shift angrily. 'I believe he wanted to add a codicil.'

'But that's no—' Fane began, but once again Jennifer impatiently broke in.

'I wouldn't be surprised if Father didn't even sign this so-called new will,' she said grimly, and surreptitiously jabbed Colin hard in the ribs with her elbow. 'In which case his old will still stands,' she added with malicious glee, her eyes fixed on Keira's face.

Keira paled perceptibly. If that was so, then the land would be lost . . .

'But Mr Harwood *did* make a new will,' Colin said, and felt the woman beside him fairly vibrate with anger. Too late now to play her silly games.

'So where is it?' Fane asked grimly. It took Keira a moment to realize that he'd asked the question of her. She gave herself a mental shake and turned to look at him, surprised at the anger she could clearly see in his face.

'I don't know,' she said again, perfectly truthfully. 'Lucas didn't tell me where it was.' Then, as his eyes narrowed in even more out-and-out suspicion, she asked abruptly, 'Did he tell you?'

Fane shook his head. 'No,' he said quietly, more thoughtfully. 'He didn't.'

Jennifer could hardly contain her glee. This was going even better than she'd planned. And if her father really *had* kept the will so safe that it couldn't be found . . . she'd be rich!

Fane stared hard at Keira, trying to read her mind, to see what was going on behind the beautiful face, battling to keep the suspicion from tearing him apart. She *looked* as puzzled and surprised as anyone about this sudden glitch. But was she?

'I think it might be best,' Colin said, 'if we make a search of the house. Our best efforts must be put into finding the will.' He sounded very much like a legal man all of a sudden, and Keira glanced at him uncertainly.

'You want me to search the house?'

'I think we should *all* search the house,' Fane said with grim emphasis. He didn't want to believe it of her, but who else could have masterminded this coup? And if she had done it, it was so diabolically *clever* . . .

Keira looked at him with deeply puzzled eyes. Why was he looking at her so oddly? He looked cold and . . . *furious.* But what had she done?

'All right,' she said, trying to figure it all out but getting hopelessly confused. 'We'll search the house.'

'First,' Fane said, looking around, 'let's get rid of the bystanders.'

He approached the vicar and murmured a discreet warning that the family was ready to read the will. A small whisper went quickly around the room and it began to clear, mourners tactfully taking their leave of Keira, who shook hands and thanked them all for coming, all in a state of numb shock.

She just couldn't understand why Lucas had kept all the copies of the will. It was not like him to be so careless about something so important. He must know that, in case of fire, for instance, it was sheer folly to have all the existing copies in one place. And if the old will did stand . . . the reserve would have lost the land.

No. It didn't bear thinking about. They would find the will. They had to! She stiffened in determination, unaware that Fane was watching every look on her face. His heart sank at the grim light of battle in her eyes. It could only mean that his damned suspicions were right.

Over in the corner, Jennifer rounded on Colin viciously. 'Why didn't you say that my father never signed the new will, you imbecile? I'd have everything then, everything my father left me in the old will! I'll see you ruined for this!' Her voice was a poisonous hiss.

Colin summoned up every last inch of guile and acting ability in him. It wasn't hard — he was fighting for his life now. 'Why didn't you tell me that that was what you had planned?' he said angrily, the surprise attack silencing Jennifer as nothing else would have done. 'I'm not a mind-reader! If you'd told me that you thought you could invoke the old will, I'd have told you that it's impossible.'

Jennifer stared at him, wondering briefly where the worm had suddenly got his backbone. Then, as the import of his words finally sank in, he had the satisfaction, at least, of watching her eyes become wary and unsure.

'What do you mean? Why not?'

'Because,' Colin explained with feigned patience, 'when a man marries, it immediately makes null and void any existing will.'

Jennifer stared at him in infuriated silence. Finally, as the last of the guests filed out of the door, Keira and Fane going with them to see them off the premises, she snarled angrily, 'Why didn't you tell me that?'

She didn't notice her husband, sitting quietly on the settee, listening to every word.

'Because I thought you must have known it!' Colin said. 'I thought you had something else in mind. A legal wrangle that would hold up the release of your father's assets for years . . . Like I said, I'm not clairvoyant!'

Jennifer's hand itched to slap his silly, stupid face, but she knew she had to act cool. The others would be back at any minute. 'What happens now?' she asked sullenly.

'If the new will can't be found, then your father will be declared to have died intestate.'

'Meaning?'

'Meaning,' Colin said, trying hard to keep the gloating from his voice, 'that the widow will get far more than Lucas had originally planned to leave her. These things can vary, but in some cases the widow can get everything.'

'*Everything*?' Jennifer yelped.

Colin, realizing his life was still in her hands, so to speak, quickly lifted his hand to placate her. Behind him, he could hear the others returning.

'In this case, perhaps half will go to the widow, the other half to be divided between you and Fane.'

'Half?' Jennifer snarled. 'Never! I'll drag her through every court first!'

As she saw her brother walk through the door, she quickly turned away. Damn it, she had to *think*!

'Right then.' It was Fane's voice, cold and deliberate. 'Let's get organized. Bessie, I want you to go out and get all the servants you can find and ask them to come in here.'

Bessie cast Keira a puzzled glance, but after a brief pause she nodded in assent, and Bessie hurried out.

Fane watched Keira's face closely, his eyes as watchful as those of a hunting hawk.

Once again, she was aware of him holding something back. Something that seemed to make him fairly vibrate with tense, powerful energy. And, although she didn't want to believe it, she couldn't help but feel that it was anger. He was furious about all this. But why? They both knew what Lucas had put in the will; he'd told them plainly and clearly, after all. And if it turned out that they couldn't find the will, well, they'd still be able to work it out just as Lucas had wanted it.

She couldn't understand why he was looking at her as if he wanted to kill her.

Slowly, in groups, the household staff came in. With all the gardeners, Bessie, Sid and the dailies, it made quite a group. When they were all gathered, Fane spoke crisply, coming to the point immediately. 'It seems that nobody can find a copy of my father's latest will,' he said bluntly, and, behind her, Keira could hear Bessie give a gasp of surprise. 'So we're going to search the house from top to bottom. I want you to organize yourself into groups of two and each take a room. No room is to be left unsearched. You're looking for a fairly bulky, typewritten document, signed by my father and two witnesses.' He glanced at Keira, almost as if he expected her to demur, but she only looked back at him with a wary, worried look in her eyes.

As well she might!

'Begin in the attics,' he said, 'and work your way down methodically to the basements, please.' The milling group of men and women slowly filed out, whispering amongst themselves.

'That was hardly discreet.' Colin Rattigan was the first to speak in the now deathly quiet room.

'There would have been no keeping it quiet anyway,' Fane said, still watching Keira, still half expecting her to say something. Anything. Anything at all in mitigation. But there was nothing.

'I'll get onto the legal end, of course,' Colin said. 'See if your father employed any other legal firms. He might have sent the will to them.'

Fane nodded. 'And check with his banks. See if he sent it to them for safekeeping.'

Colin nodded. He glanced at Jennifer, then quickly away again. The sooner he was out of this mess the better. But he'd set one of his junior clerks onto the task. If he was any judge of man, Fane Harwood would be checking up on their progress daily, and he wanted him to be reassured that all due searches were being made. It would give him, Colin, valuable time to make his getaway.

'Well, I'd best get onto that straight away. Er . . . you will let me know if anything turns up here?'

Fane nodded. But he didn't expect the will to be found in the house. And seven hours later, after every stick of furniture had been moved, every carpet lifted, every cupboard, drawer, nook and cranny diligently searched, he would be proved right.

But, right at that moment, Colin took a hurried leave, and Keira walked to the settee and slumped down, exhausted, next to Patrick.

Patrick took one look at his wife's feverish eyes and rose silently. He took a quiet, murmured leave of Keira, while Jennifer moved restlessly from foot to foot.

'I think it's time we left,' Patrick said firmly. He knew Jennifer was desperate to stay, to see what became of the search, but right now he'd had enough. Jennifer had gone too far this time. It was obvious, to him at least, that she was in some sort of criminal conspiracy with the solicitor.

Fane came over to his sister and kissed her cheek. 'I'll call in later, all right?' he murmured. He knew that all this uncertainty must be hitting her hard. He knew how much importance Jennifer gave to money and status.

Jennifer nodded grimly. 'All right.' But they needn't think they'd heard the last from her!

Keira watched them go, and then walked to the drinks tray to pour herself another glass of cognac. It was her third, but she felt she needed it.

Desperately.

When she turned back, the glass raised to her lips, Fane was watching her.

'Want one?'

Fane shook his head. 'No. We have to talk, you and I.'

Keira's breath caught as he walked slowly towards her. He was dressed in a black suit, of course, and in the gathering dusk the firelight played across his face, casting deep shadows that made him look more hawk-like than ever. His eyes were no longer deep chocolate brown but near black, and they glittered like jet.

Her heartbeat began to race. It was his nearness that was causing it, she knew, and felt ashamed. This was the day of her husband's funeral . . .

'Keira, you must tell me the truth about this damned will,' Fane said, reaching out to take her hands in his. Instinctively, motivated by a sense of guilt, she took a step back.

'Don't. Don't touch me!'

She bit her lip as Fane reared back.

A strange look flickered across his face — it started out as stricken surprise, turned to anger, then settled into grim understanding.

'I know,' he said, walking a little way from her and turning to face the window. Outside it began to rain, heavy and grey. 'I feel it too. You think I don't feel as guilty as hell? I wanted you from the first moment I saw you — when you were marrying my own father, for pity's sake!'

His voice wavered and he ran a hand wearily through his hair.

Keira sighed. 'I'm sorry it all happened, if that's any help to you. I'm sorry Lucas asked me to marry him, and I'm sorry I said yes. I'm sorry he was so ill and never told us. I'm sorry Jennifer hates me. I'm sorry that I love you.'

There. The words were out. She hadn't meant to say them, but now that she had she was not sorry.

Fane eyes widened, incredulous. Then, in the next instant, he wasn't incredulous at all. Why should he be so surprised that she loved him when he already knew, had known for some time, that he loved *her*?

He just hadn't wanted to admit it.

But what did it matter now? Now that she had stage-managed this 'lost will' fiasco.

'It won't do us any good,' he said at last, and with a bitter laugh, Keira tossed back the last of her cognac.

'I know.'

Fane walked towards her, but as she visibly tensed, he veered off slightly towards the fire and stood staring down at the hypnotic flames instead. Overhead, he knew, the house was being turned inside out in a search for a will he felt sure had long since been destroyed.

Keira would never be stupid enough to leave a single page of it unburned.

At last he looked back at her. She was nursing the empty glass, her fingers closing and unclosing around the short stem in convulsive, subconscious movements.

She looked so beautiful.

But he couldn't think of that now. He couldn't think of their love, not when it was so hopeless. So unwanted. It would rip him apart.

'But you're not sorry about anything else, are you?' he said at last.

Keira's head jerked up. What was he talking about now? She looked at him, wanted him, needed him, and shook her head.

'No. I'm not sorry he left me some land,' she agreed at last, her voice defeated and yet strong at the same time. It was the one and only good thing that had come out of this whole tragic, painful mess, and she was determined that Lucas would have his final wish. Over the years Lucas had come to love the wildlife that had she had helped to flourish, every bit as much as she did herself.

Fane nodded, seeing how her chin jutted out at a determined angle, and how her eyes at last took on a glimmer of life. 'And you'd do anything for the sake of your precious nature reserve, wouldn't you?' he asked, but he already knew the answer.

Keira sighed. 'It's a huge part of my life,' she said simply. 'Love me, love my dreams . . .'

But Fane couldn't let love come into it. If she thought she could cheat Lucas and get away with it, she was in for a surprise. And he was the man who was going to give it to her.

He had no other choice. No matter how much it would be like tearing out his own heart.

For a long moment they looked at each other. Then Fane gave a bitter, bleak smile. 'So nothing's really changed?' She was behind this damned will business; she'd as good as openly admitted it, damn her eyes. Was there no end to her treachery?

Keira shrugged. 'It seems not.'

But they both knew that *everything* had changed.

They just didn't know what they were going to do about it. What they *could* do about it . . .

CHAPTER 13

Barely a week later Fane slipped the car into second gear as he approached the turn to Upper Rousham and then quickly into first as he saw Keira striding along the road. Her legs ate the pace at a fast but natural gait, her body moving with unconscious grace with every step she took.

When Keira heard a car idling to a stop behind her, its throaty purr telling her at once that it was a sports car, she stopped, and turned around apprehensively. Their eyes met at once through the windscreen.

Fane leaned across the gearstick and thrust open the passenger door. 'Get in.'

Keira hesitated. She came reluctantly around the door and bent to look inside, one hand nervously clutching the car roof. She let her eyes skid away from the banked embers in his and examined the Jaguar's immaculate interior. The dash was wood-panelled, the upholstery pristine cream leather. The carpet was bottle-green, to match the body's paintwork.

Then she looked down ruefully at her mud-caked wellingtons. She'd been over by Fishpool Spinney, examining the small area of marshland there. The frog and toad population looked healthy enough, and the resident kingfisher certainly seemed happy with the minnow and gudgeon population.

'I'm all dirty,' she said, then blushed as his eyebrow rose at her choice of words.

'You said it,' Fane replied, so expressionless that it cut through her like a scalpel.

Keira glanced at him quickly, her breath trapped in her throat. A nasty feeling began to uncoil in the pit of her stomach. Looking into his eyes, as carefully blank as his voice, she knew that something was wrong. Very wrong.

She swallowed hard. If she was going to have to go into battle with this man yet *again,* she wanted to do it on her home ground. She straightened and moved a step away. 'I have work to do. I can't afford any time off for a spin in the country.'

Fane's lips twisted. 'Especially in a petrol-guzzling pollution machine like my car?' he asked grimly.

'You said it!' Keira shot back, then sighed, instantly regretting it. She was not, after all, a raving zealot who thought all cars should be torched. Just that people should be educated and made aware of the harm cars could do when used to excess.

Despondently she watched him pull away, but the car only idled to the side of the road and pulled off onto the grass verge. When he got out, uncoiling himself from the low bucket seat with all the grace of an indolent panther, she felt her throat constrict. He was dressed in black jeans and a thick warm black sweater, and the slight breeze was ruffling the hair back from his well-defined temples.

He looked . . .

Keira quickly turned away and climbed the wooden fence, setting off across the fields towards the plot of land that Lucas had given her in his will. It was long past time she gave it a thorough check. She'd need to take soil samples, and, more importantly, river-water samples . . . But, no matter how desperately she tried to school her mind along business lines, her senses weren't having it.

She could hear him coming up behind her, but even if she'd lost her hearing she'd have known instantly that he was there. Every sensor under her skin was pulsing the message of his proximity. She would swear she could smell him — the primordial scent of a hunting male.

'You promised a tour of the reserve, remember?' he asked as they drew level, being deliberately cordial. 'We might as well kill two birds with one stone.'

Keira ran her tongue tip over lips gone seriously dry. 'Fine,' she said, keeping up her regular walking pace, skirting the fields at the edges, checking the hedges as she went and making a mental note of the now-abandoned birds' nests she saw there. A good selection of hedge sparrows, of course, some chaffinches, one or two yellowhammers . . .

But she couldn't concentrate. Damn him!

'So, what was it you wanted to see me about?' she asked, since he seemed to be in no hurry to talk, and her nerves couldn't take the silence any longer.

Fane glanced across at her stubborn, set face, and smiled bleakly. 'You've searched all the outbuildings?'

Keira frowned, nonplussed. Whatever she'd expected him to say, it had hardly been that! 'Outbuildings? What for?'

Fane's lips twisted. 'Father's will, of course.' How easily she forgot!

'Oh. Yes, I had them all searched the day after . . . the funeral,' Keira said. It was just about the will. She felt herself relax a little.

'Let me guess,' Fane said, still in that aggravatingly polite tone. 'It hasn't turned up?'

'No,' Keira said shortly. She was getting tired of this. The way Fane was acting, anyone would think that *she'd* deliberately hidden the damn thing.

'You don't seem all that concerned,' Fane commented, pausing as she climbed over a stile in the hedge before quickly following. He was not about to let her get away from him. 'Surely you've contacted your own solicitor by now?' he fished. 'To see how you stand from a legal point of view?' His tone had a grating edge now, and she paused, turning to look at him curiously. What on earth was wrong with the man? His hands were clenching and unclenching by his sides, and he was walking with a jerky, energy-consuming gait that told her he was still dangerously tense.

'I was waiting to hear what Mr Rattigan turned up,' Keira said truthfully. There was no point getting ahead of herself. She was sure the will would turn up *somewhere* after all.

Fane drew up beside her, his lips twisting into a mocking smile. It made her itch to slap it off his face, even as she puzzled over what had put it there.

'That might prove . . . difficult,' he warned her coldly, watching her like a hawk. 'Since Mr Rattigan has disappeared,' he added silkily. 'Convenient, isn't it?'

Keira gaped at him. 'Disappeared? What do you mean, disappeared?'

Fane's eyes narrowed. Her lips had fallen open in surprise and her eyes were slightly rounder. Even her irises had contracted a little. 'Good grief, you really are a good actress, aren't you?' he said in reluctant admiration.

Keira felt her teeth come together in an annoyed click. 'If you say so,' she said shortly. 'But, since I haven't got the faintest idea what you're double-talking about . . .' She turned and marched away, her mind working furiously.

Rattigan had gone? Why? Where? And what did that have to do with Lucas keeping all the copies of the will? It just didn't make sense.

For a moment Fane watched her leave, torn with the desire to just let it go. He almost wanted to let her have her own way; he himself could go back to London, and the office, and forget he'd ever met her. Except . . . his life would be empty without her. And besides, his father was relying on him to see that justice was done. He'd never meant for Keira to have half of his fortune and land, and Fane would see to it that the scheming witch didn't get it if it was the last thing he did!

'If we were in a theatre, I'd be applauding like crazy,' he called to her retreating back, and quickly caught up with her. She made no move to try and out-distance him, he noticed, and he could only admire her cool courage, even as he silently cursed her for it.

'This is beginning to look familiar,' he added, looking around at the lie of the land as he drew level with her, his long legs easily eating up the distance.

'It should do. It's the land your father left to me,' Keira said simply. 'I wanted to check it out.'

She yelped as a hard hand suddenly curled around her elbow, the strength of his grip swinging her around in mid-stride and almost making her fall. Instead, she cannoned into his solid chest and let out a small gasp of surprise and . . . pleasure. Then her eyes darkened angrily. 'Just what the hell do you think you're doing?' she snapped, trying to twist her arm free and failing miserably. 'Let go of me!'

But Fane was in no mood for games. He was staring at her in open fury now. 'You have some gall! So you're going to "check out" the land, are you? Don't you feel even the least little bit guilty?'

'Why should I?' Keira fumed. 'Lucas wanted me to have it!'

'Yes. But only this! He never meant for you to get half of everything!'

Keira stared at him as if he'd gone mad. 'What are you talking about? Half? Of course he didn't want me to get half. That's . . . that's millions of pounds, for crying out loud. You know the sum of money he wanted to donate to the reserve. You were there when he told us exactly what he was putting in the will.' Her voice was rising angrily now.

Fane's fingers tightened on her arm, unknowingly leaving small bruises in her tender flesh. 'That's right. I was there. So don't think you're going to get away with this,' he all but snarled.

'With what?' she screamed, totally frustrated now and at the end of her tether.

Fane's eyes narrowed suddenly. He noticed how high her colour was, the storminess in her eyes and the raggedness of her breathing. If he hadn't known better he could have sworn she was genuine.

With a snarl of disgust and disbelief at his own weakness as far as this woman was concerned, he all but threw her arm away from him.

Keira felt a wave of pain hit her. It was almost as if he couldn't bear to touch her.

'Oh, you've been very clever,' Fane said bitterly. 'I haven't been just sitting around twiddling my thumbs the last few days, though for all the good I've been able to do I might as well have been. As you know only too well, the will isn't with any of my father's banks, solicitors, or friends. It's gone, and you and I both know it's never going to turn up again, don't we?'

Keira felt her breath leave her in a whoosh. She'd been hoping against hope this last week that Lucas had sent at least one copy of the will to a bank or another solicitor. It was, after all, the sensible thing to do. But now . . .

'It doesn't make sense,' Keira said slowly. 'Lucas wasn't the kind of man to be so careless. He *must* have put it somewhere safe. Have you checked the safe at Green Acres?'

Fane turned away, his shoulders slumping in disappointment. 'Oh, stop it,' he growled. 'It's wearing thin.'

Keira stared at his profile, totally at a loss. 'Fane,' she said at last, taking a calming breath and mentally preparing herself for the worst, 'will you kindly just tell me what this is all about? What do you think I've *done*?'

He turned, then, his eyes blazing. 'You know damned well what you've done. I don't know how you persuaded my father not to let Rattigan have a copy . . .' Suddenly he stiffened, his eyes widening in surprise. 'Or perhaps Rattigan *did* have a copy all along. And you got him to destroy it and then disappear. Is that how it worked, Keira?'

Keira felt suddenly cold. Although she didn't know it, every tint of colour fled from her face.

'You think I arranged for the will to disappear?' she said, her voice barely able to raise itself above a whisper.

Fane almost groaned. The look of pain and hurt in her eyes seemed so real that even though he knew she was conning him, had to be playing the game out to the very last throw of the dice, he *still* wanted to reach out and comfort her.

He gave a slight shake. Was he insane?

Keira took a step forward, her hand reaching out to his shoulder, to touch him, to ask him *why* he was doing this to her, but his head reared back at her movement and her hand quickly fell away, leaving the gap between them unbridged.

'So, that's it,' she said listlessly. She turned and walked off, her legs feeling like lead. She automatically took a footpath through a small wood, aware that he was following but uncaring now. The day seemed to have been leached of all colour and life. She felt as if she were walking through a black-and-white photograph of something that had used to be her life.

So. The man she loved hated her. Well, she could live with that. She'd have to. She still had her life's work. At least the reserve would never let her down, rip her heart out and watch her bleed.

A few minutes later she emerged onto the land bordering the Westcombe Nature Reserve and glanced around. Lucas had chosen it well. With more than six miles of the River Cherwell winding and twisting through it, it would provide valuable habitat that the rest of her river-free reserve badly needed.

Fane, following her doggedly, watched her walk to the riverbank and look down into the weed-choked water. She looked pale and somehow . . . drained.

She stiffened as she felt him move silently to stand beside her. When she chanced a quick look at his grim profile, she could see that he looked as miserable as she felt.

'Don't think you can just walk away from me,' he said quietly. 'I'm not going to let you. Oh, I know it's not going to be easy. The team of top-flight solicitors I talked to yesterday made that more than clear. But I can at least string it out. Make you wait for it.'

'Wait for what?' Keira asked, too weary now to even try and figure out what he was talking about.

Fane waved a hand vaguely at the river. 'This.'

Keira's head reared up, and he turned to face her, a savagely satisfied smile on his face. 'Yes, I thought that might shatter your calm a bit. After all your planning and scheming you don't like to think you might not get your way so easily after all. Do you?'

It almost killed him to think that she cared so much about the reserve but so little about him.

Keira could do nothing but look at him helplessly. Everything she wanted to say sounded pitifully inadequate. Finally she just sighed, a heart-wrenching, defeated sound. 'Why are you being like this?' she asked at last, her voice a mere wisp of sound.

Fane laughed. It was as bitter as the look in his eyes. 'Why am I being like this?' he repeated in disbelief. 'Because you've cheated your husband, that's why. My own father. And,' more agonizingly still, 'you've cheated me.'

'No, I haven't!' she cried, stung to her very soul. 'What makes you say that?'

'Because the will's missing!' Fane all but shouted at her, tired of her stalling. 'Which means that my father died intestate. Which means, as his widow, you get the lion's share of all his money and all this damned land!'

He felt like killing her. And making love to her. And, most absurdly of all, like crying. He'd have willingly bought her all the land her greedy little heart could have desired — all she'd had to do was ask him. Love him. Marry him. 'I'd have given you anything you ever wanted,' he said, hardly realizing he'd spoken the thought out loud. 'Don't you see? If only you'd trusted me, I'd have given you everything I had.' And, as owner of Harwood Construction, that was a lot.

Keira felt herself swaying under the weight of so much astounding information all at once. Only one thing, out of it all, shone with such blinding evidence that it left her feeling shell-shocked. He loved her! He really, truly loved her! He'd have given her everything. But all she'd ever wanted was the man himself. And now, understanding what the disappearance of this will truly meant, it was no wonder he thought she was responsible.

But she *wasn't*!

'Fane,' she said, desperately reaching out for him, but he was already backing away. On his face was a mixture of pain, love and despair. And determination.

'You're not going to get away with it,' he said, his voice as grim as death. 'If I have to drag you through every court to the highest in the land, the highest in Europe . . . If I have to spend every last million I have in legal fees, I'll see my father's assets tied up in court for years. Years! I'll starve you and your precious reserve out of existence!'

He turned and stalked away, pain and wretched anger in every inch of his body. But even as he walked away from her the memory of her stricken face remained with him like a tormenting ghost. He knew why he was being so vindictive, of course. Because he loved her so much. It felt as if the weight of it was driving him into the ground.

And as she watched him go, her mind racing, vainly trying to find explanations, desperately trying to find a way out, Keira knew why he was being so ruthless too.

And her heart ached. 'Fane, I love you,' she called, her voice forlorn and hopeless on the wind.

But he heard it. And it drove yet another little nail into the aching coffin of his heart.

* * *

Blaise put the final touch to the cottage roof — a deep arrow of shadow cast by a Douglas fir tree — and stepped back from the easel.

Yes. The painting was complete.

Unlike the *Plough and Man* — the title of her first Rousham painting — which had a feeling of wildness and naturalness to it, the atmosphere of this painting was totally different, as it was meant to be.

If the ploughman had represented man's relationship with the land, this painting represented man's homemaking urges. The cottage looked thick-walled and sturdy — as it was. And the garden, even on the eve of winter, still showed the care and attention lavished on it by the owner. A viewer, coming new to this painting, would be able to close their eyes and see how it would look with the coming of spring.

Or, at least, that was what she hoped.

Now the canvas cottage had smoke curling from its chimney and rising into a threatening sky. But in six months a viewer should be able to expect the painting to mature with the season. For the smoke to be gone. For the cherry tree off to the right to be out in candy-pink blossom. For the daffodils to be blooming around the tree trunk.

She sighed in happiness. Another major work completed. Utterly different from *Plough and Man*, and yet part of the same world.

She'd have to think of a name for it. *Cottage and Man*? Perhaps she could start off a whole series. The mill in summer. *Feeding Man* might make a good title for that. The Penda Stones in winter. The pub, on bonfire night, with fireworks overhead and revellers spilling out, beer glasses in hand, to watch the bonfire burn. *History and Man*?

'Hello, you look like the cat that got the canary.'

The final word came out like 'cannery', and Blaise looked up with a huge grin on her face to see Aidan, who must have opened the gate and walked up behind her without her realizing it. He stood with his coat slung across his shoulder, his hair curling with the dampness of sweat.

She pointed to the painting. 'It's finished. What do you think?'

Aidan looked at the painted cottage and garden on the canvas, and then lifted his eyes to scan the real thing in front of him.

He was silent for a long time, and then shook his head. 'I don't know how you do it.'

Blaise smiled, a touch unsurely. 'Do what?' she asked tentatively.

Aidan looked from the cottage and back to the canvas again.

'A photograph would capture how it *looks*. But . . . even though you haven't copied every stick and stone exactly . . . you've made it look how it actually *feels*.' He shrugged, a touch shamefacedly, and laughed. 'Does that make any sense?'

Blaise turned and threw her arms around him, hugging him as tightly as her meagre muscle-power would let her. With her cheek pressed to his, she laughed.

'That's the nicest thing anyone's ever said about my work. And, yes,' she drew away to look at him, noticing an odd look of relief pass over his face as she did so, 'it makes *perfect* sense.'

Aidan grinned, then glanced up at the lowering sky. 'We'd better get the painting inside. It's going to rain.'

Blaise yelped in alarm and grabbed the precious canvas, running to the door. Aidan watched her scuttling retreat, and laughed.

He'd never felt so happy in his life.

He followed her, shutting the door behind him and moving into the living room to throw another log and scuttle-full of coal onto the fire.

Blaise collapsed happily into his old but comfortable sofa and watched him.

'Lunch?' she asked brightly, when he turned back to her, and then suddenly wondered why. Why had she waited until he was looking at her before speaking? She felt a frisson of . . . something . . . move up her spine.

For weeks now, in fact ever since they'd first met, she'd known there was something about Aidan that was different, that set him apart from other men. That she loved him was only one of the things that made him special. That he was kind to animals, that he loved the land, that he was as strong of spirit as he was of body — all of that set him apart.

But there was another thing too . . .

If only she could grasp what it was.

'Hmm. Welsh rarebit?' he asked, the words coming out with their usual susurration.

Blaise smiled. 'Lovely. I'll do the toast; you cut the cheese.'

'You're on.'

They moved to the kitchen in perfect harmony, Blaise humming 'Red River Valley' as they set about the simple domestic chores. She could see the happy years stretching ahead of her now — either in this cottage or in hers. A son or daughter sitting at the table, legs swinging, hungrily chivvying them on to get the food ready faster. At Christmas time they'd decorate the tree together, and Aidan would stand at the head of the table to carve the turkey.

Her humming grew louder as the fantasy-within-reach grew around her.

'Not finished the toast yet, slowcoach?'

Blaise peered into the toaster. 'Not yet. It's just getting brown. Have patience, man!'

Aidan grinned, and put the plate of sliced cheese on the table. 'Tea?'

'I thought you'd never ask,' she said, and poked out her tongue.

Aidan made a quick grab for it, his hands surprisingly fast, and caught her tongue tip between his finger and thumb.

Blaise choked, and laughed.

'Now what are you going to do, clever clogs?' he teased.

Blaise slowly lifted one hand and tickled the inside of his wrist. A long, tender look passed between them. He released her tongue and she sucked it back into her mouth, relishing the taste of his skin that still lingered on her taste buds.

Aidan caught his breath, then turned to the kettle.

Blaise popped up the toast, laid the cheese across it and took it to the grill.

'You know, I think I'll do the stones next,' she said, looking up at his back, waiting for his comment. 'I think they'll be much more dramatic in winter than in spring or summer. Don't you?'

Still no answer.

She watched him reach up for the sugar. 'Aidan?'

No answer.

The frisson down her back suddenly cemented. She felt her whole body jerk in sudden realization.

'Aidan!' she called his name loudly.

Nothing.

'Aidan!' she called again, a great shout of sound.

Nothing.

Blaise leaned one hand on the table. She felt just a little dizzy.

He was deaf. Aidan was *deaf* . . .

And all this time she hadn't noticed. What kind of an idiot was she? He must have thought she was so stupid. Why hadn't she known?

Her colour drained away. Had she ever embarrassed him with her clumsiness? When they'd gone to the pub for the first time . . . had she said anything or done anything to make him feel uneasy? Oh, how could she have been so selfish? How could she love him so much and not be aware of his needs?

He turned to look at her. 'Would you like some lemon with this? I bought one fresh from Marge yesterday. She'd had a dozen sent in and then couldn't get rid of them fast enough— Blaise? What's wrong?'

Blaise shook her head. Her eyes were wide, blue and dazed. 'Oh, Aidan, I'm so sorry,' she whispered, appalled. 'I never realized . . . I didn't mean to do anything to upset you . . .'

Aidan frowned. 'What the hell are you talking about?'

And the slightly slurred, mispronounced words made total sense now.

She felt tears spring to her eyes. This was the man she loved, with all her heart, body and might, and she'd never even suspected his secret. Why *had* he kept it secret? Then she mentally shook her head. What did it matter now? She had more important things to think about. Like how she had never done anything to make it easier for him. Never comforted him when he must have needed it. Never tried to make life simpler for him. Never . . .

'Why didn't you tell me?' she asked, her voice as stricken as the look on her face. And she realized . . . he couldn't hear her voice. Had *never* heard her voice.

She went white.

'Oh, Aidan . . .' She moved around the table, holding out her hand.

Aidan stiffened and went suddenly pale. He took a step away.

'So you know?' he asked, his voice strangely harsh. He knew that some of the villagers must have realized about his deafness before now, and it had never really bothered him. He wasn't keeping it a secret, exactly, just not broadcasting about. But somehow, now it was *Blaise* who knew about it, he felt . . . vulnerable. Guilty. Ashamed. Angry. Confused.

Blaise faltered to a halt. 'That you're . . . deaf.' She forced herself to say it calmly. Clearly. 'Yes. I only just this moment realized. Oh, Aidan, why didn't you tell me? I could have . . .'

Loved you better, was what she'd been about to say.

But Aidan didn't give her the chance.

'You could have what? Pitied me a bit more? Fussed around me like a mother hen with a disabled chick?' He spat the words out angrily. 'No thanks.'

'But—' She stopped, confused, as he moved quickly around the table.

'I don't want your pity,' he snarled, grabbing her elbow in a tight vice. 'And I'm sorry if you feel you've made a right fool of yourself.'

He began to march her across the kitchen.

Blaise was too stunned to even think of protesting.

'But I did try to warn you that you weren't quite getting the bargain you thought you were,' he continued, taking a detour into the living room to pick up the still-wet canvas, 'so you have only yourself to blame.'

He had her elbow lifted so high she almost had to stand on tiptoe to walk.

'But, Aidan,' she cried out as he marched her into the hall, 'I never thought that . . .' But then she realized he was looking straight ahead, to the front door, and so he couldn't be reading her lips.

She tried to dig her heels in, but he was too strong for her. The rug beneath her feet slipped and bunched up, and he gave her another strong yank. She tugged backwards as he put the canvas down to open the door, but still she couldn't break free.

He was going to throw her out, and there wasn't a damned thing she could do about it!

With the door open, he thrust her firmly outside. She stumbled onto the step, almost fell, righted herself and swung around.

'Aidan, oh, please, don't do this . . .'

But his head was turned away from her as he reached back into the hall to retrieve the canvas.

When he thrust it into her arms she was staring at him, tears running from her lovely blue eyes, her face a mask of misery.

'I never meant to hurt you,' she said forlornly, and saw his eyes widen.

His face tightened. Then he smiled grimly.

'Lady, you don't have the power to hurt me,' he lied viciously, and slammed the door in her face.

CHAPTER 14

Keira rose, a little apprehensively, as the secretary answered the discreet buzzer on her desk.

'Mr Knighton will see you now, Lady Penda,' she smiled, her made-up eyes frankly curious as she watched Keira enter her employer's office.

Keira remembered Martin Knighton from the time he'd handled her father's affairs, and the intervening years had added just a few touches of grey to his sandy hair. His blue eyes were as kindly looking as ever.

'Please, Lady Penda, take a seat.'

Keira did so, gratefully. Her legs were feeling just a little weak-kneed.

Martin retook his seat behind the small, cluttered desk and looked at her, silently questioning.

Keira took a rather deep breath, and began at the beginning. From Lucas's proposal of marriage — and why he'd made it — to the wedding, to Fane's arrival, Jennifer's continued disapproval and, finally, the fiasco of the missing will. Throughout it all, Martin remained quiet, only taking the odd note or two.

Finally, Keira fell silent.

Martin leaned back in his chair, his face still a picture of circumspection. 'And you say your husband told both yourself and your stepson what he intended the contents of his new will to be?'

'Yes. He wanted to leave a sum of money to me,' she quickly told him the amount and watched him write it down, 'and a certain piece of land.' Again she specified its exact boundaries, watching his eyebrows elevate slightly. It made her flush, and feel oddly defensive. 'We chose which parcel of land Lucas wanted to leave to the reserve very carefully. That's how I remember it so well.'

Martin nodded, still scribbling busily. 'Yes, yes, I imagine that was so.' Behind the deceptively kind blue eyes, Keira could feel his mind working like a buzz saw. It wasn't altogether a pleasant feeling. 'But, apart from your stepson, there were no other witnesses to this conversation?'

Keira shook her head.

'And the day before your husband's death, he definitely said that the missing solicitor,' he checked his notes, 'Colin Rattigan, was coming with the new will for him to sign?'

'Yes.'

'Do you know who the witnesses were?'

Keira blinked. She hadn't even given that a thought, but now her eyes sparkled with hope. 'Of course!' she said, breathing a sigh of relief. 'He must have asked somebody at the house to witness it. Bessie, perhaps . . .'

No, Bessie would have said something. But there were always the gardeners. It would have been simplicity itself for Lucas to get two of them together to witness the signing of the will. Most of the lads came on a daily basis from the surrounding villages. By now they must have heard the rumours going around about the missing will. Even if they might be feeling a little reluctant to come forward and actually *volunteer* some information, if she asked Sid to have a discreet word here and there, she'd be bound to discover who they were. 'I think I may be able to locate the witnesses,' she said at last. 'That will help, won't it?'

Martin nodded thoughtfully. 'And it's been over a week now, and nobody has been able to locate the missing will?'

'No,' Keira said ruefully. 'It's not in the house. We've practically done everything but strip the wallpaper off the walls. It's not at the Heronry, that's for sure.'

'And you say your stepson has made due enquiries of all possible outside agencies?'

Keira's lips twisted into a curiously painful, bitter smile. 'Oh yes. Believe me, if it was out there, Fane would have found it.'

Martin nodded with a rather knowing smile of his own. 'Quite so.' He had no doubt that the son had been quite frantic! 'What he told you about your husband dying intestate is correct. If you apply to the court and convince them that all due search has been made, all best efforts exerted in an attempt to find the will, and the said will is still not forthcoming, then the court will rule that Lucas Harwood died intestate. Now, as to the *exact* amount you, as the primary beneficiary, will receive — that's debatable. Had your husband had no living children or immediate family, of course you would almost certainly have received everything. As it is, I can confidently predict that you will easily be awarded at least half of—'

Keira held up her hand abruptly. 'You don't understand,' she interrupted firmly, her voice cool and confident and perfectly calm. It succeeded in silencing the solicitor at once. 'I want Lucas's last wishes to be carried out. I want the sum of money and the land he promised me, and nothing more.'

For a moment, Martin Knighton looked at her in well-concealed horror. He fiddled with his pen. His kindly blue eyes looked a shade less kindly. 'You do realize, of course, that you are legally entitled to so much more than that . . .'

'But I'm not morally entitled to it,' Keira pointed out quietly. 'Oh, yes, I know how pompous that sounds,' she said wryly as she watched even his poker face twitch in surprise. 'If my friend Jane were here, she'd tell me that my ridiculous and outdated sense of duty was getting the better of me again.' Keira smiled. Then her face became suddenly sombre. 'But I respected and trusted my husband. He never let me down, and I have no intention of letting him down now. So, I came here to ask you to do whatever it is you have to do to see to it that my husband's last will and testament is properly executed.'

Martin Knighton was an excellent judge of character, and he knew when it was possible to cajole a client and when it was not. He inclined his head. 'Very well. But in all probability it will take some time. If your stepchildren contest any legal actions we might propose, your husband's estate could be tied up in court for years.'

Keira winced, remembering Fane's bitter parting words to her. 'I want to avoid that at all costs,' she said quickly. 'Perhaps we can arrange a meeting at the Heronry with all the parties concerned? If we can just sit down and calmly and sensibly talk about it, I'm sure Jennifer and Fane will agree to whatever legal proposals are needed to see that everybody gets their share.'

Martin's lips twisted. 'I hope you're right.' But, where sums of millions of pounds were concerned, it had been his experience that people were not apt to be reasonable. 'If you could let me have the addresses of all the parties involved, I will write to them and ask them to attend a meeting at your home on . . .' He consulted his desk calendar, made a few calculations and said, 'An afternoon early next month? That will give me time to make some preliminary notes, find a few answers to some of the more complex legal questions, and set a few things in motion.'

Keira nodded, more relieved than she'd ever felt before, and got gratefully to her feet. 'That will be fine.'

Martin rose courteously to see her out. An interesting woman, Lady Penda. Curiously . . . noble. It was an odd word to use in this modern day and age, but it seemed to fit her. Too bad. He could have made her a fortune.

* * *

Blaise absently stroked Keats's head, only half hearing the satisfied rumbling purr rising up from the vicinity of her lap. Her fingers curled around the silky ears and tickled the chin almost of their own accord.

For her mind was miles away from the task of petting her beloved cat.

It was firmly on Aidan Shaw.

Blaise had stumbled from his cottage in a daze, the canvas, which moments earlier had seemed so important, clutched, forgotten, in her hand.

She'd felt oddly disjointed as she'd walked the short distance to her own cottage. Her legs had felt rubberized, and, looking back on those few awful minutes, she could only be thankful that she hadn't met up with a villager intent on a chat and a get-together.

Even now, Blaise was no fit company.

The cat on her lap mewed in bliss and stretched, her claws pumping Blaise's leg. Even to the four-inoculations-at-once Blaise was insensible.

She still couldn't figure out what had gone wrong.

Well, she knew what was *wrong*. But not how it had got to be that way so quickly, and without her ever being aware of it. Aidan didn't trust her.

Blaise shuddered as she remembered his hand on her arm, the grim anger on his face as he'd hauled her out of his home. Even now, a day later, she could still feel the imprint of his strong fingers on her flesh.

Aidan — strong but gentle Aidan — had never been quite so rough with her before.

But even then, a small voice reminded her, he hadn't actually *hurt* her. At least, not physically.

Being ejected from his home and his life, however, had been the cause of more mental anguish than she'd ever thought it possible for one person to bear.

Blaise heaved a sigh, making the grey she-cat on her lap look up at her with curious green eyes.

Blaise, too, looked up, as a shadow passed the window at the end of the garden, but it was only the baker's wife off to do the church. The wreaths of holly were obviously giving her trouble, because she paused to wince and pull the sleeve of her heavy coat a little further over her wrists.

Christmas is coming, Blaise thought with a start.

And then, rather woefully, she wondered what she was going to do with it. On her own. Before, she'd had her mother. Despite her illness, Mary Clayton had loved mistletoe and mince pies, carols coming from the radio kept constantly by her bedside, and the gaudy, colourful hangings Blaise had habitually hung up in her bedroom.

Before yesterday, Blaise had confidently expected to spend this Christmas with Aidan.

Even though they'd known each other only a couple of months, she realized now how perfectly natural it had seemed to take their perpetual togetherness for granted.

Just a day ago she would have sworn they were meant for each other. That a kindly fate had guided her to Upper Rousham. That the man of her dreams, the man of her destiny, had been waiting here for her.

And she still thought it.

Suddenly she stopped stroking the cat's head.

What had really changed?

Had she stopped loving him?

Had she hell!

Had she stopped wanting him?

Even the thought of touching his bare skin, of unbuttoning his warm checked shirt and running her fingers across the wide expanse of his muscled chest had her fingertips tingling in pleasurable anticipation and her insides flooding with honeyed warmth.

Had she stopped needing him?

She gave a short bark of laughter. Miserably contemplating a Christmas without him answered that question. She needed him like a desert traveller needed an oasis.

Keats heaved a heavy sigh, but curled her nose into her tail and began to doze.

Blaise continued to sit and stare out of the window.

Nothing in *her* had changed. Nothing *for* her had changed.

The only difference that she could see lay in increased knowledge. Now she knew he was deaf. Before, she hadn't. And now she knew that Aidan believed it was all over between them just because of it.

Blaise frowned.

She could understand why he hadn't wanted to broadcast his personal life to the village. She could understand why he had opted for the life he had. She could understand why he was so shy, so reclusive, so . . . wonderful.

But she couldn't understand why it should now all be over, just because she'd unearthed his secret. What difference did it make?

She couldn't see one.

But Aidan obviously could.

What?

She closed her eyes, so tired she could feel herself wilting. She hadn't slept, or eaten, since Aidan's outburst. What had made him so angry?

She replayed the scene over and over again. It wasn't easy — shock had blanked out great portions of her memory — but one thing became very clear. He hadn't wanted her pity.

Blaise frowned at that sudden realization. Had she ever felt pity?

No.

She could remember feeling like a right chump, because she hadn't realized before that he had no hearing. And she remembered feeling so upset because of all the things she might inadvertently have done that would have made life more difficult for him. The times she'd talked when he couldn't see her lips. The way she'd all but dragged him to the pub — which must have been something of an ordeal for him.

And she remembered thinking how much she loved him. For his courage and bravery. For the way he'd met the challenges of his disability and so magnificently overcome them.

She could remember feeling proud of him.

But pity?

Blaise shook her head, her frown turning to a scowl. No. Never pity. Who could pity Aidan? The man was like a force of nature.

So just what was his problem?

And then, like a blast of cold air, she remembered something else. The fear in his eyes.

Fear. Did he think she was going to blazon his secret all over the village? Take out an advertisement in the local paper?

Blaise gave a growl of anger, and Keats smartly jumped off her lap. Freed of the warm ball on her lap, Blaise leapt to her feet and began to pace.

The grey cat crept to the fire and curled up, her wary green eyes watching her mistress pace up and down.

Blaise sighed deeply. No, she couldn't believe Aidan thought so little of her. She might not be the brightest person around, but she knew when a man respected her.

But then, she'd also thought Aidan loved her.

No. She shook her head. She couldn't deal with *that* now. One thing at a time.

Why the fear in his eyes? She knew that there must have been a bit of talk in the village — for surely most people by now had guessed about his disability? And it was only human nature that people would discuss it behind his back. But it would soon have died down. And she knew these people now. They were kind-hearted and generous-natured.

No. It couldn't only be that which bothered him.

He didn't want pity. And he was afraid. What *had* he been thinking when he'd taken her by the arm and thrust her from his house?

And then, like a gauzy curtain suddenly lifting, Blaise understood.

And she stopped dead, threw back her head and let rip with a growl of sheer rage.

She stormed to the door and, oblivious of the freezing cold fog, left her coat hanging in the hall and slammed the door behind her.

Keats leapt to the windowsill and watched her march down the path. The cat's ears flattened and she gave a meow of encouragement.

Blaise marched off grimly down the pavement. Old Mrs Grimmet, shuffling up the lane, holding onto the walls for guidance and support in the thick fog, started as a golden-headed figure stormed past her.

'Oh, hello, dear,' she called.

'Hello, Mrs Grimmet,' Blaise said through clenched teeth, and was quickly swallowed up in the white haze.

The old lady watched her go, noticing the tense young shoulders coupled with the arm-throwing march, and suddenly grinned. Gone to give that Aidan Shaw a good talking-to, she'd be bound. Old Mrs Grimmet nodded. About time too. That man needed a good woman to take him in hand.

She frowned. It was obvious the artist lady was made for him. She, and all the other ladies of the village, had watched their romance with nothing but growing fondness and approval.

Something had obviously provoked an argument between them, though. Mrs Grimmet remembered her barneys with Cyril, her husband of the last sixty-two years, and smiled gently. There was nothing like a good argument followed by a passionate reconciliation to keep life spiced up and interesting.

As the no-nonsense tap-tapping of Blaise's footsteps echoed eerily up the street the old woman wondered if she should warn the artist lady that Aidan was deaf. She might not have realized it yet. No, perhaps not. It was none of her business, after all.

Blaise's determined march began to falter as she was forced to peer through the fog to check that she was at the right cottage. Then she saw the outline of the little cherry tree Aidan had planted last spring, and nodded.

Right, then.

She strode to the door, pondered politely knocking, then growled again. Why should she knock? This was *her* home too, damn it. In every way that mattered. She thrust open the door, slammed it behind her, and then laughed. Rather grimly. Of course, he couldn't hear her grand-slam entrance. Just as he wouldn't have heard her knocking.

But she would make her presence felt in other ways. Yes indeedy.

Blaise thrust open the kitchen door, mouth open, ready to blaze away with all guns.

It was empty.

Undeterred, she swivelled and turned to the living-room door, which was slightly ajar, and pushed it open.

He must have caught the movement in his peripheral vision, for he turned his head. From his position on the sofa in front of the fire, their eyes met.

Aidan leapt lithely to his feet. The suppleness and economy of his powerful grace reminded Blaise of a springing wolf, and she felt a swift pang of desire lance through her, turning every atom of her being into quivering alertness. Beneath her blouse, she could feel her nipples begin to throb.

'What the hell do you want?' he snarled.

Not the most auspicious of greetings, but then she wasn't there to be courted with chocolates and flowers.

Blaise slammed the living-room door behind her, just because she felt like it.

She saw his eyes follow the savage movement of the door, and then felt her throat contract with emotion as his eyes returned to hers. They were such beautiful eyes. Green and brown and . . .

Stop that, she thought savagely. First things first.

She marched up to him, swung her hand back, pivoted on her toes and thrust herself forward with every ounce of strength in her. She swivelled her arm around, suddenly — of all ridiculous things — remembering her games teacher's instructions for throwing the discus.

Blaise had never been good at throwing the discus, but right now the remembered instructions on how to get the maximum whiplash effect came in very handy.

Her open palm connected with his cheek with a very satisfying 'thwack'.

'Ouch!' Blaise yelped, her hand tingling as if she'd just submerged it in ice water.

Aidan's head whipped back.

She began to hop on one foot, shaking her hand like a dog shook its head after being stung on the nose by a wasp.

Aidan turned back to look at her. His eyes were wide with surprise. On his reddening cheek, a pale hand print stood out in stark relief.

'Ouch, bloody hell, that *hurt*,' Blaise yipped.

Aidan blinked. 'I dare say it did,' he muttered, and lifted his hand to touch his own smarting cheek. He rubbed it, more thoughtfully than anything else.

Blaise glared at him balefully. 'I hope your teeth are loose!' she snarled.

Aidan blinked. Again.

'I don't think so.'

'Pity. I'll have to try a clenched fist next time.'

Aidan continued to stare at her blankly, then his stunned surprise started turning to anger. 'Just what the hell is all this about? What's got into you?' he demanded.

Blaise's mouth fell open. 'What's got into me?' she squeaked. 'What's got *into me*?'

She barely knew where to start.

'You . . . you . . . stupid . . . insulting . . . pig-headed . . . oooh!' She pushed him with all her might, her two hands connecting solidly with his chest, overbalancing him. She watched his arms windmill helplessly as he fell back on the sofa, and smiled with happy anticipation. That was better.

She stood over him, arms akimbo, watching with satisfaction as his wide eyes turned to her lips. Good. She wanted him to catch every last syllable of this.

'I come to this village, still grieving for my mother, alone and friendless. And I meet the man I've been searching for, without even realizing it, for all of my life. Kind. Gentle. Handsome. I came to start a career and found not only artistic inspiration but a man I can share the rest of my life with. A man who touches horses like I touch paints to canvas. A man who's found his niche in life and has it all ready and prepared for me. A man I love as much as I am capable. A man who has only to touch me to fill me. A man who has only to caress me to set me on fire. A man I would be honoured and privileged and proud to call my own. And what happens?'

She paused for breath, very much aware of the sudden leap of hope and love in his eyes. And, although it gave her courage to continue, it also fuelled her anger.

'Well?' she demanded. 'What happens? I find out he's deaf, that's what.'

She saw his eyes flicker, and growled. 'Yes, I thought so. And what does this wonderful man do when I discover what he's been trying so hard to keep from me? Does he rely on me to carry on loving him? Does he honour me by believing in me? No. He assumes I won't want him anymore. He believes I'll suddenly stop loving him. He takes it for granted that I'm a shallow, petty-minded, bigoted, worthless lump of a human being and chucks me out of his home like unwanted rubbish.'

'Now wait . . .'

'And so, with typical male *stupidity*,' Blaise huffed, 'he thinks to himself, Right. Before she can tell me to take a hike, I'll get rid of *her*. Oh, very clever, Aidan,' she snarled. 'Very macho. It didn't occur to you that you were ripping my guts out, did it?'

Aidan struggled to get to his feet, but she quickly pushed him back again, launching herself onto his lap, her knees in his stomach.

She heard his breath leave him in a painful 'whoomph' and pressed him against the backrest of the sofa, her hands on his shoulders, bringing her face to within inches of his. He smelt of soap and leather, very faintly of horses, of the earthy land, and of another, wholly male scent that was all Aidan. She took a deep breath through her nose, and sighed.

'Well, I've got news for you, Aidan Shaw,' she said, reluctantly dragging her thoughts back to the task at hand, her blue eyes blazing like Ceylon sapphires. 'If you think you can insult me in that way and get away with it, you'd better think again. If you think you can just throw my love back in my face and tell me to peddle it somewhere else, you don't know me as well as you thought. And if you thought you were going to be able to put me off with insults and rejection, and that I'd just crawl away like a dog with my tail between my legs, I think it's about time you learned differently.'

Her palms, warmed by his body heat through the thick plaid shirt, suddenly curled into the material, and with a dramatic wrench she pulled her wrists apart.

Unfortunately, the buttons didn't fly apart to reveal his manly chest as they always did in the films. Instead the shirt just ripped a little at the shoulder seams.

Blaise snarled, and quickly attacked the buttons, undoing them as if she hated them (which she did) and looking as if she was demented to get her hands on his flesh (which she was).

'Blaise, darling, I never meant—'

'Shut up!' Blaise yelled at him, but there was the sunshine of laughter in her eyes now.

His shirt unbuttoned at last, she leaned forward and bit one nipple. Hard.

He jerked underneath her, his arms raising to press gently against her taut shoulder blades as she released her teeth.

'Blaise . . .'

'Shut up.'

She thrust the shirt aside and ran her tongue across the undulating line of his muscles to the other nipple. There she laved it lovingly, lavishly, pressing the very tip of her tongue into the button of flesh, burrowing in like a mole for the winter.

Aidan groaned. His big body shuddered and his hands spasmed against her back. His head lolled back helplessly against the sofa. His throat, stretched taut, made too tempting a target.

Blaise lifted her head and kissed his Adam's apple into submission, while he swallowed hard and moaned softly through his parted lips.

Now for the rest of him.

She thrust her hands down between them and attacked his belt buckle. Aidan moaned as her knuckles brushed clumsily against the bulging hardness of his manhood.

'Blaise, you're driving me crazy.'

'Shut up.'

'Let me help . . .' He lifted his buttocks, thrusting his jeans past his thighs.

'Thanks,' Blaise muttered. 'Now shut up.'

She slithered down his body, tugging off his boots and jeans, running her hands up his leg, digging her fingers into his calf muscle and making him yip, just as a reminder that she was still as mad as a hornet at him.

Then she leaned forward and bit his inner thigh. Gently. She slipped her fingers into the waistband of his boxers and slid them down, pressing her lips against him, moving higher, then a little higher, her hands on his knees, firmly thrusting them apart.

Aidan bucked on the sofa, his back arching off the cushions, his mouth falling open in a very satisfying groan of ecstasy as Blaise took one silky ball of flesh into her mouth. It felt like silk against her lips and she sucked hard, loving the way his breath caught and then moaned out of him, like a man being tortured.

By her side she saw his hands curl, white-knuckled, around the sofa's armrest.

And she smiled. Not easy, given the circumstances, but she managed it.

Now Mr Aidan high-and-mighty Shaw would see who he thought he could just chuck out of his life.

Blaise stood, stripping herself in record time.

Aidan's dazed eyes feathered open just in time to see her gloriously naked, silhouetted in gold against the flames of the fire.

Her skin was pale as milk, the hair on her head and at the junction of her thighs a warm barley-gold.

'Blaise, you're beautiful.'

'Shut up. No, wait, say that again.'

Aidan didn't smile. His eyes were deadly earnest. 'Blaise, you're beautiful. I love you. Forgive me.'

Blaise swallowed hard. Her mouth went suddenly dry.

'Of course I forgive you, you big oaf,' she managed to croak, and then moved to him, her hands tender on his bare skin as she moved herself up his body. Their skin rubbed together like satins from the same bolt of cloth. Her breath feathered over his face as she positioned herself over him. Their eyes met, like sky and earth. Part of one planet.

'I love you so much.'

'Oh, Aidan. I know you do. And I love you too. Believe it. Oh, please, *please,* never doubt it.'

Aidan's strong hands went tenderly around her waist, pulling her closer, his eyes as steady as rock.

'I won't,' he whispered, 'not ever again. I swear it.' The words were as slightly slurred and as oddly pronounced as ever. And the most beautiful sounds Blaise had ever heard in her life or would ever hear again.

Tears swamped her eyes, then overflowed, and she quickly leant forward to kiss him. Her lips tasted of the salt in her tears, and his arms tightened around her.

'I'm sorry,' he whispered wretchedly. 'I never meant to make you cry.'

Blaise lifted her head abruptly. 'Shut up!' she snarled, but somehow the command had lost some of its bite. Then, with a swiftness that took his breath away, she impaled herself on him, her head thrown back in a fierce growl.

Her inner muscles welcomed him with a clenching joy that had him screaming a great shout that echoed around the room, filling her ears with sweet sound and his own ears with triumphant vibration.

'Oh, Aidan,' she said, her thighs gripping his, her flesh quivering.

'Shut up,' Aidan whispered, and, taking her in his strong arms, he lowered her to the rug in front of the fire, still deep inside her, and pushed ever deeper into her with one powerful surge.

Blaise felt the marvellous weight of him on top of her, and gave a brief cry as he filled her to the limits of ecstasy. She felt the brush of his hair on her face and opened her eyes to gaze deeply into his.

Her legs curled around his back, keeping him a passionate prisoner, locked inside her. She didn't think, in that moment, that she would ever be persuaded to let him go.

Her hands raked across his broad shoulders in lustful punishment as he withdrew, then clutched him in appeasement as he surged into her again. She felt herself contract and expand around him as he throbbed like iron velvet deep inside her.

Blaise could feel, hear and see every detail.

She could feel the individual tufts of lambswool in the rug against her back, shoulders, buttocks and thighs. She could feel the sweat-slicked glide of their flesh wherever it touched. She could feel the slightest touch of his lock of dark hair whenever it brushed against her own forehead.

She could hear the crackle of the fire as the resin in a piece of wood hit the bare flame. She could hear a clock ticking somewhere in the room. Outside, she could the drip, drip, drip of a leaky piece of guttering. She could hear every harsh breath he took. It seemed to affect her own breathing, until her own sighing, moaning breaths became co-ordinated with his.

And she could see him. The way the green flecks in his hazel eyes blazed when he pushed into her and then banked when he withdrew. She could see the taut muscle in the planes of his cheeks clench as he moved atop her. Looking in his eyes, she could see her own soul.

This man was in her.

Of her.

'Aidan,' she said, just to hear the sound of his name on her lips.

Aidan didn't need to take his eyes from the blue depths of her own to know she'd said his name. He could hear it. In his head. In his heart.

Where it mattered.

A starburst of heat made him tremble, and he felt his body begin to break apart.

Blaise felt her very womanhood enter the decreasing spiral into the final, shattering climax of passion.

Her fingers dug into his back, becoming warm with his lifeblood. She gave a great, feminine call of triumph as she felt his strong, masterful body erupt in the weakening spill of desire.

Her own body shattered into myriad pieces of sensitized light that radiated out of her being. The ecstasy was so great that for a bare instant of time she thought it must kill her.

And she wouldn't have cared.

Then she felt his weight collapsing upon her, warming her, keeping her whole. She felt her own thrashing legs fall apart in exhausted, satisfied defeat. Her thundering heart calmed under the reassurance of his own loud beats. His head fell to her shoulder, his hair silky against her chin and cheek.

Silence.

Outside, the fog began to lift. A weak sun trickled lemon light onto the naked, entwined lovers.

The clock continued to tick ponderously.

Eventually, reluctantly, Blaise finally stirred.

Aidan bent his elbows and lifted himself to look down at her. She looked so fragile and crushable beneath him that he made a sound of apology and moved to lift himself from her.

But her hands quickly clutched his shoulders. 'No. Don't leave me.'

Aidan smiled, and relaxed a little, but was careful to keep most of his upper weight on his bent elbows.

'I won't leave you,' he said. 'Not ever again.'

Blaise nodded. 'You'd better not. Or next time I *will* use my clenched fists!'

Aidan rubbed his cheek, surprised to find that it *was*, in fact, still a little tender.

'In that case . . .' he said, his voice full of laughter and just a touch of anxiety, 'perhaps you'd better marry me? I wouldn't want you to get mad at me again.'

As her eyes widened, he added hastily, 'Besides, now you've had your wicked way with me for a second time, you have to make an honest man of me. I can see this lovemaking of ours becoming a habit.'

Blaise began to laugh.

An honest man?

'Well . . . I suppose I shall have to, then,' she said, heaving a long-suffering sigh. 'After all, *some* poor woman will have to take you on . . . Ooh! That tickles. Aidan. Stop it . . . *stop it*!'

CHAPTER 15

'So, what's next on the agenda?' Blaise asked cheerfully, looking out across the rich ploughed fields. By her side, Aidan took a deep breath of the crisp, frosty air, his eyes narrowed against the pale sunlight as he looked out across the rolling acres.

'The next thing we do is the spring chain harrowing,' he mused, in his mind's eye already harnessing the horses to the wide chains.

'Chain harrowing?' Blaise looked up at him questioningly. Huddled into her coat, her toes warm and snug in her boots, she felt as happy as a skylark in summer. Her heart was singing — not a high alto, just a happy, contented little hum. Her eyes sparkled.

All was right with her world.

'Hmm. The winter frosts help break down the earth, but it needs a little help. Come March, if it's dry enough, I'll team up two horses, attach them to a chain harrow and go over it. It breaks the soil down into a finer consistency, just right for sowing. It's lighter work than ploughing.'

'So the horses won't mind?'

Aidan suddenly laughed. 'The horses don't mind working, sweetheart. If they're cared for and kept in good hard condition.'

'Hard condition?'

Blaise was fascinated by this new language she was learning. After all, Aidan was going to be her husband come May — the month they'd both settled on as their ideal time to marry. And she wanted to learn everything about the way he lived his life.

In her turn, she would teach him how to paint. 'Hmm. By hard condition I mean that their hides, or their skins, if you prefer, need to be kept good and hard, so that when they sweat the harness doesn't rub them sore. It's the same sort of thing with men who do manual work. The skin on their hands and feet becomes toughened and conditioned.'

Blaise nodded thoughtfully. 'I never thought that the same thing might apply to horses.'

'Well, it does.' He smiled indulgently.

'It all sounds so . . . foreign to me.'

Aidan smiled understandingly. He loved watching her face — the way it moved when she talked. 'Don't worry. It's not as complicated as it sounds. It's basically good common sense. Like bringing out buckets of water when you're turning the lucerne.'

Blaise turned a beady eye on him. 'You're doing this on purpose,' she accused, and gave him a playful punch in the ribs. 'What's lucerne, why does it have to be turned, and why do you need plenty of buckets of water?'

Aidan grinned. 'Lucerne is a crop, like hay. It's grown green and lush in the summertime and then cut, to preserve its oil. Once it's been in the field for some time, the sun dries the top of it but underneath it's still green. So it needs to be turned with a swathe turner — or side-delivery rake, if you want to get technical. And, because it's summer, the horses sweat a lot and need to drink a lot. So you have to make sure they get plenty to drink. If there isn't water available on site — and there usually isn't . . .'

'You have to give them buckets of water,' Blaise finished for him, grinning from ear to ear.

'See? What's so hard to understand about that?'

'Nothing. So all you do is make hay when the going gets good?' she asked archly, giving him a mischievously twinkling look.

'And plant potatoes in April, and spring drilling — planting barley and corn to you city-slickers — and then digging up the potatoes, and then making the hayricks with the help of a hay sweep, and fitting the horses with a breechen so they can walk backwards, and then harvesting the corn, which needs three horses and a bogey, and—'

'Bogey?'

'Making sure the binder isn't stretched too tight, or it'll make life very difficult indeed. Then there's the wagons that need maintaining, and the thatching I have to do to keep the final haystacks weatherproof, and then, in the autumn, there's the hazel wood I have to cut to use as pins, and then, after all that, we're back to square one and it's ploughing time again.'

'Is that *all* you have to do?' she asked, trying her best to look scandalized.

'Well, then there's the agricultural shows — Keira likes me to bring home the ribbons and cups if I can; it reflects well on both the home farm and the nature reserve. Then there's the local charity events . . . It's amazing how much a well-turned-out carthorse and a pound-a-ride buggy trip can accumulate in a day. And then of course there's the—'

Blaise, given no other choice, stood on tiptoe and kissed him hard. As a way to shut a man up, it had its compensations.

Aidan leaned against the stile, his hands pulling her hard against him, the kiss deepening.

When Blaise finally turned away, her eyes were periwinkle-blue and quite satisfied.

'Now, suppose I tell you all about painting? Most people think it's a case of dabbing oils on canvas, but there's a whole lot more to it than that. The techniques are quite fascinating, and you have to know a fair bit about chemistry and . . .'

* * *

Patrick Goulder put the last of his clean shirts into the suitcase propped open on his bed and then looked up as he heard the bedroom door whisper open. He was just in time to see the appalled look in his wife's eyes disappear behind a hard smile.

'Pat.' Jennifer's hands clung to the door handle. 'I didn't know you had a trip coming up. Where are you off to now? Glastonbury, to see if all those religious—'

'I'm not going on a field trip,' Patrick interrupted quietly, and reached behind him to the open drawer to pull out a third pair of trousers. 'I'm leaving you.'

The blunt, stark words sounded very strange in the familiarity of her bedroom.

Jennifer felt her throat tighten and go painfully dry.

She licked her lips nervously. 'I see.' The words, she was astounded to realize, came out quite clearly and calmly. 'Do you mind telling me why?'

Her husband glanced up, his normally placid face wearing a look of total surprise. 'Oh, come on, Jen. Are you honestly trying to tell me you don't know why?'

Jennifer's hands tightened on the door handle. She opened her mouth, then closed it again, since her brain refused to come up with any words in self-defence.

Patrick silently resumed his inexorable packing.

Jennifer blinked, hopelessly grappling to find some sort of anchor. This was just too sudden. She didn't know what to make of it.

She'd met her husband of the last nine years when she was chairing an Oxford charity committee. Patrick had been ideal husband material — older than her, but not too much, imminently respectable, very intelligent. Someone her father would approve of, that society and her circle of friends would approve of. Reasonably good-looking, with reasonably good prospects. And, as time had passed, she'd found that she actually *liked* him too. Very much, in fact. There was a kindness, a quiet gentleness about Patrick that had always been missing in her life. Her marriage, or so she'd always thought, was a successful one. True, there were no children yet, but there was plenty of time . . .

Except suddenly there wasn't.

'Patrick,' she said quietly, 'I don't want you to go.'

Her husband looked at her again, not in surprise this time, but more in genuine curiosity. For a long, long moment his eyes searched her face questioningly, and then he sighed.

'No,' he said, his voice a defeated, flat monotone. 'I think you honestly don't.'

But he reached behind him to transfer his shaving things into the small toiletries bag resting on the bed. His side of the bed, Jennifer noticed with a pang. The side he always slept on.

'Pat,' she said appealingly, moving further into the room.

She was dressed as exquisitely as always, in a cream two-piece suit with a chocolate-brown blouse. Her hair was caught up in an elegant chignon and her make-up was, as ever, perfectly applied.

Patrick watched her approach with wary but firm eyes.

'Pat, what's this all about?' she wheedled, beginning to feel the first pangs of real fear. Even to her own ears, the question sounded pitiful.

Patrick sighed. Deeply. 'You know what it's about. This obsession with money. Or with your father's money, to be more precise. Not to mention this ridiculous feud with Keira Harwood.'

'Don't call her that,' she flashed immediately. 'Fane always calls her Keira Westcombe, and so do I. You know she only married Father for his money. She was no wife to him.'

Patrick quickly straightened up, and winced as he did so.

His back's playing him up again, Jennifer thought, and wondered where his back-rub cream was.

'Your father married her because you left him no other option,' Patrick said bluntly, making *her* wince. 'If you hadn't gone ahead with that ugly scheme of yours to get power of attorney, he'd never have proposed to Keira in the first place.

But what really matters, or what *should* matter, is that he wanted Keira to have that land. He approved of the nature reserve, and, incidentally, just in case you're interested, so do I.'

Jennifer simply stared at him in absolute astonishment. 'You never said anything about that before,' she gasped accusingly.

Patrick smiled wryly. 'You never asked me, Jen,' he said, and there was something in the quiet chiding of his voice that made her heart suddenly begin to ache. It was an astonishing feeling. One that was utterly new to her.

'So you're taking her side?' she demanded, a red flush quickly passing over her face, then just as quickly disappearing, leaving her chalk-white.

Patrick felt his resolve weaken, and quickly reached for his socks. 'I'm not on her side,' he denied wearily. 'Nor am I on yours. For once in my life, I'm on *my* side.'

Jennifer literally gaped at him. This didn't sound like her Pat at all. What the hell was going on?

'What do you mean by that?' she asked in an appalled whisper, not at all sure that she wanted to know.

Patrick put the last of his things into the suitcase and snapped it shut. The finality of the sound made her wince. 'I mean that I'm tired of not being enough for you, Jen,' he said grimly. 'I'm only a don, but you want me to be dean. I'm not rich enough for you. I can't provide you with the big country estate you think is your right, so you have to take it from your father's wife. I just don't measure up.

'Well, I'm tired of it, Jen. I'm tired of your obsession with your father, and his money, and his last wife. And this latest stunt of yours is the final straw. Do you think that I don't know that you and that damned Rattigan man are in some sort of cahoots? He, at least, has had the good sense to disappear before things get too hot.

'Haven't you understood yet that you might have gone too far, Jennifer? This time you've left yourself wide open to a possible criminal prosecution. You've lost all sense of reality, and I want out. And I'm getting out.'

He hoisted the suitcase off the bed as Jennifer stared at him in utter amazement.

'And I'm going to stay out, Jen,' he said quietly, 'until you get your act together. I want a wife, a partner, a friend, a lover. Not an embittered, jealous, discontented spouse.'

As he walked towards her she straightened expectantly, but he merely passed her as she stood, mutely shocked and swaying in the doorway, and didn't give her so much as a single backward glance.

* * *

Aidan lifted the top strand of barbed wire and put his boot on the bottom one. Blaise lithely climbed through the gap, deftly avoiding snagging her coat.

Once she was through, Aidan pressed down the top strand and, with careless bravado, stepped his long legs over it. Blaise winced, but was relieved to see him come through undamaged.

He caught her look and grinned. 'Don't worry. For all the years I've been doing that, I've never yet come a cropper.'

Blaise held out her hand. 'Ah, but I've got a vested interest now, remember?' She moved towards him and saucily cupped him in her hand, loving the way he drew in his breath in a ragged gasp. 'And I don't want damaged wedding goods come May.'

'Wretch,' Aidan said thickly, and reached to cup her breast in his hand in retaliation. Even through the layers of clothing separating them, they both felt her breast harden and swell against his touch.

'Enough of this,' Blaise said. 'Or we'll both be running to get back to the privacy of the cottage. And won't that give our neighbours something to talk about?'

Aidan grinned. 'Speaking of which, we'll have to have a word with the vicar. Sort out a definite date, and get the wedding banns announced.'

Blaise sighed. 'I didn't know that was still done.'

Aidan grinned. 'In Upper Rousham it is.'

They were heading for the stones. They were never far away, those Penda Stones, and there were not many places on Westcombe land where you could look about you and not see their brooding presence somewhere in the distance.

As they started up the gentle slope that would bring them to the top of the field that looked directly down onto the megalithic monument, Blaise glanced quickly towards a small spinney — barely more than a few walnut trees — just off to their right.

Aidan noticed her sudden frown immediately. 'What's up?'

'I thought I heard something,' she said, then quickly glanced at him, her eyes anxious as she realized how insensitive that might sound.

Aidan understood her fear in a moment, and laughed. 'Don't be so daft. You are *allowed* to hear things, you know! Just because I can't doesn't mean I don't want you to tell me all about it. I want to know what hearing things means to you. I want to know everything about you . . .'

Blaise immediately understood what he was trying to say. She, too, felt just the same. She wanted to crawl under his skin and absorb every minute detail of him. 'Is that why you took up farming? Because you didn't need your hearing to do it?'

Aidan laughed. 'There are lots of jobs that don't include the need to hear things, sweetheart. No, I took up farming because when I was just a lad of six or so, my mother and I moved onto a Yorkshire farm. She was housekeeper-cook there, and the farmer was one of those die-hards who'd never converted to tractors after the war.

'His sons had all been raised as horse men, and so, when I was constantly about underfoot, it was just a natural progression that he and they taught me how to handle the horses too. And I loved it. I loved the life, even getting up at the crack of dawn on a bitter Yorkshire winter morning to do the mucking out.'

'I'm surprised you managed to find another job with horses,' Blaise mused out loud. 'I dare say there aren't many places that still farm with draughts. I take it that there wasn't enough room for you to stay on at the farm in Yorkshire when you left school? That you had to leave?'

Aidan, for the first time since she'd known him, looked away from her. If she spoke now, she knew he wouldn't know. It was such an unusual thing for him to do that she openly frowned.

And then she heard the sound again. This time she was sure of it. It was the unmistakable sound of someone crying. A woman.

She touched Aidan's arm. He turned, his mouth already open to tell her something, something important, but she spoke before he had the chance.

'Aidan, I think there's someone in trouble up there.' She nodded towards the spinney.

Aidan frowned, then quickly set off up the hill. Aware that she might have given him the wrong impression, Blaise broke out into a run to catch him up. But by the time she'd done so they were already at the first tree, and Aidan stopped so suddenly that Blaise cannoned into the back of him.

Still trying to get her breath back, Blaise looked around his broad shoulder and saw what he had seen.

There, on the wet and cold grass, her back pressed against the broad trunk of a walnut tree, sat Keira, hugging her knees and sobbing.

Hard.

Her nose ran, and she quickly reached into her coat to pull free a handkerchief. Although she must have been aware of their presence, she didn't look up, or speak. She was probably incapable of speaking, Blaise thought.

These were no pretty little tears. They were shoulder-heaving, stomach-wrenching sobs.

Aidan looked at Blaise helplessly, and Blaise gave a slight movement of her head that could have meant anything but which he understood immediately. She moved slowly forward, bending down on the wet grass and moving across to take the other woman gently by the shoulders.

Keira made a superhuman effort to stem the tears, failed, and leaned forward to sob against Blaise's shoulder.

Gradually, after a while, the sobs subsided.

Keira leaned back against the trunk, mopped her face, and gave Blaise a rather wan smile.

'Sorry about that. I didn't mean to interrupt your walk.'

Blaise smiled. 'You didn't. I wasn't sure . . . I mean, we didn't know if we should . . . interfere.'

Keira gave a ragged breath and shrugged her shoulders. 'It's all right. I just needed a good cry, that's all, and now I've had one. So. That's that.'

She put her hands behind her and pushed up, getting rather unsteadily to her feet. Her face was still pale and tear-ravaged, but Aidan was relieved to see that the desperate look was beginning to fade from her eyes.

For all the years he'd worked for Keira, he'd never seen her in such a state.

They had started off, that first year, very much as employer and employee. But as time had progressed, and Aidan had begun to realize that she'd meant what she'd said at their initial interview — that she had no intention of interfering with his running of her home farm — their relationship had mellowed into one of mutual respect, liking and finally, inevitably, a friendship.

Aidan had always admired the way she'd turned her estates into such a financial success as well as a worthwhile enterprise. He respected her dedication and approved of her goals. And, besides all that, he *liked* her. There was nothing of the landed gentry about her. Nothing superior. She kept her warm heart well hidden, but it was obvious to anyone who knew where to look for it. In short, he'd come to understand her.

Now, he nodded across towards the stones. 'You often come here, I've noticed.'

Keira smiled. It was still a little wobbly, but it was at least genuine. 'I know. My father spoiled me rotten.' She laughed self-deprecatingly. 'He told me tales as a little girl about how the stones had been built for the first Westcombe princess by King Penda. When I was little, I used to bring all my friends from school here and we'd play our games. Knights of old, with wooden swords and all that. And we girls were damsels in distress, naturally, being sacrificed to imaginary dragons.

'It's not surprising that I grew up thinking of them,' she looked at the ancient ring of stones thoughtfully, 'as my private property. Of course they're not,' she added hastily. 'They belong to the nation. But they are under my stewardship, and even now, sometimes I still feel as if they talk to me. Comfort me. Give me a proper perspective on things . . .' Her voice faltered. 'That's what I was doing this morning.'

Blaise and Aidan exchanged glances. The last thing they wanted to do was intrude, but if Keira needed someone to talk to . . .

Blaise had heard only yesterday about the rumours circulating that her husband's will had gone missing. It was common knowledge that all the staff at the big house had been turning it upside-down trying to find it without, apparently, any success. No doubt the legal wrangle that must be causing was enough to fray anybody's nerves.

Keira caught the sympathetic look and smiled wryly. 'Sorry. I'm being a wimp. It's just that . . . things are getting me down a bit.' She glanced up at her horse man and realized that she was being rather selfish. 'Aidan, this affects you too, in a way, so you have a right to know.' Blaise noticed that Keira looked at him carefully as she spoke.

With a jolt, Blaise suddenly realized that Keira knew all about his deafness. And then, just as suddenly, she relaxed. Of course, Aidan would have told her about it when he first applied for the job as her head horse man. It would be just like him to have been scrupulously honest about it. And Keira obviously hadn't cared.

It was at that moment that her respect for Lady Penda slid unobtrusively into the beginnings of a valued friendship.

'It's about Lucas's land,' Keira said, forcing her voice to come out calm and clear. 'You remember I told you some time ago about Lucas donating that patch of land near the lower forty?'

Aidan nodded, curious. Unlike Blaise, he hadn't heard the rumours about the crisis up at the big house.

'I know you had ideas about setting up an experimental East Anglia-style farming regime out there . . .' Keira's voice trailed off for a moment, and then she shrugged. 'I, too, was thinking along the same lines. Butterflies . . .'

Lovely swallowtail butterflies . . .

She blinked and shook her head. 'But I think it's only fair to tell you that we might have to wait a long time before we can move on that now. I'm afraid I've run into . . . legal difficulties.'

Aidan, Blaise noticed, was watching her very closely. More closely than just lip-reading required, surely? 'Do you mind if I ask what kind?' Aidan asked quietly.

Keira laughed. It was a bitter, strangely painful laugh. 'Not at all. Lucas made a will leaving the land to us. The reserve, that is. But none of us can find a copy of it. The solicitor who drew it up is missing, and I've had to call a meeting for tomorrow to see if we can sort it out. Fane and Jennifer have already agreed to attend, and my own solicitor will be there. But I'm not optimistic that we'll be able to sort it out amicably or quickly. Jennifer is . . . well, determined that I should get nothing, and Fane—' Keira broke off as her voice began to wobble ominously again, and merely shrugged instead.

Blaise sighed, feeling deeply depressed. Aidan had talked to her a lot about what good, solid conservation work the nature reserve was doing, and, like her future husband, Blaise was an ardent supporter of it. It would be such a shame if Keira had a setback now.

Keira surreptitiously wiped the fresh tears from her eyes and took a deep breath. 'I have this feeling . . .' She shook her head. 'I don't know. I know it's defeatist thinking, but I just have this strange feeling I can't shake that . . . well, that we're going to be locked up in the courts for years. If only Lucas had told me where the will was, or had filed it with his solicitor, none of this would be happening. I just don't understand it.' And then, unable to stop herself, she added heart-wrenchingly, 'Fane thinks *I'm* behind it all.'

Her voice caught on the man's name, and Blaise's wide blue eyes took on a shocked, then deeply sympathetic look. Keira was in love with Fane Harwood. Oh, the poor woman . . . No wonder she'd been sobbing her heart out just now.

Blaise glanced at Aidan, wondering if he understood — and she saw at once that he did.

But, when he spoke, surprisingly it had nothing to do with Keira's emotional state.

'What does your solicitor say about this will business?' he asked, his voice as clear as Blaise had ever heard it. But he was looking at Keira with such a strange, almost alarmed look.

Keira sighed and explained about the consequences of her husband having died intestate. 'But I'm not going to try and get half of the estate,' she added tiredly. 'I only want what Lucas wanted me to have, but even that will be too much for Jennifer. She's sure to fight me in court all the way. And Fane . . .' But Keira couldn't even *think* about Fane. It hurt too much.

She looked defeated already, Blaise thought. And it was Fane Harwood who had put that defeated and haunted look in her eyes, not the possibility of a protracted court battle.

'I don't want you to worry about it, Keira,' Aidan said, with such a finality and surety in his voice that it made both women look at him in surprise. Aware of it, Aidan opened his mouth once again, as if to say something important, and then very visibly changed his mind. 'This meeting you're having to sort it all out, it's tomorrow, you say?' he asked slowly, his shoulders slumping a little, as if he'd just made a decision he'd rather not have made.

Blaise wondered what was going on, and Keira looked equally puzzled.

'Yes. Two-thirty at the Heronry.'

Aidan nodded and sighed lightly. 'All right. Don't worry about it anymore. Things will turn out fine, you'll see,' he promised. He'd have loved to reassure her more, but, much as he wanted to, he knew he had some serious thinking to do first.

Keira drew in a deep breath and shrugged. 'Well, you might be right. And one thing's for sure — I can't sit around here bawling my eyes out all day.' She laughed, a little self-consciously. 'I have herons to count. The annual census is long overdue.'

She gave them a much more jaunty smile, but the defiance was obviously forced. Blaise gave her a brilliant smile back, trying to give her new-found friend a boost.

Keira set off determinedly towards the south, back to the Heronry. Blaise watched her go and sighed deeply. 'I hope it all works out for her.'

But Aidan wasn't watching her. He was thinking of something else. Of someone else. Of Lucas Harwood, in fact . . .

* * *

In his hotel room in the Bahamas, Colin Rattigan stood on the balcony sipping a sun-downer. The sun was warm on his shoulders; the sea view was spectacular.

But he was almost out of money, he still had no idea how to go about getting a false passport and false identity papers, and he was already missing England and, most surprisingly of all, his dusty, old-fashioned office.

He was also terrified every time he spotted the uniform of a Bahamian police officer.

But, as miserable and as lost as he was feeling, he knew that he could never go back.

He was in exile for the rest of his life.

* * *

Keira's spirits began to lift as she toured the veterinary hospital. She bent down to inspect the injured hedgehogs, who should, in the wild, have been deep in hibernation by now. Then she checked the huge map on one wall that detailed all the findings of injured animals on Westcombe land. Which were very few, she noted, profoundly satisfied.

Just then the door opened and Steven walked in. He was wearing a bloodstained white coat, and she surmised he'd just come out of surgery.

At the sight of her his eyes lit up, and he hastily got out of the gory garment and pushed it into a big plastic bin.

'Keira, how was the census?'

She smiled. 'We're up five. Two, I think, are a mated pair, one's a juvenile male — probably one of last year's fledglings. He should be on the lookout for a mate come spring. Before long we're going to have the biggest heronry in the country.'

Steven nodded and smiled. He knew that the herons held a special place in Keira's heart. 'Glad to hear it. The magpie situation's under control, by the way.'

Keira nodded, trying to force her mind to concentrate on the daily run-of-the-mill business that went hand in hand with running the reserve.

But Steven knew her too well to be fooled. 'Keira, what's wrong?' he asked softly.

She glanced at him with some surprise at his astuteness. 'Nothing,' she lied, then sighed as Steven gave her a telling, slightly hurt look. 'It's just that we might lose Lucas's acres, that's all.'

Steven's face fell. 'No. We can't. I've had reports about that injured buzzard we released. There's a long, low patch of land, right in the middle of Lucas's donation, that's ideal habitat for her. I've had several reports come in from twitchers saying that she'd successfully been catching rabbits over there.'

'Well, let's hope it all sorts itself out at the meeting I've arranged for tomorrow.'

Steven frowned as he recognized the same tone of defeat in her voice as Blaise had done earlier, and he walked towards her. Gently, he turned her around to face him.

'You know, if there's anything I can do . . .'

'She can always ask me,' a freezing voice whiplashed through the quiet office, making both of them jump and swing around.

In the doorway, dressed in black jeans and a thick white sweater, Fane stood watching them, his lean, saturnine face looking more hawkish than ever. His eyes glittered with the cold, hunting gleam of a bird of prey.

His eyes dropped pointedly to Steven's hands, still holding Keira's upper arms, and the vet flushed, his hands falling away. Then he rallied. 'I hardly think so,' he snapped. 'You're the one *causing* the problems in the first place. Turning to *you* is the last thing she'd do.'

Fane pushed away from the door with such speed that he was halfway across the room before Keira quite realized what was happening. Beside her, Steven gave a start, then stiffened, turning to face the menace head-on.

Keira felt her nerves snap. 'That's enough!' she said sharply. Fane stopped dead in his tracks.

'Steven, I don't need anyone to fight my battles for me,' she rebuked him sharply. Why did grown men have to act like schoolboys? The vet gave her a half-angry, half-resigned look, and shrugged.

Fane merely looked at her, his eyes unreadable. 'I need to talk to you,' he said quietly, firmly, ignoring the other man altogether.

'It's a bit late for that, isn't it?' she said coldly. 'I've already got the message. Loud and clear.'

'I'll . . . see to the badgers,' Steven murmured, leaving discreetly, if unwillingly.

For a long, long moment they simply stood and stared at each other.

Fane felt the tension stiffening his sinews. She was looking at him as if she hated him. No, that was not quite true, he suddenly realized, with a pang of unease. She was leaning against the cluttered desk, her shoulders drooping wearily. In her eyes was a look not of hate but of deep disappointment. And yet it was so unlike her to admit defeat. Perhaps, after all, her conscience was playing her up, he thought grimly.

But Fane hated that look of despondency. Her passion he could cope with. In spades. But this . . .

'I want you to understand why I can't let you get away with this will business,' he began. 'I don't know what legal tricks you have up your sleeve for tomorrow, but I just wanted to make my position clear before we get into it officially . . .'

Keira folded her hands over her chest. Her chin angled up. 'Oh yes? Please, do enlighten me, then, by all means. But please don't feed me any guff about it being the *principle* of the thing,' she warned him bitterly. 'All you're interested in is building some unwanted and unnecessary housing estate on your father's land! More money for the coffers and damn the consequences! Why don't you just admit it?'

Fane sighed. 'So that's what's been bothering you all this time?' His lips twisted bitterly. 'I should have known you'd assume the worst of me! As a matter of fact, I don't have any plans for my half of the land. I never *have* given any serious thought to a big housing development.'

Keira felt her heartbeat stop, then start again. For one second she yearned to believe him. Then her face creased into a look of scorn. 'Oh, come off it. Don't you think Lucas told me about your building projects? He told me all about how you were trying to get him interested in construction again . . .'

'Yes, I was,' Fane snapped. 'I was trying to get him out of a rut I thought he'd fallen into. I didn't know he was dying! I was trying to pique his interest, get the old blood flowing again. But I only had plans to build a few houses — two or three, here and there. Big houses that blend in with the environment. Nothing for you and your precious, all-important reserve to worry about.'

But, even as he felt the familiar helpless anger wash over him, he had to admit how absurd it was to be jealous of a wildlife reserve. But . . . oh, if only she cared half so much about *him* as she did about . . .

Keira found herself breathless. Was he serious? Had she misjudged him about that?

Fane watched the nuances of expression crossing her expressive face. He waited, unconsciously holding his breath.

But Keira didn't know what to say. So, she might have been wrong about his greed. But they both knew he was still convinced she was a gold-digger of the first order.

'Oh, go away, Fane,' she said tiredly. She watched, without surprise, as his eyes blazed angrily.

'You think you can dismiss me just like that?' he said, his voice dangerously low and soft. He felt his muscles bunch, ready for action. But what could he do? Oh, he could kiss her, and they'd both flame up, and then she would have him moaning in desire and agreeing to anything. She could wrap him around her little finger . . .

It wasn't an unpleasant prospect.

He took a deep, calming breath, shaken by his wayward thoughts. 'We're getting nowhere,' he said flatly. Perhaps it had been a mistake to come here. But he hadn't been able to keep away. Even knowing what she'd done, even knowing what a fool he was being, he loved her. And he would do anything to have her. For the rest of their lives. He didn't care if he had to blackmail her, threaten her, buy her . . . so long as they were together, he could live. Apart, he knew, he would die. Slowly, by inches, and over many years, but he'd die.

Keira laughed bitterly at his words. What had he expected? 'I know we're getting nowhere,' she agreed. 'And we never will.' She loved him more than her own life, but what did it matter when he thought so little of her? She could never admit that his distrust of her was killing her. It would give him far too much power over her. Far better to keep the existing barriers between them. 'You want the land. I want the land,' she said coldly. 'One of us has to win, the other has to lose. It's that simple.'

'Granted,' Fane stunned her by saying equitably. Then he moved closer. Keira felt her body begin to burn. 'But what then, Keira?' he asked softly, his arms reaching up to take her into his soft, yet iron-hard embrace, where she knew it would feel so wonderful. 'What then?'

He lifted her unresistingly from the desk, pulling her into his orbit, her body melting at their first contact. Her eyes flared green. Her lips fell open.

Fane leaned forward and slowly, thoroughly kissed her.

It was a deep, long, promising kiss. One that threatened to suck the heart right out of her. When, at last, he lifted his head, she was already beaten, and knew it.

Fane sighed.

'It won't be long now,' he promised. 'Soon . . . soon, all the barriers that kept us apart will be gone. And then . . .' he said thickly, his eyes darkening to ebony. 'And then . . .'

He kissed her again.

And then, Keira thought, with a sigh of ecstasy. And then . . .

CHAPTER 16

Fane tossed restlessly in his bed, as, outside the Woodstock flat, the dark of night slowly, reluctantly gave way to the first glimmerings of a pearly grey December dawn.

His lean body shuddered.

In his head he could hear a voice — a deep, rumbling, *inhuman* voice.

He was walking across a giant field that seemed to stretch for ever. Suddenly, over his head, he heard the harsh whirl of flapping wings, and he ducked instinctively in the middle of the dew-soaked meadow.

A pair of herons flew over him, their grey, black and white plumage elegantly spread in flight. Their long, graceful necks curved and glinted in pale yellow watery sunshine.

He straightened and watched them fly into a tree, next to a squat, ancient-looking castle.

Again he heard a deep rumble of noise. It was not a voice, but it talked to him.

He looked around, puzzled.

He wasn't sure where he was, but all around him the lie of the land looked vaguely familiar.

The sun began to show itself more strongly over the tops of dark, bare trees. His feet began to feel icy with the penetration of the cold dew.

Suddenly he swivelled his head, as he finally located the direction of the 'voice'.

And he saw the ring of stones.

In his bed, Fane's body froze into rigidity, then slowly relaxed.

He stared at the ancient ring of stones, puzzled but willing, as they called to him again. He began to move across the field towards them, curious to find out what it was they wanted. As he walked, he looked around him. It was a typical English meadow in winter, but as he continued to walk towards the stones he began to realize that something was wrong.

He'd been walking for *hours* and yet he was getting no closer. The ring of stones still seemed to be the same distance away.

He stopped and looked down at his aching, cold feet, and then once more looked all around him. He didn't seem to have moved, and yet he was tired from all the walking. His calf muscles ached. The giant meadow just rolled on and on . . .

In his bed, Fane rolled onto his side, a small frown tugging at his dark brows.

The stones called again — louder this time, and more insistently. And as the sound rolled across the ground it seemed to reach him with a physical touch. He felt the noise change into feeling, and creep up his legs. It was warm, and heavy, and made him feel languorous.

And then he understood that the stones were female. He felt himself harden, and his heart started to pound.

He ran a hand across his forehead, not surprised to find that he was sweating. His hand dropped, falling back across his chest, brushing against his nipple as he did so. Underneath his thick sweater, the button of flesh was hard.

He looked at the stones — and was sure he could see a faint glow coming from them.

He knew what they were now. The Penda Stones.

The Keira Stones.

He moved towards them again, and this time he could feel that he had help. Behind him, a firm wind pushed at his back. From the stones themselves, he could feel a magnetic pull.

This time, as he walked, the stones got nearer.

The ancient rumbling voice rose steadily in pitch until it became like the whine of a roaring wind.

And yet there was no breeze. The air seemed unnaturally still.

As he reached the first seven-foot stone, he stopped. The rock was grey, covered with lichen and leaning at an odd angle. He could feel the eons and ages rising from it like wafts of timeless perfume.

These stones had been steeped in history when the conqueror came from Normandy. They'd been ancient even when King Arthur had freed Excalibur from the stone. They were already old while the Romans constructed their straight little roads towards Londinium.

He swayed, feeling slightly giddy.

They wanted him . . .

Fane felt himself lurch, and suddenly shot upright in bed. For a moment he had to clutch the side of the bed, convinced he was about to pass out.

Then he blinked in the darkness. Confused, disorientated, he rubbed a hand over his eyes and discovered, somewhat ruefully, that they felt as if they'd just been gritted.

He turned, his blinking eyes seeking out the faint glow of green light emanating from his alarm clock.

The time was twenty past six.

Outside it was still dark, but grey-dark, not pitch black. Dawn was marching on.

Just a dream, then. He leaned back against the pillows, but even as he did so he felt the restless urge to be up and about. In his body he could feel the echo of the dream, his skin still rippling to an imaginary touch. His body felt hard, poised, *ready*.

He sighed, trying to laugh at himself and scoff at the fantasy of the dream, but he couldn't quite manage it. He cursed himself softly as he rose and headed determinedly for the shower. There, under a chilly spray, he lathered and scrubbed himself vigorously.

Somewhat to his surprise, the languorous sensation of the dream wouldn't leave him.

Restless, he donned grey corduroy trousers, white shirt and black thick-knit sweater, and padded, still barefoot, into the kitchen.

As he passed a mirror, he suddenly did a double-take. Black, white and grey. Like the herons that had flown past him in his dream. He shook his head, angry at the way the fantasy persisted in lingering.

He had other things to think about today. Like going to the Heronry this afternoon for this legal meeting of Keira's. He had to make sure nothing went wrong, that she and her solicitor didn't pull a fast one. That damned legacy of his father's had caused him enough trouble already. He wanted it dealt with, once and for all, and he was bloody well . . .

Suddenly he thought he heard the 'voice' again. So strong was the sensation of sound in his mind that he hesitated as he was about to plug in the kettle.

He leaned a little uneasily against the marbled worktop. Stupid. There was no ancient sing-song voice of the Penda Stones in his head. He was in an expensive flat in Woodstock, for pity's sake, not out in the fields . . .

Outside, a lorry rumbled by. He smiled, relaxed, and reached for the bread bin. Toast was what he needed. That, and a level head.

He set about hunting out marmalade and tea, but the dream wouldn't leave him.

As he brewed and buttered, he began to smile. He didn't need to be a psychologist to understand or interpret the dream, of course. The Penda Stones represented Keira Westcombe. She wanted him, and he wanted her. Hence the feeling of being drawn like a magnet towards the ring of stones on her land. She also wanted to defeat him. Hence his feeling of helplessness and confusion.

Well, once this fiasco about the will was settled, he could say a final and proper goodbye to his father, and then . . .

Keira.

He felt a pang. Deep inside, he felt again the pull of the stones. It was so strong that for a moment he wondered if he was still dreaming. But no. He knew he was wide awake.

But dreams were supposed to fade with the morning. Not continue . . .

He swore softly under his breath and took his meagre breakfast to the table. He sat, lifted the first slice of toast to his lips and then slowly put it back down again.

He remembered the first time he'd seen the stones. He'd intended to explore them closer, and then, for some reason, he'd turned away. Even then he'd felt, *instinctively* sensed, that the time wasn't right. That the stones didn't want him yet.

He shook his head angrily. The dream had really rattled him.

Almost against his will, he wandered over to the window and pulled the curtains aside.

It was slightly more grey than dark now. On the other side of the street another intrepid early riser had put on his or her lights. The row of orange streetlamps reflected a foggy day. A milk float purred its way electrically up the road.

He sighed, drew the curtains fully back, and leaned on the windowsill, feeling the cold air coming at him through the glass. And suddenly he needed to be outside. Where the fog could moisten his skin. Where the cold air would advertise his breath. He felt cooped up, caged . . .

He walked to the hall, calling himself all kinds of a fool as he did so, but nevertheless thrust his feet into a pair of warm boots. Facing the rack of coats in the hall closet, he hesitated, and then reached for a long, heavy black winter coat and shrugged into it. He grabbed the car keys and sprinted lightly down the three flights of stairs.

Once outside, he got out the E-type and, with a silent apology for any slug-a-beds he might be waking, reversed the car noisily out of the garage, and with a roar pulled out onto the open road.

A few minutes later he was not surprised to find himself heading towards Upper Rousham, although he was pretty sure he'd made no conscious decision about where to drive.

He frowned, then laughed. He probably *had* done more mad things in his life before than to drive in the fog at seven o'clock on a cold December's morning at the whim of a dream. He just couldn't think of any at the moment.

He drove slowly and with care, but there was little traffic about, and when he turned in at the village the fog was just beginning to lift a little. A lemon-yellow light was rising in the east.

He slowed to glance at the big house, but could only make out a few squares of yellow light in the distance. He imagined the kind of breakfast Bessie would be cooking, and felt his stomach rumble. A strange kind of homesickness seemed to grab him. Ridiculous, of course. The Heronry was not his home.

Behind the house, grey flapping shapes were beginning to move in the trees. The herons were up and about and ready to fly off to catch their breakfasts. The sight of them sent a strange feeling of kinship shivering through his veins.

Fane shook his head with a grim, rather bleak laugh. Mad. Totally mad.

* * *

Keira paused, her nose quivering. She was in the walnut spinney overlooking the Penda Stones, and her delicate nose picked up a distinctive, hot stink on the air.

Fox.

She crouched, turning on her torch to check the undergrowth. She found the fox run easily, just by following her nose. No doubt the fox had been after one of the pheasants that had wandered onto her land from her neighbours' copses and spinneys.

She herself didn't raise pheasants — she certainly didn't believe in blood sports or shooting game, and pheasants, as a native of warmer climes, didn't do particularly well in English winter woodlands anyway.

But she couldn't blame a bird for wanting to escape from the shotguns of the surrounding land and seek sanctuary here. Any animal, bird or fish was welcome on her land, so long as it didn't threaten the ecosystem.

Keira rose, nodding. Probably the vixen down from Fishpool Spinney. The one who'd successfully raised three cubs last year.

She set off, emerging with some relief from the trees into the open field. Although it was now nearly seven-thirty, and dawn had fully broken, it was still a fairly gloomy day. Just what she didn't need. With the court case preying on her mind, she was dreading this afternoon. A sunny day would have gone a long way to lifting her spirits.

As it was, the fog had just about managed to elevate itself into a mist, but in the dip in the field it still clung thickly, like a cotton-wool soup, around the ring of stones. Their grey heads rose above the mist like ancient teeth.

She paused and glanced hopefully at the lemon sun, shining across the wet fields. There must have been a frost earlier on, but already the day was warming up fast.

She might just get her wish for a bit of cheering weather after all.

Keira set off across the field, intending to go through the ring of stones and on to the other side. She wanted to check the river there. She had a water-sampling kit already with her, compactly tucked away in the voluminous pocket of her oilskin coat. She had to keep an eye on her fellow farmers. Seepage into the water table was the last thing the reserve needed.

* * *

Fane had parked up near the far end of the village, and had climbed the stile that led onto the Penda footpath with a feeling of half-amused, half-shivering resignation. He'd resolutely told himself he shivered because of the damp cold air, but he knew he was lying.

Ever since he'd woken he'd been plagued by a feeling of . . . inevitability. He'd thought he had life more or less summed up by now. He'd worked hard and made more money than most people dreamed of. He was successful.

He'd also pleasured, and been pleasured by, any number of women, who were all now happy to call him a friend. He'd been determined that his bad experience with one woman would not sour him for life, and he'd succeeded. Even when his own father had married a woman young enough to be his granddaughter he'd been prepared to at least try to give her the benefit of the doubt. No, he had nothing to reproach himself with. He'd made himself a good life, and he believed he had a good philosophy to go with it. He'd been quite content with it all. And he'd arrogantly and confidently believed that that had been all there was to it.

Until the day he'd gone to a church to witness a wedding. Until this morning, when a dream that he couldn't make himself believe was just a dream had brought him to a cold, foggy field.

He sighed, but nevertheless faithfully followed the footpath towards the Penda Stones, walking briskly. Within ten minutes he was on the crest of the far hill, looking down at the stones.

Or rather, the top half of the stones.

He caught his breath at the sight. A lemon sun bathed the ancient ring in eerie light as the fog danced at the feet of the stones like an ancient slave.

For a moment, just a bare instant, he couldn't move. And then the echo of the 'voice' stirred in his memory, and he found himself walking towards them.

Of course, his rational mind came up with all sorts of excuses. For as long as he'd been in the area he'd never actually got around to exploring the stones up close before. So it wasn't surprising that he should want to do so now.

And, it had to be said, an early-morning visit to an ancient site had its attractions.

But as he drew closer to the stones the shivering sensation in his stomach intensified. It was not unpleasant. Nor frightening. Just . . . *there.*

The stones, looming closer, seemed almost welcoming, as if greeting him. He paused at the first stone — which was no taller than himself, and lichen-free — and the difference between the reality and the fantasy of his dream made him smile. He reached out and touched the stone. It felt cold and clammy to his fingers. Rough-textured.

'Hello,' he said, then blinked. Now why on earth . . . ?

With a slight, fatalistic shrug, he stepped past the stone and into the centre, the fog closing around him like a curtain.

Keira approached the circle from the other side, moving past the biggest of the stones first — a seven-foot, lichen-covered stone leaning at an odd angle, which most experts thought had probably been the first stone set. The foundation stone. It had always been her particular favourite.

The whiteness of the fog was much thicker here, she noticed. She slowed, as always, awed by the atmosphere the megalithic monument roused in her blood.

Although she'd seen the Penda Stones fog-shrouded many times, this morning felt like the first time. She could feel the twin, opposing forces of the cold fog and warm sun on her hands and face. The long grass that grew here swayed as she walked over it.

And then suddenly, like a ghost, she saw a tall, dark-shrouded figure looming up ahead of her.

For a moment her heart leapt.

Penda!

And then she was inwardly laughing at herself. Of course not Penda.

But someone . . .

Fane heard a small sound and quickly turned around.

Emerging from the white mist, he saw a dark swathe of hair and a pair of sea-green eyes.

He was not, somehow, surprised to see her.

The two came together.

Fane! Keira's breath caught. What was he doing here? Why hadn't the stones warned her?

She took a step back, but it was too late. Much, much too late.

His hands reached out and caught her wrists. His fingers were like warm bands of steel.

Between the inches separating them, the fog swirled. A sudden shaft of sunlight found a chink and pierced straight to her eyes. It dazzled her, and she blinked. But as quickly as it came the beam of light was obliterated by the fog again.

Fane caught his breath. The sunlight had turned her eyes to emerald.

'What are you doing here?' Keira asked, her numbed brain finally engaging, and coming up with some sort of coherent thought. The skin of her wrists felt hot where his fingers gripped her.

Her knees felt shaky. Her heart matched.

'The stones told me to come,' Fane said simply.

Keira gasped, then seemed to sway. 'I don't . . . believe you,' she whispered helplessly.

Fane pulled gently but irresistibly on her wrists. Her feet dragged across the grass. He bent his head over hers, his eyes seeking hers out.

'Yes,' he said softly. 'You do. The stones aren't just yours any longer. They're *ours*.'

Slowly, he let his hands fall away from her, and Keira felt herself freed. And yet she knew she wouldn't be able to move out of the circle of the Stones. Not yet. Not until fate had had its way with her.

Fane's dark eyes shone like black fire in his face, piercing the whiteness of the fog like jet. She saw his shape shift, and then she realized he was shrugging out of the long black coat he was wearing.

Fane spread the huge waterproof coat on the grass between them.

For a second Keira's heartbeat faltered. She opened her mouth to speak, but before she could say a word — any word — that might save her, he was holding her again. This time she was pulled against him so hard that she felt her breasts flatten against his breastbone. The breath left her in a 'whoosh'. Her neck whiplashed back, and her mouth fell open in surprise.

Before she could draw breath, his lips were on hers. His tongue duelling with hers, winning, being defeated, and winning again. She felt the strength of him in his arms around her waist, smelt the raw animal power of him through her nostrils.

Her legs gave way, and instead of holding her up he collapsed with her onto the black coat and the yielding fresh green grass underneath.

His hands cushioned her fall and then moved inexorably from her waist to her stomach, which quivered and trembled, and then up. Higher. His fingers thrust away the thickness of her coat, seeking the body warmth beneath.

She was wearing her usual 'working' clothes: a pair of jeans, a thick flannel shirt — one of her father's — and a chunky woollen sweater that Bessie had knitted her for Christmas years and years ago.

Through the layers of clothes her body reacted eagerly to his expert touch. Her breast swelled and burgeoned in his palm, the button of flesh pressing hard and insistently against his hand.

Beneath his lips, he felt her moan.

Fane lifted his head to draw in a deep, ragged breath. His head was throbbing. His senses shimmered. His body trembled wildly.

'I've waited so long,' he said thickly, then bent his head again, unable to bear his lips being away from hers one instant longer.

A lock of hair from his forehead fell against her own, its dark, thick, silky touch making her shudder with pleasure.

His hands went down to her waist, finding the snap of her jeans, releasing it and pulling her shirt free. The foggy touch on her bare skin made her gasp for a moment, and then his hand was on her bare midriff, his fingertips providing four solid points of heat that flamed through her like a furnace.

He pushed the loose sweater up to her shoulders, bunching it around her neck, and dragged his lips reluctantly away from hers.

His head dipped lower. Through the flannel of the shirt his mouth found her nipple. Against his lips he felt her swell and harden.

Keira's head thrashed from side to side against the coat, her hair coming free from its ponytail and splaying around her like strands of raven gossamer.

She gasped, her eyes opening to look up, dazed, into a grey infinity.

Fane's fingers struggled with the buttons of her shirt for a moment, but then he had them free, and was pushing one half aside to bare her left breast.

Her skin erupted into gooseflesh as it made contact with the air, and then erupted in a different way as his lips found the warm valley of her breasts. She felt his tongue lave its way up her sternum as, beside her, her hands compulsively gripped great clumps of heavy dark coat.

Fane sucked one dark aureole of flesh into his mouth, nipping the hardness between his teeth, his tongue pressed hard against her. Deep in his body, something roiled. It made him gasp, and jerk in helpless, vulnerable reaction.

Beneath him, he felt her buck — a wild, spasmodic movement that made him growl in approval and answering need.

His knee nudged hers apart. Against the restraining pressure of his trousers he felt himself throbbing. A primal, lava-hot need demanded that he rip the barriers that separated them. He needed to be inside her. He *had* to get inside her now, or perish.

Keira felt her legs tremble. His knee between her thighs, she could sense the vulnerability of her womanhood. The opening to her body was guarded by mere scraps of silk and denim. She could feel him throbbing against her. Powerful, velvet over steel, demanding entry, insisting on possession . . .

And, deep inside, a hot, warm, honeyed welcome began building . . .

Fane fumbled with the zip of her jeans, pulling the garment roughly down to her knees. He leaned over her, covering her cold flesh with his own, warming her.

His own trousers ripped as he pulled and struggled free, and with a cry of triumph he once again thrust her legs apart.

Keira gave a great shudder, then her body went suddenly still.

Fane's eyes opened and he lifted his head to look at her.

His face looked taut; the hard planes of his cheeks were stretched tight. His mouth was grim and yet slightly open with a vulnerability about his lips that she'd never noticed before. His eyes, though, held hers like magnets.

Keira's own eyes widened.

Now.

Now . . .

She gasped, then cried out as he plunged into her, filling her so completely that she was sure she could feel him in every inch of her.

Her body shuddered around him, hot, contracting, enslaving . . .

Fane cried out, his voice harsh in the quietness of the air. It was a sound of primordial triumph, and at the same time a scream of defeat.

He pulled away on bended elbows, and then thrust into her again, his hips grinding against her own, his body covering hers, keeping her warm but pinned, like a sacrifice, to the ground.

Keira screamed in pure ecstasy as she felt the hard, hot length of him deep inside her. Her heels drummed against the earth in helpless reaction. Her back arched, then fell flat as he withdrew, then arched again at his implacable invasion.

And how her body loved its marauder!

Fane groaned, deep in his throat. It sounded, even to his own ears, much like the 'voice' of his dreams.

He looked up and around at the stones, then felt his body clench as it demanded more. Always more . . .

He lunged again, deep, hard, sure. And again, and again.

Keira writhed beneath him, her hands clinging to his broad shoulders, her fingers digging into his flesh.

Hers.

He was all hers. As he'd always meant to be hers.

'Fane!'

He heard her shout his name, her voice a cracked, ecstasy-thickened sound that he'd always longed to hear. Now, with her pinned beneath him, around him, *absorbing* him, he was finally free of the memory of her walking down the aisle in a floating white wedding dress on the arm of his father.

Now she belonged to him.

His.

He thrust powerfully into her again, his jaw clenched tight, beads of sweat pouring from his brow. A hot, hard inner core was building inside him. Making him feel heavy. Languorous . . .

'Keira!'

She gasped at the sound of her name on his lips. He'd made it sound like a curse, as well as a blessing, and she was glad.

Why should she be the only one to suffer?

She tightened her muscles around him, clenching as savagely as her fit young body would allow.

Fane screamed, then snarled, his eyes shooting open. Ebony locked with sea-green. Sea-green melted into grey. Ebony glowed into gentleness.

He moved harder, thrusting ever deeper, ever faster, striving for the explosion that would destroy and heal them both.

Around her the stones seemed to whirl in a giddy sort of dance. Keira felt her body begin to convulse as pleasure undreamed of, unimagined, began to implode within the core of her being.

She felt a great rolling wave of ecstasy, coming at her from some inner place that roared into reality. Her legs thrashed, her booted feet finding bare grass and gouging a dark, earth-coloured rut into the ground. Her hair splayed around her, across her face, across the coat and onto the grass, like a black silken web.

Her eyes shot open, her hands leaving his shoulders to cup his face.

'Look at me,' she demanded, her voice a broken whisper that nevertheless still had the ability to command him.

Fane opened pleasure-dazed, pain-triumphant eyes. His nostrils flared, his body heaved, and his lips opened to let forth a long, low moan of surrender.

She could feel her insides flood with their mutual harmony, and she gave a great, screaming cry of feminine triumph that lifted above the stones and floated free into the field.

A family of rooks lifted from a bare sycamore and rose, calling, into the air.

The lemon sun began to shine more strongly.

The fog began to lift, leaving the lovers exposed in the circle of stones.

Keira felt his weight collapse against her, and she breathed a ragged, satisfied sigh.

Her body relaxed against the earth.

Fane let his head fall, exhausted, against her breast, and breathed deeply.

Wearily, he smiled. So, he hadn't been able to wait until all the other debris that littered their lives had been cleared away after all.

Perhaps it was just as well. He was perfectly willing to believe that the Penda Stones knew best. Time and timing, was, after all, their speciality.

CHAPTER 17

Fane glanced across at his sister with a puzzled expression on his face as he neatly pulled in between the impressive double gates that led to the Heronry.

'You've been very quiet,' he said, careful to keep his voice neutral. She didn't suffer interference in her affairs easily but, ever since he'd picked her up at her Oxford home, his sister had been rather less than her usual voluble self.

And it surprised him. When she'd accepted his offer to drive her over, he'd expected to have his ear chewed all the way from Oxford to Upper Rousham.

But his sister had been pale and tight-lipped as she'd climbed into the car, and had remained that way throughout.

Now, in answer to his half-question, she merely lifted one shoulder in weary silence.

Fane sighed a little and pulled the car to a stop next to some forsythia bushes. Whatever was bugging her, it had to be something major. Otherwise she'd have been spitting venom about Keira for the last ten miles.

He and Jennifer had never been close; Fane was the first to admit that. And since he'd left home and become so busy setting up and then running Harwood Construction, globetrotting and working ridiculous hours, he and Jennifer had only ever spoken to each other half a dozen times at the most.

Since neither of them was a particularly good letter writer, Fane felt he was in no position to even take a guess at what was eating her. Sad, but true to say, the Harwood family had never been close. Hard to say, now, who was primarily at fault for that, but he suspected that they'd all played a part in putting the distance between themselves.

He glanced at his sister again, wondering if he should say something. He'd been so sure that Jennifer would be spitting mad and in a fighting mood by now. After all, Keira Westcombe was her nemesis. And right now she was trying to pull a fast one and grab the lion's share of their father's wealth. It was just not like Jenny to take it lying down.

Fane had no illusions about his sister. Even growing up, Jenny had placed so much emphasis on the material things of life. She'd always wanted to have the biggest, most expensive dolls. The most lavish presents. At twelve, a pony had been a must. At seventeen, a new car, not a second-hand one, had been demanded, and received.

He could still remember her mammoth spending sprees, when their father would hand over his gold credit card with a sigh and Jenny would come back with dresses, shoes, hats, scarves, jewellery, perfumes, handbags and all manner of other feminine fripperies, a triumphant and happy smile on her face.

Now she looked up at the elegant, lovely house, her face expressionless.

Getting more and more unnerved by her unnatural silence, Fane switched off the engine and released the seat-belt, turning to look at her with a frankly worried expression.

'Look, Jen, if this is getting too much for you, you don't have to come in. I don't expect much will happen anyway. Keira will get her tame lawyer to try and make us agree to Father having died intestate, and I'll stall, and that will be that.'

Jennifer, in spite of herself, smiled. It was a grim, rather forlorn smile. One that didn't sit at all well on her normally confident and slightly supercilious face. 'I dare say.'

She sighed wearily. 'Well, we might as well get it over with.' She pushed open the door and extracted herself from the low-slung sports car with less than her usual grace.

She looked tired, Fane thought. And her make-up was heavier than usual. Hiding purple-tinged bags under her eyes that hinted at sleepless nights, perhaps?

'That doesn't sound like you,' he persisted. 'I thought you'd be breathing fire by now. Aren't you worried about what she might do next?'

Jennifer slammed the door shut with her first display of real emotion. 'I don't give a damn what scheme *she*,' Jennifer tossed her head in the direction of the house, 'is trying to pull now. I've got other things to think about.'

Fane literally gaped at her in astonishment. And seeing the look of total amazement on her own brother's face was the last straw for Jennifer.

'So you think I'm worthless too, is that it?' she asked, her voice beginning to break. 'Well, if my own husband thinks I'm nothing but a stupid, money-grabbing bitch,' to her horror she felt her chin begin to wobble and her eyes cloud over, 'then I suppose I shouldn't be surprised if my little brother thinks so too, should I?' she wailed, reaching into her handbag for her handkerchief.

Fane came quickly around the car, feeling at a total loss. He had no idea what to do now. Helplessly he stood beside her, one hand on her arm, watching anxiously as she howled into her handkerchief. He tried to think of something to say, but since he had no idea what was going on he decided silence was probably better.

Eventually the storm passed. Jennifer sniffled and reached into her handbag, snapping open a compact and tut-tutting at her smudged make-up. She smiled somewhat ruefully at the state of her nerves as, with a slightly shaky hand, she repaired her face as best she could. Then she snapped her handbag shut and turned, giving her brother as open and honest a look as either of them could ever remember.

'Patrick's left me,' she said simply. Only the shadow of pain in her eyes betrayed the fact that she wasn't as impervious to the statement as she might have wished.

Fane sighed heavily. 'I'm sorry. I had no idea you two were . . . in trouble.'

Jennifer gave an ironical half-laugh. 'Neither did I.'

Fane looked at her speculatively. 'You love him, don't you?' It was not, on the face of it, as stupid a question as a stranger might think. And, perhaps thinking of the way she'd rather cold-heartedly selected Patrick as the man to marry, Jennifer didn't feel in the least indignant at being asked such a question by her own brother.

Instead, a strange, thoughtful expression came into her eyes. 'You know,' she said, as if just making some surprising discovery, 'I think I do.'

Fane smiled. He couldn't help it. 'Then why don't you do something about it?'

Jennifer laughed, a much more bitter laugh this time. 'Like what? I don't even know where he's gone.'

But Fane was already shaking his head. 'That won't do. A woman like you could find out where he's gone in zero seconds flat.'

Jennifer nodded reluctantly. 'I know. Perhaps I'm too scared to find him. Perhaps I just don't have the guts. What if I try and persuade him to come back and . . . fail?'

They were both silent for a moment. Failure wasn't something Jennifer was used to dealing with. Except recently, she amended, grimly but honestly. First she'd failed to get power of attorney over her father's fortune, thus failing to stop him making a fool of himself over the Westcombe woman. Then she'd failed to get the old will reinstated. Now she'd failed in her marriage.

'They say these things come in threes,' she murmured mysteriously.

Fane gave her a sharp-eyed look. 'Threes?'

Jennifer bit her lip. She was feeling particularly vulnerable just now. She was pretty sure their father hadn't told Fane about her bid to get power of attorney, and right now her brother was the only friend she had. She didn't want to turn even him against her, so she was hardly about to tell him that she was behind the disappearing will business. She was not that much of a reformed character!

But . . . 'If I get Patrick back, I'll have to promise him that I'll change,' she murmured, thinking her way through. 'And Patrick's too clever to be fooled by a good imitation. I really *would* have to rethink my whole way of life.' It was a daunting, terrifying thought.

Fane smiled wryly. 'Good luck.'

Instead of it crushing her, she found a reluctant smile coming to her lips. Fane's words had the effect of making her backbone stiffen in answer to the challenge. Her spirit, bruised and dampened, began to rally a bit.

She lifted her chin and looked at the house, then sighed. 'Well, I suppose we'd better get this show on the road.' But she had little appetite for the fight ahead.

* * *

Aidan checked his appearance for the last time, feeling a little uncomfortable in his one good suit. He fiddled again with his pale blue tie. He looked like a dog's dinner. He grimaced at his reflection and then shrugged.

He walked to the hall table and lifted the heavy brown paper envelope. It was the same envelope that Blaise had noticed the day Lucas Harwood had visited, and he found himself glancing down at it apprehensively.

He'd much rather not be doing this. His whole instinct was to just keep his head down and carry on quietly getting on with his life, as he had been doing ever since coming to Upper Rousham. But with Keira in such a mess he knew he couldn't justify doing nothing . . .

Oh, well, there was nothing else for it.

He left the cottage, tucking the envelope under his arm, and set off determinedly for the Heronry.

* * *

'Fane and Jennifer are here, luv,' Bessie said, coming into the library a little tentatively. 'But they're just standing by the car talking. Shall I go and open the front door?' she offered, glancing at the sandy-haired solicitor nervously. Martin Knighton, who'd taken a seat at the big oak table and was currently looking through some papers, glanced up briefly.

Keira, standing by the fireplace, sighed. 'No, leave them be. They'll ring the bell when they're good and ready.'

'Probably discussing strategy,' Martin said with a slight smile. The solicitor was quite looking forward to seeing their faces when Keira dropped her bombshell. Not many contentious relatives had wealth handed to them on a silver platter. It should be interesting to see how they took it. With suppressed glee, or rampant triumph?

Just then, the doorbell chimed, its melodic tones echoing off the hall walls, and Bessie hastily withdrew.

Martin leaned back in his chair. 'You know, there's still time to change your mind about this. Your husband's last will still hasn't shown up.'

'No, but I know he made it, and he wanted it honoured,' Keira said stubbornly. 'I found two of the gardening lads who told me that Lucas had asked them to witness him making a codicil. And that was the day he died.'

Martin sighed, knowing when to accept defeat. He looked up, automatically straightening his shoulders for even a non-existent battle, as Bessie showed their two visitors in.

Keira's eyes went immediately to Fane, of course, and then just as quickly turned away. She wanted to forget that this morning had ever happened. And she wanted to remember every detail of it for the rest of her life.

After all, it might be the only thing left to her. Once he knew he had won the fight, would he lose interest? To some men, the fight was the game. And Fane fought so very well . . . and loved so very well . . .

But she couldn't think about their rapturous union right now. She couldn't think of him as a lover, but as the man who mistrusted her. The man who thought so little of her.

Instead she looked at Jennifer, expecting spitting venom and instead finding weary blankness.

She's been crying, Keira thought instantly, then wondered if she was imagining things.

She felt a pang of guilt and then quickly quashed it again. In a few minutes Jennifer would know she was going to get all that Lucas had wanted her to get, and that would surely banish any tears.

In that, unknowingly, she was doing the other woman an injustice.

'Martin Knighton — my solicitor — this is Fane Harwood, my . . . stepson, and Mrs Jennifer Goulder, my . . . er . . . late husband's daughter,' she mumbled hastily as Jennifer shot her a warning look. It would most definitely not do for Keira to call her her stepdaughter!

Martin half rose, nodded politely, and resumed his seat.

Fane glanced at him speculatively. Only one legal expert, then? He'd been half expecting Keira to have an armada of legal heavyweights with which to impress and, hopefully, subjugate.

'Please, have a seat,' Keira said, indicating the comfortable and spacious eighteenth-century chairs that were set strategically around the impressive library table.

Jennifer took the seat directly opposite the lawyer, her chin angling up in defiance. Fane noticed it, and couldn't help but feel relieved. It meant that she was beginning to get some of her old spirit back.

'Mr Harwood, Mrs Goulder,' Martin opened the meeting politely. 'As you know, my client and I have asked you to come here to . . .' He paused as the sound of the doorbell echoed clearly once more out in the hall.

Keira glanced towards the sound just a little impatiently. She was not expecting anyone, but if there had been some sort of emergency any of her staff wouldn't think twice about calling into the house, expecting her to be available and ready to help.

It looked as if just such a crisis had occurred, for the next moment Bessie opened the door and nodded somebody in.

Keira rose from her own chair as Aidan Shaw walked in, looking decidedly nervous. For a moment Keira was puzzled, wondering what was striking her as so odd. And then she realized he was wearing a suit. It was so unlikely that her first thought — that there'd been some sort of farm accident, or that one of the horses was ill — quickly withered.

'Aidan?' she said, more surprised than annoyed at the interruption.

Aidan glanced at the people seated around the table and sighed. His eyes briefly met those of Fane, who was looking at him speculatively, and a ghost of a smile crossed his face.

Fane felt an answering smile come to his own lips. Somehow, he wasn't *surprised* that Aidan Shaw had turned up here. Now why was that?

'Keira,' Aidan said, by way of apology, 'I hope you don't mind, but I wondered if I could sit in on this . . . er . . . meeting.'

Jennifer half turned in her chair, wondering what business Keira's horse man thought he had butting in on a purely private family council-of-war.

Keira, too, looked surprised. Then she remembered meeting him and Blaise yesterday, and how she herself had said that this could affect him. After all, he had a stake in the land too.

Even so . . .

She glanced at the others, wondering how they might feel about having a witness present. Things might get a little heated, after all, and people tended to say things they might later regret. Then, remembering just in time that Aidan needed to see her lips, she turned back to him to say doubtfully, 'I'm not sure that I have the right to—'

But Aidan held up his hand. 'I think I might be able to help.'

Martin Knighton, who didn't know Aidan from Adam, raised an inquisitive eyebrow.

In the end it was Fane who broke the slightly uncomfortable silence. 'Well, I, for one, have no objections,' he said, wondering even as he spoke why he felt the way he did. There was something about Aidan that he liked and trusted.

Aidan glanced at him, both gratefully and thoughtfully.

Keira waved a hand. 'Well, in that case . . . er, take a seat, Aidan, please.' She held out the chair next to hers. She could do with a little moral support.

The table now reminded Keira of a scene from Victorian melodrama. Martin, as the legal man, sat in solitary splendour with the window as a backdrop. A few chairs away sat Fane and Jennifer, the orphans and aggrieved parties. Then there was another gap of two chairs, then Keira and Aidan. The villains, she supposed.

Martin tried again. 'Now, to get down to business . . .' He coughed and pulled a document towards him. 'Lady Penda has written down all that she can remember of her late husband's will. That is, the will he told Mr Fane Harwood and his wife that he intended to make. Naturally the will of a man as wealthy as Mr Lucas Harwood is a complicated document, and she can't remember many of the finer details, but . . .'

He handed the document across to Fane, who hesitated, rather surprised at the way the meeting was shaping up. Almost reluctantly he took the proffered document and quickly scanned it.

Intent on watching Fane, everyone at the table missed the way that Aidan's shoulders tensed at the mention of the missing will.

Fane quickly read it through, a slight frown forming across his brows as he scanned the document. 'That's how I remember it too. Except that Dad also wanted to leave a hundred thousand to the Salvation Army.'

Keira clicked her tongue. 'Of course. I knew he'd made a bequest to a charity, but I couldn't remember which one.'

Wordlessly, Martin made a note of it.

'Now, Lady Penda has informed me that she wants, in every way possible, to see that her late husband's wishes are carried out.' Martin's somewhat dry voice carried on smoothly, the man himself seemingly oblivious to the effect his words were having on the assembled people.

Jennifer blinked.

Fane felt his breath become trapped in his lungs.

Aidan, alone, failed to look surprised.

'Since there is no will, or at least it can't be found,' Martin pressed on, 'the easiest way will be to petition the courts that Lucas Harwood did, in fact, die intestate. Then Lady Penda can settle the money and land on you and your sister as set out in the missing will.' He had been addressing himself primarily to Fane, but here he glanced across at Jennifer.

Fane began to smile wearily. 'I don't think so. What's to stop Keira keeping the lion's share once she has her hands on it? Possession is nine-tenths of the law, or so I've been told.'

Aidan raised his eyes from Fane's lips, looking up into his face with a look of total surprise. For some reason it made Fane angry, and he glowered back. Just because Aidan was so obviously blindly devoted to her, it didn't mean that he, Fane, had to be so naive. And he actually loved her, damn her eyes!

Keira, oblivious to the two men silently feuding across the width of the table, felt her own spirits sink. But really, she told herself angrily, she had no excuse for being surprised. He already thought she was a schemer and a gold-digger. Why not a liar and a reneger of promises as well?

Martin sighed deeply. 'Really, Mr Harwood, if we can't conduct this meeting with at least a modicum of trust between the parties involved . . .' He spread his hands in a world-weary fashion.

Jennifer's lips twisted. 'Where millions and millions of pounds' worth of inheritance, land and property are concerned, would *you* trust anybody?' she asked scornfully.

But Patrick would, she thought, suddenly going pale. Patrick had all but admitted that he'd always liked Keira Westcombe. How he'd have hated all this . . .

She bit her lip, half wishing the jeering words unsaid.

Both Fane and Martin opened their mouths to speak, but it was another voice, strangely slurred and oddly accented, that got in first.

'What would happen if you found Lucas's will?' Aidan asked quietly.

The solicitor glanced at him a little impatiently. 'Well, it would be probated and that would be the end of it,' he said, with a shade of exasperation. Luckily he'd said it to Aidan's face, so the horse man understood. And nodded.

He could see now for himself just what Keira was up against. If he let things go on like this, Fane and Jennifer would have her tied up in the courts for years.

'Then it's just as well I brought this, isn't it?' Aidan said, and pushed the big brown envelope into the middle of the table.

Keira had vaguely noticed that he was carrying something, but now, along with the others, she stared at the brown envelope in sudden surprise. It looked so ominous, just lying there.

Martin was the quickest to react and hastily pulled the envelope towards himself, opening it and drawing out the document within. 'What is it?' he asked, even as he glanced at the first typewritten page.

'Lucas's will,' Aidan said bluntly.

Keira gasped. '*You* had it?'

Aidan nodded, but made no other comment. Fane suddenly sat forward on his seat, his eyes fixed on the other man.

'Why the hell was it in your possession?' he asked, his voice hard with suspicion and . . . something else. A vague kind of doubt that made him less aggressive than he might otherwise have felt justified in being, under the circumstances.

Aidan looked at him levelly. And again, as on that other day, when they'd first met, Fane felt a strange kind of . . . kinship with this quiet man of the soil.

‘I had it because Lucas gave it to me,’ Aidan said simply, meeting Fane’s eyes and not flinching so much as an eyelash.

Martin, impervious to the byplay, was reading busily.

‘So Lucas gave it to you for safekeeping,’ Keira said, but was still obviously puzzled. Why had he given it to Aidan of all people?

And then her brain gave her a well-deserved kick. Abruptly, a huge smile of relief began to cross her face.

Fane noticed it at once, and stared at her, fascinated by the light in her eyes.

‘This means that everything’s all right!’ Keira said, her voice nearly a yelp of pure relief and happiness.

Jennifer and Fane were both struck at once by the sheer, genuine exuberance of it.

Jennifer all but gaped at her. ‘You really meant it, didn’t you?’ she said, so surprised and shocked she could barely speak at all. ‘You were going to give us the money.’

Keira laughed. She couldn’t help it — the other woman looked so poleaxed! ‘Of course I was.’

Jennifer slumped back in her chair. So Patrick was right. About Keira, about . . . everything.

She was a jealous, manipulative woman. She’d been terrified that her father was about to make a fool of himself with his plan to donate land to the Westcombe Nature Reserve. She’d so easily convinced herself that it couldn’t possibly be a genuine act of sincere respect on her father’s part. That he couldn’t possibly agree with the reserve and its aims. Oh no. She’d immediately assumed the worst. That another woman was scheming to make a fool out of her father and get her hands on his money. Because she, Jennifer, had always thought money was all-important, and that everyone else must think so too.

But money couldn’t buy her happiness. Even now, knowing she was a rich woman, it wouldn’t bring her husband back to her.

Only she could do that . . .

She leaned back in the chair, a thoughtful, increasingly hopeful look flooding her eyes.

Martin, coming to the end of the will, read the signature and those of the two witnesses, then turned the page and began to read the codicil . . .

Fane was still staring at Keira with a half-stricken, half-jubilant look deep in his eyes. He, too, understood in that one blinding flash what a complete idiot he'd been. But was it too late?

Keira! Oh, Keira, what a mess he'd made of things.

Martin read to the end of the codicil and slowly looked up. But he looked neither at Fane, Jennifer nor Keira.

Something in the quality of his silence suddenly brought everyone to rigid attention. All eyes moved to Martin, and then, in suspenseful curiosity, to the man he was staring at.

Aidan.

Martin said quietly, 'You are the Aidan Shaw mentioned in this codicil?'

Fane frowned. Codicil?

Aidan nodded simply. 'I am.'

Martin half smiled. 'You can, of course, provide proof that you are who this document says you are?'

Aidan smiled grimly. 'Aye, I can. I have a birth certificate at home.'

Keira glanced at her friend, a puzzled look on her face. But it was Jennifer who asked the obvious question, not with belligerence but with understandable curiosity.

'What has this man got to do with anything? Who is he anyway?'

Martin glanced at her. 'Your father, Mrs Goulder, added a codicil to the will. The bequest of land and money to his widow remains the same, but the remainder of his estate is to be left in a straight three-way split. To be divided equally among his children.'

For a moment, nobody spoke.

Then Fane slowly leaned forward. 'But that doesn't make sense. There's only the two of us.' He waved a hand at Jennifer. 'How can that be a three-way split?'

Martin smiled. He'd never enjoyed a legal meeting so much. 'According to this document, your mother,' he nodded to Fane and his sister, 'was Lucas Harwood's second wife. When he met and married her, he was already divorced from his first wife, who had retained custody of their son. Your elder brother. Or half-brother, I should say, to be more exact.'

Fane glanced from Martin and looked, very slowly, at Aidan. His eyes were dark with surprise and shock, but also with wonderment.

'You,' he said simply.

Jennifer nearly fell off her chair. A little slower on the uptake, it had taken her a few seconds to let it all sink in.

She, too, stared at Aidan.

'Aye. Me.'

Keira let out a long, fulminating breath. 'I don't understand. Why didn't Lucas tell me about you? That you were his son, I mean?' She felt as if she were in some kind of mental boxing match. Everybody was dealing her body-blows, and she was beginning to feel distinctly winded.

Aidan sighed. He supposed he'd better make a clean breast of it. 'I don't think he knew that I was his son — at least not until the very end.' Seeing that this statement made everyone stare at him in amazement, he took a deep breath and plunged reluctantly into the whole story.

'When my mother and moved to Yorkshire I lost all touch with my father. It was only when Ma died, and the farm became too over-manned to keep me on, that I thought about making a big change in my life, and part of that meant contacting my father. You can understand how I felt when I read Keira's advert for a horse man right next to the village where my father lived.'

Everyone was listening with rapt attention.

'I intended to introduce myself, like,' Aidan said, acutely uncomfortable at being the focus of so much attention. 'But after a while I couldn't see that it mattered. I was happy working the farm and horses, and if Lucas knew who I was, he might feel obliged to . . . well, change things. Besides, he was an old man, and I was . . . well . . . I hardly needed a dad at my age.' Aidan shrugged. 'I just thought it best to let sleeping dogs lie. But then he married Keira.'

He said it simply, but nevertheless both Fane and Keira winced slightly.

'And that got him to thinking about making his will, I suppose. And he didn't want to leave me out. He must have tracked me down somehow, because the day he died he came to see me . . . and gave me that.' He nodded at the will.

There were many things they had talked about on that first and only visit which Aidan never intended to tell anybody. His father had told him how guilty he'd always felt, about the pain he'd caused both Alice and Aidan. He'd admitted frankly to making many mistakes. And Aidan, too, had apologized. For living near him for so long and never letting him know who he was.

Now, when he thought of all the time they'd wasted, it made him feel unbearably sad.

'He said he wanted to make up for not being there when I was growing up,' Aidan said concisely. 'That's why he showed me the will. So I'd know that I was to get the land and the money. I suppose he wanted me to know that he'd always thought of me as his son just as much as . . .' He glanced at Fane, and didn't bother to complete the sentence.

Martin glanced at the will. 'The codicil names a particular acreage that is to be left to you. I take it he thought that was the best farmland that he owned?'

Aidan nodded. 'Aye, I dare say he did. He knew by then what he could leave me that would suit me best.'

Fane slowly slumped back in his chair. 'Everything makes so much more sense now,' he said, but there was a certain bleakness in his voice, and Keira glanced across at him, a shiver of unease running down her spine.

'Well,' Aidan said, pushing his hands down on the table and rising abruptly, 'I have to get back to the horses.'

Martin looked at him in surprise. 'You're leaving? But . . .'

Aidan glanced at the will. 'You have everything you need, don't you?'

Martin blinked, and nodded.

Aidan glanced at his brother and sister. 'And you aren't going to cut up about it, are you?'

Jennifer openly grinned. Her inheritance may have been reduced but she had gained in the form of a brother, and she was genuinely pleased about it. With a start, she realized she was starting to change already.

Fane merely shook his head. But he'd be calling on his brother soon. They had a lot to talk about . . . The thought of having an older brother to talk to and visit with was a warming one.

'Then . . .' Aidan shrugged, wanting nothing more than to get out of his suit, away from this emotion-laden atmosphere and back to his horses.

'I'll see you out,' Keira said, hastily rising to follow his retreating figure. He was out in the hall before she caught hold of his arm, and he turned, jumping a little at the sudden grip.

Keira looked at him helplessly. 'I don't quite know what to say. Oh, Aidan, I'm so sorry about you and Lucas. At least Fane had a chance to patch things up with him, but you . . . you and your father must have seemed miles apart.'

Aidan smiled. 'It was as much my fault as his. But we had a long talk that morning, you know. It . . . well, it felt good.'

Keira nodded. No doubt the two men had opened their hearts to each other — or at least as much as each man was capable of. And whatever wounds there had been were obviously on the mend.

Which reminded her . . . 'Does this mean I've lost my most valuable horse man?' she asked, a little apprehensively but with a twinkle of genuine happiness in her eyes. 'I don't know what land he left you, but now that you and Blaise are together you might want to be solely independent?'

But Aidan was already shaking his head. 'He left me that parcel up by the back spinney. The one with the semi-drained water meadow.'

Keira nodded.

Aidan scratched his chin thoughtfully. 'I always thought that water meadow would make an ideal lake,' he said. 'It would take about a month to dig it out, and then, well, I'm not an expert, but I imagine you could plant it out with reed beds, near the back brook?'

Keira's eyes began to shine. 'We could get corncrakes back. And bitterns . . . But, Aidan, that's *your* land now. Not the reserve's. You must do with it what you think best. You don't owe me anything, you know.'

But Aidan was already smiling. 'What with my job working your farm, and owning my own land, not to mention the rest of my inheritance, I doubt Blaise and I will starve. We can afford to donate the odd lake or two to a good cause.'

Keira smiled and impulsively reached up to hug him. Fane, standing in the doorway watching them, smiled ruefully, with a growing pain-pleasure that was fast making him feel distinctly shaky.

'Well, we'll have to get used to him, I suppose,' Jenny said by his side. But her eyes, which were watching her newly discovered older brother hug the woman she had hated with a passion, were gentler than Fane could ever remember seeing them.

Keira pulled away, her eyes shining. 'Well, you'd best be off to tell Blaise the good news. It might take a month or two to become official, but you're now a wealthy landowner in your own right. Think she'll mind?'

Aidan grinned. 'I suppose I'll get my ear bitten off for keeping secrets, but . . .' his face took on the look of a man very definitely in love, '. . . we'll kiss and make up!'

Keira laughed and watched him leave. As she turned, Jennifer stepped forward. 'Time I was going too. I'll wait for you in the car,' she tossed over her shoulder to Fane.

Keira hastily made to open the door for her. As they passed, Jennifer paused and then, a little reluctantly, stopped.

The two women looked levelly at one another. Then Jennifer's lips twisted wryly. 'Well, I don't suppose we'll ever be friends, exactly,' she said, 'but I don't see why we should go on being enemies.'

And she held out her hand.

Keira, after one surprised moment, took it, a tentative smile creasing her face. 'I agree.'

Fane watched them shake hands, and moved aside to let Martin pass him.

As Jennifer left, Martin drew up beside Keira, his face a picture of amused reluctance. 'I know, I know. I'll start getting on with this, shall I?' He held up the will.

Keira nodded. 'Yes please. And don't lose it!' she called after him, before turning and shutting the door.

Fane watched the smile fade from her face, and turned to walk back into the library. He heard her shut the door behind them, and he walked heavily to the window. It overlooked the terraced garden leading down to the fish ponds.

'Well, that's that, then. Another afternoon of revelation and shock. Just an average day in the Harwood family saga,' he drawled.

But Keira couldn't joke about it.

'Yes. Everyone seems to be sorted out. Aidan and Blaise are happy, Lucas must be happy, and even Jennifer's mellowed.'

'Which just leaves us,' Fane said, turning to look at her. She was wearing a mint-green two-piece, and her hair was caught back on her head in a raven roll of dark silk. Silver and jade earrings swung whenever she turned her head, casting shadows on her creamy neck.

'And, since it seems to be the afternoon for confessions, I think now's as good a time as any for me to make mine,' he said quietly.

He'd known, ever since admitting to himself how wrong he'd been about her, that this moment was inevitable. And if she couldn't find it in her to forgive him — and why should she after the way he'd behaved? — then he was just about to have his heart amputated.

He took a steadying breath.

'When I got Dad's letter about the marriage, I tried to give you the benefit of the doubt. I got to the church, full of self-righteous intentions of not judging you until I could see for myself just how things were. But when I saw you walking down that aisle and our eyes met, it was like being sliced in two by a huge sword. And every time I saw you again I bled a little more. Soon I began to need to hate you, just for my own self-protection.' He ran a hand through his hair, his fingers shaking. 'At first it was easy to convince myself you were a lying little schemer, marrying a man old enough to be your grandfather just to get his money. You even admitted it, more or less!'

He half laughed, remembering the times she'd taken the ground out from under him. 'But then it got harder and harder to keep on kidding myself that I despised you. You were so obviously devoted to the nature reserve. You so genuinely cared about the people in the village, people who relied on you for their housing and their living. I couldn't maintain the fallacy that you were the cold-hearted wicked witch I needed you to be. So I fell more and more hopelessly in love with you. And then Dad died, and another barrier shot up between us. And still I kept on falling more and more in love with you.'

Keira took a step towards him, her own heart crying out to him that he needn't tear himself apart like this, but he quickly held up a hand. 'No, I need to say this.'

He half turned back to the window, as if he couldn't quite bear to look at her.

'I'd just get to the point where I didn't think it was possible to love you any more, and what would happen? You'd do something to prove me wrong. That day you threatened that ridiculous fox hunt, for example. And then . . . reprieve! Or so I thought. The will went missing. Who else but you had a motive for destroying it? I could whip up anger over that and protect myself with it for months — or so I thought. And then, this morning,' his voice became gruff, 'in the circle of stones, I realized I'd never be safe from you. I couldn't even make myself *want* to be safe. This morning I knew I would love you for ever. Just like those stones will stand for ever.'

Keira gave a silent cry. She felt the ice that had encapsulated her heart for so long melt in a sudden flame of joy.

She took another step towards him.

'I tried to tell myself you were just like my fiancée,' Fane said bitterly, 'but I knew from the first moment that you were nothing like her. Now I can't even remember the colour of her eyes. But I'll be seeing your eyes from now until the moment I die.'

Keira took a few more stumbling steps towards him. 'Oh, Fane!'

'No! Don't. I don't deserve your forgiveness.'

Keira began to laugh. 'In that case, I don't deserve yours, either!' she said giddily. 'If you were putting up barriers between us, I was busy building Hadrian's Wall!'

He turned from the window, his eyes full of hope so dreadfully suppressed that she felt tears fill her heart. 'Don't you see, Fane, I'm as much to blame as you are? I immediately convinced myself you wanted to build office blocks and factories right next door to my reserve! I told myself you wanted to drag Lucas back into the world of big business just to line your own coffers. I lay awake at night, imagining you with every good-looking woman from here to Oxford . . .'

Fane laughed. 'Are there any? I haven't been able to see any woman but you. Not from the moment you walked down that aisle on my father's arm, dressed in white . . .'

Keira was already walking towards him, *running* towards him, and his arms were lifting, ready to catch her.

'Oh, Fane!' she cried, launching herself at him, feeling her feet leave the floor just as her heart similarly took flight. For a long moment they just stood there, bound together, her cheek pressed to his, their eyes brimming with the brightness of tears.

Then she sighed. 'I keep remembering that moment too,' she said soberly, pulling her head away to gaze into his darkening eyes. 'But I know how we can exorcize it.'

Fane swallowed hard. 'You do?' He could barely whisper the words. So much depended on her being right. The rest of their lives depended on her having the answer.

She nodded. 'It's so simple. I walk down the aisle on *your* arm.'

Fane drew in a deep, ragged breath. 'Promise?'

Keira nodded. 'Whenever you like.'

'I want to do it now,' he yelled exuberantly. 'Right this moment.'

Keira laughed. 'I don't think the vicar is in. But I've got the keys to the church . . . How about tomorrow?'

Fane stared deeply into her eyes. 'It's all right, then?' he said at last, as if hardly able to believe it.

'Yes.'

'You and me . . . no more . . .'

She quickly put a finger to his lips, stilling them. 'No. No more.'

She lifted her finger from his mouth and replaced it with her own lips.

Beneath their soft, cushioning, sweet pressure, Fane groaned helplessly, and his arms tightened compulsively around her, almost crushing the breath from her lungs.

But it didn't matter.

They'd come through every storm life had been able to toss at them, and they were together at last.

And this time they'd let nothing come between them again.

THE END

ALSO BY FAITH MARTIN

HILLARY GREENE SERIES

Book 1: MURDER ON THE OXFORD CANAL
Book 2: MURDER AT THE UNIVERSITY
Book 3: MURDER OF THE BRIDE
Book 4: MURDER IN THE VILLAGE
Book 5: MURDER IN THE FAMILY
Book 6: MURDER AT HOME
Book 7: MURDER IN THE MEADOW
Book 8: MURDER IN THE MANSION
Book 9: MURDER IN THE GARDEN
Book 10: MURDER BY FIRE
Book 11: MURDER AT WORK
Book 12: MURDER NEVER RETIRES
Book 13: MURDER OF A LOVER
Book 14: MURDER NEVER MISSES
Book 15: MURDER AT MIDNIGHT
Book 16: MURDER IN MIND
Book 17: HILLARY'S FINAL CASE
Book 18: HILLARY'S BACK

JENNY STARLING MYSTERIES

Book 1: THE BIRTHDAY MYSTERY
Book 2: THE WINTER MYSTERY
Book 3: THE RIVERBOAT MYSTERY
Book 4: THE CASTLE MYSTERY
Book 5: THE OXFORD MYSTERY
Book 6: THE TEATIME MYSTERY
Book 7: THE COUNTRY INN MYSTERY

MONICA NOBLE MYSTERIES

Book 1: THE VICARAGE MURDER
Book 2: THE FLOWER SHOW MURDER
Book 3: THE MANOR HOUSE MURDER

WRITING AS MAXINE BARRY
THE LYING GAME
AN OXFORD REVENGE
AN OXFORD SCANDAL
AN OXFORD ENEMY
More coming soon!

FREE KINDLE BOOKS AND OFFERS

Do you love mysteries, historical fiction and romance? Join 1000s of readers enjoying great books through our mailing list. You'll get new releases and great deals every week from one of the UK's leading independent publishers.

Join today, and you'll get your first bargain book this month!

Follow us on Facebook, Twitter and Instagram @joffebooks

We hate typos too but sometimes they slip through. Please send any errors you find to corrections@joffebooks.com. We'll get them fixed ASAP. We're very grateful to eagle-eyed readers who take the time to contact us.

Printed in Great Britain
by Amazon

45706293R00192